Tasmina Perry is the author of the huge *Sunday Times* bestsellers *Daddy's Girls*, *Kiss Heaven Goodbye* and, most recently, *Perfect Strangers*. She left a career in law to enter the world of women's magazine publishing, going on to become an award winning writer and contributor to titles such as *Elle*, *Glamour* and *Marie Claire*. In 2004 she launched her own travel and fashion magazine, *Jaunt*, and was editing *InStyle* magazine when she left the industry to write books full time. Her novels have been published in seventeen countries.

Tasmina lives with her husband and son in London, where she is at work on her next novel. For the latest news, competitions, travel ideas and much more, visit

www.tasminaperry.com

Escape with Tasmina's other novels . . .

Daddy's Girls
Gold Diggers
Guilty Pleasures
Original Sin
Kiss Heaven Goodbye
Private Lives

Tasmina Perry

Perfect Strangers

headline
review

First published in 2012 by HEADLINE REVIEW
An imprint of HEADLINE PUBLISHING GROUP

First published in paperback in 2013 by HEADLINE REVIEW
An imprint of HEADLINE PUBLISHING GROUP

2

Cataloguing in Publication Data is available from the British Library

ISBN 978 0 7553 5850 2

Typeset in Sabon by Avon DataSet Ltd, Bidford-on-Avon, Warwickshire

Printed and bound in Great Britain by Clays Ltd, St Ives plc

Headline's policy is to use papers that are natural, renewable and
recyclable products and made from wood grown in sustainable forests.
The logging and manufacturing processes are expected to conform
to the environmental regulations of the country of origin.

HEADLINE PUBLISHING GROUP
An Hachette UK Company
338 Euston Road
London NW1 3BH

www.headline.co.uk
www.hachette.co.uk

In memory of my friend Clare Swillingham.

Prologue

He woke to the sound of screaming. He lay there in his bunk, staring up at the mottled ceiling, and listened. Sighing, he lit a cigarette and blew the smoke out in a hazy stream. At first, the sounds of the correctional centre had terrified him; the unearthly shrieking, the begging, the promises and threats. What would drive a man to snap like that? What had happened to him to make him claw at the walls? But slowly, like everything else, it had just become part of the routine, an inevitable piece of the landscape, like the chirp and twitter of the dawn chorus in the country.

'Gimme a straight razor!' bellowed the desperate voice. 'I'll cut my own throat right here! Please, just let me do it!'

Maybe the poor guy was trying to get sectioned to the psych ward. He'd heard the food was better down there. Or maybe he'd just woken up and realised where he was. That much he could identify with – especially today.

'Happy birthday,' he whispered to himself with an ironic smile. 'And many happy returns.'

Swinging his legs out, he shuffled over to the sink, rubbing the short grey stubble on his chin. He smiled. There, propped up against the warped plastic mirror, was a carton of cigarettes. No bow, no fancy wrapping, but touching all the same, even if your only birthday gift had come from a three-hundred-pound biker named Tyler. And it was the thought that counted, right? Especially here. Inside, your own

1

thoughts were about all you had. They didn't go big on personal possessions in lockdown; just one more thing for the Bulls to take away from you.

Of course, it hadn't always been this way. There had been a time when he had been the Man Who Had Everything. As he soaped up his beard, he thought of his last birthday: the party at the Long Island beach house, the path down to the shore lit by thousands of candles, tables of the finest caviar and champagne, five hundred guests, all leaders in their own fields: politicians, tycoons, media barons, each one jostling to shake his hand, to squeeze his arm, trying to strike a deal. But that was all over now. All over.

He picked up his half-blunt plastic razor and began to shave with slow, careful strokes. Money could fix most things in here – a bigger cell, TV; he'd even heard they could get you a woman if you paid enough – but no one ever paid another man for a wet shave in the Pen. That would be tempting fate. *They call it swimming with sharks on Wall Street*, he thought grimly. *Those pale-faced preppies wouldn't make it to chow in here.*

He peered into the mirror, noting the deepened lines around his eyes.

A year, had it only been a year? That morning of his last birthday, he'd been in Sag Harbor, a beautiful early summer morning. He'd come down to breakfast and Miriam had left his gift on the marble counter, beautifully wrapped in delicate blue tissue paper. He remembered how his heart had leapt when he had seen what was inside – a beautiful antique cigar box, polished ebony with ivory inlays and a tiny gold key in the lock. It was just exquisite, exactly what he'd wanted. And inside, he had found a single crisp dollar bill: a private joke between husband and wife, Miriam's way of saying, 'You'd rather have a dollar in your hand than any of these beautiful things.' Of course, they both knew it wasn't the money he cared about. It was what money could *give* you.

Not the trinkets, not the yachts and the houses, but the respect, the position, the power. Once you rose above a certain level, money was just zeros on a spreadsheet, but when people knew you had money – or thought you did – they treated you differently. They treated you like a king.

He patted his face dry and began to dress: starched collars and cuffs, a crisp crease in the leg; he paid extra to the Bloods who ran the laundry. Inside, it paid to look after yourself, to stand out from the crowd, make people see you meant business.

Taking a deep breath, he walked out on to the landing, his shrewd eyes instantly assessing the cons leaning against the railings. By now, he knew all the faces. Two gangbangers, three murderers, a slew of furtive wannabes. All white skin of course – the administration wisely segregated the landings along racial grounds to minimise gang conflict – but there were still warring factions even on this floor. Currently the Nazis had beef with the bikers and the Russians wouldn't deal with the Italians, but that could all have changed by the end of the day. Violence in jail was fluid, sudden, and it all came down to one thing: money. Who owed whom. And everyone owed someone something – even him. *Especially* him.

He spotted Ty standing talking to one of the Russians. This was a Category 5 security establishment, so all the foreign nationals convicted of federal offences – drugs, violence, money laundering – were dumped in with the rest of the scumbags. And the celebrities. Celebrities like him. He guessed they put him in a cell with Ty as a punishment, a way of saying, 'Don't think you're special in here.' In for running a meth lab in Atlanta, the biker had half killed two cons and wounded a guard in his first month. But, to his surprise, Ty had been polite and respectful, showing the terrified new guy the ropes, telling him what to do, who to speak to, how to survive. One night, he had asked him why.

3

''Cos you the man from the TV.' Ty had shrugged. 'You're someone, y'unnerstand?'

Oh, he understood all right. That was exactly the principle he'd used in business. It wasn't *what* you could give your clients, it was what they *thought* you could give them, that was what made them queue up to invest, that was what made them shower you with gifts: the holidays, the Cubans, even on occasion their wives.

'Hey, Mr Hollywood,' said a voice behind him. His shoulders tensed, expecting a blow – but all he felt was a hand on the shoulder. He looked up to see the wide smile of Uri the Bear. Somehow the sight of the Russian gangster's leering face was worse than being stabbed.

'Uri, how are you?'

'Fine. Good,' he said in his strong, stilted accent.

Uri's hand remained on his shoulder. 'There is some business I wanted to discuss with you.'

He nodded. He had been expecting it.

'Shall we take a walk?'

'Of course.'

They walked slowly along the landing – no one hurried here; why would they? – flanked by Uri's ever-present body-guards, one of whom had been rumoured to have strangled a child at the behest of a Mafia boss. But then prison was full of rumours like that.

'How have you been this month? Safe? Well?' asked Uri, an eyebrow raised.

Of all the dark souls in the correctional facility, Uri frightened him the most. His face was scarred and there was a tattoo of a dragon peeping out from beneath the collar of his prison-issue denim shirt, but Uri Kaskov was not your standard prison predator. Uri was educated, ambitious and more cold-blooded than anyone in the Pen. Which was why he had approached the Russian with a proposition. Uri could provide something he wanted – protection – and he could offer Uri something in return. The penitentiary was not so different from Wall Street – it was just one big trading floor.

'Yes, I'm very well, thank you, Uri,' he said.

Uri the Bear paused for a moment. His pockmarked face looked quizzical.

'Then that means our deal is working. You remember how I agreed to protect you from those animals down there?' He gestured to the floor below, where the black gangs roamed. 'And from the scum up there?' He pointed to the Bulls walking the gantry. 'And, as I understood it, from the number of very wealthy people who wish you harm?'

He nodded back at Uri, remembering the first few weeks of his time at the correctional facility. It had been a time of fear. Not a day went by here without some episode of violence. Men were stabbed over a simple disagreement in the laundry. People were killed because of vendettas from the outside. And he knew that he could be next. Uri was right. Countless people hated him on the outside. Rich people, vengeful people. People who wanted to see him dead. And they could reach him inside the prison, because within these walls, everything was possible for a price.

'Yes, of course, you have done a very good job, Uri. I have no complaints.'

'Of course not. No, the complaint is on my side.'

He swallowed, glancing nervously at Uri's bodyguards.

'Complaint?'

'The deal has been rather one-sided, don't you think? I have delivered my part of the bargain: here you are, fit and healthy. But where is my money?'

'Money is no good to you in here, Uri. When you get out . . .'

'That might be sooner than we both expected.'

He looked at Uri. The Russian was inside for fifteen years for extortion and racketeering. The authorities couldn't get him on any of the bigger charges, but he was still expected to do a decent stretch of time. So why was he getting out sooner? What deal had he pulled?

He felt the Russian's strong hand on his shoulder again as they walked into the yard.

'I want you to start making arrangements to transfer the money to a friend of mine,' said Uri.

His heart was beating faster now. He hadn't risen so high in the business world without being able to read people, and Uri's manner was hostile, the squeezing fingers cruel. Yes, he was a brute, a gangster, but until today he had been respectful, jovial even. Something was wrong.

'Well, that might take a while,' he said. 'I have to contact someone. He might be difficult to reach. I just need a little more time.'

Uri's grip tightened.

'You don't have the money? Don't tell me it's like the rest of your empire. *A mirage.*'

'Of course I have the money.'

'Then I want it. Including the interest.'

'What interest?' he asked nervously.

Uri laughed.

'We've heard you talking about how much money you have stashed away. Under the circumstances, I think the price of my protection just went up.'

He cursed himself. Sometimes he let his mouth run away with him. He had a fan club inside the facility, convicts who idolised him for what he had done, and sometimes it was hard not to bask in their worship and boast about his achievements.

'Okay, so let's talk,' he said, trying to keep his voice even. 'I just need to make a few phone calls. Give me some time.'

Uri had steered him past the baseball field, behind the bleachers out near the fence. A quiet part of the yard. The gun towers could see them – but would the guards be looking? It was a warm day, and a bead of sweat had begun to trail from his hairline down the back of his prison shirt. But despite the heat, he had gone suddenly cold.

Uri's dark eyes were full of menace. 'No more time. I want that money,' he said, moving his hand slowly up the base of his neck. 'I want it now.'

He felt his blood pumping in his ears, and his vision began to swim.

By the time the guards spotted him, he was dead.

1

She closed the bathroom door and locked it behind her. Her heart was beating hard and she felt sick to her stomach. Sitting down on the edge of the bath, she squeezed the bridge of her nose. *Don't let me cry, not in front of these people.*

Since the scandal twelve months ago, Sophie Ellis had discovered reserves of strength that she didn't know she had. But today it was taking every ounce of it not to break down in front of all the gawkers. They were all out there in the living room and the kitchen, eating their canapés and judging her, their oh-so-sympathetic words of condolence loaded with hidden meaning.

'How are you coping?' they'd said after the service. Meaning: how can you afford this funeral after your father ruined the family?

'It was so sudden, a heart attack with no warning,' which meant: you should have seen it coming. And 'Shame Charles couldn't make it,' which was really code for: look at how your friends have abandoned you now you've lost all your money.

Well, she wasn't going to give them another reason to pity her, she thought, breathing deeply to steady herself. The people on the other side of that door knew enough about her family life. They'd read about it, gossiped about it, held the Ellis family's misfortune up as a mirror against their own lives and given thanks, with barely disguised *schadenfreude,* that it hadn't happened to them. And now Sophie wanted to keep something hidden – her pain at losing her father, the one man she knew would always love her – and she couldn't.

Smoothing down her black pencil skirt, she fumbled in her make-up bag for some concealer and looked in the mirror. Her skin was pale and her amber eyes had lost their sparkle. No wonder: the last few days had been a strange limbo. She hadn't slept properly either; despite wanting to numb the pain with sleep, it just hadn't come.

Behind her, on the wall, she could see a collection of family photographs in sleek black frames. It was like her whole life flashing before her. Peter Ellis, proud and weather-beaten on his little sailing boat, *Iona*. Sophie and her parents, tanned and happy in Barbados, rosy-cheeked and smiling in Klosters. They had been wealthy, yes. But what did money matter when her father was gone? She could win the lottery tomorrow but never get that life back.

Sophie had adored her father and he had loved and indulged her in return. There had been the zippy BMW as her eighteenth birthday present, the Chelsea flat at twenty-one. Peter had even supported her when she had dropped out of university to take up modelling. When that hadn't quite worked out – someone should have told her *before* she had given up college that she just wasn't that photogenic – along with all her other career ideas, Daddy had stepped into the breach with a generous allowance in return for some event planning at his City accountancy firm. He had always been there for her, always.

'We'll get through this,' he'd told her with his quiet certainty. 'Nothing matters as long as we've got each other.'

She let out a sob, covering her mouth with her hand. It just wasn't fair.

'Sophie? Are you in there? Is everything okay?'

She could hear the brusque rap of knuckles on the bathroom door.

'Hold on, I'll be right out.'

She took one last look in the mirror, then unlocked the door. Her best friend Francesca was waiting for her, solemn but sleek in a charcoal trouser suit, accessorised by a black dahlia in the buttonhole and a diamond the size of a quail's egg glinting on her ring finger. Not so long ago, people would comment that she and Francesca looked like sisters. They had their hair dyed the same honey blonde at Richard Ward's salon in Sloane Square. The same racehorse physique, slim and long-legged, the same glowing, tanned skin. The *Evening Standard* magazine had even run a feature on them a couple of years earlier. 'Chelsea Girls!' the headline had screamed, before outlining their carbon-copy CVs: a little modelling, a spot of party planning. Five per cent work, ninety-five per cent pleasure.

Her life was quite different from her friend's now.

'There you are. We've been looking everywhere for you.'

'I've just been freshening up.'

'Are you sure you're all right?' queried Francesca. 'You do look a little pale.'

'Well, it's my father's funeral. I thought I'd go easy on the Fake Bake this morning,' she said, attempting a smile.

She took a fortifying glass of wine from a passing waiter as they walked into the living room. It was packed with people from the golf club, people from Daddy's sailing club, people from Mummy's Cobham circuit, their plates piled high with sandwiches, their glasses filled with wine. Half of them were studiously trying to avoid Sophie's gaze, the others shooting her doe-eyed looks of pity.

'Come on, Fran, show us the ring.'

Sophie spun around to see Megan and Sarah, her house-mates from her flat in Chelsea. Francesca had just become engaged to Charles, a friend of Sophie's ex-boyfriend Will, and her friends were anxious to hear about it.

Francesca held up her hand to display the rock. Her

happiness and self-confidence were quite dazzling, thought Sophie, feeling herself shrink into the shadows. Megan and Sarah squealed.

'It's enormous, Fran. What is it, five carats?'

Sarah reverently stretched out one finger to touch it as if it were magic.

'Six, I think,' said Fran thoughtfully. 'Flawless. Pear-cut. He got it just right, although God knows I dropped enough hints.'

'Don't they say that men have to spend two months' wages on their fiancée's engagement ring?' Sarah looked up, her eyes wide. 'He must be earning a fortune.'

'Charlie's doing okay,' Francesca smiled.

'Although I've heard that the bonuses have been cut this year,' added Sarah. 'Bloody Americans, they had to get greedy and screw it up for the rest of us, didn't they?'

Sophie didn't want to get into a discussion about finance or greed at her father's wake.

'So where did he propose, Fran?' she asked, trying to change the subject.

Her friend launched into an expansive description of her 'super-romantic' weekend at an exclusive country-house hotel: two days of spa, sex and Michelin-starred dinners. It sounded very much like the weekends Sophie used to spend with Will, all except the six-carat ring at the end of it. Not that she wanted to think about *him* today, either.

'When he took me out into the rose garden at midnight,' continued Francesca, 'then produced a Cartier box, I couldn't believe it.'

'I'm really happy for you,' said Sophie honestly.

'Well, obviously you're all invited,' said Francesca. 'We were thinking a winter wedding in the sun.'

'Where did you have in mind?' asked Megan.

'I want the Turks and Caicos. I'm not bothered about a church wedding and I never wanted to wear a big puffy meringue dress.'

'The Aman resort out there would be just perfect,' said Sarah.

'I know, I've already made enquiries,' smiled Francesca.

'Then I'd better start saving,' said Sophie, making a quick mental note of how much it was all going to cost her. The hen night – or more likely weekend – was bound to be somewhere splashy, the wedding gift list registered at Harrods or Thomas Goode.

'Soph, Charlie is paying for all the accommodation, so you'll only have to find the air fare.' There was a slight air of superiority mixed in with the familiar pitying tone but Sophie chose to ignore it. Francesca had her faults, but at least she was here, and she appreciated the gesture.

'And if that's a problem, I'm sure we can sort something out. Someone must be flying private. I'll ask around, see if you could cadge a lift . . .'

Sophie raised her hand to stop her. 'Don't worry, I'll manage. I wouldn't miss it for the world.'

And she meant it. She didn't care how much it was going to cost her. She didn't care if Will was going to be there with a new pedigree girlfriend. She didn't care if she had to go without food for a week, if that was what it took. For one weekend she was going to get her old life back, no matter what it cost her.

It wasn't until three o'clock that the last of the mourners left. The catering staff bustled about clearing away the half-empty wine glasses and stiffening sandwiches. Sophie found her mother standing alone in the conservatory at the back of the house, staring out into the garden. Julia Ellis had always been what people called a handsome woman; not beautiful, exactly, but striking, with high cheekbones and a long, elegant frame. She had certainly been the one to turn heads at the black-tie dinners over the years. But today she looked ten years older, the lines around her mouth seemed more pinched and her eyes were rimmed pink.

She turned around to give her daughter the slightest of smiles.

'It went as well as could be expected,' she said coolly.

'I think so,' said Sophie reassuringly. 'People weren't exactly here to enjoy themselves. But it was a decent turnout.'

Julia snorted. 'I see the Derricks, the Smyths, even the bloody Fosters stayed away – Annabel Foster has never had a migraine in her life and yet she develops one this morning, *I don't think so.*'

Sophie kept silent.

'Look, this place is a mess,' said Julia, turning to face the kitchen. She began collecting glasses of warm white wine and taking them to the sink. Growing up, Sophie had never known Julia to lift a finger around Wade House, their eight-bedroom Arts and Crafts house in one of the most fragrant parts of Surrey. But since the army of home help had disappeared, she had grudgingly taken on the role of housewife. Not that her efforts had stopped the house from falling into slow disrepair. Without the cleaners, the decorators, the interior designers and landscape gardeners, Wade House was wilting. Damp patches had appeared in dark corners, once-white walls looked smeared and grey. The lawns were limp and untidy, while the pond, once a clear sheet of turquoise water, was covered in a thick crust of moss. It was a high-maintenance house that needed money to be spent on it – and money was one thing they didn't have.

Yet Julia had refused to sell it. Even when the golf club memberships had to be sacrificed, and the weekly shop switched from Waitrose to the closest branch of Lidl. Sophie knew that by holding on to the house, Julia Ellis was holding on to the past, but the time had come to let go.

'Mum, don't you think we should talk about what we're going to do now?' she asked as she helped to clear up.

Julia didn't appear to hear her, thrusting the glasses into

14

the soapy water, oblivious to the white suds that were spilling up the front of her good black dress.

'I hear Francesca is getting married,' she said. 'To a friend of Will's, I believe.'

'Charlie Watson. They met at Will's birthday party last year.'

'I'd thought Will might have come along today,' said Julia casually.

'Why would he?'

'Because you went out with him for long enough. He always got on with your father.'

'Mum, I haven't spoken to Will in six months.'

Julia gave a small, hard laugh. 'I suppose you're right. Why should he be any different to anyone else?'

When the Ellis family had received the news that Peter's investments had gone seriously wrong, Will Lewis hadn't ended his relationship with Sophie immediately. No, instead he had taken her out for a slap-up meal at Hakkasan. Afterwards, in bed, he had held her, stroked her hair, reassured her that nothing would change. For a short time she had believed him. But over the weeks he began to see her less and less. Like the fallout from the scandal, the repossession of the cars, the fading of Wade House, it took time to crumble.

When he finally told her, three weeks after her twenty-sixth birthday, that he was too busy to sustain a committed relationship, Sophie had accepted it as an inevitability. No one wanted anything to do with the Ellises any more. It was as if their poverty was catching.

Julia put the glass she was holding down on the counter-top and turned to look at her daughter.

'Isn't it about time you got yourself a nice man?'

By nice, she meant rich. Julia had always judged Sophie's boyfriends by their jobs, their prospects, their backgrounds, and had always impressed on her daughter the importance of a *good marriage*. Will had been a particularly great catch in her eyes. An Eton-educated investment banker who had bought a duplex in Chelsea with his bonus, he had been perfect husband material and she had been more devastated than Sophie when their relationship had ended.

Looking back, Sophie could see that Will's success and desirability hadn't made her especially happy; in fact, it had fed her insecurities and made her quite neurotic. For the entire duration of their relationship she had spent a fortune on buttery blonde highlights and lived on little more than miso soup and salad, thinking that being blonder and slimmer than everyone else was the way to hold on to her man. If nothing else, she was glad that tyranny was now over and had no desire to jump back into it.

'Mum . . . we've been through this,' she pleaded.

'What? You're still young, you're pretty enough. And you're not exactly going to get your old life back any other way, are you? Don't expect there to be any money in the pot, Sophie. There's no life insurance. Your father left us with nothing.'

The way she spat out the word 'nothing' made Sophie's stomach turn over. Growing up, she had wondered if her parents had ever really been in love. Once or twice she had suspected her mother of having affairs, but Peter and Julia stayed together and the danger had passed.

'Mum, please. Can't you leave him alone on today of all days? He made one bad investment, that's all. There's no need to hold it against him in life *and* death.'

'One bad investment? He gave every penny we had, everything we had worked for, our entire life savings to *that man*.'

Her mouth twisted into a snarl. Julia Ellis still couldn't say his name.

'He was only trying to do his best for us.'

Julia was unrepentant. 'He was foolish, he was greedy, he was reckless and now he has ruined my life.'

Sophie felt her temper flare. 'Greedy? You were the one who wanted the big house, the exotic holidays. Dad would have been happy with a little house by the river so long as he had his boat and he had us.'

Her mother rounded on her, her small, even teeth bared. 'Don't pretend that you didn't enjoy the high life,' she snapped, her voice quivering with anger. 'Would you have preferred to go to the local comprehensive rather than Marlborough? To go to Margate on holiday rather than Mustique? You had the best education, the money, the lifestyle. We spoilt you, and you were every bit as angry as I was when it was all gone, so don't throw this back at me and blame my so-called greed.'

Sophie closed her eyes and for a moment she was somewhere else. On the Thames on her dad's boat. A tinny radio drowning out the noise of the engine, the air sticky with summer heat and dragonflies. They had got as far as Old Windsor when Peter Ellis had told her that his safe investment hadn't been as safe as he'd thought. Along with thousands of others across America and Europe, he was the victim of a $30 billion Ponzi scheme, and he was unlikely to get a penny of his money back.

'*You're kidding?*'

She could hear her voice now, bristling with annoyance and panic.

'*How could you let this happen?*'

'*But none of it matters, Sophie. So long as we have each other.*'

Back then, she hadn't believed him. *Daddy, I'm so, so sorry*, she thought, feeling ashamed of how she had behaved, how she had thought that money was the only thing that mattered.

There was the crashing sound of a glass smashing, and Sophie opened her eyes. Her mother was leaning against the Smallbone kitchen units, her face creased. For a moment,

Sophie didn't know what to do; she couldn't remember Julia Ellis ever giving in to emotion. Even at the graveside she had been composed and upright.

'He's left me, Sophie,' sobbed Julia, her voice barely audible, sliding down to the floor. 'He's left me.'

Sophie knew what she meant. *He's left me to this.*

Julia hadn't coped with the fallout of the scandal at all well. At one point she'd even left Wade House, packing a small suitcase and telling her husband that she couldn't take it any more. She'd returned within forty-eight hours, presumably realising there was no hope of a big divorce settlement, and retreated into a shell. Sophie hadn't missed the bottle of antidepressants in the bathroom cabinet, the bottle of gin in the closet. What if her husband's death pushed her over the edge?

She knelt down beside her mother, feeling her own mood soften.

'Money comes and goes. Nothing matters so long as we've got each other.'

She meant every word she said. So many things had been put into perspective in the last couple of days. The importance of family above everything was one of them.

'But the house,' sobbed Julia. 'There's a mortgage on it. I'll never keep up the payments.'

'So we'll sell it,' said Sophie defiantly. 'We'll buy something just as lovely, just a little bit smaller.'

Julia nodded without lifting her head from her knees.

Outside, the sun emerged from behind a cloud, sending a shaft of late afternoon light into the kitchen. As it warmed her face, Sophie felt a strange, calm optimism.

They'd had such a run of bad luck, things had to get better soon. Surely.

2

She was late again – she was always late. Ruth Boden peered out of the black cab's window as the streets of Mayfair sped by. *Come on, come on*, she thought angrily as a white delivery van moved out in front of them. *Not today, I can't be late today of all days*. She glanced down at her phone to check the time – it was only five past, not actually late, not really – and wondered if she should send him a text, say she was running behind. No, that would look unprofessional, and that was the last thing she needed.

'Oh God, come on,' she muttered to herself as they stopped at some temporary traffic lights. 'Why are they always digging up the goddamn roads?'

'Tell me about it, love,' said the cabbie. 'I tell you, since the bleeding recession, there's more holes in London than they got in Calcutta.'

Ruth smiled politely and willed the lights to change. She was due to meet Isaac Grey, the *Washington Tribune*'s editor-in-chief, and although she knew him well, it was still important to make a good impression, especially when there were rumours flying around that the *Tribune*'s London office was about to be restructured. It was, on paper at least, a huge opportunity for Ruth. She'd been the star London reporter for five years, and ever on the job, she'd been up since six chasing a lead. This morning the lead had come from a contact in the Met who had rung to say that some hotshot American lawyer had been found hanging in his million-pound flat; a sex game gone wrong, he'd said. It had sounded too juicy to ignore, so Ruth had shot over to Westbourne Grove, only to find that it was an overdose, the man had been revived by the paramedics – and to cap it all, he wasn't even American, he was Canadian, for Chrissakes!

Ruth shook her head at the memory. It was obviously useful having contacts within the police force and she was well aware that the detectives liked having her around – the sassy American journalist who always spelt their names right – but sometimes Scotland Yard's efficiency left a lot to be desired. Ruth had been brought up on the stories of Sherlock Holmes, and she couldn't help feeling disappointed that there seemed to be very few Inspector Lestrades left in the force. Even worse, this morning's wild goose chase had made her late.

The black cab's tyres gave a little squeal as they pulled up outside the restaurant.

'Thanks so much,' said Ruth, pushing a twenty-pound note into the cabbie's tray before slamming the door and running up the marble steps, her heels clacking on the stone.

Isaac was waiting for her in a private booth, flicking through his BlackBerry, his trademark scowl on his face.

'So sorry, Isaac,' she said, leaning over to air-kiss him. 'Got called out to a big story on the other side of London.'

'I hope it was good,' he said as she slid into the red leather seat beside him. Isaac Grey always seemed to be pissed off about something – Ruth remembered he'd had that same pained expression the day he'd interviewed her at the *Tribune*'s office twenty years before. His hair had taken on more silver and the lines around his mouth had got deeper, but time certainly hadn't mellowed him. 'Goddamn BlackBerry,' he muttered. 'Ten times a day I dream about smashing it with a hammer. And now they tell me I should be tweeting.'

Isaac was as old-school as they came, a battle-scarred newspaperman who rolled up his sleeves and had ink on his fingers. She knew he loathed the onset of digital media – she'd once heard him yell, 'You can't wipe your ass on a JPEG' across the office – and he hated answering to younger, slicker Harvard grads who knew nothing about the editorial side of the business and were now questioning his methods about generating revenue for the business.

'So,' said Isaac, finally putting his phone down. 'Can we expect another one of your world exclusives?'

Ruth allowed herself a smile. Three months ago, she had scooped all of the other papers when she had broken the story of Kirk Bernard, a New York hedge-funder now based in London, who had been burgled at knifepoint in his Mayfair home. The level of violence and the fact that a rich foreigner had been targeted sent a twitter of anxiety around both sides of the Atlantic. Bernard's valuable art collection – most notably, a Rubens and a Monet sketch – had been stolen, almost certainly to end up in the private collection of some super-rich Eastern European gangster – or so the tabloids had speculated. But Ruth had discovered that the paintings hadn't been stolen at all. Bernard had simply hidden them in the attic for a few months, claimed the insurance, then hung them back on the wall, maintaining they were clever reproductions. Unfortunately his wife liked to throw dinner parties, and a guest at one, a visiting professor from the Sorbonne, had noticed that the 'replacement' paintings were suspiciously accurate. When Ruth had interviewed Bernard in Pentonville pending his deportation, Bernard had simply snorted and said, 'Who gives a shit if they were real or not? To me, they're just cheques with faces.'

On that occasion, Isaac Grey had sent her a magnum of champagne, but Ruth was hoping for something more substantial today.

'You know me, always on the lookout for a scoop.'

'Uh-huh. So how's things?'

'Great,' she said breezily.

He took a sip of the red wine that the sommelier had handed him.

'You know we go back a long way.'

She tried to keep her face as impassive as possible. They'd had a brief affair soon after she had begun at the *Tribune*, when Isaac's recent divorce and Ruth's eagerness to please the boss had spilled over into an out-of-hours relationship. The fling had lasted weeks, and within six months Ruth had been posted to Kosovo. At first she had thought it had been a rather extreme reaction to their break-up, but the truth was that Isaac had known about her desire to become a foreign correspondent and had done everything in his power to make that happen. For that she would always be grateful.

'So I thought I'd give you a heads-up about some changes that are happening,' said Isaac. As always, he was impossible to read. But she'd heard rumours that the *Tribune*'s London bureau chief, Jim Keane, was ready to move on. As his number two, she'd be in pole position to take over.

'How old are you, Ruth?'

Her heart gave a little jump. So he was cutting to the chase before they'd even ordered their first course.

'An experienced forty-one, Isaac, as well you know,' she said smoothly.

Ruth held her breath. She had dreamt of this moment her entire career, throughout that time in the Balkans, then stationed in Cape Town – her bag permanently packed as she waited for a call from the foreign desk, day or night, dispatching her to Namibia, Mozambique or Angola. And now finally London, covering all those dreary weddings, openings and parties that passed for news stories, hoping against hope that one day it would all be worthwhile and she would finally get the position she deserved: bureau chief of one of the most important territories in the world.

'I won't bullshit you, Ruth,' said Isaac. 'There's talk about shutting the bureau down.'

For a moment she couldn't take in what he had just said.

'You're closing us down?' she croaked.

Isaac looked apologetic.

'We're not the *Herald Tribune* or the BBC. We're smaller, leaner, and to be frank, we're struggling financially. We can't afford to keep a team out here.'

Ruth couldn't believe what she was hearing. 'But this is London. The financial capital of the world. America's ally . . .'

'Which is exactly why we've kept it going so long.'

She was still shaking her head. 'I don't believe this. I thought it was going so well. The Bernard story . . .'

'Ruth, one great story does not pay the rent on an office in Victoria. You know it's all about the bottom line these days, and the London bureau doesn't generate anything that we can't get from local stringers and freelancers.'

'Local stringers?'

She had worked with them many times before – fixers, interpreters, hacks from the native newspapers. They were often difficult and unreliable; he couldn't seriously be thinking of handing the *Tribune* over to them?

'Isaac, local reporters have their place,' she said, trying to keep calm. 'But they are never going to be as impartial as a *Tribune* journalist. Remember Kosovo?' She had been shortlisted for a press award for her balanced reporting. 'Local journalists are more likely to be biased because of their politics, their allegiances.'

'London isn't Kosovo, Ruth.'

He put his hand on the tablecloth.

'The view from upstairs is that we don't need *Tribune* journalists out in the field any more. Not in English-speaking territories anyway.'

'This is just cost-cutting.'

'To an extent, yes it is. I'll be honest, we're not getting enough from you to justify the upkeep of the goddamn photocopier. Ruth, the media is changing. It's the new way, kiddo: they want blogs and as-it-happens tickertape crap. Citizen journalism – stories phoned in, seconds after the thing has happened. No one wants investigative journalism any more.'

'Bullshit,' snapped Ruth, before she could stop herself. She'd been up since six and she was in no mood to mince her words. And what did she have to lose anyway? 'Don't try and dress it up as the fallout from the digital revolution. You're just cutting corners, pure and simple. You're taking away the real journalists and bringing in interns to write cuts jobs from the internet and press releases. And relying on the general public to send in their cell-phone videos isn't *reporting*. I can't believe you don't agree with me, Isaac.'

'It's not me you've got to convince, Ruth. I answer to the goddamn management consultants right now, just like everyone else.'

Another time that comment might have gained some sympathy from her – but not today.

'So what about opportunities in Washington?'

Isaac shifted uncomfortably.

'We're downsizing over there too, not recruiting newbies.'

'Newbies! I've got nearly twenty years' hard news experience.'

She closed her eyes for a moment, considering the alternatives. Freelancing? Writing about relationships for the women's glossies? She'd come here expecting a promotion. Instead, she was being retired. Washed up at forty-one. She had devoted everything to her career at the expense of other areas of her life – most women her age were married, settled, they had kids. She knew the window of opportunity for motherhood was closing quickly, and while that thought occasionally saddened her, she consoled herself that she had her career. *But no.* After all her hard work, twenty years of dodging bullets, pounding the pavements, her reward was going to be – *nothing*?

'Listen, nothing has been decided yet,' said Isaac. 'As I said, I'm just giving you a heads-up. There is a possibility that we might keep a bureau chief in London if we can show it's worthwhile.'

'But that's Jim's job.'

'Not necessarily.'

She raised her eyebrows. Was he suggesting her?

'I want the best person for the job in that role. If you can prove to me that that person is you, then I will move Jim on. There's possibly an opening coming up soon in Shanghai that I think he'd be perfect for.'

It was a tiny chink of light, but it was something.

'So when will you be making a decision?' Ruth asked, trying to keep her excitement in check.

Isaac closed his eyes and rubbed his forehead with one finger.

'I don't know. Within a few weeks. Half the publishers are on vacation until Labor Day.'

Ruth began to speak, but Isaac silenced her with a shake of his head.

'Don't think you're getting a free run at this, though,' he said. 'I'll be giving Jim the same pitch: there is only money for one of you – and even then you've got to make it pay. I want to see a shitload more stories coming from the London bureau – good stuff, real scoops, none of this red-carpet crap – otherwise I'm going to cut you off at the nuts and I won't feel the slightest qualm about it. We clear?'

Ruth nodded, her smile leaking through. Stories were what she was good at. 'We're clear.'

'Okay then,' said Isaac, snapping his fingers for the waiter. 'Let's order some steak.'

3

Her hand caught the alarm clock's *off* button on the third ring. Sophie stifled a yawn, and reluctantly crawled out of bed. She was not usually a morning person. She had always been a 'five more minutes under the duvet' kind of girl, but since the funeral she had felt a renewed sense of purpose. Life seemed more urgent, as if there were so many things to do, and right now was the time to start making them happen. It was either that or curl up into a ball – and Sophie wasn't prepared to give in to that urge.

Walking into the bathroom, she turned on the shower as hot as she could stand and stepped inside. She let out a high-pitched squeal, but forced herself to stay under the scalding water until her head cleared, then she carefully scrubbed herself with some peach-grain body lather and washed and conditioned her hair. By the time she was dried off and wrapped in her fluffy robe, she felt ready for the day.

Taking the few steps back into the bedroom, she folded up the sofa bed to transform it back into her living room. Her Battersea studio was the tiniest space – but it was her own space, she reminded herself, remembering the day when the For Sale sign had gone up outside her old Chelsea flat. She cried herself to sleep that night, but she had been adamant she was not moving back to her parents' house. After the financial problems began, the atmosphere at Wade House had become depressing, not to mention that she did not want to be a daily reminder to her father that he could no longer provide for her. Instead, she offloaded her entire designer wardrobe of dresses, bags and shoes to the second-hand dress agency on the King's Road and the money was enough to pay for the deposit and twelve months' rent on this place. Although it was small – no bigger than the dining room in her Flood Street apartment where she had thrown her weekly pre-Raffles dinner parties – it was bright and sunny, which gave the illusion of more space, and it was in a decent spot too – two streets away from the park and a ten-minute bus ride from Chelsea. Her old life might have gone, but with her new address, at least she had a view of it from the other side of the river.

She sat down at her little dressing table and chose a lipstick. Even her make-up had been scaled back, but she'd always had too much of that anyway – too much of everything really. Sophie knew she had always led a privileged life, a safe life. She had always stayed well within the bounds of what was expected of a pretty girl of her class. Her default setting was shy, and for many years she did not have the confidence to do anything but conform. There was never any teenage rebellious phase; she had never done anything unexpected. If everyone was wearing pearls, she would wear pearls. If everyone was learning to ride horses, she signed up. She applied to one of the Sloaney universities, and when everyone started dating men from the City, she found herself a banker boyfriend too. Sophie couldn't remember a time in her life when she had done anything daring, or even out of the ordinary. She had always just been a leaf bobbing along on the stream.

Leaning forward into the mirror, she stared at her reflection. Well, now it was time to take her own path. The past few days had gone by in slow motion, and her grief still felt raw. But Daddy was gone and one thing was clear. Not only was she going to have to look after herself; in a reversal of the parent–child dynamic she had grown up with, she now felt completely responsible for her mother. For a start, it meant that she had to make some money. For the last few months she'd got by on what a Burlington Arcade jeweller had given her for her diamond stud earrings and Cartier watch – a present from Will two Christmases before – but that money was dwindling and she'd have to start paying more rent soon.

She dabbed her lips and forced a smile, then grabbed her gym bag. She picked up her iPod and phone, zipping them up inside her make-up bag, a hard-won habit she'd developed to keep them safe from wet towels and puddles in the changing room.

Glancing at her bookshelf, she saw the faded spine of *I Capture the Castle*, the book her father had given her for her last birthday. Smiling sadly, she opened it up to read the inscription Peter had scribbled on the title page.

To my dearest S, read this and think of our castle. Happy birthday. All my love always, Daddy.

It wasn't a first edition or collectable; just a rather dog-eared second-hand copy with the name of the previous owner scribbled inside. Sophie had loved its faded green cover with its line drawing of a peacock peering down at a creepy castle, because it showed her Dad had been thinking of her. He could have bought her some fancy perfume or something – not that they had any money for luxuries, as her mother was constantly reminding her – but instead he had remembered that *I Capture the Castle* was her favourite book, and had written a message only they would understand.

Sophie and her father had talked of their castle since she was a little girl and he had told her bedtime stories of sailing off to exotic shores. 'One day,' he had said, 'we will all live in a pink castle on a desert island where no one will ever find us.' That was never going to happen now she thought grimly, throwing the book in her bag and heading for the bus.

There were closer gyms to Sophie's flat, but the Red Heart was owned by Sharif Khan, an old friend from the Chelsea nightclub scene, who had offered her free membership in return for helping out behind the reception desk once a week. Sharif was a serial entrepreneur who had gone bankrupt many times before, and he knew more than most that she needed a lifeline.

'Hi, Mike,' she said, grabbing a plastic cup of water as she grinned at the short-haired man behind the desk.

'How are you, Soph?'

She guessed his concern was genuine; Mike had filled in for her last week, so no doubt Sharif had told him why she was away.

'Glad to be back,' she smiled.

'I'm so sorry about your dad.'

She nodded. Mike was a nice guy, but she still didn't feel comfortable discussing it.

'Thanks,' she said, then lowered her voice. 'Listen, Mike, do you think Sharif might give me any more hours here?' She enjoyed her time at the gym more than anywhere else, and if she needed to get a job, where better?

Mike looked doubtful. 'He's been cutting hours the last couple of months. I mean, I'm on my own here this morning. Still – seeing as it's you, he might sort you out with something.'

'Well shout me when he's in,' she grinned. 'I can only ask, right?'

Fastening her hair into a ponytail, she limbered up by doing a few stretches on the mats, then headed over to the treadmill. Sophie always felt better, more focused and in control, when she was working out. The gym was the one place in the world where she felt truly good about herself. No one cared about your bank balance here, where you lived or who you were married to. It was all down to how much work you put in. You could have arrived in a Ferrari, but if you were flabby, unfit and bursting out of your cycling shorts, you'd still wish you had the hard pecs and toned arms of the woman with the pushbike next to you.

She tried to empty her mind, enjoy the run as usual, but that nagging problem kept popping back into her head. She needed to make money. But how? Her CV was embarrassingly scant, and six years had gone by since she had dropped out of her English course at Oxford Brookes. After the modelling, and the obligatory stint travelling around Australia and South East Asia, Sophie had pulled another favour and landed a job running the door at one of the Chelsea night-clubs the young royals liked frequenting. Truthfully, it hadn't gone well. There were some girls who revelled in being a clipboard Nazi, but Sophie wasn't one of them, feeling too mean to turn anyone away – and had eventually been fired for letting in the 'wrong sort'. Her next bright idea, working as a gallerist, had also been a professional dead end. The art history course in Florence had been a lovely six months but hadn't actually led to a job, as the London galleries were all full of beautiful rich girls with MAs from the Courtauld Institute. So once again Sophie had fallen back on Daddy, and she had to admit that hadn't been a roaring success either. The irony was that she had really enjoyed organising events for his firm – the Christmas dance at Il Bottaccio, a trip for wealthy clients to Cowes Week – but a mishap involving a missing consignment of canapés at the summer garden party on the lawns of Bingley Manor had led to Peter Ellis's office manager calling her a *dippy cow* in front of everyone. Sophie had quietly resigned, half thinking the woman had a point. Maybe she wasn't much good at anything; maybe her mother was right: the only way Sophie would ever get on in life was to find herself a decent husband.

She punched angrily at the treadmill's buttons, forcing herself into a sprint. No, that kind of negative thinking wasn't helping, and it certainly wouldn't pay the rent. And then there was food, gas and electricity, council tax, and there was no way she was giving up her skinny lattes in the morning.

Frustrated, Sophie moved on to the cross-trainer and the weights, pushing herself harder and harder.

She had always been slim and athletic, a member of the netball, tennis and hockey teams at school, but lately she had been spending more time than ever working out. She might be feeling emotionally fragile, but at least her body was strong and healthy. Over the past few months she had seen her shape change too. She was at least a dress size bigger than she had been when she was going out with Will and had starved herself into size eight designer dresses, but now she was leaner and more toned than she had ever been.

Finally Sophie let herself rest, towelling her face and taking a long drink of water. She puffed out her cheeks, and as the endorphins coursed around her body, she could feel her mood lift.

'Excuse me. You don't know how to work this, do you?'

Sophie glanced up to see a glamorous brunette. She was about ten or fifteen years older than Sophie; her hair was immaculate, freshly blow-dried and bouncy, her face unlined but with that suspicious hint of Botox waxiness. She was the stereotypical Chelsea housewife, except there was something exotic about her, an accent that Sophie couldn't quite place.

'It's a bit embarrassing,' said the woman. 'I've never been on this one before.'

'Don't worry, it's new,' smiled Sophie.

She knew the equipment backwards. Not just because she worked out here so often – it had been a condition of starting at Red Heart that she take a basic gym instructor's certificate for occasions just like this.

'It's a rowing simulator – not like those old-fashioned straight-pull rowing machines; it works the exact muscles you use sculling or rowing. Here, hop on,' she said, showing the woman how to operate the machine. 'Can you feel that stretch along your quads?' she asked as the woman pulled back on the virtual oars.

'It's good,' she said. 'I take it you work here?'

'Yes. Sort of. Part time anyway.'

'Well that's perfect, because I'm actually looking for a personal trainer. I don't suppose you'd be able to squeeze me in?'

'No, I didn't mean—'

'I know, I'm too old to get a body as good as yours, but we can try, huh? How much do you charge?'

Sophie stared at her. She was kidding, right?

'Two hundred pounds an hour,' she said. It was meant to come out as a joke, but the woman didn't even blink.

'Could you do Thursday?'

'Thursday?' Sophie looked at her, expecting her to start laughing, but the woman's expression was serious.

'I know it's short notice, but I'm heading to the South of France and I need to get in shape for my bikini. Are you available?'

The woman's startling green eyes challenged her to say no. This was clearly someone not used to being turned down. Sophie hesitated. After all, she wasn't strictly speaking a personal trainer, but it *was* the one thing she did know an awful lot about. And two hundred pounds an hour! A few sessions at that rate and she'd definitely be able to stay in the little Battersea flat, maybe even think about upgrading back to Chelsea.

'Okay. Thursday it is.' The words came out of Sophie's mouth before she could stop them.

'Excellent,' said the woman. 'Let me take your details.'

Her Chanel quilt bag was hanging off the treadmill behind them. She reached inside and took out her diary.

'I don't even know your name,' she said without looking up.

'My name's Sophie Ellis.'

'I'm Lana,' said the woman, scribbling in her book with a silver pencil. 'Sophie, you're a lifesaver. An absolute lifesaver.'

And here I am thinking exactly the same thing, thought Sophie.

4

With a pencil wedged between her teeth, Ruth scrolled through the news stories on her computer screen. She had five pages open, all from different news outlets reporting on the same event.

Nodding to herself, she took the pencil and annotated the spidery flow chart in front of her with more circles and arrows, and when she had finished she tapped her knuckles against the desktop with satisfaction. She had been working on something all morning, trying to draw together a seemingly disconnected collection of names and events – and it all seemed to be coming together. Well, possibly. Of course, now she had to back up her theory: she needed documents, photographs, maybe even get an interview, someone on the record. But there was a story there. She could feel it.

She sat back and took a sip of her now tepid coffee, thinking of her father. Art Boden had been a newspaperman too. Not a hotshot editor at the *New York Times* or the *Washington Post* – no Woodward and Bernstein fame for him – no, Art Boden had been the news editor on the flyspeck *Greenville Chronicle*, 'a small-town paper for a small town', as he had always put it. But despite his small circulation, he was passionate about what he did. He loved the chase, the story, the joy of conjuring something from thin air, and as far as he was concerned, there was only one way to find the biggest scoops: instinct. It was a word he drummed into Ruth summer after summer when she had interned at his paper during college. 'Instinct, Ruthie,' he'd say. 'You either got it or you ain't and it's something all the fancy journalism schools in the world can't teach you.' Well, right now, Ruth's instinct was telling her she had something. She hoped it wouldn't let her down, because she desperately needed something right now.

'Ruth, meeting room!' Chuck Dean, the *Trib*'s junior reporter, called as he walked past. 'Jim wants a catch-up.'

Ruth rolled her eyes. *I bet he does*, she thought as she gathered up her notes. Jim had been putting more and more pressure on them to produce 'significant' stories, but only Ruth knew why. The problem was, however, that Jim's sudden enthusiasm for scoops had coincided with a sudden dearth of decent stories. Nothing had appeared on the wire services, nothing much in the national inkies. The July and August holiday months were notorious for being a slow news period, but the past few weeks had seen a particularly dry patch.

Ruth closed the door behind her and sat in the last chair around the cramped meeting table. If it hadn't been so pathetic, she would have laughed. When she was growing up, Ruth had always assumed the life of a foreign corre-spondent would be terribly glamorous – she had imagined herself riding in the back of bullet-scarred jeeps or exchanging war stories with grizzled old hacks by the pool of some hotel in Singapore or Guam – but here she was, crammed into a tiny rented room, sitting on a rented office chair with the foam leaking out the side. *Not much of a bureau to close down*, she thought grimly, looking around at her colleagues. The *Washington Tribune* London office consisted of Chuck, an eager but mousy Yale graduate; Karl, a forty-ish veteran of British local newspapers; and English rose Rebecca, who acted as Jim's PA and occasionally filed a story on travel or fashion. And then there was Jim Keane himself. If you met

Jim at a party, you'd guess he was a banker or a corporate lawyer. In his neat suits and club tie, he had all the polish – and sense of entitlement – of the preppy Ivy League classes. He was a fixture on the Hampstead intelligentsia circuit, and had written a rather pompous and self-regarding book called *Sarajevo: City Under Siege*, despite having been stationed in Bosnia for all of a week, just as the war was dragging to an end. Ruth had taken a great deal of pleasure seeing it in the window of one of Soho's remainder bookstores a few months later, but Jim still seemed to believe he was Hemingway reborn.

'All right, people, before we start, let me say I know all the excuses,' said Jim. 'You're going to say that it's summer and that nothing ever happens in summer. You're going to complain that there're no stories out there, or that there's nothing to grab them Stateside. But' – he tapped his signet ring on the desk – 'we need to work, guys. You'll all know that Isaac Grey has been over to London, and I want to show him just what we can do.' He looked around the room. 'So what have you got?'

As Ruth had guessed, it was pretty slim pickings. The announcement of a new Cy Twombly show at the Tate Modern, a rumoured meeting between the Secretary of State and the Foreign Secretary about the situation in Iran, some royal tittle-tattle. If this was all they had, then perhaps Isaac was right to consider closing the London bureau.

'Ruth?'

She looked down at her notes and pulled a face. She had wanted to keep this new story under wraps until she had researched it some more, nailed down something more concrete, but they clearly needed something right now. She took a deep breath.

'Well I guess everyone has read the latest on the Watson story?' she began, looking around the table. Sebastian Watson was a senior City banking executive who had been caught out with an escort girl. It had been the splash of one of the Sunday tabloids a few days earlier, and, it being a slow news week, the other papers had waded in, generating enough bad publicity to force Watson's resignation from his two-million-a-year job.

'There was more on the wire this morning,' nodded Chuck. 'Apparently his wife has left him.'

Jim steepled his fingers together and raised his eyebrows. 'And?'

'I think there is a bigger story here,' said Ruth, noting Jim's patronising smile. Even before Isaac had effectively put them in competition, Ruth and Jim had had an uneasy relationship, with the bureau chief never missing an opportunity to subtly undermine her in front of the staff. She told herself that it was because he was threatened by her, and while it no longer upset her – you couldn't be in this business without a thick skin – she never felt entirely comfortable in his presence.

'How big, exactly?' said Jim. 'Sebastian Watson's story has no resonance Stateside at all; he's British, barely a celebrity. It's business gossip at best.'

'Agreed, but Watson himself isn't the story – it's the escort girl. She's twenty-five and from Chesterfield, a town about twenty miles south of Sheffield.'

'I don't see how—'

'Hear me out,' said Ruth quickly, opening a file and spreading out copies of various newspaper cuttings.

'Look at this one. Three years ago, the German finance minister was caught entering a west London hotel with another escort girl. There was little coverage about it in the UK, but the German press got hold of the story and it forced his resignation from the Bundeskabinett.'

She tapped another cutting.

'Bill Danson. Gubernatorial hopeful. Five years ago he's in London on a business trip and he gets caught with some racy blonde in Chelsea. He pulls out of the governorship race. Are you noticing a pattern?'

She could feel the eyes of her colleagues on her; she knew they were intrigued, but it was Jim who counted. Everything had to go through Jim, and right now her superior didn't look impressed.

'So some high-profile men got caught with their pants down.' He shrugged. 'It happens. I could add dozens more mug shots to your collection if I had enough time.'

'Yes, but it's the background of the girls that I'm interested in. The Danson scandal was one of the first stories I covered when I came to London, so I pulled out my notes and looked.'

She flipped her notebook open and pushed it into the middle of the table.

'The girl involved in that story was also from Chesterfield. In fact, all three girls, Seb Watson's hooker, the German guy's and Danson's, all came from Chesterfield, and they are all roughly the same age.'

'So what does that mean?' asked Rebecca.

'It means I'm off to Chesterfield if that's where all the racy birds are from,' chuckled Karl.

Ruth ignored him.

'It means that these girls know each other. I bet you a hundred bucks they are old friends. Maybe went to school together. I haven't had time to look into it just yet, but—'

'And the story with interest and significance to a US audience is . . . ?' asked Jim.

'We have a US candidate for governor who's had his career destroyed, Jim. If I can just have a little time to join the dots . . .'

Jim pulled a face and shook his head.

'It's too thin, Ruth,' he said briskly. 'We can't waste time on maybes at this point.' He stood up, putting his desk diary under his arm. 'And that goes for the rest of you too. I want more than this; bigger stories, stronger leads. We need to do better, much better, yes?'

The team mumbled assent without much enthusiasm and Ruth watched him walk out of the meeting room, her stomach knotted in anger. She couldn't believe he would turn down a story with such potential just because he wanted to undermine her chances of getting the bureau job. She quickly gathered her cuttings and followed him to his office.

'Can I have a word?' she said, knocking on the door frame.

'What?' he asked impatiently.

Ruth closed the door.

'What's really wrong with the escort story?'

Jim shrugged. 'Nothing. I just think it's too spurious to waste a week on. Need I remind you that this bureau may not exist in September? We need to generate something pretty good and pretty damn fast to even have a chance of stopping that from happening.'

'Exactly,' said Ruth. 'This is the sort of story the mother ship wants. Exclusives, scoops, not rehashed press conferences or interviews that any stringer could bring in.'

'And what scoop are you picturing here, Ruth? A picture of three trophy blondes in their school uniforms?'

She took a breath. *Don't rise to it, Ruth*, she told herself.

'Look, I think these girls were honeytraps. I always felt that about Danson's girl. Say they all knew each other, say they were recruited by some Mr Big – some go-to man for help setting honeytraps for influential men – that's dynamite. It's a global news story, especially as one of the players was a potential governor.'

'Danson? He's old news, years old. He's not even in public life any more.'

'He would have been a good governor, Jim,' she said feeling the words come out of her mouth too quickly. 'If he was the victim of a sting, that is still going to cause one hell of a fuss.'

Jim levelled his gaze.

'It's a no, Ruth. I want you to work on an Angela Ahrendts profile in time for London Fashion Week.'

'Oh come on, Jim!' said Ruth, throwing her hands up. 'Let Rebecca do that. She loves fashion. I don't know a Burberry tote from a Walmart carrier bag.'

'I'm not sending a twenty-seven-year-old to interview the hottest American CEO in London. This is a good story for you.'

Ruth glared at him. 'A good story for you, more like.'

'What's that supposed to mean?'

Ruth knew she should hold her tongue, but she couldn't stop herself. 'You know Isaac wants the best person for the job in this role. You are sacrificing the good of the newspaper for your own personal ambition.'

Jim's eyes opened wide.

'And how am I doing that, exactly?'

'By sabotaging my story ideas. I am the only one who generates exclusives on this team.'

His face reddened with anger. He looked as if he was about to scream at her, but then his eyes closed, and when they opened, his expression had softened.

'Do you know what I think, Ruth? I think Shanghai is a good opportunity for you. You're a field reporter, you thrive on chasing down a big story.'

'Exactly, and that's why—'

Jim cut her off.

'London doesn't need a hotshot reporter, Ruth, it needs an editor. Someone who can liaise with the stringers, co-ordinate the bloggers. Someone with an eye on what Washington needs in the twenty-first century.'

Someone to go for long lunches with pretty PR girls and your broadsheet cronies, thought Ruth.

'Is this how it's going to be, Jim?' she asked. 'Are you really going to make it a competition?'

Jim smiled, a lopsided, nasty smile.

'It's always been a competition, Ruth. And frankly, you don't have what it takes to win.'

5

Sophie turned off the engine of her moped and glanced down at the address written in her diary. *This can't be the place, can it?* she thought, looking up at the virgin white stucco building across the road. She had been to some very impressive homes in her time, town houses in Chelsea, estates in the country, villas abroad, but none had been quite as grand and as exquisitely elegant as the one before her now. Egerton Row was one of the most exclusive streets in south-west London, tucked away in a quiet enclave off Brompton Road. Lana's detached house looked freshly painted, with slate steps, manicured window boxes on the Juliet balcony and miniature privet hedges standing like sentry guards either side of the shiny black door. *Recession, what recession?* thought Sophie, as she locked her helmet into her scooter's storage box.

Then again, she had to admit she was benefiting from all this surplus cash too. In the three weeks since she had met Lana, Sophie had made over fifteen hundred pounds from the woman and her wealthy friends for yoga and fitness sessions. She had quickly got over her embarrassment at being their 'hired help', as one client had ungraciously called her, and instead had felt empowered at bringing so much money in so swiftly. It had been enough to get her moped taxed and back on the road, to pay off the interest on her credit card bill, and to pay for a plane ticket for her mum to go and visit a friend in Denmark, which had been the first time she had seen Julia smile since the funeral.

To be honest, Sophie didn't know why she hadn't thought of becoming a personal trainer before. She'd spent years keeping her body in tip-top condition and had the figure and athleticism to show for it. It made total sense to turn her prime asset into a career.

Lana opened the door dressed in black cycling shorts, her long chocolate hair tumbling over the straps of a hot-pink cropped Lycra vest top.

'Come in, come in,' she purred. 'Sorry I had to ask you to come to the house, but I'm mad, mad busy.'

'Wow!' said Sophie as she followed Lana inside. 'This place is amazing.'

If the exterior of Lana's house was stunning, the interior was something else. The entrance hall was double height, with a white marble staircase curling off to the right, a grand piano standing centre stage and a stunning collection of art on the walls. Sophie still hadn't worked out what Lana did for a living, but assumed that the money came from her husband Simon, who apparently did something in the money markets.

'I suppose,' shrugged Lana. 'We only bought it recently, and there's so much I want to do. I wanted to get the renovation work done while we were away, but I think this is maybe a six-, twelve-month job. Don't you think it's looking tired?'

Sophie didn't think anything of the sort. It seemed perfect to her eyes, all sparkling white paintwork, varnished wood floors and artfully arranged furniture; her idea of a dream house. It was a shame how Lana's wealth and the ease with which she could spend her husband's money had anesthetised her to its beauty.

'So where do you want to do this?' she asked.

'There is a studio downstairs,' said Lana, 'but it's a lovely day. Would it work to go for a run?'

Sophie nodded. Much as she would have liked to see the studio, she knew she was here to work. Improving Lana's cardiovascular fitness was a good idea, and her client was right: the sun was out and the morning air not too warm yet.

They took the back streets towards Hyde Park, crossing Brompton Road, then snaked down Ennismore Gardens towards South Carriage Drive. They didn't talk much, but when Sophie did say something, it was to praise Lana's work rate. She knew from personal experience how women with rich partners, no matter how beautiful, tended to be insecure, and needed constant compliments and reassurance. But in Lana's case, no false flattery was required. She was long-legged, fit and light-footed, and had no problem keeping up with Sophie's pace. They were inside the park now, running down the shaded path between two lines of sycamores.

'So how long are you away for?' Sophie said it lightly, but she had been dreading the answer. She was just getting used to the income from Lana's daily sessions, and despite getting some response from a notice for 'Ellis Training' she had pinned on various café notice boards around South Kensington, she knew she wouldn't be able to charge them a quarter the rate she was getting from Lana and her friends.

'We'll be away all of August. The French way,' replied Lana. 'We can start again in September, though? I don't want you getting so booked up you can't fit me into your schedule.'

'Actually, it will give me the chance to do some training myself. Take a few courses.'

'Qualify, you mean?' said Lana with the hint of a smile.

Sophie felt her cheeks burn with embarrassment.

'Don't worry. Your secret is safe with me. Qualifications?' She waved a dismissive hand. 'All I care about is if someone is good at what they do, and you're the best trainer I've worked with, Sophie.'

The compliment was gratefully received. Sophie had quickly found out that the relationship between client and trainer was quite an intimate one, and had hated feeling a fraud in front of Lana over the past three weeks. Still, she was doubly determined to get certified. After all, what if Lana injured herself and complained that Sophie wasn't qualified? No – it was best to do a personal trainer course as quickly as possible.

They stopped by the bandstand and began stretching exercises.

'So what did you do before? Before the training, I mean?' asked Lana.

'A little bit of work for my father,' replied Sophie vaguely.

Lana laughed. 'Don't be embarrassed. It's not as if most of the girls in Chelsea have professional careers. I think they are just killing time waiting to find the right husband.'

Sophie gave an ironic smile.

'That used to be me.'

Lana glanced at her.

'So what happened?'

Sophie sighed.

'Which bit do you want to hear about? The bit where my dad lost all his money, or the bit where he died of a heart attack?'

Lana looked sympathetic.

'I'm so sorry. When did this happen?'

'Just a few weeks ago. It's all still a bit raw, to be honest, which is why it's been good to throw myself into something like this. And you're right, I *am* good at this and it's been a nice feeling recognising it. I have to say, I've been enjoying myself for the first time in a while.'

'I bet you're hearing some hair-raising stories, too?'

Sophie burst out laughing. Lana was right. Most of her

clients had been shockingly open about their marital problems: how they felt neglected by their husbands, how they were convinced they were all having affairs.

'I guess I'm cheaper than a shrink.'

'Well, I'm sure you've only heard the tip of the iceberg,' replied Lana. 'You wouldn't believe what really goes on behind closed doors. All those women in their lovely houses, with every luxury and nothing to do all day; yet they're still miserable, aren't they?'

They exchanged a look, and for a minute Sophie wondered if Lana was talking about herself. On the surface, Lana had exactly the sort of life most of Sophie's friends aspired to – the big house, the 4×4, a wardrobe of Dior – but who ever really knew how happy someone was?

'All right,' said Sophie with purpose. 'Enough chat. Two-hundred-metre sprint, then a circuit of the park. Let's see what you've got, Lana.'

They ran for an hour, Lana impressing Sophie with her general fitness and willingness to push herself – not something she saw with other rich housewives at the gym. For them, Sophie got the feeling, personal training was just something you did, an expected activity for a certain type of rich woman along with tennis and charity lunches. Finally they jogged back to Egerton Row, where Lana handed Sophie one of the white towels she had left in the hall.

'So I'll see you in September,' said Sophie, wiping her face. 'It must be one hell of a place in France if you're prepared to say goodbye to this.'

Lana puffed out her cheeks and looked at Sophie.

'Listen, I have an idea. Why don't you house-sit for us?'

Sophie gazed at her in amazement.

'Here? For you?'

Lana threw the towel over her shoulder.

'Why not? For insurance purposes, it would be good to have someone at the house.'

'But you hardly know me. I could run off with all that expensive art in your hallway.'

'I see you more than some of my closest friends.' Lana smiled slowly. 'Besides, I have a very sensitive alarm system and a housekeeper who lives out but who can check you don't throw any wild parties.'

'But what if you needed to come back to London?'

Lana laughed. 'Darling, I can't see that happening. But if I did, I wouldn't throw you out. It's plenty big enough for two.'

'What about your husband?'

'You're unlikely to see him. He works mostly out of Geneva these days.'

'Lana, I couldn't . . .'

'Sophie, you would be helping me,' she insisted. 'And you can use the studio for your training.'

Sophie understood Lana's gesture. It wasn't pity or charity, it was generosity. From Sharif's no-strings-attached job offer at the gym to the man in the newsagent who gave her two months' credit for the glossy magazine habit she couldn't relinquish, kindness had come from the most unusual places since her world had turned upside down. And now Lana was making an offer she felt certain came from the same sense of simply wanting to help.

'Well I warn you, I'm no domestic goddess, but I can water the plants, take messages if you like . . .'

'That's sweet, but I have a housekeeper for all that,' smiled Lana. 'I fly to Nice early Thursday morning. You're welcome to move in any time after that. Any questions?'

Sophie looked around at her dream house and couldn't keep the smile off her face.

'No, actually, I think I'll be fine.'

6

Ruth twisted around in front of the mirror, her arms tied in knots trying to reach for the zip. *Stupid things, why do they make them so hard to put on?* Finally she got the black dress straight, smoothed down her short blond hair and gave her lips one last slick of gloss. *There*, she thought, *that's the best you're going to get*. Looking at herself in the mirror, she winced at the reflection. She looked like a dominatrix. Perhaps it was the knee-high boots *and* the tight black dress. If she'd have been at home, she might have changed into something else, but she had left work so late, the only option had been to get ready in the ladies' at the restaurant; she had to go with what she'd brought. Maybe she shouldn't have rushed. Ruth seriously doubted David was even here yet. He was at his desk at seven and rarely left before ten; that was standard working hours in the City, so a financial journalist like David had to work the same beat. At least that was what he told her. Of late Ruth had begun to have doubts about her boyfriend. They had been dating for two years, and he had yet to invite her to meet his parents, they rarely spent the entire weekend together; hell, it was the first time she had seen him this week.

Of course, Ruth would never usually complain about that. She had always tried to keep relationships at arm's length; work always had such a habit of getting in the way of her love life that she found it easier not to bother cultivating it. But she liked David. He was smart, sexy and handsome, with dark cropped hair and the clean-cut, regular features of a talk-show host. More importantly, they understood each other. He was as devoted to his career as she was to hers – he planned on being business editor of *The Times* within two years and editor-in-chief another three years after that. What she needed to work out was whether he was just as devoted to her. She wasn't looking for a ring on her finger, but what was it her mom always used to say? 'You've got to shit or get off the potty.'

'Just go and have fun,' Ruth told herself, blotting her lipstick and heading for the ground-floor cloakroom. Dropping her bag off, she rode up in the lift to the dining room on the twentieth floor. It was a pretty swish restaurant they were meeting in – so maybe things were looking up in her relationship after all. Stepping off the elevator, she almost whistled at the view. Ruth never tired of the otherworldly futurescape of Canary Wharf: the chequerboard yellow lights of the offices and the clean modernist angles of the architecture. It was like a science fiction film set come to life, a strange secret city hidden away around the corner from the rest of London.

The maître d' pointed her towards the bar area, where she saw David almost immediately. He was sitting at the bar laughing – with a pretty girl in a miniskirt. *Great*.

'Oh, hi, Ruthie,' he said, rising from his bar stool as he spotted her. 'Come and meet Susie, she's a lobbyist with Lorna Steele.'

Of course, thought Ruth, *a PR girl. Aren't they always?* Not a great beauty up close, but blonde and young enough to flatter David, that much was obvious. The girl clearly caught the look on Ruth's face, because she stood up.

'Listen, I've got to be going,' she said quickly, picking up her clutch.

'Stay for another one,' said David.

Susie shook her head.

'It's late. Lovely meeting you, David. You too, Ruth,' she added, before swaying towards the lift on five-inch heels.

Fifteen years younger and ten times as hungry. What hope is there for the rest of us? thought Ruth, watching her leave. Her long legs, her tight ass. It didn't help that David was three years younger than Ruth. He'd once called her his cougar and she'd sulked for three days. At least he'd laid off that line of teasing ever since.

'So, want a drink?' said David, slightly too eagerly. It looked as if he was on his third, at least.

'Why don't we eat?'

He laughed. 'You're joking, aren't you? We'll have to take out a mortgage just to get a starter.'

'But it's fine to buy overpriced cocktails with Susie?'

His handsome features frowned.

'What's got into you?'

Ruth stopped herself. After her confrontation with Jim, the last thing she needed tonight was a public row. She just wanted a nice night out, to have fun, for David tell her everything was going to be all right. And she wasn't going to get that by screaming at him for talking to some floozy.

She waved a hand. 'Sorry, sorry,' she said, capitulating. 'Just a bad day at work.'

David raised a finger to get the barman's attention.

'Vodka tonic. Double. Slice of lemon.'

He turned to look at her.

'So come on, tell me. What's happened? Jim Keane's been dick-swinging again?'

'Is my working life so predictable?'

She took the vodka and sipped it slowly as she told him about the editorial meeting at the *Tribune*, about the escort story she had been working on, and how Jim had nixed it before she had time to investigate it properly. David leant forward on the bar, his eyes twinkling with the same excitement as she had felt earlier today when she'd been piecing together the story. Sometimes it was good dating a journalist – the same hunger for news.

'Bloody hell, if you're right that's a fantastic story,' he said. 'Not just for the *Tribune*, but for the Germans, for us, for anyone. I can't believe he doesn't want to follow it up.'

Ruth stabbed at the lemon in her drink with a swizzle stick.

'We're both on trial for the bureau chief job, remember? And I have more to prove because he's already in the job. He's not going to want me to get the glory, is he?'

'So don't tell him,' said David. 'Write it under the radar. Smile sweetly, do the Angela Ahrendts profile and whatever else Jim throws at you. In the meantime, you find your scoop, then file it directly to Isaac.'

Ruth shook her head. She had already thought of that approach and dismissed it.

'I don't know. Isaac is going to see right through that. And Jim will go ballistic. In fact he'll probably have me fired.'

David gave a low, slow laugh. 'It's every man for himself now, sweetheart. And as for Isaac, if he's got a shit-hot story on his hands, he won't give two hoots who you shafted to ring it in.'

Ruth smiled. She knew they were talking about dirty office politics but David made it sound acceptable.

'You're a ruthless sonofabitch, you know that?'

'I'll accept that as a compliment,' he grinned.

Ruth finished her vodka. She was already feeling better, that stupid little PR girl a distant memory. She looked over towards the restaurant hopefully.

'Aren't you hungry?' she said.

David slid his hand up her thigh.

'Yes I am,' he whispered. 'Why don't we go back to mine and get a takeaway?'

'Let's go,' she said, reaching out and taking his hand.

David lived in one of the anonymous modern apartment blocks a short distance away from the restaurant. Ruth had enjoyed the walk along the river, her arm looped through his, not talking, just relishing the intimate air of expectation. They rode up in the lift, then David stopped to push the key in the lock, fumbling and cursing as he failed to get it in. Smiling, Ruth came up behind him and brushed her lips across his neck. He smelt good – a familiar tang of soap and expensive cologne.

'Can I help?' she murmured. After feeling frustrated at work, paranoid about the girl at the bar, suddenly Ruth felt sexy, in control. David turned and she kissed him, slowly at first, teasing him, barely touching his lips, until the kiss grew deeper, more fervent. Groaning, David twisted the key and they stumbled through the door into the darkness of the small foyer, kissing, laughing, needing to touch, taste the other. Her hands held his face and he moved his mouth to suck the tips of her fingers, sending urgent shots of lust round her body.

'Get this dress off me,' she purred, feeling the heat between her thighs.

'You need to get pissed off about work more often,' smiled David as he unzipped it, slipping the fabric from her shoulders, stroking her bare skin with his palms.

Unhooking her bra, she crawled on to the bed, feeling his hands behind her, peeling down her panties and slipping them off over her long, slim legs. She lay back, watching him undress, and stretched her arms above her head, closing her eyes in lazy, lustful anticipation of what was to come.

Kneeling on the mattress, he parted her thighs, then dipped like a cat to take a long, slow lick between her thin strips of pubic hair. She gasped as his tongue entered her and seared across her swollen nub.

He worked his way up her torso, slowly sucking and kissing each nipple in turn, then eased himself on top of her, his scrub of chest hair brushing against her breasts, as his hard cock pushed into her wetness.

'Yes,' she gasped, arching her back as his lips brushed her neck. She circled her hips, her hands pressing against his back, feeling his skin bead with sweat under her palms. They moved in perfect motion until slowly, teasingly, he pulled out of her, stroking her clitoris with the tip of his cock as he moved position. He gave a deep, animal thrust back into her and she moaned in desire. She felt so exquisitely full of him, a hot, rippling arrow of lust ripped through her core. And when she came, the orgasm shook her like she had touched a live cable.

Finally David cried out and collapsed on top of her, his muscles shaking. For a moment they lay there in silence, then they both smiled, slowing their breathing.

'You're a wildcat sometimes, Boden, you know that?'

'I try,' she smiled.

She felt her breath regulate, feeling much more calm, the stresses of the day all but gone. David rolled over to face her, propping his head up with the pillow, and looked at her earnestly.

'Why don't you move in here?' he said, his voice unusually hesitant.

She was determined to remain cool, despite the surprise of his offer.

'Because you've never asked,' she replied calmly.

His lips curled into a half-smile.

'I'm asking now. It makes sense.'

She laughed. 'You mean sex and home-cooked dinners all on tap within a one-mile radius of work. You're such a caveman.'

He laughed.

'You'd never make a home-cooked meal.'

'You're right there.'

There was a long pause.

'So what's your answer?'

'I don't know,' she said finally.

He looked hurt.

'You don't . . . know?' he asked.

Ruth pulled a face. Wasn't this exactly what she'd wanted from him earlier in the evening?

'I can't give you an answer because I don't know what's happening in my life right now,' she said. 'If I lose my job, there's a good chance I'll be leaving London.'

'That might not be such a bad thing.'

It was her turn to look wounded, but he put out a hand to stroke her cheek.

'I've always wanted a spell working Stateside,' he said. 'New York, Washington. It could be good for us both.'

'It might not be that simple,' said Ruth. 'If they close down the London office, the only job I know of is in Shanghai, not Washington.'

He frowned.

'I don't want to go to Shanghai,' he said, smoothing her hair back. 'And I don't want you to go to Shanghai.'

'Neither do I.'

Her words surprised her. Five years ago, maybe even two, such an opportunity would have made the hairs on her neck stand up. But things had changed, *she* had changed. She was tired; she had no more desire to go racing off to China than she had to go to the moon. The truth was, her battle to impress Isaac wasn't just about keeping a job – it was about keeping the job she had now. She looked into David's handsome face. Was it time to settle down, put down some roots? And suddenly she knew: what she really wanted was to make a home, not just a base from which to work. It was as if she had floated right around the world, and like a feather falling to the ground, she had chosen to stop here. She pulled David closer, nuzzling into his chest.

'Right now, I don't want to be anywhere else.'

7

There was a note leaning against the marble counter-top in the kitchen. Sophie put down her suitcase and picked it up.

Make yourself at home! The fridge is stocked – help yourself to anything you can find, and if you get bored, there's a few things on the mantelpiece you might enjoy. Have fun! Lana xxx

A slow smile spread across Sophie's face.

'Bloody hell,' she whispered. 'This really is home.'

The Filipino housekeeper cleared her throat, standing by the front door.

'Madam, is it okay if I now leave?' she said, picking up her canvas tote.

'Sorry, of course it's fine,' said Sophie, a little too enthusiastically.

'I be on holiday now for a few days,' she continued in her halting English. 'But there is food in house, okay?'

'No worries. No worries at all.'

She waited until she heard the front door close shut before she let loose an excited scream.

'I don't believe it,' she said to herself as she began to look around the house. 'I just don't believe it.'

Lana's home was a palace. The drawing room was like something from a more genteel age, with hand-painted wallpaper, cream carpets, long mint-green drapes and an amazing mottled green and white marble fireplace that looked as if it had been carved from Stilton. There was a piano room, a dining room with a table that seated twenty, and a luxurious sunken living space, with sofas not much smaller than Sophie's Battersea flat. The studio in the basement was better equipped than a hotel gym, and there was even a plunge pool down there. It wasn't just a house that said money; it said taste or at least an expensive interior design job. Sophie couldn't believe Lana wanted to change a thing.

She moved upstairs to explore the master bedroom with its emperor-size four-poster and views over the square. The guest rooms were equally impressive, effortlessly fitting modern furniture into the period features of the house. There was even a nursery with a fairy-tale mural along one wall and a cot in the shape of a carriage. In the final bedroom, a huge suite in the eaves with a claw-foot bath under the skylight, Sophie threw herself on the bed, laughing out loud at the crispness of the expensive linen.

She felt giddy with excitement. It wasn't as if she hadn't experienced luxury before, but she supposed her brief brush with relative poverty had made her appreciate the beauty of Lana's home all the more. Pulling out her mobile phone, she scrolled to Francesca's number, desperate to share her excitement with someone.

'Fran, is that you? It's Sophie.'

'Darling, can I call you back? We're in Browns Bride and I am about to try on the most amazing Alberta Ferretti dress.'

'Sorry,' said Sophie, her excitement fading a little.

'I'm just freaking with the choice,' said Francesca in a conspiratorial whisper. 'The Lanvin I've just had on was incredible. The Valentino with the cap sleeves was adorable too and I've not even started with Wang or Monique Lhuillier.'

'You carry on,' said Sophie brightly. 'Do you want to meet up tonight? You can tell me more, and besides, I've got something fabulous to show you.'

She could hear Fran's mother in the background, ordering Francesca to get off the phone. Francesca was her only daughter and she was taking the wedding *very* seriously.

'I don't know, Soph,' sighed her friend. 'All I'll want to do tonight is flop.'

'Come on, Fran. You'll like it.'

'All right,' she said after a long pause. 'Where? Don't think I'm coming all the way to Battersea, because I'm exhausted as it is without trekking south of the river.'

'You don't have to,' said Sophie, trying to suppress her smile. 'I've moved. To Egerton Row.'

'*Really?*' replied Francesca, her interest clearly lifting a notch.

Smiling, Sophie gave her friend the address and said she'd expect her later.

By the time Sophie made it back down to the kitchen, she felt quite light-headed. She crossed to the fridge, an enormous American-style brushed-steel refrigerator with two doors. One side was filled with fresh fruit and vegetables, much of it in the distinctive brown and green Whole Foods packaging; the other was given over to exotic-looking fruit juice, bottles and bottles of sparkling water and at least a dozen bottles of white wine. Sophie pulled one down and looked at the label.

Château Olivier 2005.

'Gosh,' she said.

At her mother's insistence, Sophie had taken a wine-tasting course a few years back – 'You don't want to look stupid at a dinner party, do you, darling?' Julia had said – and to her surprise, she had really enjoyed it, partly because it was run by a handsome older man named Charles whose enthusiasm for grapes was infectious, and partly because Sophie discovered she had a natural flair for tasting. Encouraged by Charles, she began reading up on grape varieties and the history of vineyards. She was only a keen amateur, but she enjoyed her little hobby: the imagination she'd always wanted to channel into writing or art had found an outlet in wine appreciation. And if she remembered correctly, Château Olivier was one of the finest Sémillons in France.

She looked around the fridge for something cheaper, as she did not want to abuse Lana's hospitality, but every bottle reeked of quality. And Lana *had* said to help herself, hadn't she? *I'll only have a glass, anyway*, she thought as she rummaged in the drawers looking for a corkscrew. She quickly opened the bottle and splashed the wine into a big glass. It was delicious; clean and flinty. She held on to the glass as she lugged her suitcase upstairs. Lana hadn't specified where she should sleep, but there was something magical about having a bath under the stars, so she chose the room in the eaves.

She unpacked, hanging her few outfits in the empty wardrobe as she ran a bath, then when it was ready, climbed in, sighing with pleasure. There was only a shower at her little studio, and she could no longer afford the pharmacy of bath oils Lana had sitting next to the tub. *I feel like Julia Roberts in* Pretty Woman, she thought, sipping her wine and giggling to herself. She stayed there, topping up the water, until her fingers started to crinkle, then towelled herself dry and pulled on her best underwear. It felt appropriate to the surroundings, after all. It was just then that the doorbell began to ring downstairs. It took Sophie a moment to remember she had invited Francesca over.

Wrapping herself in a robe, she padded downstairs, opening the door to her wide-eyed friend.

'How the bloody hell can you afford this?' said Fran as she pushed her way inside.

Sophie laughed.

'Don't get too excited, I'm only house-sitting.'

Sophie filled her in on her new domestic arrangement as she took her on a guided tour of the house, loving every squeal of delight and envy that Francesca let out as she showed her the bedrooms, Lana's huge dressing room, even the long garden at the back of the house. Finally, they sat down at the breakfast bar in the kitchen and Sophie poured her friend a glass of the Sémillon.

'So you're going to live this Lana woman's life for the summer?' said Francesca, sipping her wine. 'Who is she?'

'She's Spanish. Or Majorcan, I think. Beautiful, anyway, and very stylish, very nice. Her husband has some money markets job, works in Geneva apparently.'

'What's his name? Charlie might know him.'

'Simon Goddard-Price.'

Francesca pouted.

'Never heard of him. Have you Googled him?'

'Tried that,' said Sophie between sips. 'Couldn't find much beyond mentions in the business pages.'

Francesca nodded sagely. 'You know some people actually pay a publicist to keep them out of Google searches? Charlie told me. They must have serious money if that's the case.'

'That makes sense,' nodded Sophie. 'Lana doesn't seem the sceney type. There's a heap of invitations on the mantelpiece she didn't seem that bothered about going to. Said I could go along if I fancied.'

'Really?' said Francesca, sliding out of her seat. 'Let's have a look, then.'

She retrieved the invitations and spread them out on the kitchen counter.

'Bloody hell, Soph,' she said. 'These are some of the hottest tickets in town. Oh my God, look at this!' she gasped, snatching up one of the cards and holding it out to Sophie. 'It's for Victor Yip's fortieth!'

'Who's Victor Yip?'

Francesca gaped at her.

'You don't know who Victor Yip is? Chinese gazillionaire, Sophie. Like, only the richest man in London right now.'

Sophie frowned, feeling totally out of the loop.

There was a time when she knew all about the hottest clubs, bars and parties to be seen at. She'd pored over *Tatler* and *Harper's* and had enthusiastically thrown herself into London's summer season – attending everything from Henley to the Cartier polo. But Lana's invitations hadn't registered at all.

'I thought that steel magnate, wossisname, was the richest man in London.'

Francesca rolled her eyes. 'Get with the programme, Soph.'

Sophie caught the look on her friend's face.

'Whatever. We can't go,' she said firmly.

'Why not? There's a plus one.'

'We can't go bowling up to someone's birthday party just because we've got the invitation. It's a personal party; he invited Lana, not us.'

Francesca sighed.

'Well, what about this one, then?' she said, pointing to another card.

'The Chariot Dinner,' read Sophie, craning her neck. 'What's that?'

'God, it's like you've been living in Burkina Faso, not Battersea. It's only one of the biggest fund-raisers in the calendar. Do you know how much it costs to go to this? It's ten thousand a plate. We're talking hedgies, oligarchs, the mega-connected. Not even *I've* been to this, Soph.'

Francesca's expression changed as she picked up the invitation. 'Oh look, Soph! *It's tonight!*'

Sophie took the invitation out of her friend's hand.

'Well, we've missed it. It started at seven.'

'The *meal* was at seven for seven thirty,' corrected Francesca, snatching the card back. 'We don't want to go to that anyway, I've got ten pounds to lose before the wedding, remember? But the party will go on all night.'

She looked at Sophie with puppy-dog eyes, clutching the invitation to her bosom.

'Please, Sophie, can't we go? It will be amazing. Last year Beyoncé did a set and Daniel Craig was the master of ceremonies for the auction. Who knows how they'll top that this year. We *can't* miss it.'

Sophie hesitated. She could do with a really fun night out. And seeing Daniel Craig or some other celebrity hottie would be the icing on the cake of a pretty extraordinary day so far. Maybe it was the wine, maybe it was the excitement of feeling back in her old life, but suddenly she felt uncharacteristically bold.

'All right, let's do it,' she said, putting her wine glass down decisively.

'Yay!' squealed Francesca, clapping her hands together.

'Well we can't go like this. It's black tie. But if we go via your place, I could borrow something there.'

'Sod trekking all the way back to my place,' said her friend. She took a long slurp of wine. 'The solution is right here.'

She stood and pulled Sophie up by the hand.

'Oh no, no, no,' said Sophie, as Francesca led her up to Lana's enormous dressing room off the master bedroom. 'We *can't*.'

'Why not?' said Francesca bluntly. 'Lana's in France and we're here with a party to go to and nothing to wear.' She pulled a faux weepy face and then swept into the room, running her fingers across the racks of silks and chiffons.

'This is heaven,' she squealed, picking up a lizard-skin Blahnik heel and pushing her foot into it.

'Come on, Fran, don't,' said Sophie. 'This is not my stuff.'

'Chill out,' said Francesca. 'It's not as if I'm planning on selling them on eBay; we're only borrowing them for a few hours. We'll get everything dry-cleaned afterwards; Lana will never know.'

'Even so . . .'

'You used to be so much fun,' said Francesca wearily.

At school, Francesca had always been the most rebellious of their group of friends, and she had a way of making anyone who didn't want to go along with her schemes feel stuffy and boring. She had certainly always been able to talk Sophie around; the truth was, Sophie had been painfully introverted and strait-laced when she had first arrived at Marlborough, and Francesca had brought her out of her shell, with the result that she found it almost impossible to say no to her friend.

'Come on, Sophie. You *deserve* a good night out.'

Sophie couldn't disagree with her there. She reached out to touch a rack of evening gowns. The closest thing she had to a party dress in her little wardrobe upstairs was a black jersey wrap – not exactly 'dress to impress' by any stretch of the imagination – and her ballet flats were comfy, but it wasn't the sort of thing that turned movie stars' heads.

Francesca pulled out a beautiful midnight-blue gown with sequins sewn in swirling patterns down the length of the delicate material.

'This would be perfect for you, why don't you just try it on?' she urged.

Sophie felt a flutter of anxiety, but then she pictured herself wearing it, sipping a cocktail and laughing at some film star's joke.

'Well, it couldn't hurt just to see how it looks,' she said.

'That's my girl,' smiled Francesca.

Sophie shrugged off her robe and quickly slipped into the dress, looking at her reflection in the full-length mirror. She almost gasped; it was beautiful. Flowing, very flattering and the sequins twinkled like stars when she moved.

She felt a flutter of excitement, of mischievousness. Grinning, she turned to Francesca.

'So which shoes do you think I should wear with this, then?' she asked.

8

Sophie was having second thoughts. As she tottered across Waterloo station's busy concourse on five-inch heels, she felt overdressed and unbalanced. She clutched the hem of her dress – Lana's dress, actually – desperate to keep it off the smeared floor. Three of the sequins had already come off in the taxi, and she was pretty sure that the fabric was too delicate to dry-clean.

'Why did you let me wear these bloody shoes?' she hissed at Francesca. 'I can barely walk.'

'You're wearing them because they're beautiful, and they make your legs look thinner.'

'But no one can see my legs – they can't even see the shoes.'

Francesca stepped daintily on to the escalator and tossed her long hair back.

'Stop complaining,' she smiled. 'This party is going to be fabulous, *we're* going to be fabulous. And remember, you're Lana Wosserface, otherwise we'll never get in.'

'Oh God,' Sophie whispered to herself as she looked towards the entrance. The party was being held in the old Eurostar terminal – according to the invitation, actually on the platform – and the archway that had previously been the security screening area was the only way in. It looked incredible: the whole structure had been covered with shimmery blue material, and a bright blue carpet had been rolled out to meet the bottom of the escalator.

'Be cool,' said Francesca as they walked up to the clipboard girls standing behind the velvet rope – who were dressed in azure sequinned minidresses, like sexy mermaids. Fighting the urge to run away – not that she could have run in those shoes – Sophie simply smiled at them and handed over the invitation. She had spent enough time on the other side of the rope to know that people on the door can smell fear.

'Lana?' said the girl, looking her up and down. Her expression was serious. Sophie's heart was pounding, fearing they were about to get caught out. 'I'm afraid you've just missed dinner. But I'm sure we can get someone to sort you out some food,' she said sympathetically.

'Don't worry about food,' smiled Sophie, realising they were in.

'Have a good time,' grinned the clipboard girl.

Sophie beamed. 'We will.'

Her jaw almost dropped as they walked inside. The whole of the Eurostar terminal had been transformed into a fantastic dining-room-cum-nightclub. The track had been covered over and turned into an ad hoc dining area, with huge flower arrangements in the centre of each circular table, the blue and white flowers mixed with peacock feathers. At the far end of the platform was a flashing dance floor and a stage, and suspended from the hangar-height roof were thousands of glowing blue lanterns. It was so magical it almost took Sophie's breath away.

'Is that who I think it is?' she whispered, staring at the stage.

George Clooney was standing at a podium offering a weekend on a yacht in the Caribbean as an auction prize, which brought on a flurry of frantic bidding.

'And you wanted to stay in tonight,' giggled Francesca. 'This is the party of the bloody decade!'

She walked over to a board which had the seating plan laid out on it.

'According to this, we're on table 53,' said Francesca.

'No, Lana's on table 53,' corrected Sophie. 'And she's probably been seated right next to her best friend. We can't just go and sit down in her spot, can we?'

Francesca sighed.

'I suppose not. Anyway, dinner's over. I think the live act is about to come on any minute. That Damien Hirst-customised Range Rover has got to be the star prize, hasn't it?'

Sophie watched in amazement as a white 4×4 drove on to the stage and parked up next to George Clooney's podium. *What credit crunch?* she thought.

'Listen, I've got to pee,' said Francesca. 'Get me a drink, would you? Nothing with any calories, think of the wedding dress, okay?'

Sophie looked after her friend anxiously, feeling exposed and fraudulent.

'May I offer madam a Silver Fir?' said a handsome waiter carrying a tray of glasses containing something that looked cool and green.

'Yes, certainly,' said Sophie, reminding herself that she was playing a role. She needed to behave as if this sort of thing happened every day. *In fact, shouldn't I look a bit bored?* It was a hard look to pull off, especially as this had to be the most exciting party she could remember going to. She had already seen two actors – three, if you counted the master of ceremonies – and one woman who she recognised as a fashion designer. Every other person looked as if they could be – probably *were*, for all Sophie knew – talented, famous or both. She was certainly glad that Fran had talked her into wearing this dress; at least she fitted in among the acres of couture. God, she thought suddenly, was her dress couture? Didn't they cost like fifty grand each? She consciously held her drink further away from the fabric, which suddenly felt even more flimsy than before. Knowing her luck, there would probably be only one of them in existence and word would get back to Lana quicker than you could say 'house-sitting charlatan'.

'It's quite a party, isn't it?'

Sophie turned to see a man watching her with evident amusement. He was handsome, with dark blond hair pushed off his face, lightly tanned skin and bright blue eyes that seemed to assess everything. Francesca would have noticed his sharp navy suit, and the chunky watch, but Sophie reminded herself that she wasn't interested in that sort of thing.

'Yes, it's fun,' she said, sipping her drink nervously. She wasn't sure whether she was supposed to be wildly enthusiastic or feign indifference.

'They must have raised about twenty million tonight.'

'Really?' said Sophie, then remembered her cover story and tried to look as if twenty million was a trifling sum. 'How much did the car go for?'

'Well, I bid fifty grand, but I stopped listening when it reached two hundred.'

'Lucky escape, then,' said Sophie without thinking.

He gave a smooth, easy smile.

'You've got me. I always bid first on the star item because I know someone will outbid me. Besides, it would have taken me three months to ship the thing home.'

'To America?' she said, flushing slightly. *Of course he's American, you idiot*, she scolded herself.

'Is it the accent?' smiled the man, then held his hand out. 'Nick Cooper, from Houston. Well, I'm from some no-account backwater actually, but Houston's where I'm based right now.'

'Sophie Ellis. I'm from a backwater too. Surrey.'

Nick frowned.

'Isn't Surrey like ten miles from London?'

'When you're in Chelsea, that's like being a hillbilly,' she laughed, widening her eyes.

'I see,' he drawled. 'Moonshine and 'gators, that sort of thing?'

'Very similar, although it's more like Pimm's and ponies.'

'I clearly haven't ventured far enough outside the Riverton,' he said, name-checking one of the most deluxe hotels in town.

'You should,' she giggled. 'Actually no, you're probably better off staying at the Riverton.'

He laughed, his blue eyes flashing.

'Listen, can I get you another drink?'

'Yes, that'd be nice, one of those silver things, please.'

Wow, he's good-looking, she thought as she watched him move through the crowds. And rich enough to bid on a car he obviously didn't even want. Her mother would be very pleased.

'Soph, you'll never believe it!' Francesca rushed up to her, her eyes frantic. She looked close to tears.

'What? What's happened?'

Francesca held up her mobile. 'I just spoke to Charlie. He's had his briefcase snatched.'

'Oh no. Is he okay?'

Francesca nodded and bit her lip.

'Yes, he's fine, but he's shaken up, I can tell.'

Sophie pulled her into a hug.

'It's okay honey, as long as he's not hurt, that's the main thing.'

Her friend pulled back.

'No, you don't get it,' she snapped. 'That's not the bad part – he wants me to go and give him my set of house keys.'

Sophie immediately saw that what she had assumed was teary concern for her fiancé was in fact fury at Charlie's poor timing.

'You're not leaving?'

'I *have* to, apparently,' said Francesca, throwing her hands in the air. 'He's with clients from Hong Kong and he doesn't know what time he's finishing.'

'Why doesn't he just come to yours when he's finished?'

Fran pulled a face and shook her head. Sophie had always thought her friend wore the trousers in her relationship with Charles, but it was clear now who was in control.

'Come on, let's go,' said Francesca, turning towards the exit.

Just then, Sophie spotted Nick weaving back through the crowd holding two drinks in the air, and she caught Francesca's arm.

'Listen, Fran, do you mind if I stay? I can come out and find a cab with you . . .'

Francesca frowned. 'I can't *leave* you here.'

'Why not? I'll be fine.'

Over Sophie's shoulder, Francesca spotted Nick approaching and her face twisted.

'Oh, I see, it's like that, is it?' she said tartly. 'It's all right for some, isn't it?'

Sophie knew she forgave her friend for too many tantrums, too many sarcastic remarks – at the end of the day, she was grateful that Fran did not abandon her when she moved out of Chelsea, and with it her old lifestyle. But this time she was going to put her foot down.

'Come on, Fran. Don't be like that. We've just got here.'

'Fine. You stay and have all the fun,' said Francesca bitterly before striding off.

'Fran!' called Sophie. 'Don't . . .'

'Is there a problem?' said Nick, handing her a drink.

'I hope not,' she said, running to follow her friend, but Fran had got lost in the crowd. Sighing, Sophie returned to Nick.

'Who was the blonde?'

'Fran? An old school friend.'

'She seemed pretty pissed off.'

Sophie laughed wearily.

'She can get like that,' she replied diplomatically.

'Do you need friends like that?'

His honesty disarmed her.

'That's the thing about boarding school, you get thrown together. I guess she's like the sister I never had. Maybe we don't have as much in common as we used to, we've grown apart, but I couldn't imagine her not being around.'

She looked at Nick and shrugged. She couldn't believe she was telling this complete stranger things she hadn't even really admitted to herself.

'Well, I'm glad you stayed,' he said, clinking his glass against hers.

'What's the toast?'

'To old friends. And new ones,' he said playfully.

They were disturbed by a voice behind them.

'Nicky boy, I don't believe it.'

There was a man standing there with his arms open. He was tall, muscular, with dark tousled hair and a scrub of stubble that made him rough around the edges. But his black suit fitted his broad shoulders perfectly, although he wore it with white sneakers. New money, definitely, thought Sophie. She had met his type many times before in the Chelsea clubs. He probably had a yellow convertible Ferrari double-parked outside, cocaine in his pocket and a model waiting for him in the loos.

Nick looked as pleased about the interruption as she was.

'Hey, Josh,' he said without enthusiasm. 'I'm surprised to see you here.'

'How come?' said Josh, his voice cocky, with a soft Scottish burr. 'Everyone's here tonight, aren't they? If there's a better place to do business, then I want to hear about it.'

He turned his attention to Sophie, his intense grey eyes disarming her.

'I'm sorry. We've not been introduced. Josh McCormack. I'm an old friend of Nick's, aren't I, Nick?'

'Sophie Ellis. Hello.'

He turned and ignored her, which irritated her more than it should have.

'So how long are you in town for?' he asked Nick.

'Just another few days. Then back to Houston.'

'So how was Paris? How long were you there for in the end?'

'Four months. On and off.'

'That's right,' said Josh, nodding. 'You said you might stay a while when I saw you. Was it fun?'

'Well, it was business, not a holiday.'

Nick took a sip of his drink and let the silence hang between them.

'Well, I'll leave you two love birds alone,' said Josh finally. 'Nice to meet you, Sophia.' He pulled out a card and handed it to her.

Joshua McCormack, Bespoke Horologist.

'Bespoke horology?' she asked. 'What's that?'

The corners of his mouth curled upwards.

'Watches. I source them, buy them, sell them to a very select and demanding client list.'

'I thought the richest men in the world wore Timex these days,' said Nick.

'Not everyone, my friend,' said Josh, patting him on the shoulder. 'I see Sophia here with a Patek Philippe Gondolo. Rose gold. Alligator strap. Sexy. Stylish. Call me if you need anything sorting out.'

He winked at her and she felt herself bristle. He couldn't even get her name right, and he was clearly trying to sell her something.

'Enjoy the evening,' said Nick, raising his glass.

Josh grinned and disappeared.

'You don't like him much, do you?' smiled Sophie as he went.

Nick shrugged. 'He's all right, I suppose, a bit of a bullshitter. I wouldn't buy a watch off him, put it that way. What was it you said about your friend? I think we've grown apart.'

Sophie smiled.

'So what do you do that takes you to Paris?'

She'd been trying to avoid the question, as 'What do you do?' was the classic cocktail party way of sussing people's worth; she had learnt that particular lesson at her mother's knee. Whether you were a surgeon, hedge-funder or astronaut, your occupation was an instant, silent indicator of how much money you made and, in her mother's case, whether you were worth talking to. But still, Sophie was curious.

'I'm in investments.'

Sophie waited for him to say something else. When he didn't, she burst out laughing.

'What's wrong?' he frowned.

'Why is everyone who works with money so guarded? Is it perhaps because you don't want us to see that what you do isn't actually very glamorous?'

'Ouch. You wound me,' said Nick, mock-hurt. 'For your information, my work is pretty interesting.'

'Yeah, *right*,' said Sophie. 'My last boyfriend worked in the City. Listening to him talk about work was about as exciting as watching croquet.'

'I thought the British loved croquet.' Nick smiled.

Sophie grinned.

'Okay, then,' he sighed. 'I buy and sell companies. Mainly in the oil and gas sector. Also oil and gas royalties, mineral rights. Hence I live in Houston, rather than New York.'

'And what's that like? You're living in the desert, right?'

'The desert!' he laughed, almost choking on his drink.

'I've seen pictures of Texas,' replied Sophie. 'The orange soil. Scrub, cactus, blue skies, all that?'

'Not Houston,' said Nick, shaking his head. 'It's pretty green,' he smiled. 'Real hot, but green; we got a subtropical climate, it's on the banks of a bayou.'

'I guess I'm not as well travelled as I thought.'

'Travel's overrated,' said Nick. 'When you do what I do, you see a lot of identical minibars and not much else.'

He led Sophie over to a table and they sat down. Everyone else seemed to be up on the dance floor now throwing shapes to Michael Bublé, but all Sophie wanted to do was listen to Nick. He told her how he'd been to India, the Australian outback, Afghanistan; he'd even been fishing in the Faroe Islands: 'An amazing place, but I wouldn't recommend it unless you really like eating baked puffin or whale meat.'

In return, she told him about her six months in Florence, the tiny apartment overlooking the Ponte Vecchio, the family Christmases at the Sandy Lane hotel in Barbados, a ski trip to Jackson Hole with Will and his friends the New Year before. She told him only the good stuff, obviously. It was such a magical evening, she didn't want to ruin the mood with tales of her dad's death and her money problems. She had spent so long feeling sorry for herself lately, it was fun to just imagine herself in Lana's life for real, pretend that everything was wonderful and effortless and sparkling. There was no harm in that, was there? And she loved the way Nick listened to her stories – *really* listened to them. Every other boy she'd dated in the last ten years only seemed to want to talk about themselves: who their friends were, what kind of car they were driving, what japes they'd got up to at university. She supposed that was the difference: Nick was a man, not a boy. And damn, he was sexy.

'And what do you do, Sophie Ellis?'

She paused.

'I'm just setting up my own business, actually. Personal health and fitness.'

It was economical with the truth. But it was still the truth.

'That's a growing market.' He nodded approvingly. 'And how's it going?'

He looked into her eyes, and for a moment Sophie wondered if he was really asking about the business or about herself.

'It's early days yet,' she grinned. 'But I think it has potential.'

Just then the lights went down and Michael Bublé was frozen in a solitary spotlight. Everyone turned to look at him, holding their breath in anticipation, then the band kicked into 'Haven't Met You Yet' and the dance floor erupted. Nick grabbed Sophie's hand.

'Come on, I like this song,' he said, dragging her through the crowd.

'No, Nick,' she laughed. 'I can't dance, not in these shoes anyway.'

'That's okay, it's up to the man to lead, right?'

He pulled her close and she felt his strong body against hers, then he spun her round and dipped her.

'I feel like Fred Astaire,' she giggled.

'I think you mean Ginger Rogers,' he replied.

She laughed.

'That feels good.'

'What?'

'Laughing.'

'And what about this?'

He pulled her closer, resting his hand on her bare back.

'That's pretty good too.'

'You know, you do have very long eyelashes,' he said, gazing into Sophie's eyes.

'And no one to bat them at.'

'Not until now.'

Was he teasing her? Or was he really enjoying their time together as much as she was? *Come on, Sophie*, she said to herself, *take it slow*. She inhaled and let herself relax, resting her cheek against his shoulder as they swayed. She hoped Nick liked her. She'd been wary of men since Will had so unceremoniously dumped her. There had been no dates. No sex. She had trusted no one to get that close, expecting more disappointment. But this one seemed different.

The song ended and Nick whispered in her ear.

'Shall we get out of here?'

She looked up at him.

'Yes please,' she said.

They walked down past the clipboard mermaids and up on to the concourse. Nick began to head across towards the taxi rank, but Sophie took his arm and steered him through the station's ornate marble main entrance.

'Let's walk,' she said.

It was a clear night and still warm; it seemed a shame to let the magic go so soon. They walked arm in arm on to Waterloo Bridge; the evening air was soft against her cheeks, and the light riverside breeze ruffled her dress.

'Look at that,' she said, nodding upstream towards the lit-up Houses of Parliament and the London Eye. 'Best view in London.'

'Damn.' Nick whistled. 'I see what you mean.'

They stood there, breathing in the night air, Sophie feeling his warm body against hers. She felt electrified by his presence and yet it felt so comfortable.

'Why have I never noticed this before?' said Nick quietly.

'Men like you probably don't go to Waterloo station very much.'

He smiled.

'I guess not. So where are you taking me next?'

'What do you want to see?'

'Something British. Best London pub?'

'It's way past closing time,' she said, glancing at Big Ben, whose black arms were both pointing up at midnight. 'Besides, I'm not exactly dressed for it.'

She looked at him for a moment. 'You really want to see London?'

'Sure, but not the cheesy tourist version. Things only someone who lives here could tell me about.'

'All right, but you can pay the fare,' she said, putting her arm up to hail a taxi. 'I'm going to take you on a tour of my favourite London places. Now pay attention, because I'll be asking questions later.'

She pointed out Somerset House as they crossed the bridge, 'the most romantic place to go ice-skating at Christmas', then the old Strand 'ghost station' where they filmed movies, and the National Portrait Gallery, home to Sophie's favourite painting – Branwell Brontë's portrait of his sisters. They took a detour along Jermyn Street so Sophie could show Nick two of her favourite shops: a cheese vendor and a hat maker within twenty yards of each other.

'Hey I love those hats the businessmen used to wear,' said Nick enthusiastically. 'What are they called again?'

'Bowler hats. You should get one, it'd turn heads in Houston,' she said.

Then she directed the cabbie down to the Mall, past the Palace – '*We have* to see Buck House, you are an American,' she teased.

As they sat back in the cab, London was looking its most magical. The stateliness of the grand houses, the dark lure of the park, then an illuminated cavalcade of gleaming shop fronts, whirling traffic and the milky light from an almost full moon.

Finally they stopped at a late-night tapas bar in Belgravia Sophie had frequented in her Chelsea days and drank slightly rough red wine at a cramped corner table. But Sophie didn't notice the surroundings, she was having too good a time. Nick was smart and charming and unlike so many men she had met in the upper echelons of society, keen to hear her opinions and stories. In between, he told her about his life, his comfortable childhood in 'nowheresville' River Oaks, his growing annoyance at having to spend half his year in the air and his deadline of forty when he wanted to give it all up. Sophie laughed at that one.

'Men like you never want to give up. You all say you do, but you love it too much.'

'It's what we work our asses off for, to retire to the country with a couple of pigs and a chicken.'

'No it isn't,' said Sophie. 'You're in it for the competition. I saw it with my dad, with his friends and with my ex. After a certain level of salary, money becomes meaningless. You might as well pay guys in the City in coconuts – all they care about is being the guy who has the most coconuts at the end of the year.'

Nick laughed.

'Maybe you're right. And what's your ambition, Sophie?' he asked.

'I always wanted to live in a castle. By the water, like the sea or a lake that turns pink in the sunset,' she said, blushing slightly. 'Maybe I have a princess syndrome,' she laughed.

The crowd in the bar had thinned and the waiters had started putting the chairs on the tables.

'Well, I guess that's our cue,' said Sophie, standing up and feeling an ache of sadness that the evening was coming to an end.

'So where do you live?'

'Not far. Just off Brompton Road.'

'Well in that case, how about I walk you home?'

She was about to complain that it was too far to walk, that her shoes were too high, but she didn't want the night to end. At the back of her mind a little voice told her to beware;

that this could be just a quick fling, a holiday romance, a one-night stand with a handsome stranger who would be back in Texas by the end of the week, but she could only throw caution to the soft, balmy evening wind.

They walked up towards Belgrave Square and cut across Sloane Street, Sophie still pointing out landmarks, like the flat John Barry had shared with Michael Caine where he had kept the actor awake composing 'Goldfinger'. She felt light-headed, and when Nick took her hand in his, it seemed like a perfectly natural thing to happen. She let it stay, enjoying the warm, firm clasp of his fingers. She caught herself and realised she was happy. It wasn't an emotion she had felt in a long time. Her grief and anxiety about the future had blocked out the light, but tonight she realised that something simple like holding hands with a man you liked was enough to make life feel good again.

'So what's a girl like you doing being single?' he asked her finally.

Sophie paused for a moment.

'Who said I'm single?' she chided.

She caught his look of disappointment and continued.

'Yes – I'm single,' she grinned. 'And what about you, oil man? You must be what, thirty-two, thirty-three?'

'Thirty-two actually. Hard work, it's taking its toll.'

'So how come you haven't settled down with those pigs?'

He stole a sideways glance at her and sighed.

'I'm not one of those commitment-shy guys you read about in women's magazines. I guess I've just spent the last ten years working my butt off to make something of my life. Besides . . .'

'What?'

'Well, I know this sounds conceited, but . . .'

'But?'

'But I guess it's difficult finding someone who likes me for me.'

'You mean the money?'

'Exactly. I mean, there's a lot of gold-diggers out there,' he said frankly. 'If I hadn't met you at a fancy ten-thousand-bucks-a-plate dinner, if we'd bumped into each other ice-skating at Somerset House, I'd have pretended I was a waiter or a struggling poet with not a bean to his name.'

'Really?'

'Sure. My dad had four wives, count 'em. Even my own mom, she squandered the family money, parties every weekend, keeping up with the Joneses, all that crap. It's just nice to meet someone, you know, who's successful in her own right.'

'Listen, Nick,' she began, but stopped herself. She wanted to tell him that her dress was borrowed, that she lived in a tiny flat in Battersea, that she didn't have a penny. But what good would it do? And anyway, finally there it was, Lana's huge white house looming up in front of them like a big full stop.

'Well,' said Sophie. 'This is it, then.'

'This is yours? Hey, not bad.'

Sophie felt a sinking feeling. She wanted to blurt out that she was only house-sitting, that she wasn't a high-flying businesswoman, but he was so nice, why ruin a perfect evening? And he would probably never call again anyway.

'It's been a good night, Nick. Thanks.'

'Maybe. But it could have been better.'

Her smile faltered.

'How?'

'We never did this.'

Nick stepped towards her, his hand touching the curve of her cheek, his lips on hers, soft and warm. Hers eyes closed as she savoured the taste of him, then all too soon it was over. She knew he was waiting for her to invite him inside. But she couldn't. He would know in an instant that the house was not hers. The photographs of Lana and Simon. Her bedroom, still with that temporary vibe of a holidaymaker. *Don't break the spell*, said a voice in her head. *Keep it as a perfect memory.*

'Good night, Nick,' she said.

'Is that it?' he asked, his disappointment evident.

'Well, I thought you were going back to the desert.'

'Not straight away.' He smiled, reaching into his jacket and pulling out a red pigskin diary.

'Here,' he said, opening it and showing her the page for the next day. 'You see that?' He pointed to the blank space. 'That's for you. And the next day and the next.' He looked at her, suddenly anxious. 'If you want it, that is.'

'Yes,' said Sophie, and she stepped forward and kissed him again. 'Yes I do. Very much.'

9

The sun was leaking through the curtains in the Wellington Suite of the Riverton Hotel. Sophie kept her eyes closed, wanting to savour the feeling for a few seconds more. Still pleasantly fuggy from sleep, she felt the crisp sheets on her skin and the soft pillow under her bed-head hair. Most of all, she wanted to relish the feeling of Nick's naked body next to hers, his arm casually thrown around her, his leg hooked over hers, their bodies still entwined even in sleep.

I think, she smiled to herself, *this is what they call a whirlwind romance.* Nick had called her that night; in fact he'd called her moments after he'd left her on Lana's doorstep – 'just to wish you good night' – then first thing in the morning to tell her that the sun was out and that it was a perfect morning for croissants and coffee. He came to collect her in his silver sports car, casual and sexy in a navy polo shirt, and drove her to a café with checked red tablecloths, hidden away down by the river, which he said reminded him of his time in Paris where his apartment had had a view of the Seine.

Neither of them had wanted the date to end. When Sophie had suggested that she had clients to see, Nick had insisted that she cancel them all. They got back in the car and followed the river all the way out to Eton, where they drank Pimm's and lemonade watching the sunlight glint off the Thames.

The next few days had followed a similar pattern. Nick was attentive and fun, calling or texting throughout the day, sending her flowers or arranging a lunch date. And they had spent every evening together at the sumptuous suite he kept at the Riverton. Sophie smiled to herself again, remembering the fourth night, the previous evening, when she had finally succumbed and allowed him to seduce her, slowly, gently, sensuously. She could feel herself becoming turned on at the memory of him undressing her. He was obviously a practised and skilful lover, taking his time to explore her body, kissing every inch of her, every secret place, making every nerve ending pulse with pleasure, making her come with such a fierce intensity she had felt faint and dizzy afterwards. At some point they had called room service. They had made love again and then taken a long, sudsy bath together, and in the early hours of the morning had fallen asleep, their limbs tangled beneath the starched white hotel sheets, their bodies tired, depleted and happy from sex.

And yet, still she felt a tightness in her stomach. It had been perfect, this whirlwind romance, apart from one thing. She still hadn't told him the truth about Lana's house, how it wasn't really hers, how she was only house-sitting, or the fact she was actually a personal trainer – an unqualified personal trainer at that.

I'll tell him, she said to herself. *I'll tell him tonight.*

'What time is it?' said Nick sleepily, stirring at her side.

'Six forty,' she said, kissing his shoulder. 'I have to go.'

'You're kidding me. What's so important?'

'I've got a client to see and I have to go back to the house and prepare. You've been distracting me too much.'

'Who's the client? Can't they wait?'

'Some hedge-funder. I have to take the meeting.'

Stop it, she scolded herself. *Stop lying.*

Then again, Olivia Isaacs *was* a hedge-funder. One who was getting married and who wanted to get into top shape so desperately she was prepared to pay Sophie £200 an hour for the privilege. This was their first session, and Olivia was potentially a big money-spinner for Sophie; she still hadn't taken her personal trainer's course, but she couldn't look a gift-horse in the mouth, could she?

'How about I distract you?' growled Nick, his nose nuzzling into her ear.

His lips moved to hers, plucking them with delicate kisses as his hands traced the curves of her body. She groaned with arousal. She was tempted, so tempted to stay, but if she could not drag herself away from him, if she let him make love to her, she would miss her appointment and lose a client.

She laughed softly and pulled away.

'Sorry, stud, you'll have to wait.'

He frowned.

'You don't think last night was a mistake, do you?'

'Far from it,' she said. 'It was incredible, and there's nothing more I'd like than to stay and finish what you just started. But I've got an important meeting at eight thirty. I have to go home, prepare . . .'

'Well how about later? I could come to your house at five.'

Sophie felt a rush of panic, but she knew she couldn't put it off any longer. *If he really likes you, he won't care you don't own the house*, she thought, not exactly convincing herself.

'Okay. There's something I need to talk to you about before you go back to Houston anyway.'

She hoped he could not detect the hesitancy in her voice.

Nick sat up on one elbow.

'Say, why don't you come?' he said.

'To . . . Houston?'

'Sure, why not?'

She gaped at him. What was he suggesting? A new life? With him in Texas? *Don't be silly*, she told herself. *He's not proposing; this is just a mini-break for him.* She bent to give him a long, lingering kiss.

'I'll call you to make a plan later,' she whispered, then, catching sight of the time on the bedside alarm clock, swore and ran for the shower.

Her luck was in: she jumped into the lift just as the doors were closing. She ran through the lobby and immediately found a cab waiting outside the door. Maybe she wouldn't be late for Olivia after all.

'Where to, love?' said the driver, rolling his window down.

'Kensington High Street,' she said breathlessly, quickly opening the door and jumping inside. She slumped in the back, letting out a long breath, and watching gratefully as the London streets slipped by.

'Whereabouts you want exactly, darling?' said the cabbie into his mirror as they passed the Royal Albert Hall. 'Only there's roadworks up by the hotel; if you want near the church, I'll have to go round.'

It was only then that Sophie realised she didn't know the actual address. She dug around in her bag for her mobile phone; Olivia had texted the details to her. Where the bloody hell was it?

'My phone,' she groaned, picturing it on the bedside table. 'I must have left it at the hotel.'

She banged on the glass.

'Sorry, can you turn around? I have to go back to the hotel.'

'You sure? We're almost there.' He frowned, then glanced at her in his mirror and blew out his cheeks. 'It's your fare, love. But I'm leaving the meter on.'

He changed lanes, swinging the cab around the Wellington Arch roundabout and back towards the Riverton. The traffic was beginning to build up on the way to Hyde Park. Stop, start. Sophie looked at her watch, mentally calculating the likelihood of arriving at Olivia's on time. *Pretty bloody slim*, she thought with a grimace. And these ladies didn't like to be kept waiting. Even those that didn't have high-flying jobs in finance always seemed to have a packed schedule, and woe betide anyone who made them late for their appointment with their nail technician.

The cab swung across Park Lane and pulled up in the forecourt of the hotel.

'I'll be two minutes,' said Sophie, opening the door.

The cabbie shrugged and tapped the meter. 'Well you'd best hurry then, aincha?'

Sophie burst through the revolving doors, startling a woman in a mink, and ran for the lifts. Sod's law, this time, there were none waiting. She pressed the button repeatedly. 'Come on, come on . . .' she said through gritted teeth.

Bugger it, she thought, yanking open the door to the stairs. It's only three flights. She took them at a run, two steps at a time, swinging round the banisters, trying to ignore the pain in her legs and lungs. *You're supposed to be a personal trainer, remember?* she scolded herself.

Finally there it was: the third floor. She pushed through the fire door and turned left, dodging a housekeeping cart and sprinting to Nick's suite. The door, of course, was closed.

'Nick!' she called, knocking on the door and panting. 'Let me in, I've left my phone!'

She waited, but there was no reply. Had he left already? No, he couldn't have done; more likely he'd just gone back to sleep. 'Nick!' she called, knocking louder now.

Just then she noticed that the maid with the housekeeping cart was watching her.

'Hello,' said Sophie, slightly embarrassed. 'Erm, my boyfriend must have popped out or something. I've left my phone by the bed. I don't suppose you've got a pass key or anything?'

The woman looked at her warily.

'Honestly. You can call downstairs if you like, his name's Nick Cooper.'

The maid hesitated for a moment, then, with a shrug of resignation, slotted her key-card into the door.

'Thank you,' mouthed Sophie and pushed inside. There was a lamp on inside the suite and she could hear the sound of dripping water.

'Nick?' she called, but there was no reply. She walked through the bedroom towards the bathroom. He wasn't in bed, although the duvet had been thrown back and the sheets looked crumpled. The drip-drip sound was louder now.

'Nick, are you still here?'

She stopped and stepped back as she felt a squishiness under her feet. The carpet between the bedroom and the en suite was sodden.

'What the hell?' she whispered. The en suite door was slightly ajar and she gave it a gentle push.

For a moment she couldn't understand what she was seeing – or perhaps her brain didn't want to process it. It was as if she was frozen in the moment, caught in a bad dream. Nick was lying on the floor of the bathroom, naked except for a white towel that had become unfastened at the waist. His eyes were closed, his head lolled lifelessly to one side. The bath had overflowed, surrounding his body with a puddle of water stained red with blood.

'Nick!' she gasped sinking to her knees to cradle him.

Blood was oozing from a wound on his head. The floor was studded with shards of green glass like angry teeth glaring at her.

'No, Nick, please, no . . .' she sobbed, putting her hand over the wound, as if to join the two sides together again, but it was too big, too wide. Too bad.

'Help! Somebody help me!' she screamed, as loud as she could. 'I need an ambulance! Please, someone!' Helpless tears were streaming down her cheeks as she looked at his lifeless face. 'Someone. Please! He's dying,' she choked.

But she could tell that he was already dead. His skin was still warm, but Nick had gone, she could feel it in her heart.

Suddenly there was a blur of activity; hands were lifting her, pulling her away from him.

'No!' she cried. 'I can't leave him! He needs me!'

There were people in the room, noise, raised voices. The maid was crying, a man in a suit barking orders.

'Help him!' screamed Sophie, her voice barely audible through the sobs.

Vaguely, she could hear words being spoken in her ear. Kindly, reassuring words: 'It will be okay', 'There's nothing more you can do', 'The police are on their way'; the sort of things that people said in movies when someone died. Sophie sat on the bed, staring down at her trembling, red-stained hands, her whole world frozen in time, her body weighted by a dim, fearful awareness that the worst was yet to come.

10

Ruth was in Starbucks buying her first macchiato of the day when she got the call. Flinging five pounds at the barista, she ran out on to the street to hail a cab. She couldn't have moved any faster – a trail of coffee had spilt on her white shirt – but still, by the time she she made it to the hotel, it was already a no-go area. Two white police vans were parked on the street and a uniformed officer was checking ID as guests went into the Riverton. Worse, there was a Channel Five film crew setting up on the steps. Not exactly the exclusive she had been led to believe.

Cursing, Ruth pulled out her mobile, but before she could dial the number, she heard a low whistle. Turning, she saw a familiar face: DC Dan Davis, lurking by the side door. He beckoned her over.

'What's that film crew doing here?' she hissed.

'It's a free country, Ruth. Or hadn't you heard?' said Davis, a smile on his face. 'I can't help it if that nice bird off the telly turns up, can I?' He craned his neck around to look at the pretty newsreader standing on the steps.

'I thought we had a deal,' said Ruth.

'Of course we do, darlin',' said Davis, holding the door open for her. 'You'll always be my number one, you know that.'

Ruth took a deep breath. She knew she shouldn't let her frustrations show; besides she should be grateful. Dan Davis was one of a handful of officers she had courted over the years, spending hours in coppers' pubs listening to their war stories, putting up with their ham-fisted attempts at seducing her. It was the price she paid for getting phone calls like the one in the coffee shop. Well, that and all the fat envelopes filled with cash.

The payola to the police wasn't the part of her job she felt most proud of, but it was the way things got done, exchanging tips, *incentives*. And it was the way Ruth Boden had carved herself out an enviable position as one of the Met's pet reporters; at least amongst the troops, where it counted. People like Dan Davis knew what she was after – anything juicy, particularly anything involving Americans, and on the phone this morning he had convinced her that he had something good.

'Well I hope this isn't going to be like that Canadian and his failed suicide attempt,' muttered Ruth as Davis led her down a dark corridor and into a service elevator.

'All a bit of a misunderstanding, that one,' he said, standing a little too close to her. 'Besides, I wanted to see you, didn't I?'

Ruth forced a smile. It wasn't that Dan Davis was bad looking; in fact he had lovely green eyes and floppy dark hair: the sort of colouring they called Black Irish back home. But he was young; he couldn't be more than about twenty-six, although it was always hard to tell their age with coppers. The ancient, grizzled ones with the bags under their eyes and the broken veins on their noses always turned out to be about forty. She supposed the job did that to you; it wasn't as if journalists came out the other end looking particularly youthful either.

'I'm always glad to see you too, Dan,' said Ruth, truthfully. She had no intention of sleeping with him, but he was always good for an ego boost. 'I just don't like to have my time wasted.'

'Well, you'll like this one,' he said. 'There's claret everywhere.'

'Claret?'

Davies rolled his eyes. 'Blood. Fella had his head stoved in, didn't he?'

'So who is he?' she asked, turning to him.

Davis smiled, and Ruth could feel her heart rate increase. Just from the width of his grin, she could tell it was a big story.

'American businessman,' said Davis. 'He must be worth a bit if he can afford one of the suites.'

'Is that where he was found?'

The detective nodded.

'Told you it was worth your taxi fare. I hope you're going to be grateful.'

'You know I'm always grateful,' said Ruth, making a mental note to put in an expenses claim. She was going to have to take Davis and his pals to one of those grubby table-dancing clubs they so enjoyed. At the very least.

'Any idea about the doer?'

'The girlfriend found him. Claims she left the hotel to go to work. Came back after she'd forgotten something and found him dead on the bathroom floor.'

'Do you believe her?'

'She's just some pretty posh girl. Not your average murderer, but a crime of passion? Maybe.'

'What's she called?'

'Ruth, come on.'

'Please, Dan. I'll find out another way, you're just saving me time.'

The detective sighed.

'Sophie Ellis.'

'Is she around?'

'No, she's just been taken to Paddington Green,' he said, leaving the lift and leading her into a small room filled with shelves stacked with bed linen. Ruth looked around; this clearly was not the crime scene. She turned to look at Davis. She hoped he wasn't expecting her to become grateful right now.

'Here,' he said, handing her a white forensics overall. 'You'd better put that on. Don't want you contaminating the scene, and besides, I'm taking a bloody great risk bringing you up here. At least if you're dressed as a SOCO, my boss probably won't notice you.'

Awkwardly, Ruth climbed into the suit, knowing Davis was enjoying watching her. *It's the price you pay*, she reminded herself, the excitement of being so close to such a juicy story overriding any annoyance.

'Sexy,' said Davis as she tucked her hair inside the suit's hood.

'I try,' she said, pulling up the mouth mask.

His expression turned serious.

'All right, here's the rules. I'll walk in, you wait a few seconds and follow me inside. Try and look busy, like you're looking for fingerprints or something, have a butcher's at the scene, then back out the same way. Don't hang around, but don't make it look obvious. We clear?'

Ruth nodded. 'Crystal.'

She shuffled along behind him, the swish-swish of her suit making her feel extremely conspicuous, but at the same time, her heart was beating with excitement. Police had allowed her on to crime scenes before, but never a murder like this. Clearly, Davis sensed that linking his name to this in the press could be very good for his career, or else he expected a fat wodge of cash; otherwise he would never take such a risk. They ducked under some police tape – the whole corridor had been sealed off – and walked towards the only room which was open. Ruth hung back at the door as instructed, then stepped inside. There was one uniformed policeman by the door, three scene of crime officers and two plainclothes detectives talking to Davis, but they all completely ignored her.

She quickly took in the hotel suite: it was clearly an expensive room. The bed was unmade, and there were some scattered papers and clothes, perhaps enough to suggest a disturbance but not enough to think that there had been a fight.

'Are you looking for Pete?'

Ruth turned towards the voice, but hampered by her suit, she almost stumbled over a table, and a hand shot out to steady her.

'Careful, we don't want any more casualties today,' the voice said gruffly.

Ruth pulled down her mask and saw a forty-something detective; he was better dressed than most coppers – a well-cut grey two-button suit with a plain navy tie – but she could still tell he was 'on the job'.

'No, yes,' she stuttered. 'I mean yes, I'm looking for Pete. Have you seen him?'

The detective inclined his head toward the bathroom. 'In there, but watch your step, okay? The floor's wet.'

Ruth nodded and put up her mask, hoping she had just come across as some green graduate on her first crime scene. *A little old for that, aren't you?* mocked a voice in her head. *Come on, concentrate.* Taking a deep breath, she walked over to the bathroom and peered around the door. It was a good job Davis had prepared her. Most of the white tile floor was covered in blood, smeared with footprints. Two more scene of crime officers were kneeling down, bent over the body. Ruth couldn't see the body's face, but the bare upturned foot, its heel surrounded by congealed blood, was enough for her. She turned and walked straight out of the room, holding her breath all the way. She ducked back under the tape and strode down the corridor, almost stumbling into the linen room, where she tore off the suit and shoved it in her tote bag.

Calm, calm, she told herself, inhaling deeply. Ruth had been a reporter for twenty years and she considered herself to be quite hardened – she'd covered road accidents, natural disasters, she'd even been to a refugee camp in Somalia, all in the line of duty. It was not the first time she had seen a dead body either. In Kosovo and Congo she had seen some terrible things, but still, nothing could prepare you for the sight of a murder victim. She trembled, feeling disturbed and upset, and almost ran to the service elevator, focused only on getting outside. Pushing out through the door, she gulped in the fresh air, glad to see the trees, the walls, the rushing traffic. She turned into a side street and sank on to the steps of a red-brick town house to collect her thoughts. There was one image fixed in her mind: the man lying there on the cold tiles, his toes pointing up towards the ceiling. Who was he? How had he been killed, and had posh, pretty Sophie Ellis done it?

But now Ruth could feel her journalistic instincts taking over. A dead American in a top London hotel wasn't exactly Watergate. It wasn't even as potentially explosive as her escort story, not for the *Washington Tribune*, which liked its stories to have a political spin. But she was here, now, in the thick of it. She had seen the body and had the name of the suspect.

She reached into her bag and pulled out her mobile, quickly scrolling to the entry marked 'Squirrel'.

'Robbie, it's Ruth,' she said quickly. 'I need a favour.'

'Really?' said a weary voice. 'And here was I thinking you'd called to wish me a happy birthday.'

Robert Sykes was the society editor of *Class* magazine, the ritziest glossy on the newsstand. He had been to school with one of the royals, and thanks to a brother who had done time for drugs, knew everyone from criminals to the highest-ranking aristos in the country. Ruth had met him years ago on a press junket to Budapest, and ever since, he had been the man she called whenever she needed the skinny on anyone wealthy and British. Robbie always knew where the nuts were – hence Ruth's affectionate nickname.

'Jeez, is it really today?' she said, her heart sinking. 'I'm sorry . . .'

'See?' he said. 'A real friend would have known my birthday is in November.'

She gave a low laugh. 'Robbie, this is important.'

'It always is,' he said, then paused, obviously catching something in her voice. 'Ruth, are you all right?'

'Yes, I'm fine. I just need some info on one Sophie Ellis. Ring any bells? Rich girl with a wealthy boyfriend?'

'I think you'll find there are roughly a zillion rich girls called Sophie in London, darling.'

'Can you get me details?'

'And what has this Sophie Ellis done?'

'And have you steal my exclusive?' she smiled.

'Darling, you know I have to stop fraternising with the enemy. If my editor knew . . .'

'All right, all right,' she said, making a note to increase that expenses claim. 'You know it'll be worth your while.'

He sighed.

'The name doesn't ring any immediate bells. I'll have a little nosy around. I prefer single malt, by the way. Scotch, not bourbon. You can give it to me over dinner at Scott's.'

'It's a date,' she smiled, knowing how much fun she had on her nights out with Robert and his partner Stephen.

Ruth stood and snapped her phone shut, briskly walking back towards the road. Suddenly, she felt a lot better. Suddenly, she was back on the hunt.

11

The policewoman had been very nice. She had given Sophie a blanket for the ride in the car down to the station, and had even brought her a cup of tea.

'Hot sweet tea,' she had said cheerily, as if it was a panacea for all the ills in the world.

The drink was nearly cold now, and had done little to make her feel better. Sophie picked up the polystyrene cup and ran her thumbnail across it, scoring lines into the material. *When are they going to come?* She had been sitting in this little room for an hour at least, just her, a table and an old plastic chair with cigarette burns on it.

A policeman had interviewed her briefly at the hotel and asked her if she wouldn't mind continuing the questioning at the station. She had agreed, coming down to the ugly concrete police station on Harrow Road with the WPC, where she was told to wait for the detective in charge. But where *was* he? The longer Sophie sat there, the more distressed she began to feel.

At the hotel she had been bewildered and in shock, but now, sitting in this empty, soulless interview room, the reality of what had happened was beginning to sink in. Nick was dead. *Dead.* She couldn't close her eyes without seeing the image of his lifeless body, the blood from his wounds colouring the water on the wet bathroom floor. She felt numb, confused and just needed to talk to somebody to try and make sense out of what had happened. Who would want to kill Nick? And what for? Was it an ex-girlfriend, jealous of his relationship with Sophie? A business associate? Somebody he owed money to? She knew that she had had a deep and intimate connection with Nick over the last few days, but there was so much she didn't know about his life. She'd watched enough cop dramas, though, to know that people were most often killed by someone they knew. *Someone like you, you mean?* she thought with a chill.

Just then the door was pushed open and a tall man in his early forties walked in. His smart dark suit did nothing to detract from the tired, unhappy look about him. A slightly older woman carrying an armful of folders came in behind him.

'I'm Detective Inspector Ian Fox,' said the man as they both sat down opposite her. 'This is DS Sheila Field. Sorry to keep you waiting so long,' he added. The tone of his voice – firm and serious – scared her.

'What's happening?' said Sophie, anxiously looking from one to the other. 'Have you any idea who might have done this?'

The two police officers exchanged a look.

'That's what we're hoping to work out, Sophie,' said Fox.

The woman passed the inspector a blue file and he opened it, taking a pen out of his inside pocket.

'Okay, first of all, we'd like to ask you some questions. Is that okay?'

Sophie was immediately on her guard. The way he'd said it sounded carefully phrased. Did they suspect her of anything? At the hotel, when she had first seen Nick on the bathroom floor, her immediate, instinctive response had been to cradle him. Her hands had tried to knit his wound back together, although even in her distraught state she had known that the gesture was useless. But in the police car going to the station she realised the dangerous position she was now in. She was Nick's lover. She had found him dead. Her fingerprints were all over the suite and now his body. Even she could see that looked suspicious.

'Should I have a lawyer?' she asked quietly.

'That's your right. Would you like one?' said the policewoman flatly.

Sophie hesitated, then shook her head. Lawyers were for people who had something to hide; that's what her mother had always said. She just wanted to tell them the truth, and the truth was that she loved Nick and had been devastated to find him dead.

'I'm just here to help you find whoever hurt Nick,' she said in the most controlled voice she could manage.

Fox nodded.

'So let's start with everything you know about Nick and what happened to him.'

Sophie took a minute to compose herself before she had to relive those moments again.

'It started off a perfect day,' she said, puffing out her cheeks as she tried to contain her emotions. 'We woke up at about six forty. He wanted us to spend the day together, but I had to leave early for a meeting. I had a shower and left his suite at about seven twenty and got a cab to High Street Ken. But I had forgotten my phone so I asked the cabbie to take me back to retrieve it.'

She wiped at her cheek, feeling a tear trickle down.

'I was gone, maybe thirty minutes,' she said, her voice trembling now. 'That's all. When I returned to the hotel room, he was like that.'

Fox looked at her for a moment before he spoke.

'Why don't we go back a bit? Tell me how you met, what was the nature of your relationship?'

She watched as Fox turned on a tape recorder. Slowly, haltingly, Sophie told them how she had met Nick at the party, how they had spent the week together, the places they had been, anything she could remember. The woman sergeant was scribbling down notes in one of her files as Sophie unfurled the story. When she had finished, Fox folded his hands.

'What was Nick's full name?'

It seemed a strange question to ask.

'Nick Cooper.'

'Is that what he told you?'

'Yes, why?'

'Sophie, do you know why Nick gave you a false name?'

'I'm sorry, I don't understand you.'

'We opened the safe in the hotel suite. His passport was inside and the name on this passport was Nick Beddingfield.'

Sophie shook her head vigorously.

'You're mistaken. His name was Nick Cooper.'

Fox shrugged.

'His passport said otherwise.'

'Maybe it was . . . maybe he had changed his name or something. People do, don't they? For legal reasons, sometimes?' She looked from Fox to Field and back again. 'Why would he lie to me?'

'I don't know, Sophie. But we'd like to know why too.'

'Nick Beddingfield,' she repeated slowly, staring at the grainy wood of the tabletop. Her head was beginning to swim. She felt dizzy now. Sick, wounded. Could it be true? But why would the police lie? So what else had he been lying about? She made a mental trawl of the last few days, looking for clues, contradictions, inconsistencies in what they had talked about. Had it all been lies? Even his feelings?

'Is he really from Houston?' she said, feeling her eyes cloud with tears.

'We're making enquiries.'

The air seemed to have been sucked out of the room and her tongue was dry.

'Could I have a drink, please?'

DS Field got up and returned with a plastic cup of water. It didn't seem to make much difference; it still hurt to swallow.

'Here's the problem I have, Sophie,' said Fox. 'You claim that you have only known this man, what is it? Five days? You also claim you don't know anything about him – you don't really know where he's from beyond perhaps Texas, you've never met any of his friends or family, you don't even really know what he does for a job. And yet, you're basically living together.'

'Not really,' said Sophie. 'I mean, I stayed in his room a few times . . .'

'All a bit quick, isn't it?' said DS Field.

'Quick?'

'Well, you meet him on the Thursday, by the Monday you're shacked up together.'

'We weren't shacked up,' protested Sophie. 'I'd just been seeing him—'

'And had he been to your place?' interrupted Fox.

'No. He didn't—'

'So you're boyfriend and girlfriend, but he's never been to your flat. Why not?'

'I never said we were boyfriend and girlfriend,' said Sophie, her voice rising. 'And I didn't . . .'

I didn't want to take him back to my flat, she finished the sentence in her head, *because then he would have known that I was just some ordinary girl, scraping a living as a gym instructor.*

'I didn't take him home because I was house-sitting for a friend. It didn't feel right to take him there without permission.'

Fox made a note in his book.

'What do you do for a living?'

'I'm a personal trainer. Well, a gym instructor,' she added with panic.

'And where have you been house-sitting?'

'Sixteen Egerton Row, Knightsbridge.'

'Smart area. Who does the property belong to?'

'Lana Goddard-Price. She's out of the country.'

'Do you have a contact number for her?'

'In my phone. She's one of my clients.'

Fox fixed her with his hard gaze.

'Do you think Nick was targeting the property?'

Sophie glared at him.

'He was not a thief,' she said defensively. 'Nick was smart and generous and rich . . .'

'So is that why you were interested in him?' asked Field flatly.

'No. I was in love with him.'

Tears welled in her eyes. She had a sudden urge to call her mother, but at the thought that she was still in Denmark she felt suddenly, frighteningly alone.

'After five days?'

Hostility prickled in the air. All she wanted to do was get out of the room.

'Did you have sex with Nick this morning?' pressed Fox.

She felt her face flush.

'We had sex a couple of times through the night. This morning we just fooled around. Kissed.'

'There were fragments of a wine bottle on the floor. Do you know where that could have come from?'

She paused to think.

'Maybe from last night. We had a bath together and ordered some champagne. The bottle would have been left on the side.'

'And where did you leave Nick this morning? In bed or in the shower?'

'In bed.'

'Did you argue?'

'No.'

Fox looked straight at her.

'Did you hit him in the bathroom with a wine bottle?'

'You think I did that?' she croaked. 'I told you I loved him.'

'Please, Sophie, answer the question. Did you hit him?' pressed Fox.

She felt nauseous, faint. She gripped the sides of the chair, feeling the burns under her fingers.

'I think I need a lawyer.'

12

Sophie was still shaking as she pushed out through the glass doors of Paddington Green station. She felt dirty and violated, but above all tired. She walked down the steps, filling her lungs. It wasn't exactly fresh air – she could see cars rushing along the Marylebone flyover in front of her – but it felt good after the stale rooms and corridors of the police station. *Police station*, her mind repeated. How had she come to be here? She was a good girl, she'd never even been in trouble at school, despite Francesca's best efforts.

All she had done was walk into that hotel room and find Nick, her lover, lying on the floor. That was her only crime. And yet they were treating her as if she were some deranged killer. They had taken swabs from her mouth for DNA and they'd taken fingerprints and made rumbles about doing a police appeal in the Scotland Yard media suite within the next twenty-four hours.

'Don't worry. Hopefully you won't see the inside of that place again for a little while.'

Edward Gould put a reassuring hand on her shoulder. He was one of her father's old college friends and one of the top criminal defence solicitors in the country, or at least that was what her mother had told her on the phone, when Sophie had managed to contact her in Copenhagen.

'Bear in mind they haven't charged you and we have no date for another interview yet.'

She found little comfort in his words.

'Yet? You mean I'm going to have to go back?'

'Possibly,' he said guardedly.

'You mean probably.'

Gould raised his eyebrows.

'The truth is that you are going to be on their suspect list until they get more information about Nick's life. You'll only be eliminated when they find another lead.'

Panic swelled inside her. She couldn't go back in there, she couldn't.

'But that's not fair, I haven't done anything!'

Gould shrugged.

'No, it's not fair,' he said brusquely. 'Not if you're innocent. But at the top of any suspect list at the beginning of an inquiry are partners, the person who finds the dead body and the person who last sees the victim alive. You're unfortunate enough to be all three, Sophie. For now, you're going to be the one under the microscope.'

She was grateful to Edward Gould for arriving so quickly and for effectively forcing the police to release her, but he did not have a sympathetic bedside manner. She knew his type; most of her father's friends had been like this, Oxbridge-educated and of a generation that kept a stiff upper lip no matter what.

'But they think I'm innocent,' protested Sophie. 'They want me to do an appeal to ask for witnesses.'

Gould's head gave a short shake.

'Doesn't necessarily mean they think you're innocent. Sometimes they use a press conference to put suspects under the spotlight. They'll have a criminal profiler watch it, analyse your responses, your behaviour under pressure. It's a useful psychological tool for creating a suspect profile.'

'A *suspect profile*. So you think they might arrest me?'

'The police will certainly be gathering as much evidence as they can: witness statements, forensics, whatever background they can find on the victim. They won't be idle, you can be sure of that, and as soon as they feel they have enough to prosecute, they will.'

'But what about me?' she repeated, in panic.

Gould hesitated.

'Sophie, the British justice system is founded on the strongest principle: innocent until proven guilty, and it will be the police and the Crown Prosecution Service's task to produce evidence which proves who did this. And clearly, as you did not, they will certainly struggle to find a case against you.'

She wondered whether her solicitor actually believed in her innocence.

'But they're going to pin it on someone, aren't they?' she said, with an air of resignation. She'd had plenty of time to think about it while the police sorted out her paperwork. A murder at the Riverton was high profile. 'It's not good for the Met, it's not good for the hotel. Not good for London tourists.'

'Of course the police and the CPS are going to want a successful conviction. But they don't want to go round throwing innocent young women in jail either.'

Gould glanced at his watch.

'Look, I have to get back to the office. When your mother called, I came down immediately, but I'm in the middle of a trial at the Old Bailey, you understand?'

She nodded, glad that her mother had arranged for him to come. It wasn't as if she had a criminal solicitor on speed dial. Before today, the only thing she'd ever done wrong was exceed the speed limit.

Oh yes? said a mocking voice in her head. *You've spent the last week lying through your teeth.*

She closed her eyes. Uncomfortable as it was, it was true. She'd taken on another woman's home, her clothes, lied her way into a party, then told her new boyfriend a string of lies about who she was, where she lived, what she did for a living. Perhaps that was what had brought her to this horrible concrete police station in the middle of London, dried blood under her fingernails. Maybe it was all karma.

A taxi had pulled up to the kerb.

'Go home, Sophie,' said Gould. 'Get some rest. We'll talk again tomorrow.'

She nodded sadly and watched the car drive away, suddenly feeling very alone.

Where was home, exactly? Where should she go? She thought of Lana's stuccoed townhouse and shivered. A week ago she thought it had been the answer to her prayers, but now it was like an empty shell, filled with her own guilt and echoes of Nick's footsteps on the pavement outside. Returning to her parents' place held even less appeal; Wade House would be empty and somehow even more sad than the last time she had been there for the funeral. Julia Ellis had agreed to come back from Copenhagen but would not be home until morning.

Sophie threw her bag over her shoulder and crossed the road towards the Edgware Road tube station. It was packed with rush hour crowds, and being surrounded by the swell of people going about their ordinary lives somehow made her feel better. She got off at Sloane Square and walked the rest of the way home to Battersea, wanting some early evening air to clear her mind. She had been at the police station all day, and the sun was beginning to fade, sending smudged ribbons of peach and lilac across the sky. The heat of the day was still coming up from the sun-warmed pavements, and the summer smells of cut flowers and fresh tarmac mingled with the fumes of the cars rushing past. As she approached Albert Bridge Road, she could even hear a few birds still singing in the park, but none of it made her feel at home. She felt alien, and disconnected. Nothing seemed to make sense any more, nothing looked as it should. Only a few days ago, she had been so sure of everything. It had really felt as if her life had finally turned a corner: a new job, a new exciting life in London – a new boyfriend. The last image of Nick jumped into her mind and she shivered. It was horrible, truly horrible. Who could have done such a thing? She genuinely had no idea: DI Fox was right, she didn't know much about this man she had professed to love. But she had felt so sure of the connection between them, and you couldn't fake that, could you?

She shook her head. All she wanted to do was sleep. Her eyes were heavy and her mind was so foggy that she could hardly think. Her body, usually so strong and vital, felt weak and depleted.

She came to her building and fumbled in her bag for her keys. The policeman – or had it been the woman? She couldn't remember; the whole thing was a terrible blur – had made a big deal about how Sophie had never invited Nick back here. She supposed she could understand that, given the circumstances. But that was just dating, wasn't it? Who really told a new partner everything about themselves in the first week? 'Hi, my name's Sophie, I've had my heart broken twice, I'm still hung up on my ex and I once thought I'd caught an STD, but it was only thrush.' People only revealed the best version of themselves in the early days of a relationship, because if everybody was that honest, nobody would get beyond the first drink.

She pushed open the door and walked into the communal hallway, a large if rather shabby room dominated by the wide staircase. For some reason, Sophie's mind flashed on to the memory of her first visit here, walking through the hallway with the letting agent and her dad. Peter Ellis had sniffed the musty air and whispered in his daughter's ear: 'I think I can smell the last tenant.' Sophie had giggled then. Her dad had made her laugh a lot; it was one of the things she missed most about him. After his financial troubles, he always seemed preoccupied, but he always had time for a joke, even if it was just something corny. Back then, she hadn't really tried to understand how he must have been feeling; struggling to keep everything together, fighting to keep his family afloat. Had he felt as wretched, as helpless, as she did now? At least he had faced it with a smile.

After checking her pigeonhole for mail – nothing, why would there be? – she began to climb the stairs.

She stopped on the second landing, holding her breath. Somehow, she knew something was wrong. She walked slowly down the corridor towards her flat, all her senses jangling, ready to run at any moment. She tried to dismiss the feeling, believing it was just the tensions of the day making her nervous. But she stopped dead in her tracks when she saw her front door. It was open, the wood splintered around the lock.

She hesitated and then crept inside, every nerve-ending jangling.

'Who's there?' she called. 'If there's anybody in there, I've already called the police.'

She edged forward and ducked her head around the door frame, expecting to see – what? A burglar in a black balaclava and stripy jumper? There was nobody there, but the place was a mess. A complete and utter mess. Someone had been there, pulling out drawers, turning over chairs; they'd even upended her bookcase. There were clothes everywhere, and her duvet had been torn open. *Why? What do I have that anyone would want? I don't even own a TV.*

Had it been the police? But surely they weren't allowed to tear down curtains or slash pillows open? This was trespass, vandalism. There were laws against that, whether you were the police or not.

Another thought hit her that turned her cold. Had it been Nick's killer? But why? What on earth could they have been looking for? Did they think she had something of his?

Whatever Nick had done to get himself killed, perhaps they thought she knew about it.

Her heart was pumping fiercely. 'What do you want?' she yelled out loud, her voice trembling.

She went to her top drawer, where she kept her valuables. It had clearly been rifled through, but her small bag of sentimental jewellery was still there. Feeling a sense of relief, she saw her passport too, and the key fob which gave internet access to her bank account. Instinctively she grabbed everything and stuffed it into her bag, then got out of the flat, not wanting to spend another second in there.

She tried to regulate her breathing with deep yoga inhalations, but she was fighting a losing battle and a sob stuttered from her throat, slow at first, before the dam burst and her body released some of the tension and hurt she had been bottling up since that moment she had walked into Nick's hotel room.

'What do you want from me?' she screamed, slumping down to the landing floor, holding her knees tightly as tears plopped on to her jeans. She sat there for a minute, letting the fraught emotion drain from her body. When she had finished, she blew her nose and looked at the destruction of her flat again.

Without thinking, she pulled DI Fox's business card from her pocket and used her mobile to dial his number.

'Fox,' said a tired voice finally.

'Mr Fox, it's Sophie Ellis. I've just got home.'

The policeman evidently heard the wobble in Sophie's voice.

'Is everything okay?'

'Someone's broken into my flat, torn it apart.'

'A burglary?'

'Yes, I suppose,' she said uncertainly, looking around. 'The front door was open.'

'It was open?' said Fox. 'Was anything taken?'

He sounded genuinely concerned, the hostility from their earlier encounter gone.

'I don't know. I don't think so,' said Sophie, her voice shaking. 'I mean, there's stuff everywhere, I can't really see . . .'

'I'll try and pop by later, or I can send a colleague over.'

'Thank you.'

'Sophie, are you sure there's nothing else you want to tell me?'

She hesitated. 'What do you mean?'

'You've just found a dead body and your flat has been ransacked. Maybe now is the time to tell us everything you know.'

'I've *told* you everything,' she said, immediately regretting the call.

'Are you sure? Even the smallest detail might be important. Your flat has been turned over for some reason—'

'I've told you everything. Please come. I'm afraid. What if they're still watching the building?'

'I need to finish some things at the station, but I'll be there as soon as I can. If you don't want to stay there alone, go to the nearest public place. Is there a local pub or Starbucks you could sit in for an hour or so?'

'Yes, I suppose.'

'Go there. Call me again to tell me where, okay?'

She put the phone down and tried to stuff Fox's business card back into her purse. She felt some resistance in the notes compartment. She had never been good at detoxing her wallet; it was constantly fit to burst with tube tickets, old receipts and business cards. She pulled them out and they fell on to her lap like confetti.

One small white card stared at her.

Joshua McCormack, Bespoke Horologist.

It took a second to place him, and then she remembered. The cocky charmer at the Chariot Dinner.

At the time he had seemed inconsequential; they had chatted for barely five minutes, she had not seen him for the rest of the night and Nick had not mentioned him since. And yet in the short time that Sophie had known her lover, Josh McCormack, horology consultant, was the only person she had met who had known Nick prior to his trip to London. He was the only person who might be able to tell her something about him that she didn't know and who might have some information that could help solve his murder.

It suddenly seemed of vital importance to speak to him. She paused before dialling, and then punched in the digits. Finally he answered. The voice sounded groggy, clotted with sleep.

'Yeah. Hello.'

'Is this Josh?'

'That's right.'

'It's Sophie Ellis. We met at the Chariot Dinner. I had a blue dress on. I was with Nick . . .'

'I remember,' he said flatly.

'He's dead, Josh. Someone has murdered Nick.'

She felt icy cold as she said the words. There was silence at the other end of the phone.

It hadn't occurred to her that she might be the one to break the news to him. Surely he'd seen the *Standard*, watched the news . . .

'What happened?' he said finally.

'I spent the night with him last night. I left first thing this morning. When I returned, he was dead in the bathroom. He'd been attacked.'

She surprised herself with the flat, matter-of-fact way in which she told the story, as if it was a news report she had read, not a traumatic event she had experienced that morning and had had to keep reliving all day at the police station.

'Are you a suspect?'

'I didn't do it,' she said, rounding on him. 'All I did was

110

find his body. Josh, I need to talk to you. You're the only person I know who knew Nick.'

'Hang on, sweetheart, don't drag me into this,' he replied, his voice becoming more animated.

'Josh, please.'

'I talk to you. You talk to the police. The next thing I know, the police are sniffing around me for a witness statement. I'm sorry to hear about Nick, I really am, but I don't need this. I'm leaving town tomorrow. Sorry.'

'Did you know Nick Cooper isn't his real name?'

'No, I didn't. I barely knew him.'

'Josh. Please. I'm begging you. Just ten minutes of your time.'

'I said I'm busy.'

'Please,' she repeated, her fingers gripping the phone.

There was another long pause.

'Ten minutes. No longer,' he said finally. 'And get some beers on the way over. Stella.'

'I'm not Ocado,' she said impatiently.

'I thought I was the one doing you a favour?'

'I have to be back home in an hour. Where should we meet?'

'Do you know Fleet Reach, by Stamford Wharf?'

It rang a bell. If she got a taxi there and back, she could make her meeting with Fox.

'Get a cab to Lots Road. You'll see the Nancy Blue by the wharf.'

'I'll be there as soon as I can.'

13

Ruth had been waiting in her car outside Sophie's flat for over an hour. She had spent the last twenty minutes cursing herself: what if the girl had gone straight to her mother's or to stay with a friend? She tried to convince herself it would have been better to catch her as she was leaving the police station, but experience had taught Ruth that was usually a waste of time: the suspect was invariably with a protective family member or legal adviser and was certainly not in the mood to talk. No, it was best to catch them alone when they were vulnerable, and her flat seemed like the best bet; with the *Tribune*'s resources, it had not been hard to find out where she lived.

It was getting dark. Ruth looked up at the Battersea mansion block, which was a bit run-down for a socialising Chelsea girl; on the wrong side of the river, too. Then again, when Robert 'Squirrel' Sykes had called to say that he had tracked Sophie Ellis down, he did mention that she had disappeared off the social scene after her family had run into financial difficulties. Ruth wondered whether the police had heard about the Ellis family money problems. It would certainly strengthen their case against her. After all, the victim had been a rich man – had he been killed after some struggle over money or an attempted theft? But Ruth's gut told her different. She'd looked at Sophie's Facebook page: lots of pictures of her and her friends drinking cocktails or going out to fashionable nightclubs. This girl didn't seem the type to steal a chocolate bar, let alone kill anyone.

'That's her,' she whispered, sliding down in her seat. She recognised the girl walking up the street from her photographs; it was definitely Sophie Ellis – and she was alone. That was good. Ruth would wait for her to get inside, then ring the bell. She guessed Sophie would be too polite, too British to slam the door in her face. So that was their best suspect? Seeing her in the flesh only reinforced Ruth's feeling about Sophie: an ordinary preppy girl who had got mixed up in something terrible, not some murderous, Machiavellian gold-digger. In many ways, the blonde was exactly as she'd imagined. Tall and slender, with long tousled hair; she looked as if she'd walked straight off a catwalk, not out of Paddington Green interrogation room.

Ruth looked at her watch: she'd give her ten minutes. She popped a piece of nicotine gum in her mouth. Giving up smoking was proving to be an uphill struggle. She'd tried an electric cigarette but felt as if she was smoking a tampon. As for the gum, she was popping so many they were starting to give her the shakes.

She was about to go to Sophie's flat when she saw her leaving.

'Shit,' she mumbled, grabbing her handbag from the front seat of her Ford Fiesta.

Slamming the car door, she darted across the road, a moped beeping furiously as it nearly ran over her.

'Miss Ellis, wait . . .' she said, waving at Sophie.

The young woman hovered on the pavement as if she was undecided whether to wave back or sprint in the other direction.

'Sophie, please, I need to talk to you.'

Her wide eyes looked startled, afraid, although up close, her pale face was even more beautiful. Ruth extended her hand.

'My name is Ruth Boden. I'm a journalist with—'

Sophie was already shaking her head.

'I'm sorry,' she said, beginning to walk away. 'I don't think it's a good idea to talk to you.'

But Ruth was used to getting knocked back.

'Sophie, please, I'm not a grubby tabloid hack. I'm with the *Washington Tribune*. I know the police have questioned you, but I believe you are innocent and I thought I could help with the American side of the investigation.'

Sophie's shoulders visibly relaxed at the word 'innocent' – it was one of the tricks Ruth used to get a subject on-side. But she seemed to bristle at the mention of America.

'*American* side of the investigation?' she said bitterly. 'How do I know Nick was even from Houston? He could have been from Timbuktu for all I know.'

Ruth was storing all the information in her mental database. The police had released the name of the deceased as Nick Beddingfield, but she'd had no idea he was from Houston or indeed that there were any question marks about his origins. This was good – she felt her instincts tingling – there was a good story here, she could feel it. She pulled out her business card and pushed it into Sophie's hand.

'Seriously, Sophie, if you want to find out where Nick really is from, why don't you let me help you?'

For a moment Sophie looked tempted, but then swung her bag over her shoulder and turned towards the main road.

'Sorry, I'm in a real hurry,' she said, walking away as Ruth approached. 'I've really got to go.'

'Sophie, listen to me. Everyone in this city, from the commissioner of the Met to the general manager of the Riverton Hotel, wants an arrest on this case, and right now you are the nearest thing the police have to a suspect. I can help you if you tell me your side of the story.'

Sophie stopped suddenly and turned to face her. Up close,

Ruth could see how weary she looked. There were sooty black smudges under her eyes; either she was very bad at putting eyeliner on, or she had been crying.

'My side of the story?' replied Sophie. 'My side of the story is that I have done nothing wrong – *nothing* – and yet the police might charge me with murder because it makes things easier for them. And now someone has broken into my flat and you're hassling me in the street. So all in all, I'd say my side of the story is that I want to be left alone.'

Her voice was wobbling now.

'Someone broke into your flat?' said Ruth, looking back up at the building. 'What happened?'

'They tore the place apart, that's what happened.'

'But why? What for?'

'You're the reporter. You probably have more idea than I do, because right now, I don't know what the hell is going on or why I am in the middle of it.'

They had reached the main road now and Sophie put her hand up to wave a taxi down. Ruth clasped her arm.

'Don't go, please. I can help, I really can.'

Sophie shrugged her away.

'I have to go,' she said, shaking her head. She climbed into the taxi, and as it pulled away, she looked suddenly terribly young and afraid.

'Damn it,' muttered Ruth, running back to her car as fast as her heels would allow. 'Come on, come on,' she hissed, fumbling the keys into the ignition, then gunned the engine, just turning into traffic as she saw the cab disappear down Prince of Wales Drive towards Battersea Bridge. There were a few cars ahead of her, but she could see the black roof of the cab above them. The cab turned left onto Chelsea Embankment. That made sense, she thought, cursing the darkness that was cloaking the city. She beeped her horn and overtook a minivan. Now there was only one car between her and Sophie's taxi. Chewing her nicotine gum furiously, she grinned to herself. She was back in the chase.

14

Sophie had expected the Nancy Blue to be a pub. Instead the taxi had dropped her off on a desolate stretch of the Thames close to Chelsea Harbour. No pubs, no shops, nothing. She looked around uncertainly and turned up the collar of her coat. The sun had set and a chill was in the air. This was certainly not the Chelsea that she knew and loved. There were no chic boutiques or trendy bars. Out here, where the far reaches of Chelsea met what remained of the docks, there were no street lights or houses, only abandoned wharves and industrial units, everything closed for the night – if these neglected yards and corrugated-iron gates ever opened.

She walked along the darkening road. On one side of her, faceless warehouses; on the other, the dark churning waters of the Thames. It might sparkle in the sunshine, but at night, the river looked foreboding and bone-chillingly cold. She turned to see the taxi's brake lights blinking once, twice, then disappearing around the corner. Too late, Sophie had the overwhelming sense that she was wrong to come here. She didn't know Josh from Adam. Maybe she should have told that reporter where she was going; at least then someone might be able to find her body.

And yet what was the alternative? Should she wait at home for the intruders to return? Wait for Fox? Ruth Boden was right: he could arrest her at any moment – and he had certainly given her the impression he thought she was hiding something. Anyway, why should he care whether she was innocent? All he cared about was getting a result, a conviction. No, the truth was that Sophie had nowhere to turn, and until she could find out what exactly was happening to her, there was a good chance she might end up getting the blame for Nick's death. The first thing she needed to know was who Nick was – and where he had come from.

But where – and what – was the Nancy Blue? Was it a club or a business? There was nothing that fitted any such description out here. She heard a dog bark and she jumped, one hand to her chest.

She pulled Ruth Boden's card from her pocket and punched the reporter's number into speed-dial; that way she could call her if there was a sniff of trouble. She had reached the end of the road now. There was nothing except a wooden ramp towards a small pier.

Nancy Blue: a boat! she thought, the penny dropping. Her dad would have laughed at her – that would have been his first thought. She passed a weathered sign reading 'Fleet Reach – Strictly Private'. *Very welcoming*, thought Sophie as she walked carefully over the boards.

Moored along one side of the wharf were half a dozen houseboats. The smallest was closest to the jetty, swaying gently against the upright piles. It was deep navy with tyres festooned around its outer rim and the words *Nancy Blue* stencilled on the hull. Sophie bent down to peer in through the window.

'You probably shouldn't be wearing those shoes,' said a voice, making her stumble and grab for the handrail. Josh emerged from the shadows, stepping on to the gangplank between the pier and his barge.

'Bloody hell, you scared me,' she said, looking up at his tall physique, quite menacing in the dark.

'Where's my beer?'

'I didn't have time,' said Sophie briskly. 'I haven't had the easiest day, as you can imagine.'

He gave a slow, steady tut. 'I don't know, turning up here without a bottle of wine or a scented candle. I thought you posh girls had impeccable manners.'

'Somehow I don't see you as the scented candle type,' she said.

'You don't say.'

She could feel him looking her up and down.

'Can we go inside?' she said uncomfortably.

Josh nodded and swept his hand towards the small door. '*Entrez.*'

It was surprisingly cosy inside. From the weather-beaten exterior, Sophie had been expecting something more, well, nautical. But there was a small seating area, a table and a galley kitchen towards the far end, all lit by the soft glow of hurricane lamps. It was comfortable but small and basic – clearly business wasn't that good for Joshua McCormack's horology consultancy.

'Interesting place,' said Sophie, looking around. 'Where do you sleep on this thing?'

He lifted a brow. 'It usually takes women more than two minutes to ask me that question. But if you want to know, that sofa pulls out into a futon.'

Sophie looked away, feeling embarrassed.

'You get one cup of tea, then you're out of here,' he said, squeezing past her into the kitchen area and taking down a copper milk pan. He filled it with water and lit the gas hob.

'No kettle?'

'Electricity's out. Sorry, princess.'

He looked at her through the low light. The stubble on his chin was thicker since they last met, as if he had not shaved since.

'So start talking.'

'No small talk?' asked Sophie.

'Not my style.'

'Suits me, I have to be back home for the police in fifty minutes,' she replied, sitting down at the narrow table.

Slowly, she began to tell her tale, from that first night with Nick, through their dates, to discovering the body, being grilled by the police and finally finding her flat ransacked. When she had finished, Josh came over and placed a mug of tea in front of her.

'Right,' he said, sitting opposite her. 'I'll assume for the moment you're telling the truth.'

Sophie began to object, but he held up a hand to stop her.

'Don't interrupt,' he said, his wide mouth fixed in an unsmiling line. 'My friend is dead and someone killed him. Excuse me if I'm suspicious of strangers.'

Sophie frowned. The anxiety she had first felt at being here in this small enclosed space had turned to annoyance.

'So Nick's a friend now,' she said tartly. 'I thought you barely knew him.'

Josh paused a beat.

'Figure of speech.'

'Really? If I was a policeman, I'd say you were hiding something.'

'I don't have anything to hide from you,' he said wearily. Something in the way he said it made her look at him more closely, reminding her of the way he had reacted to the news of Nick's death.

'You knew Nick Cooper wasn't his real name, didn't you?' she said slowly. 'And I don't think his death surprised you either, did it?'

'Well done, Inspector Clouseau,' he said. 'But I think you should leave the amateur detective stuff for the TV. This is real life, you could get hurt. Stay out of it.'

She knew Josh was challenging her, but Sophie wasn't afraid of him. He was cocky, maybe a little shifty; she had felt that at the Chariot party – such arrogant charmers were generally chancers and not to be trusted. But tonight that breezy confidence had been replaced by a guarded sullenness; she was sure he knew more than he was letting on, and she wasn't going to let him scare her off.

'I'm already in it, Josh,' she said flatly. 'According to my solicitor, I'm the prime suspect for Nick's murder at the moment. I don't see how it could get much worse. All I'm asking is for you to tell me what you know about Nick.'

'Look, Sophie,' he said, rubbing his eyes, 'you seem like a nice girl and I really hope the police get off your back, but I don't want to get involved in this.'

'Why not? If he *was* your friend and *if* you've nothing to hide? Or are you afraid the police might start looking at you too closely?'

Josh barked out a laugh.

'What are you suggesting? That I killed Nick?' he said incredulously.

'It had crossed my mind,' she said quietly, wondering how dangerous it was to be here.

'Well, as it happens, I have an alibi for this morning, a young lady with a flat in Camden. You, on the other hand, were right there. So if we're going to start pointing the finger, take a look at yourself first.'

He got up and went to the tiny fridge. From this distance Sophie could see it was empty except for milk and a bottle of what she guessed was vodka. He took it out and poured a good measure into a glass, not offering any to Sophie, then knocked it back, grimacing.

'So what did Nick tell you he did?' he asked finally.

Sophie looked at him. 'I didn't really understand it. He said he was in oil and gas. Trading shares, buying companies, that sort of thing.'

Josh gave a gentle snort.

'So that's not true?'

Josh poured the rest of the bottle into his glass.

'As I said, Nick wasn't a good friend. He had a lot of

business interests. So I couldn't say.'

'Please Josh, I can tell you know something.' She could feel herself getting desperate.

He lifted his T-shirt and scratched his flat, tanned stomach. Then he shook his head slowly.

'It's time to leave, Sophie Ellis. I have things to do, and playing Nancy Drew with Little Miss Pony Club is not one of them.'

Sophie stood up and stretched her hand out to plead with him.

'Please. You can't chuck me out without telling me what you know. This is my life, Josh!'

'What bit of "get off my boat" don't you understand?' he said, picking up her bag from the table and pushing it at her.

She snatched it off him. 'Fine. If that's what you want. I'm meeting Detective Inspector Fox in about twenty minutes; perhaps he'll have more luck getting information out of you.'

His grey eyes glared at her. 'Don't threaten me with the bloody coppers. By the time they get here, I'll be gone.'

'Yeah? Well then they'll just put out an ABP and pick you up.'

He chuckled.

'I think you mean APB: All Points Bulletin,' he said. 'And that's America.'

'Whatever,' she replied haughtily, turning away. She was desperate for any information Josh had, but she wasn't going to give him the satisfaction of seeing her beg for it.

'And don't fall in the river on your way out,' he said, opening and closing his hand in mocking farewell.

'Screw you,' she hissed, slamming the little door behind her.

Her cheeks burned with anger. She didn't need a cocky bastard like Josh McCormack helping her anyway, she told herself, struggling with her bag on the narrow walkway. She'd find out what she needed on her own.

Her defiance lasted just a couple of seconds. Inhaling the cool evening air, she felt completely alone and vulnerable. Inspector Fox would be waiting for her and she had nothing new to tell him. Nothing that would get her off the hook.

Glancing up, she noticed the dark shadow at the end of the street. A car? She was pretty sure it hadn't been parked there earlier.

So what? she thought, trying to quash her nerves. *It's only a car.* She forced herself to keep walking down the gantry and on to the wooden pier. She didn't want Josh to think – no, *to know* – that she had nowhere else to go. Just as she was passing the 'Fleet Reach' sign, the car's lights came on and Sophie threw up a hand, momentarily blinded. She heard the engine fire up, and the crunch of tyres on the roadway. They were driving towards her. Were they going to hit her? She suddenly understood that phrase 'rabbit caught in the headlights'. She felt rooted to the spot, unable to move. One step to the right, and she might be hit by the car. One step the other way, she could end up in the Thames.

'Move!'

Sophie felt a hand on her arm and she was pulled backwards. Suddenly the lights flicked off and Sophie could see again. She was irrationally glad to see Josh looking down at her, especially when she saw the black car parked across the road, blocking the entrance to the pier. There were two large men coming towards her, and they didn't look at all friendly.

'Keep quiet,' hissed Josh. 'Let me do the talking.'

He walked down to meet the men. Sophie could now see that one was huge, like a bouncer, with close-cropped grey hair, but it was his companion who disturbed her more. He was smaller, more wiry, but his eyes were hard, peering over at Sophie like he was examining her, looking for faults or weaknesses. For some reason, he reminded her of the crocodile from *Peter Pan*.

'Can I help you gentlemen?' asked Josh. He was back to the self-assured Josh McCormack she had met at the party, except this version was serious and unsmiling. And that gave her the sudden thought: maybe these gorillas were after Josh, not her. After all, he seemed like the type who might get into trouble with big men.

'No, it's the young lady we want to talk to,' said the smaller man. 'If that's all right with you?' He had a strange accent with an upwards glide. Eastern European? Polish or Russian, she thought.

'Well, I'm afraid it's not a good time at the moment,' said Josh. 'My wife and I were just in the middle of something.' He smiled. 'Bit of a domestic, if I'm honest. So if you could perhaps come back later . . . ?'

The small man looked at Josh, then up at the bouncer type next to him.

'A lovers' tiff, that's all it is,' he said to the big man.

'Exactly,' said Josh. 'You understand.'

The smaller man's face was cold and expressionless.

'Get rid of him, Tomas.'

The gorilla lunged forward but Josh was too quick; pivoting backwards and swinging his foot up, he caught the man mountain right between the legs.

'Run, you silly cow!' shouted Josh, grabbing her hand and yanking her along the road.

Sophie didn't need telling twice; she kicked off her shoes and sprinted as fast as her legs would carry her, her bag banging against her hip. She didn't know who those men were, but she had no doubt that they meant her harm. And she could be fairly sure that the one Josh had kicked in the balls would be pretty bloody angry if he ever caught up with them. She could see the end of the road and put on an extra burst of speed, trying to make the corner.

It was just then that she heard a deafening crack. As her body shook, she realised she'd been hit. She gasped and time seemed to stop. She closed her eyes and waited for it – a searing pain as her brain registered the wound from a bullet. But there was nothing. She tore her bag off her shoulder and saw a hole that had ripped through the fabric of the side pocket.

Josh grabbed her wrist again. Her hands were shaking but she knew she had to keep moving.

'This way,' he ordered, pulling her into an alleyway blocked by an old iron bollard. At least the men wouldn't be able to drive down here, thought Sophie. She didn't dare turn around to check whether they were still chasing; she just concentrated on running, her bare feet slapping against the cobbles, her lungs gasping. Left, right, she followed Josh through the passageways of what looked like a disused warehouse complex, her bare feet stinging on the concrete. She couldn't keep going much longer, but she knew she had to. At the end of the alleyway, Josh pulled her into another narrow passage, which ended in a locked gate. Sophie looked around desperately: there was no way out, only the alley they had just run down and, on closer inspection, the gate appeared to be rusted solid.

'Where are we going?' she panted. 'Josh, they're coming!'

'I know that,' he snapped.

'And he's got a gun.'

He flashed her a look. 'You've worked that out, have you?' he said sarcastically. Without waiting for an answer, he pulled her bag up above her head.

'What are you doing?' she objected.

'Put your foot in here,' he said, pointing to the bars on the front of the gate. 'We're going over.'

Sophie looked upwards just as Josh tossed her bag up and over the brickwork arch at the top of the gate. She quickly hoisted herself up, scrabbling for handholds, her toes slipping.

'I can't . . .' she said desperately as she began to wobble.

'Yes, you can,' he said, giving her a shove in the backside which sent her toppling over the arch and sliding down the other side, the stone scraping the skin on her right-hand side. She barely had time to draw a breath before Josh landed on top of her.

'Ouch,' she squealed.

He scrambled to his feet, pulled her up against him and clamped his hand over her mouth. Her cheek pressed against his chest and she could hardly move.

It was then that she heard thumping footsteps. There was no mistaking the sound: the men were pounding into the alley. Sophie froze, every last nerve ending tingling, ears straining, not daring to breathe, hoping against hope that the shadows would hide them.

And suddenly the footsteps were receding in the other direction. Josh didn't waste any time. He was up on his feet, dragging her along the short alleyway, but they didn't have very far to go. Sophie looked at him, her eyes wide. The alleyway ended in a flight of stone steps which disappeared into the black waters of the Thames.

'Don't think about it, just go,' hissed Josh. 'It's our only way out.'

'You *are* joking?' she whispered.

'Do I look like I'm joking?'

He grasped her arm, hard, and his eyes locked with hers.

'Listen to me, Sophie,' he commanded. 'Those men will kill you. Do you understand me?'

She began to speak, but he shook her arm again.

'Do you understand me?'

She nodded, remembering how close she had come to being shot.

'Then it's the only way. In about thirty seconds they're going to realise that we didn't go the other way and kick in that gate. And I don't want to be here when they do, do you?'

Sophie shook her head.

'Okay, let's go.'

Holding hands, they waded into the water. It was shockingly cold, like plunging into an icy bath. By the time they were up to their necks, Sophie's teeth had started to rattle. She had looped her bag around her arm, and at least that was floating a little, like a makeshift buoyancy aid. It was not her robust waterproof Prada backpack – that had ended up at the dress agency – but it was nylon, and despite the bullet hole in the side pocket, she hoped it wouldn't spring a leak.

'Keep moving,' whispered Josh, his voice shaking, but his grip on her hand reassuringly strong. 'It's not far, just down to the next pier.'

Sophie felt as if her whole body had seized up in the numbing cold. It was an effort to move her legs forward, and without Josh there, she was sure she would have gone under. *Just a little further*, she told herself. *Just keep going*. But it was so hard. Her feet were sore from the gravelly river bed, and her sodden clothes were impossibly heavy, dragging at her every move.

'That's it,' said Josh. 'Good girl, almost there.'

And then she could see the dark outline of the pier, the black wooden supports looming out of the water ahead of them. She redoubled her efforts, reaching out and clinging to the metal struts.

'Sophie, look up,' Josh said, into her ear. There was an old iron ladder leading up on to the pier. He placed her hands on the first rung and pushed her up. Her legs and arms felt like stone – heavier, even – but she struggled up and lay sprawled on the wooden deck, Josh following right behind her.

'We can't stay here,' he whispered urgently, his voice shaking from the cold. 'It won't take them long to work out where we are.'

He tugged at her jacket, pulling it over her shoulders.

'What are you doing?' she said, her teeth chattering.

'Take it off, your jeans too,' he said, pulling his own jumper over his head. 'Wet clothes will slow us down and leave a trail for them to follow.'

Sophie did as she was told, stripping to her T-shirt and pants, shivering like one of those shaved dogs you saw tied up outside fancy boutiques on the King's Road. Josh removed his own clothes, down to a pair of dark boxer shorts. He pulled a set of keys from his jeans pocket and pushed everything they had been wearing back into the water. He was just about to do the same with her bag but she stopped him.

'No, not that,' she said urgently. 'I need my bag.'

'Sophie, we haven't got time . . .'

'Give it to me. Now, Josh.'

She knew it didn't make any sense, but at that moment, her bag was incredibly important to her. She'd abandoned her flat, her family and friends, she was stripped to her underwear. That bag was the only link to her old life, a link back to a time when something made sense; she would rather face those men than leave it behind.

Josh clearly saw the determination in her face and handed the dripping bag to her.

'Come on, then,' he said, taking her hand again.

She flinched; standing in their underwear, the gesture felt too intimate, but she didn't have time to dwell on it.

'I said, let's move it,' he growled.

At first, Sophie almost fell to her knees. Her muscles had locked through the cold, but it was warmer to keep moving, warmer – and safer. She knew Josh was right about those men. They weren't going to sit down and ask them reasonable questions, like the police. They were going to kill them and dump their bodies in the river – and that was the thing that made Sophie move. She never, ever wanted to get back into that dark water, alive or dead.

'This way,' said Josh, ducking as they crossed the road and took a tiny lane up the side of a warehouse. They skirted around the back and found themselves in an alleyway, turning to the right, away from Josh's barge.

'If we can just get to . . .' he began, before immediately grabbing Sophie and pushing her into a doorway, as the dazzling glare of a pair of headlights swung into the lane.

Sophie felt sure they would have seen them, that the car would run them down. But suddenly it screeched to a halt and began reversing. In the distance she could hear the faint swell of police sirens.

'Josh! It's the police!' she hissed, almost laughing with relief. 'We have to go to them.'

'No chance. The shooters are between us and them. Come on,' said Josh, hauling her to her feet. 'We need to get out of sight.'

Reluctantly she allowed him to lead her onwards, taking each turn blindly, trusting he knew where he was going. Eventually they found themselves in what looked like an abandoned parking area, surrounded on three sides by old-fashioned pebble-dash garages with corrugated-iron doors. Josh led her to one and, fiddling around with his set of keys, pushing one key into the garage door lock.

'This is yours?'

'Get inside,' he ordered, pulling the door out and upwards. Sophie ducked under his arm and stepped inside a dark, cramped space that smelled of petrol and Christmas trees. Josh closed the door with a clang and moved over to Sophie's right.

'What is this place?' she whispered.

There was a rasping sound as he struck a match, then lit a lantern.

'Welcome to my office, Sophie Ellis.'

15

The garage was crammed with industrial steel shelves, each loaded with boxes: TVs, DVD players, even some labelled with luxury fashion brands.

'What is all this stuff?' she asked.

'Most of it belongs to a friend of mine,' said Josh in a low voice. 'Calls it his "rainy day fund". And I guess days don't get much more rainy than this.'

He reached into a box and pulled out a Ralph Lauren branded beach towel, wrapping it around Sophie's shoulders. It was only then that she realised just how cold she was, and she began shaking hard.

She glanced up at him in the low light and couldn't help but notice how good his body was: tall and well defined, with firm pecs and biceps and a taut stomach. He was not someone who lived in the gym, though, she thought idly, just someone blessed with a strong, athletic body and who looked after it. He caught her looking at him and she turned away, making a show of drying her hair.

'There's a heater in the back, and a kettle too,' he said quickly. 'No milk. But you'll have noticed it's not the Ritz.'

Sophie opened her damp bag and starting rummaging through her possessions. They were soaked, her purse, her phone, everything apart from her plastic make-up case. Thank God she'd thought to put her passport book in there

– not to mention her copy of *I Capture the Castle*. She couldn't have stood losing that.

'What are you doing?' asked Josh.

'It's all soaked, Josh,' she said, feeling herself begin to crumble. He must have heard the crack in her voice and gently took the bag from her. 'All right, don't rush,' he said, guiding her to a plastic chair and draping his own towel over her shoulders. 'Just take a few deep breaths. We've lost those guys, they won't find us in here, okay? We're safe now.'

Sophie looked at him, then gave a tight nod. She didn't feel at all safe, but she knew that panicking wasn't going to help.

'Let's see what I can find in here,' he said gruffly. He flicked on a torch and moved off behind the shelves, leaving her in the semi-darkness. *God, what am I doing here?* she thought, feeling a sudden stab of longing for her old life. Not the Chelsea one, with the flat and the money and the rich boyfriend; no, her recent life, her normal one with her little flat and her tiny seedling of a business. Back then, she had thought it mundane and unexciting, but at least no one had forced her into the river. People were always criticising ordinary life, complaining about suburbia and the daily struggle to make ends meet, but it wasn't until you had it taken away, like some trapdoor opening beneath you, that you realised just how happy you had been. Sure, Sophie had shared her dad's dreams of adventure, of escaping to exotic places, but this? Shivering in a black puddle on a concrete floor, hiding from men who wanted to shoot her dead? She certainly didn't want this. She stood up and peered around the shelves where Josh was digging in boxes.

'Who's after me, Josh?' she asked.

He looked up and his face was earnest in the torchlight.

'Whoever killed Nick, I'm guessing.'

'But why?'

He tugged a handful of white T-shirts from a box, then pulled one over his head.

'Perhaps he had something they wanted. And now maybe they think you have it. Whatever it is, they must want it pretty badly. It's the only explanation for getting shot at back there.'

She nodded, thinking.

'So who was Nick, Josh?'

'A businessman. Of sorts.'

'Of sorts?'

He sat down on a crate and puffed out his cheeks.

'He was a grifter, Sophie, a confidence trickster. *You'd* call him a con man.'

She looked at him wide-eyed.

'A con man? Who did he con?'

'People like you.'

'*Me?*' she squeaked.

'Keep your bloody voice down,' he snapped. 'We don't know if our trigger-happy friends have really gone.'

'But what did he want from me?' she pressed.

Josh paused for a moment and gave her a sympathetic look.

'Money,' he replied flatly.

'I don't believe it,' said Sophie, but deep down she knew that what Josh was saying could be true. Of course Nick thought she had money. They'd met at a £10,000-a-plate dinner, she'd let him believe she was some sort of health industry entrepreneur, and he had walked her back to 'her' £15 million home.

'Oh God,' she said.

'What?' He looked at her. 'Tell me, Sophie. We were shot at earlier, or had you forgotten? I think you owe it to me to tell me everything.'

So slowly, haltingly, Sophie told Josh about house-sitting at Lana's house, about the party invitations on the

132

mantelpiece, the borrowed wardrobe and her nearly week-long act of playing the millionaire.

'I have no money, Josh,' she said, feeling wretched. 'It was an illusion. I didn't tell him I was a broke personal trainer because I knew he'd think I was a gold-digger.'

Josh gave a mirthless laugh.

'Instead it turns out you were both playing the same game.'

She wished he would be compassionate, but then what did she expect from a man like Josh McCormack?

'What was he going to do to me, Josh?' she asked quietly.

'At a guess, the Spanish Prisoner,' he said finally.

'The Spanish what?'

'It's one of the oldest cons in the book. Basically, he would convice you he was rich, pay for everything, shower you with presents, until you completely trusted him. Then he would suddenly need money: some investment gone bad, a bridging loan on a building development – it doesn't really matter. In the old days, the con would need a ransom for a wealthy nobleman captured by the Spanish, hence the name. Anyway, you would offer the money, he would reluctantly accept – and then he'd disappear.'

'So everything he said to me was a lie?' she croaked.

Josh gave her that sympathetic look again, and Sophie began to hate him for it.

'Sophie, you're a beautiful woman.' He shrugged. 'Maybe what you two had together wasn't just work, I can't say. But that was what Nick did; he used rich women, conned them, lived off them. You asked me what his business was. That's what he did.'

For a few moments Sophie couldn't speak.

'But how come . . .' she began, but Josh held up a hand.

'Later, Sophie. If you don't get some clothes on soon, you're going to do that hit man's job for him.'

He pulled something out of a box.

'Here, try these. I can't see much, so forgive me if it's not exactly colour co-ordinated.'

He handed Sophie an armful of clothes, all seemingly brand new and covered with crinkly cellophane. Sophie held up a dress on a hanger. It had an elaborate blue and gold print she recognised.

'Versace?' she said. 'It's this season, too. How did you . . . ?'

'Don't ask,' said Josh, handing her a pair of black patent pumps. 'I've guessed the size, but there are most sizes back there. Just shout if the coat's too much as well.'

Sophie looked at her new wardrobe with disbelief. Either Josh's friend spent his weekends ram-raiding Bond Street, or he was very connected in Milan, though Sophie seriously doubted whether the top fashion houses would be happy to store their valuable stock in some run-down garage clinging to the side of the Thames.

'Josh, are these fakes?'

'At this moment in time, I thought you'd be grateful to wear anything. Fake or authentic.'

'I am, but . . .' The thing was, her knickers were still soaking, but she didn't want to point that out.

He threw her a pair of Calvin Klein men's trunks.

'Best I can do. Sorry,' he said with a half-smile.

He gave her privacy as she dried off properly and got into the clothes. He was right, she didn't care what sort they were, especially when she pulled on the heavy wool coat and wrapped her arms about herself. Finally the chill was starting to leave her bones, at least. Still, she was far from comfortable being here, stranded in some Fagin's hideout, with unknown assailants – possibly killers – on her trail. She didn't know where she was going to go next, she just knew she wanted to get out of there.

'We need to get to a phone and call Inspector Fox,' she said.

'No, Sophie,' he said. 'It's not safe to talk to the police.'

'Why not?'

'Number one,' he said, 'you said it yourself, you're the prime suspect in Nick's murder. After you called me, I went straight on the net – and Nick's death is the top news story. Number two, you say a Met inspector is going to your flat? That saves him getting a warrant. Now maybe this guy is as straight as a die, but what if he's not? He could be planting any sort of evidence in your knicker drawer. My bet is that they'll arrest you within twenty-four hours even if it's just to be seen to be doing something. And then it's in their interest to find something to make it stick. No one wants to look stupid, especially with the media watching.'

'But they're the police, they can't do that.'

He turned round and peeled off his wet boxer shorts. She tried to look away, but she couldn't resist sneaking a peek before he pulled on his own Calvins.

'Number three,' he added, oblivious. 'Even if they're not planning on pinning this on you, we really don't want the police to know where we are in any case.'

He put on a suit which Sophie noticed had a Gucci tag hanging from it.

'What's that supposed to mean?' she frowned.

'Okay. You read the papers, right? You know how they're always going on about institutionalised racism in the police force?'

'Yes?'

'Well, it's crap. "Racism" is actually just a euphemism for "corruption". There's corruption right through the force, but no one will admit it, because frankly, there's nothing anyone can do about it. In fact, if you ask me, it's the only way they can do a decent job.'

Sophie shook her head.

'I don't understand. You're saying that all policemen are corrupt?'

'Not all, no. But some are. Tip-offs, bribes, kick-backs, it all goes on. Somebody gets killed, it's on the news within minutes. I bet there were reporters at Nick's hotel when the police escorted you out, yeah?'

She had to nod; it had been horrible – shoving cameras up against the glass of the car, shouting out questions; she had felt like a criminal.

'Sophie, right now, you have thugs on your trail who have killed and will kill again. At a push, I'd say they are gangsters. Albanian, Kosovan. Russian. People like that have power, connections, even inside the police. All it will take is a call to the right person, the appropriate amount of cash – and bingo, they've found you.'

'You're beginning to make jail sound like an appealing option.'

'You're not safe there either; in fact you could be a sitting target.'

She wondered briefly if Josh was saying this from personal experience; whether he had ever seen the inside of a prison cell.

'So what are we going to do?'

'We?' replied Josh quickly.

'Sorry,' stuttered Sophie. 'I just assumed . . .'

'I've saved you from armed thugs and given you the best counterfeit Versace on the market already,' he said. 'What more to do you expect from me?'

It was true; he'd already done so much for her, but she couldn't go home, she couldn't go to the police. She had nowhere else to go.

'Please, Josh,' she said softly. 'I need . . . I need a friend right now.'

'Spare me the emotional blackmail.'

'Josh, I need you.'

He paused, rubbing the stubble on his chin.

'You didn't even bring me those beers,' he muttered under his breath.

'So you'll help me?' she said, feeling a dart of hope.

'I can't exactly go back to my houseboat, can I?' he said, looking at her. 'Thanks to you, whoever those shooters are now know where I live.'

'Exactly, so we need to find out who they are and what they want.'

He frowned, his dark brows knitting together.

'Now listen to me, this isn't a game. If I'm going to help you, you've got to tell me everything – leave nothing out, however small or embarrassing, okay?'

'Thank you, thank you,' she said, her shoulders slumping in relief.

Josh grunted.

'And you do exactly what I say, when I say, we clear on that?'

'Perfectly.'

Josh pulled a face. 'If only I could believe that were true.' He exhaled loudly. 'All right, first things first. Did Nick give you anything? A file, a computer disk, anything?'

Sophie looked down at the floor. She had been over and over this in her head.

'Nothing. I almost wish he had,' she said. 'Then it would make some sort of sense.'

'Well, it doesn't really matter. It's enough that they think you have something.'

'But what is it?' said Sophie, her voice rising. 'What was Nick mixed up in?'

'I told you we weren't good friends, not lately anyway,' said Josh carefully. 'But we go way back; once or twice we've even worked together. So when we did meet, we'd talk about stuff. The last time I saw him, I was in Paris, at a watch expo, he was in the city on business and we bumped into each other at a fashion party. He told me he'd been working in Paris and the South of France on a job, a big job. Lucrative.'

'He said he'd spent the last few months in Paris but wasn't specific about what he was doing there,' Sophie said.

Josh shrugged. 'Nick was never specific.'

'So you don't know what the job was either?'

He shook his head.

'Do you think it might have something to do with his death?'

'Who knows. But money is always a strong motive for murder. Money and women,' he added, looking straight at her.

She ignored the jibe.

'Well, he did tell me he was going back to Houston, which suggests maybe the job was finished,' she said hopefully.

'He *said* he was going back to Houston,' said Josh, raising his eyebrows. 'He was a con man, remember.'

She cupped her hands in front of her face in frustration. 'This is useless, Josh. We don't know anything, we can't tell anyone where we are and we can't trust anyone! What the hell are we going to do?'

She looked up and saw the beginnings of a smile on his face.

'I'll tell you what we're going to do,' said Josh in a low, conspiratorial voice. 'We're going to go to Paris.'

16

Ruth had been curled up in the footwell behind the driver's seat of her Fiesta for nearly half an hour. She had cramp in both legs, and as she'd had a coat over her head the entire time, she was finding it hard to breathe. This wasn't how she had planned to spend her evening. She'd pictured herself unpacking her suitcase at David's, maybe ordering Chinese in and celebrating having taken their relationship to the next level. But no, she was cowering like a wild animal in a parked car somewhere in a Chelsea wasteland.

She tensed as she heard a sharp rap on the car's window. *Don't move, don't move*, she thought, imagining an armed assassin looming over the car.

Tap-tap-tap! The knocking was more insistent now, and she could hear a muffled voice through the window.

'Ruth Boden, are you in there? It's Detective Inspector Fox.'

Fox? *Inspector* Fox?

'Hallelujah,' she muttered, and uncurled her body, throwing off the coat. Everything ached, one leg had pins and needles, yet somehow she managed to reach out to unlock the door.

'What on *earth* are you doing?' said a gruff voice.

'Hiding, what does it look like?' she said grumpily as she clambered out of the car. 'What kept you? I've been in there hours.'

She looked up to see amused eyes – and her heart sank. She recognised the face, the sharp suit instantly. It was one of the detectives who had been at the Riverton. Standing on the pavement, she kicked out her legs, one at a time, trying to get the feeling back.

'Thanks for coming,' she said finally.

'Dan Davis called me as soon as you rang him. I was on my way to Battersea and came straight here.'

He paused.

'So do you want to tell me how you've come to be hiding in the footwell of your car?'

She looked up at him.

'How about I tell you over a beer?' she said. 'I've been under that coat for almost an hour, and if I don't get some liquid down my throat, I think I might just melt here on the sidewalk.'

'Okay. Give me one minute,' he said, before walking to a squad car that had pulled up behind Ruth's Fiesta. He had a word with a uniformed officer before beckoning Ruth into the passenger seat of his own vehicle.

Ruth suggested the Cross Keys, a popular pub just behind Cheyne Walk, and on the way filled him in on her evening: her visit to Sophie Ellis's Battersea apartment and how she had followed her to this lonely stretch of the Thames.

'I was just doing my job,' she said, glancing across at Fox's face, unsmiling in the driver's seat.

'How do you know this Sophie Ellis is connected to the Riverton murder?' he said, indicating left off the main road.

'I'm a reporter,' she said with a small smile. 'Anyway, I'm right, aren't I? That's why you were going over to Battersea. To see her – she told me she'd had her flat broken into.'

Fox said nothing as he pulled into a parking space.

'Let's just get a drink.'

The pub was busy, full of loud Chelsea twenty-somethings. DI Ian Fox didn't look at all comfortable, so she sent him to the bar while she found a chesterfield sofa in the corner.

She watched him weave back through the crowds, holding aloft two overflowing pint pots. He was scrupulous in not letting the amber liquid spill on to his suit.

'So are you going to tell me what you told Dan?' Fox handed her a glass of lager, then rubbed his wet fingers with a tissue. 'You can start with why you were actually following Miss Ellis to the wharf. I assume that's what happened. You were tailing her, right?'

He had a gruffness that made Ruth feel reprimanded.

'I bumped into her outside her house,' she replied with mock haughtiness. She watched Fox nod cynically. 'She said she was going to meet someone, so as a reporter, interested in the same thing as you are – who killed Nick Beddingfield – I followed her.'

'I get the feeling you're the sort of writer who's prepared to go above and beyond in the name of a story. Like sneaking into hotel rooms that happen to be a crime scene, for example?'

'Ah,' said Ruth, feeling her cheeks flush a little. 'So you recognised me.'

Fox waved a hand as if it was nothing, but it was hard to read his expression. He had dark, brooding features that easily looked cross or impatient. She shifted position to look at him more directly.

'Sophie got a taxi from her apartment to the wharf. I parked about fifty metres from the jetty because I didn't want her to see me,' said Ruth, taking a sip of her beer. 'I was still close enough to see her disappear into one of those houseboats, and I was debating whether to go follow her when a black SUV came and parked opposite the wharf.'

'Was Sophie still in the houseboat?'

Ruth nodded. 'She was in there maybe ten minutes. When she came out, she seemed angry about something. The next thing I know, two knuckleheads had got out of the car and were blocking her way.'

'Could you hear what they were saying?'

She felt foam on her lip and wiped it off.

'No, I was too far away. And I was glad of it too. When the black SUV arrived, I thought it was creepy. I locked my car doors and was ready to speed off at any second.'

'But you stayed?'

'As you said, Detective, I go above and beyond in the name of a story.' She popped another piece of nicotine gum. 'So tell me, is Sophie Ellis your prime suspect? Do you have any other leads? And what else do you know about the victim other than the "Nick Beddingfield, businessman" statement crap you gave out earlier today?'

Fox's expression remained neutral.

'That's a lot of questions.'

She wasn't sure if he was suppressing a smile or was actually patronising her.

'I'm a journalist.'

'And you know all that the press need to know for the time being. Surely you've got enough information to file your story.'

'I don't want a story. I want *the* story,' she said quietly. 'So come on, quid pro quo. I'm telling you what happened at the wharf; you need to tell me something.'

For a moment he didn't react.

'Okay, get back to the wharf and I'll tell you what you want to know. *Within reason.*'

She clasped her hands together and leant forward. 'So this guy comes out of the houseboat and joins Sophie. Thirty-something, good-looking. He might have held her hand.'

'You think it was another boyfriend?' asked Fox.

'Hard to say.' She shrugged. 'Anyway, when one of the meatheads swings for the boat guy, he kicks him, grabs Sophie and they run.'

'Where?'

'I don't know, somewhere off to my right. I didn't exactly

have stalls seats. It was dark by then and I was watching most of it in the rear-view mirror.

Now she had his full attention.

'So why did you phone Dan Davis?'

'Because I heard a gunshot. You may think I'm some hard-hearted hack, but I was worried about the girl. You'd rather I hadn't called you?'

Fox rubbed his chin.

'Sorry, I've been on shift since six thirty this morning and I've had to deal with a body somewhere in the middle. I'd rather be at home right now – no offence.'

Ruth smiled.

'None taken, Inspector Charmer.'

Fox sat forward, a serious look on his face.

'Look, Ruth, this is my case, and tired or not, I want to find out who killed Nick Beddingfield. So to answer your question, yes, right now Sophie Ellis is our main lead, and when you called Davis and said you'd seen her at the wharf and someone was shooting at her, I considered it useful.'

'Fair enough, but the clock's ticking, Detective. I need to go and write my story. Quid pro quo, remember?'

Fox looked irritated.

'We are not partners, Miss Boden. I am a police officer and you are a journalist. I need information from you, which you are legally obliged to give me. There is no reciprocal arrangement.'

Ruth bristled, but she could tell Fox was not the sort of man who would respond well to a shouting match in a public place. *Come on, Ruth*, she thought to herself, *use your feminine wiles*.

'You're the boss.' She had very little cleavage to thrust at him, but she gave him a slow, practised smile – one meant to flatter the male ego.

'You must have a theory about it all. There was dark green glass on the floor which looked like it came from a champagne bottle. The wound on the head. On paper, it looks like a crime of passion.'

Fox paused and took a sip of his beer.

'Her story about the cabbie checks out, so she was out of the room for about thirty minutes; that's plenty of time for someone to come in and batter her boyfriend to death.'

'Does that match up with time of death?'

Fox shook his head. 'We're talking half an hour, twenty minutes either way. Forensics aren't miracle workers, they can only give a vague window. Then again, she could have shagged him, had some sort of row, whacked him and gone out to the cab, then come back and made a big dramatic show about finding the body.'

'Does the glass have her fingerprints on it?'

'Boden, I've told you enough.'

Ruth nodded and looked at him for a moment.

'You don't believe it's her, I can tell,' she said, lifting a determined finger into the air.

'Because you know me so well,' he said sarcastically.

Ruth hid her annoyance. Clearly Ian Fox was going to be a much tougher nut to crack than Dan Davis, who would tell her anything if she just smiled at him the right way.

'All right then, who owns the houseboat?'

'That won't be hard to turn up,' said Fox, glancing at her. 'Even for you.'

'Dealer, perhaps?' she said, ignoring the insult. 'Possible, I guess. Seems that Sophie Ellis was a bit of a party girl and she met Beddingfield at some fancy do. It's not a stretch to think they both did drugs. Then again, if Mr Houseboat was her dealer, it might even account for the shooting. They could have been after him, nothing to do with the Riverton murder.'

Ruth traced a fingernail through the condensation on the outside of her glass, weighing it all up. Yes, Sophie Ellis had pictures of herself on the internet waving champagne glasses, but she still couldn't see her as a cold-blooded killer – or some coked-up club hag for that matter. In her head, she could hear her dad again: 'Instinct, Ruthie.' And right now her instinct was telling her that Sophie was innocent, but she needed Fox if she was going to be able to prove it.

'So what now, Inspector?' she asked casually.

Fox finished his beer and put down the glass.

'Well I'd better get back to the river. I've got two officers scouring the streets for Ellis. I take it you're all right to get home yourself.'

'No, I mean, what about us?'

'Us?' he replied, as if she was Glenn Close in *Fatal Attraction*.

Ruth was undeterred. 'I think we can help each other, Fox. We both want to get a result on this, and if we work together . . .'

'Nice try,' he said, standing up.

Ruth sat forward, putting her hand on his arm.

'Seriously, Fox, it makes sense. Nick Beddingfield is American, right? You know that makes things difficult for you. The cops across the pond don't exactly have a reputation for being forthcoming with information to foreigners, do they? On the other hand, I work for an American newspaper – we can move things along for you.'

He looked at her for a moment, then sighed.

'Okay, give me your card. Maybe I'll call you tomorrow.'

She watched him walk out.

I hope you do, she thought to herself. *I hope you do.*

17

The garage door squealed as Josh pushed it up. Sophie winced at the grinding metal-upon-metal sound. She blinked at the grey light of dawn and peered at the empty parking lot, half expecting to see the men in the Range Rover just waiting for them to walk into their trap. But the car park was empty; they were alone.

'Come on, princess,' said Josh, heading for the road. 'It's a long way to St Pancras.'

There really had been no option but to spend the night in the garage. At least they were hidden and out of the cold – and where else could they go anyway? The first Eurostar wouldn't leave until five thirty at the earliest and they would have been too conspicuous on the streets, so Sophie had spent an uncomfortable night propped up between two plastic chairs, a pile of cellophane-covered coats serving as a blanket.

Josh had made a similar makeshift bed on some cardboard boxes and, if his steady breathing was anything to go by, had gone straight to sleep. Untroubled slumber was the mark of a clear conscience, wasn't that what her dad used to say? Sophie wasn't so sure about Josh. He could be a murderer for all she knew – he certainly wasn't the legitimate businessman he had portrayed at the Chariot party. But then neither was Nick. No, Sophie still had little idea who Josh was or what his motivation was for helping her. She knew she should be grateful – he had saved her life after all – but even so, through those long sleepless hours she had spent shivering under rustling plastic, her tired, paranoid mind had jumped to every conclusion possible: Josh was a con man after her money just like Nick (but what money exactly?); Josh was in league with the Russians (but then why didn't he just hand her over?). It had even occurred to her that he might be an undercover policeman, but what on earth for? To extract a confession that they hadn't been able to get at the police station?

By the time Josh had stirred and they had stepped out into the industrial estate, Sophie had finally come to the inevitable conclusion that she simply had no choice but to follow his lead. The bitter truth was that she had no one else to turn to: The police had been hostile, suspicious in their line of questioning; her mother was in Copenhagen; and her friends? Francesca would have had a breakdown about the fake Louboutins alone.

Sophie glanced across at Josh as they walked through the dark estate, his wary eyes searching every corner, every doorway. In the end, it didn't matter who he was or what he had done; right now Josh McCormack was her best chance of getting away from this nightmare and finding a little breathing space to decide what to do next.

As they turned a corner, she saw the black outline of the North Thames Gas Works framed against the lightening sky. They were still near the river, then. She shivered at the memory.

'You okay?' said Josh.

'I'm not at all sure about this, Josh,' she said hesitantly.

He stopped and turned to look at her.

'Fine,' he said, holding up a hand to indicate the empty road ahead of them. 'Be my guest. You want to go home, off you go.'

'I'm just not sure about Paris.'

'You're not sure about Paris?' he snapped. 'It's not exactly the way I planned on spending the day either, but as I don't fancy an early morning visit from the Russians, I think I'll keep moving. Personally, I wouldn't mind getting out of London for a couple of days, but if you want to stay, then be my guest.'

'Josh, please,' she stuttered. 'I just don't know what to do.'

His eyes were cold as he looked at her. 'Here are your choices,' he replied flatly. 'You can either come with me, or you can run off home to Daddy.'

'My dad's dead,' said Sophie. 'He died four weeks ago.'

Josh just shrugged.

'I'm sorry, but it doesn't change anything.'

He put his arm in the air as a black cab appeared around the bend in the road, its light glowing mercifully orange.

'Your choice, Sophie,' he said, opening the door.

He was right. She did have a choice. She could go back to Paddington Green, or she could go back to Wade House. But if Josh was right that the Russians could find out where she was through some corrupt policeman, then neither option seemed viable. Not if she wanted to stay alive.

She shivered at the thought of how close the bullet had come to hitting her.

'I'm coming,' she said.

Josh gave a slight nod, then looked at the driver.

'St Pancras via Pimlico, please,' he said.

Sophie waited until they were moving before she turned to Josh.

'Pimlico?' she whispered.

'Passport,' he said simply.

She frowned. 'It's in Pimlico?'

'No.' He sighed heavily. 'It's back on the boat.'

He didn't need to say that it was not a good idea to return there. She wanted to ask more, but a look at his face told her that he wasn't exactly in the mood to talk. Besides, the thrum of the cab's diesel engine was soothing and her eyelids were feeling heavy.

She jolted awake when the taxi stopped, her head resting on Josh's shoulder.

'Sorry, I . . .'

Josh ignored her. 'Wait here, okay? I won't be long.'

She watched him cross the road to a long row of white stucco town houses, not immaculate like Lana's Knightsbridge home, but rough around the edges, with peeling window frames and bikes chained to the railings. Flats, probably. Josh bent to speak into an intercom, and a tall, dark-haired man in a dressing gown appeared. His unkempt hair and scowl suggested he had been dragged out of bed – and wasn't exactly overjoyed about it. It was, after all, only quarter past four in the morning. *I'd be angry too*, Sophie thought, as Josh went inside.

She rested her head back on the seat, watching the dawn send soft golden stripes of light rising up above the Mary Poppins chimneypots into the Prussian-blue sky. She could almost feel the city coming to life around her. The hum of a milk float, the grumble of the last night bus making the final trip south of the river, the rare twitter of a bird in the spindly trees.

On any other day she would have appreciated the beauty of the summer sunrise, but right now she just wanted to get to the train station.

She started as the door opened and Josh jumped in.

'St Pancras, mate,' he said to the driver. 'Quick as you like.'

'What kept you?' said Sophie, as they set off again. 'I thought you weren't coming back.'

'How could I tear myself away?' he replied, almost smiling.

* * *

The concourse at St Pancras station was busier than Sophie had expected, especially considering it was barely five in the morning. The high hollow space was clanging with the voices and hurrying footsteps of early-bird tourists and business commuters on their way to meetings. Sophie tightened her grip on her bag and tried her best to look casual, but inside she was feeling more frightened than when they had jumped into the freezing waters of the Thames. Back then, she hadn't had any choice – it was either jump or die – but here, every one of the people in front of her was a potential assassin, every one of them could be an undercover police officer. Not that she had done anything wrong – not yet, anyway. She guessed this was how it felt being a shoplifter when you had the clothes or jewellery stuffed inside your coat and you were heading for the exit; until she actually stepped on to the Eurostar, she was just another innocent citizen wandering about a train station.

She tried to make conversation to distract herself.

'So all that fake stuff in the garage. Is it really yours or your friend's?' she asked, struggling to keep up with Josh's fast pace.

He shot her a look.

'It's my friend's.'

'But you said it was your lock-up.'

'So I'm a good friend. I help people out.'

'You're handling counterfeit goods, Josh. That's illegal.'

'Speaks she, a suspect in a murder investigation.'

Sophie looked around fretfully. 'Be quiet!' she hissed. 'You don't know who's listening.'

Josh looked at the crowd moving around them: no one was paying the slightest attention to them.

'Why is all this so important to you anyway?' he asked.

'Because I'm about to leave the country with you,' said Sophie. 'I usually like to know who I go travelling with.'

He smiled and reached inside his jacket, pulling out a passport.

'Here, take a look.'

Frowning, Sophie opened it.

'Christopher Barnard?' she said, reading the name inside. She did a double-take at the photograph, then gasped as the penny dropped.

'It's your friend from Pimlico . . .'

It was uncanny: the same dark eyes, the same thick floppy hair and brooding good looks; the two men could be brothers.

'People always say we look alike. I'm a lot more handsome, of course, but the bloke on passport control won't be looking for that.'

Sophie shook her head at him, open-mouthed.

'Josh, you *can't* go through passport control with someone else's passport!'

'Well unless you want to go back to the boat, we don't have much choice,' he whispered urgently, before giving her the slightest smile. 'And they won't notice, so long as you start calling me Christopher from here on in.'

'*Josh,*' she said. 'I'm serious!'

'Christopher,' he corrected. 'Come on, princess, just give me your passport.'

'Will you stop calling me princess! I'm not some spoilt prima donna, you know.'

'Passport. Now,' he said holding out his hand.

It was inside her plastic make-up case in her small nylon backpack. Reluctantly she unzipped it and handed the passport over. She watched, her heart sinking as Josh walked towards the ticket desk, asking herself again why she was trusting this man. For all she knew he could just disappear into the crowd, taking her passport and her only chance of escape. She hopped from one foot to the other nervously, trying to look inconspicuous as Josh went up to the ticket agent and flashed her a smile. The twenty-something girl behind the desk looked sullen – who could blame her this early in the morning? – but when Josh launched into his patter, her face lit up, her head tipping to one side, and she laughed. Sophie turned away. *Another bloody slick, charming liar. Just like his friend Nick.*

She cursed herself; she knew she shouldn't speak ill of the dead. But the truth was, her grief about Nick's death – and her feelings for him – had been tainted. It was hard not to feel bitter about the lies he had told her, not to mention the mess he had dragged her into. And now she was about to leave the country, leaving her family and friends far behind, for how long, she had no idea – and all because of Nick and whatever sordid schemes he was tangled up in. Was Josh McCormack any better, any more reliable than his friend? Probably not, but then what choice did she have but to trust another stranger?

'Here you go,' said Josh, sauntering back waving an envelope. 'Business class.' He slipped an arm across her shoulders.

'Hey!' said Sophie, shrugging him off, 'What are you doing?'

'Relax,' he whispered. 'Try and look natural. We're a young couple off to Paris, we have to play the part, okay?'

Sophie forced a smile. 'Okay,' she said, but she wasn't sure how natural she could look with her shoulders tensed and her stomach churning. She just wanted to get on the train and out of London. Her legs felt weak too as Josh steered her towards the security check. They were going to stop her, she was sure of it, glancing up at the roof, looking for CCTV cameras. Inspector Fox would certainly be wondering where the hell she was, after her phone call yesterday. Surely he'd have sent out an alert to be on the lookout for a woman meeting her description.

'What's the matter?' said Josh, drawing her to one side. 'You're walking like a waxwork.'

'What do you think's the bloody matter? We're about to

go through security and Fox will have alerted the airports, the railway stations, everywhere. They're going to arrest us, Josh.'

Josh gave a slight smile which riled her enormously.

'Sophie, the police have questioned you, that's all. You haven't been accused or charged with anything. You're hardly the outlaw Josey Wales.'

'It's not funny, Josh,' she said, glancing towards the security gate. 'Look, I'm turning back.'

He gripped her arm and pulled her into an alcove in front of a bureau de change booth, his grey eyes searching hers.

'Listen to me, Sophie. You're not on any Interpol "most wanted" list. The police almost never put out a port stop, unless it's a particularly high-profile case or they think someone's going to get killed. It's too much hassle and it costs too much money.'

Sophie's brow creased.

'You're telling me . . . I'm not wanted?'

'I doubt it very much. Sorry to disappoint you.'

'Disappoint me? You think I'm enjoying this?' she snapped, pulling away from him.

'All right,' said Josh, holding his hands up. 'Now calm down, you're attracting attention. In fact that security guard is looking at you now – don't turn around!'

'But Josh—'

'Shut up and pretend you're enjoying this.'

Before she had time to grasp what was happening, Josh had grabbed her and pressed his lips on to hers. She gasped in surprise and resisted him, but when his arms wrapped around her waist and pulled her in, she had no choice but to melt into the kiss. And as they pulled apart, she inhaled sharply. She was still only inches away from his face, still breathing the same air as he was, and could still smell him, taste him on her tongue. She stumbled back and he caught her arm.

'That shut you up,' he growled. 'Now, we've got twenty-five minutes before the train leaves.'

He grabbed her hand and led her to passport control. She was still in shock and followed in mute silence as her bag was put through the metal detector, Josh joking with the security guard, who just glanced at their passports and waved them through.

'You'd better be quick,' he said.

Josh took her bag and quickened his pace, but Sophie held his sleeve to slow him down.

'Don't run,' she hissed. 'I feel like a fugitive.'

'You *are* a fugitive,' he whispered. 'Come on, we're about to miss the train and I just want to get out of here.'

He pulled her up the ramp, running along the length of the sleek silver train. It looked so good, like a bird that would pick them up and fly them to safety. Sophie's heart was hammering now; she could hardly believe they had managed to get through security so easily. Maybe she was going to get away after all. She glanced back over her shoulder, half expecting to see dark uniforms or burly Russians chasing them, but apart from a guard with a flag, they were alone.

'You coming?' said Josh. He was on the steps of the train, his hand reaching out to her.

She had spent the past twelve hours feeling frightened, unsettled, anxious, but looking up and seeing the sign for Paris, a surge of exhilaration gripped her.

'Try and stop me,' she replied as she took his hand.

18

Ruth wandered into David's kitchen still half asleep. He was sitting at the table reading the *Financial Times* and absent-mindedly sticking a fork into a salmon fillet. Ruth opened a cabinet at random, finding only tea bags and a bottle of expensive-looking olive oil.

'Have you got any cornflakes?' she said, rubbing sleep from the corner of her eye.

'Don't do carbs in the morning, remember?' said David, not looking up from his paper.

At her own apartment, Ruth made sure she had a stash of croissants and pains au chocolat, and for a fleeting moment she wished she was back there.

'I don't know how you can eat a great big chunk of fish in the morning,' she said, turning to watch him in fascination.

'Eating eighty per cent protein in the morning cuts out the insulin spikes throughout the day,' said David knowingly. 'The spikes are what make you feel peckish and lead to snacking. It might be worth taking on board,' he said, glancing at her thighs.

As he returned to the business news, Ruth pulled a face behind his back. Ever since David had started training for the London Marathon, he had become a food bore. And while she couldn't complain about his increased stamina – the sex lately had been abundant and sensational – she wasn't sure if she could face his-and-hers salmon fillets every morning.

'Well, if I'm going to move in here, we need a stash of carbs. I'm talking Cheerios, waffle mix, the works,' she grinned, bending down to get the orange juice from the fridge. As she moved, her T-shirt lifted right up over her buttocks.

'Nice view,' he said.

'Look away,' she smiled, walking over to sit on his lap and planting a long kiss on his lips.

'So where were you last night?' he asked. 'I didn't even hear you come in.'

'Working,' she shrugged, picking a flake of fish from his plate. It was true, wasn't it? Yes, she'd gone for a drink with DI Fox, but that was all there was to it. It *was* work. Although Ruth had to admit she'd enjoyed it – it was rare she got the opportunity to screw so much information from the police. She spotted a blob of shaving foam behind David's ear and wiped it off.

'See? You need me first thing in the morning.'

He slipped his hand up her T-shirt and rubbed his palm over her nipple.

'I won't argue with you there,' he growled. Ruth giggled and pushed him away. She knew where that was headed, and she needed an early start at the office to work on last night's leads.

'Save that for later, hey?' she smiled, dancing out of his grasp. 'I've got to get to work. It's all gone crazy on my story.'

'The escort thing?' he asked, yawning.

She frowned, for a moment unsure what he was talking about. 'Oh, not that one – I'm on a new thing now. I mean the murder at the Riverton Hotel.'

'I saw the headlines about that. American bloke, wasn't it?'

Briefly she filled him in on the story as far as she knew.

'Anyway, that's where I was last night. Meeting the inspector in charge of the case.'

David folded up his paper and dropped it on the table.

'I love the way when I meet a business contact, you think I'm having some sort of affair, but when you're out socialising with the cops, it's strictly business.'

Ruth tried not to react, reminding herself that this was all new to her. She was forty-one years old and until now had always lived alone. She'd always had whatever she wanted for breakfast and she wasn't used to answering for her movements. If she was going to make this work, she had to learn to bend a little.

'This is my job, David,' she said evenly. 'You understand that.'

'All right,' he said, stretching. 'Don't get all jumpy on me. I was just saying. So the dead bloke – who was he?'

Ruth nodded, her mind flashing back to that bathroom in the hotel.

'I saw him, David,' she said quietly.

'What? Dead?'

'Dead. On the floor. It was horrible.'

'Bloody hell, Ruth,' said David, looking at her more carefully. 'Are you okay?'

She nodded quickly. 'It wasn't pleasant, but it's part of the job, isn't it?'

'Not mine, I'm glad to say. I'd much rather be looking at stock charts than dead bodies.'

Ruth poured herself some juice and told David about the incident with Sophie Ellis by the river.

'God, no wonder you were in late,' he said. 'It was quite a day.'

'I felt like someone off *CSI*. They just appeared from nowhere, started shouting in Russian and began shooting.'

David nodded thoughtfully. 'Jamie on the news desk was telling me about that the other day. Apparently there are various Eastern European gangs fighting over control of the river.'

'Control of the river? Why would they need that?'

'There's a surprising amount of trade that goes on along the Thames. A lot of cargo still gets shifted that way, so whoever controls the flow of traffic can take a cut of each transaction. It's quite creative, actually.'

'But I've seen police boats going up and down.'

David nodded. 'Apparently there aren't many of them, and the river patrol spends most of its time dragging bodies from the water – suicides and so on. Besides, according to Jamie, the gangsters don't work *on* the water. They wait until the traders come ashore, then twist their arms.'

Ruth pouted.

'That's interesting,' she said. 'I wonder if the two are connected.'

David grinned.

'There you go, I've given you a lead. Don't ever say I don't give you anything.'

Ruth ran her hand down his chest. 'I never said that, did I?' she smiled.

'So you're not doing the escort story?' He said it casually. So casually that it put Ruth on immediate alert.

'Not at the moment, why?'

'Oh, I was thinking I might have a little poke around.'

'Poke around what?' said Ruth, her back stiffening.

'Well, Sebastian Watson was the number two at his bank, and his resignation is quite a big business story for us. If it's part of a sting involving other people, then that's even bigger.'

'Wait a minute, David,' she said tightly. 'This is my story.'

'And I thought you said you weren't following it up.'

'I said I wasn't chasing it at this moment,' she said, placing her hands on her hips. 'The second they charge someone with the Riverton murder, that story is pretty much over for me and I'll be moving back on to the escort thing.'

158

He held his hands in the air.

'All right, all right. Fine.'

'What do you mean, "fine"?'

'Well, I just think it's a bit selfish of you, that's all.'

'David, I dug this story up all on my own.'

'Yes, but with this Riverton case, there's a chance you're not going to follow up the escort story for weeks, by which time Seb Watson will be old news and no one will be interested any more.'

'So?'

'So poor Watson's career is wrecked, so is Bill Danson's. I just think they should be given a chance to find out what really happened.'

'Yeah, like you care,' she scoffed.

'What's that supposed to mean?'

'I mean don't go pretending to be some great crusader fighting for justice when you've just sniffed an exclusive – *my* exclusive, in fact.'

'Oh come on, Ruth, it's not just your story, is it? Every-one's been writing about Watson. You've just found a slightly different angle.'

Ruth could barely believe her ears.

'Bullshit, David!' she snapped. 'If it was only a "slightly different angle", you wouldn't be so desperate to swipe it from under my nose.'

'Why not let me have it?' His tone softened, but she realised he was just changing tack. 'Don't you want me to get off the business pages? It would be good for me. Good for us.'

'Good for us is if I keep my job in London. And the only way I've got a chance of doing that is if I keep generating stories between now and September. I need to hold on to the escort story, David. It's my back-up.'

'Which you might never need!'

She roared with frustration.

'Ruth Boden is only ever interested in what Ruth Boden is doing,' continued David evenly. 'But if we are going to make this work, *us* work, you are going to have to start thinking about someone other than yourself.'

Her mind was reeling; she knew the argument was escalating out of control. She knew that she should stop it right there, but the touchpaper had been lit and she felt incapable of stopping the situation from exploding.

'I'm not listening to this,' she said, standing up and fuming.

'Domestic bliss,' he muttered as his knife and fork clattered noisily to the plate.

'You were the one who suggested it.'

She could hear herself, like an echo in the background, and it was a voice she did not recognise. Spiteful, unhappy and destructive. *Stop this, Ruth. Stop this*, she ordered herself, but pride and anger would not let her.

'Maybe you should go back to your own flat tonight,' David suggested.

'That's exactly what I was thinking,' she said, slamming the kitchen door behind her and feeling suddenly overwhelmingly sad.

19

'What's the matter?'

Sophie couldn't help smiling as she stepped on to the platform at the Gare du Nord.

'Nothing,' she said, swinging her bag on to her shoulder. 'Nothing at all.'

She didn't just feel safer on French soil; she felt liberated. She was in Paris, and she felt free. For the first time in her life, she had no responsibilities, nowhere to be – in fact, right at this moment no one apart from Josh knew where she was. At the back of her mind, she knew that her world had fallen apart and that her life was in danger. The two and a half hours on the Eurostar had been nerve-fraying hell – she had been convinced that she was going to be attacked or arrested at any moment – but now she was here in the City of Light, Sophie was overwhelmed with relief and something more: a sense of adventure, perhaps? She had been travelling in Australia and Asia, but she had never been to Paris before, and she felt thrilled at the whole, well, Frenchness of it all. The chatter of passers-by, the echoing announcements over the tannoy, even the clothes on the women seemed more sophisticated somehow.

'Wait here a minute,' said Josh, pulling his mobile out of his pocket. 'I've got to make some calls.'

'You've brought your mobile?'

'It's Christopher's. On loan. Mine's on the boat.'

161

She nodded. 'With the passport.'

'Which I need to get back,' he mused. 'We got through passport control this time, but who knows how easy it might be next time.'

'What were you planning? A world tour?' she frowned.

He had already stepped away from her and she did not take her eyes off him; the last thing she wanted to do was lose him.

'Let's go,' he said when he returned a few minutes later. Taking her elbow, he steered her through the high stone arch and out on to the bustling street.

'Everyone's so well dressed,' she whispered as a woman brushed past in a Missoni knitted dress, a Goyard vanity case in one hand, a miniature poodle in the other.

'Welcome to Paris,' smiled Josh, leading her towards the taxi queue. At the front was a red-faced gent in a crumpled suit, and Josh went straight up to him and began talking to him in French.

Sophie listened to his fluency in astonishment. Josh McCormack seemed rough around the edges, street-smart for sure but not a cosmopolitan sophisticate.

She felt faint embarrassment that her own French wasn't better, especially compared to Josh's linguistic skills. Then she had to admit she hadn't been the greatest student, being more interested in what parties there were to go to rather than revision to be done. The only teacher who had made any impression on her was Mr Damon, her sixth-form English teacher, who had recognised a creative flair in her and encouraged her to write short stories and poems. Not that she could ever tell Francesca or any of the other girls about it, but secretly she had harboured a desire to become a journalist or a writer. *I'd certainly have some material now*, she thought.

The ruddy-faced gentleman gestured towards the white Lada pulling up next to them.

'*Bien sûr*. Please take it,' he said, stepping forward to open the door for Sophie. She gave him a wan smile as Josh spoke to the driver and they clambered inside.

'*Merci beaucoup*,' she managed before they pulled away.

'What did you say to that man?' she asked, turning to Josh as they moved into traffic. Her French was rusty, but she was fairly sure he'd said something untrue. Josh tapped one finger against his lips and looked meaningfully at the driver, an overweight Middle Eastern man in a flat cap.

'I told him you were ill and pregnant,' said Josh.

'But that's a lie.'

'So? I'm glad we didn't have to stand around in that busy street, aren't you?'

'But you . . .'

Josh tapped her leg and she fell silent.

'Just watch Paris,' he ordered.

She did as he said and was glad of it, wondering why she had never been to the French capital before. It had always been so close, yet she had somehow never made it to this icon of chic. Unless you were connected enough to attend the fashion shows, Paris wasn't on the Chelsea-girl list of places to go: Sardinia, Switzerland, Barbados, New York. Besides, when she had travelled with Will, it was always to destination hotels rather than cities or places – in their two years together, they had chalked up stays at Leading Hotels of the World like notches on a bedpost. But this? She took a deep breath, as if to soak up the essence of Paris in one gulp. It was all just as she had pictured: the elegant grey stone buildings, the roaring traffic; even the light seemed different here.

Parked on a street corner was a black van. Standing around it were three gendarmes, machine guns strapped to their chests, and Sophie's buoyant feeling immediately left her. However inviting Paris looked, she wasn't on holiday, she wasn't here to soak up the culture and visit the Louvre.

Suddenly all of the things that had seemed exotic only a moment ago became sinister and loaded with negative possibilities. The elegant women with their high heels and paper shopping bags, the news vendor in his funny little orange castle covered with foreign magazines – they were all alien, they all spoke a different language, they could all be watching, passing on information.

'I didn't know you spoke French,' she said.

'*Un petit peu*,' said Josh. 'I had a French girlfriend once. I just picked it up.'

She wanted to ask him about her. Not because she was *interested* in what Josh McCormack's girlfriends were like, but because he intrigued her, because here she was, on the run with him, and yet she knew almost nothing about him.

'*Nous sommes ici, monsieur.*'

Sophie had been so wrapped up in her thoughts, she hadn't noticed that the taxi had stopped outside a grand white building with wrought-iron balconies at every window. She almost gasped as she clambered out of the taxi and saw the hotel's facade.

'Where are we?'

'Le Bristol,' said Josh. 'The best hotel in Paris.' Then added in a whispered aside, 'Although don't tell that to the Ritz and the Four Seasons.'

'We can't afford this, Josh,' hissed Sophie. She had about sixty pounds in her purse – probably still damp from their dip in the Thames – and had no intention of using her credit card.

'We need to stay somewhere good with a helpful concierge,' said Josh, nodding to the doorman as they pushed through the doors. 'We're not going to find that in some fleapit in the Bastille, are we?'

'And we don't even have reservations.'

'Yes we do, Miss Aniston,' he smiled.

Miss Aniston? What the hell was he on about? she thought

with alarm as Josh strode confidently up to the reception desk. Hovering behind him, anxious not to say the wrong thing, she could hear Josh talking in French to a middle-aged man with half-moon spectacles perched on the end of his nose. He had a rather severe look, but he was nodding sympathetically as Josh spoke.

'Mademoiselle Aniston, *bienvenue*.' Sophie turned to see a pretty young girl in a receptionist's uniform.

Miss Aniston – again. What on earth had Josh told them?

'Would you and your manager like to follow me up to your suite?' she asked cordially in her heavy accent. Sophie smiled weakly and tried to catch Josh's eye, but he was now on the phone barking instructions about a film premiere in an American accent.

'Suite?' she said. 'Oh, yes, yes, of course.'

They had a *suite*? What had Josh done? But she had no real option except to follow the girl, who led her to the lifts and up five floors, where they stepped into a corridor, with the deepest carpets Sophie had ever felt under her feet. At the end of the corridor, the girl stopped at a large wooden door and, opening it with a pass key, held it open for Sophie to step inside. It was stunning, stately and yet intimate, decorated in cool ivory with rich mahogany antiques and pale citron drapes. Surely this couldn't be their room?

'This is our Panoramic Suite, mademoiselle,' said the girl. 'I hope it meets with your desires. Would you like me to show you around?'

'No, no. I think I'll be fine,' said Sophie quickly. She felt strange enough being here without having to trail around after the girl. The receptionist tried to take her bag, but she declined.

'Would you like me to send some tea up to your room? Champagne? Our spa is excellent, although I am sure you have a busy day in preparation for tonight.'

'I'm fine,' said Sophie politely as Josh walked in. When

the girl had closed the door, he immediately began laughing.

'Josh! What the bloody hell is going on?' asked Sophie, watching him walking about the suite inspecting it.

'Very nice view,' he said approvingly, feeling the silk drapes between his fingers. 'I thought we might get an upgrade, but nothing like this.'

'*Josh!*'

'Oh all right, don't get your knickers in a twist,' he laughed. 'That was the call I made at the station. I rang the manager's office here at Le Bristol and said that Sophie Aniston was in town for the *Aristocrats* premiere tonight.'

'What's the *Aristocrats*? And who's Sophie Aniston?'

'You.' He grinned. 'Thought I'd change your surname to something a bit more recognisable. The *Aristocrats* is that big Tom Cruise movie out on Friday; they are having the European premiere at the Grand Rex tonight. I read it in a paper on the train. Anyway – I said you'd checked out of Le Meurice because you'd been unhappy about the size of your room. There's a lot of rivalry between the Big Six Paris hotels, so of course they were going to accommodate you.'

'But . . . there *is* no Sophie Aniston,' she said.

'There is now,' laughed Josh. 'If they were going to check on it, they'd have done it before we arrived. Obviously they've assumed you're Tom's love interest. Lucky you, eh?'

'Josh, this isn't funny. What if they . . .'

But Josh was bouncing up and down on the bed.

'Hey, come and try this. Makes a change from sleeping on cardboard boxes last night.'

She frowned, noticing for the first time that there was only one bed. Her mind flashed back to that kiss at St Pancras and she pushed the uncomfortable thought away. She walked over to the window and looked out at the view of the exquisite hotel gardens.

'So how long do you think we'll be staying here?' she asked, thinking that she never wanted to leave.

'That depends on how long it takes us to find out what Nick was up to,' said Josh.

'And how are we going to do that?'

'Well,' said Josh, picking up her bag, 'that depends what's in here.'

Before she could stop him, he had unzipped it and tipped the contents on to the bed.

'What are you doing?' gasped Sophie.

'Looking for clues,' he said, emptying her make-up bag on to the crisp white duvet.

There wasn't much to see. A book, her purse, passport, internet key fob, small bag of jewellery and an Oyster card. Josh emptied the jewellery bag into his hand. There were two small gold chains, a charm bracelet and a sapphire ring that had once belonged to her grandmother.

'Not exactly the crown jewels, are they?' he said as Sophie snatched them back from him.

'They have sentimental value.'

'I'm sure, but we can rule out Nick trying to steal your priceless stash of diamonds. That's what I'm trying to work out: what was he hiding?'

'Hiding? I thought he was after my money.'

'Lana's money, you mean,' he said absently as he picked up her copy of *I Capture the Castle* and flicked through the pages.

'Did Nick give you this?'

She shook her head.

'It was a birthday present from my dad.'

'It's a bit dog-eared, isn't it?'

'It's my favourite book, actually,' she said, taking it away from him.

'So did Nick give you anything?' asked Josh, rifling through the receipts in Sophie's purse. 'A note, a love letter, something like that?'

'Josh, please!' she said, grabbing the purse. 'I've told you,

167

he didn't give me anything. Now if you've finished raking through my life, I'm going to have a shower. I want to get the Thames out of my hair.'

Kicking off her shoes, she padded through to the bathroom, which was bigger than most hotel rooms she'd ever stayed in, even on her luxurious trips with Will.

'Don't go getting any ideas about having a three-hour bath,' called Josh. 'This isn't a minibreak. We've got a busy day ahead of us.'

'The premiere, of course.' She smiled sarcastically and turned on the taps.

It was wonderful feeling the hot water on her skin, soaping herself with peach and almond bath crème, the stresses of the past two days running away down the brass plughole. Stepping out, she dried off and wrapped herself in a towelling robe, enjoying the clean smell, and walked back into the living room, rubbing at her hair with a hand towel.

Josh was sitting at a walnut writing desk in front of a silver laptop computer. It was connected to a sleek-looking laser printer.

'Was that always here?' she said.

'They just brought it up – nothing's too good for a guest like Mademoiselle Aniston.'

She watched him do a Google search for 'Riverton Hotel murder': a shocking number of hits scrolled up.

'Good,' muttered Josh, clicking on one. 'They've released a picture of Nick.'

There was a loud clunk as the printer sprang to life, but Sophie turned away: she didn't want to see Nick's face, not right now. She picked up a peach from the fruit bowl, but she didn't feel like eating and put it back.

'No mention of you in any news stories,' said Josh. 'Let's hope it stays that way.'

He clicked about quickly, and when he had to enter something, Sophie noticed he was touch-typing.

'You're very efficient,' she said.

'You sound surprised,' replied Josh, not looking up from the screen.

'It's the barge,' she said, deciding that nothing about Josh McCormack would surprise her any more. 'No electricity, copper kettle, all that stuff.'

'So you have me down as some sort of gypsy?'

Sophie blushed.

'Not quite, just a little less technical.'

She sat down on the side of the bed and picked up the room's phone.

'What are you doing?' said Josh.

'It's gone eleven and my mum gets into Heathrow any time now, I'm going to call her, tell her I'm okay.'

Josh walked over and took the receiver from her.

'Not a good idea,' he said, putting it back in its cradle. 'The police could be monitoring her calls and trace it straight to this room.'

Sophie looked up at him.

'But you said they weren't looking for me.'

'I said it wasn't likely, but we don't know what's happened since yesterday, do we? It's safer if we stay off the grid for a while.'

'But I want to tell her I'm okay.'

Josh sighed and rubbed his chin.

'Does she have an email address?'

'Yes. I don't know how often she uses it, though. She's not exactly a fifteen-year-old girl.'

'We can find an internet café and you can email her. Perhaps contact the police inspector who interviewed you too.'

'Inspector Fox? I have his business card in my purse.'

'Given that you disappeared straight after you had your flat turned over, it's probably a good idea to tell him you're okay, save him sending out a search party. Not that I think he would.'

'But can't the police trace us from the internet café?'

'Possible, but by the time they find some grotty shop in the back of a newsagent's, we'll be long gone.'

Sophie looked around the suite anxiously.

'We're leaving?'

Josh laughed.

'Make the most of it, Miss Aniston. As soon as we find out what we need, we'll be moving on.'

Sophie nodded, not daring to admit she was disappointed.

20

Ruth rapped impatiently on the oak door. Where the hell was everyone? she thought, stepping back and gazing up at the bedroom windows, hoping to catch a glimpse of Sophie Ellis's mother. With no sign of life inside, she took a moment to admire the architecture; Arts and Crafts, she thought idly, remembering a coffee-table book she had once read on the movement. Red brick, with a sloping burnt-orange slate roof, tall narrow windows and towering chimneys, it was the sort of thing they tried to imitate on estates in Chicago and Philly, but somehow they always managed to turn it horribly twee and *Stepford Wives*-y. The real thing, however, was impressive, if a little faded round the edges. The Ellis family obviously had money.

She knocked again, harder, harder than was probably necessary, as she was still pumped with emotion from her earlier argument with David. On the journey to Cobham she had been going over and over her decision to move in with him. Had it been the right one? So far, their relationship had worked when they had kept their distance. Proximity created intimacy – maybe too much, too soon.

'Goddamn it,' she said, focusing back on work, and pressing the doorbell once more. She supposed she could have spoken to Julia Ellis on the phone – or at least called first – but she had wanted to leave the office and drive out to Surrey to clear her head, to give herself time to think.

It had been the right decision. She had been surprised how green and, to her eyes, rural it was out here, where Greater London melted into the rarefied commuter belt of Surrey. Wooden bus shelters, iron signposts, pubs with names like the Bull and Gate or the King's Head, and a noticeably slower pace of life, had gone some way to improve her mood.

Ruth walked around to the side of the house and tried the garden gate. It clicked open. *Well*, that *wouldn't happen in London*, she thought with a smile.

'Mrs Ellis?' she called, walking past a rose trellis and into the garden. 'Anyone there?'

The raised patio at the back of the house was empty – in fact, as Ruth peered in through the windows, it did rather look as though the house itself was abandoned too. Actually, it was a bit of a mess, with drawers left open and stuff all over the floor. *I thought these country types kept their houses neat*, she thought, walking back to the front of the house.

Spotting a love seat underneath the large apple tree in the garden, she went to sit in it.

'So what now, genius?' she wondered out loud, desperate for a cigarette. The truth was, it had been so easy to find the address of the Ellis family home, Ruth had rather assumed the rest would come easily too. It had taken all of two minutes to find Wade House on the internet: a quick look at Sophie's Facebook page had revealed she had studied at Tassleton prep school in Surrey, and the messages of condolence on her wall told her that Sophie's dad Peter had recently passed away; then a quick search for 'Peter Ellis – funeral – Tassleton church, Cobham' had given her the address on Meadow Lane. Thank you, modern technology.

She had set off half hoping that Sophie might even have run straight home to Mommy. If not, she felt sure Julia could help her flesh out her picture of Sophie and possibly give her a lead on where her daughter was now. One thing she was sure of: a girl like Sophie wouldn't be able to go too long without touching base with her mom.

She glanced at her watch. Eleven a.m. She was just debating whether to try the local pub, or perhaps the post office, both usually excellent sources of local gossip, when a taxi turned into the drive. She leapt out of the love seat and ran back towards the front door.

'You there!' trilled a plummy voice as the cab pulled up. 'What are you doing on my property?'

Julia Ellis stepped out of the cab and Ruth made an instant assessment. Mid-fifties, very attractive, but with a pinched and cold expression that made Ruth remember the phrase that at fifty you got the face you deserved.

'Mrs Ellis?' she said, collecting her thoughts. 'Could I possibly have a word? It's about your daughter.'

'What do you want?' Julia Ellis replied. She looked even more defensive at the mention of Sophie.

'My name is Ruth Boden. I'm a reporter.'

'Then I will have to ask you to get off my property,' said Julia tartly. 'The police are due at any moment.'

Ruth was not surprised, or even insulted. Knocking on doors that didn't want to open was her job; like a dentist, she didn't take the moans personally.

'I just wanted to ask if you had heard from your daughter since yesterday evening.'

'My last contact with her was yesterday afternoon. But I have spoken to her lawyer and we have every confidence that this matter will soon be dropped.'

Ruth saw her opening. If Sophie hadn't spoken to her mother, it was likely that she hadn't contacted anybody. With the police wanting to question her, and men with guns on her tail, it was no surprise she had gone to ground.

'So you haven't spoken to her today?'

'I left a message for her this morning to say I was on my way home. I've been in Copenhagen visiting my dearest friend. My husband passed away recently and I needed a change of scenery.'

'You haven't spoken to your daughter, Mrs Ellis, because she is missing,' Ruth said, letting the statement hang in the air.

'Missing? What do you mean?' she said, looking startled.

'Sophie has disappeared, Mrs Ellis. I think she's in trouble and I would very much like to help. I was the last person she spoke to before she went underground.'

'*Underground?*'

Ruth felt a knot of guilt. She didn't want to worry the mother unduly, but she had to make sure she got an invitation inside the house.

'A police contact of mine was supposed to meet her last night, but she didn't show up. We think she's with a boyfriend who lives in Chelsea.'

'Boyfriend in Chelsea? Do you mean Will Lewis?'

Ruth had already run a name check on the registered owner of the houseboat. It was one Joshua McCormack, not Will Lewis.

'We think she's on the run from the police,' she said. She declined to mention the armed Russians. Julia Ellis looked pale enough as it was.

'You'd better come in,' said Julia quickly, looking around as if a neighbour might have heard about the scandal.

She pulled out her keys and rattled them into the lock.

'You'll have to excuse the mess, I have been away since Thursday . . .' Julia let out a little shriek. Stepping in behind her, Ruth immediately recognised that the mess she had seen through the back windows was not everyday domestic disarray – the place had been burgled. There were papers and broken ornaments all over the hall floor and, looking through to the living room, Ruth could see a sofa on its side, with the cushions slashed open.

'No, no,' gasped Julia, her breathing becoming heavy and uneven. 'My home.'

'I'm calling the police right now,' said Ruth, pulling out her mobile.

The older woman put out a hand.

'They are already on their way,' she said, her voice shaking. 'The inspector in charge of Sophie's case is due at twelve. He wanted to talk to me.'

'Inspector Fox?' said Ruth with a start.

'That's right.'

Ruth glanced at her watch – quarter to twelve. Damn, that didn't give her much time.

Julia had walked through to the living room and was beginning to pick up some books strewn on the floor.

'I don't think you should touch anything, Mrs Ellis,' said Ruth gently. 'Why don't you come through to the kitchen and I'll make you a cup of tea while we wait for the inspector?'

Julia's eyes were wide, shocked, as she sat down at the kitchen table and Ruth filled the kettle. She looked tiny and brittle against the big oak chair.

'It'll have to be Earl Grey, I'm afraid,' she said. 'No milk you see. I told the milkman I was going to be away . . .' She stopped and turned to Ruth, her mouth open. 'You don't think it was the milkman, do you? He was the only one who knew I'd be out of the country.'

'I doubt it,' said Ruth quietly.

Julia gave a mirthless laugh.

'If whoever it was only knew we had nothing left to take. They should have tried the Hendersons up the road. She's always boasting about her silverware.'

She shook her head.

'You know, a few weeks ago, I was standing here with Sophie,' she said. 'It was just after my husband's funeral, and my daughter said that things were going to turn a corner for us. She said it with such sunniness, such confidence, that I almost believed her. But she was wrong, wasn't she? So wrong.'

Ruth rummaged around the cupboards, finally finding a set of elegant bone-china cups with a pattern picked out in gold. It was all very tasteful; in fact, from what she could see under the mess, the Ellis house was the epitome of upper-middle-class commuter-belt living.

She put the tea in front of Julia and took a seat opposite her. Julia appeared not to notice, too busy stabbing her fingers at the digits of her mobile phone. She tutted loudly when there was no reply from the person she was calling.

'Sophie, where are you?' she said, gripping her fingers around the tea cup.

'I've been trying her all morning,' said Ruth softly. 'I think her phone is off.'

Julia Ellis shook her head and then focused her full attention on Ruth. 'You said she spoke to you. Did she give you any idea about where she was going?'

'I saw her outside her apartment in Battersea, then I followed her to Chelsea. She met a man on a houseboat by Stamford Wharf. Do you have any idea who that might be?'

Julia shook her head.

'A houseboat?' There was a subtle look of distaste on her face. 'Will – that was her last boyfriend, a very nice young man – lived just off the King's Road. Not in a *boat*. I hope she hasn't got in with a bad sort. Ever since the troubles, she hasn't been herself.'

'The troubles?' asked Ruth.

'My husband lost a lot of money in a bad investment scheme,' said Julia, looking away; it was clearly not something she wanted to talk about.

'Please, Mrs Ellis,' said Ruth. 'We are all worried about Sophie. Anything you tell me could be relevant.'

Julia hesitated. 'Well, you're American, so I suppose you'll know all about it,' she said thinly. 'We lost everything through the Michael Asner Ponzi scheme. The stress of it all killed my husband from a heart attack a few weeks ago.'

Ruth tried to keep her face straight, but her journalistic instincts were tingling. Peter Ellis had invested in the Asner Ponzi scheme? Immediately her mind began to see the story laid out in print: British family wiped out by financial sting, broken-hearted father suffers heart attack, distraught daughter subsequently becomes a murder suspect. She could feel her pulse begin to race. Even for the *Washington Tribune*, with its emphasis on politics and world news, this was a better story than she had imagined. But still something didn't quite fit. The Asner scheme had been such big news when it was exposed twelve months earlier because Michael Asner, a supposedly genius investor, had preyed on the East and West Coast super-rich. It was an insiders' club for the wildly wealthy, and Asner had used their greed against them, providing high returns on investments that nobody thought or wanted to question. The news piece on Peter Ellis's funeral had mentioned that he was an accountant with a practice in the City. He was clearly a well-off white-collar professional, but he hardly fitted the Asner victim profile.

'Yes, I read about that,' she said carefully. 'Your husband was in financial services, wasn't he? Is that how he came to invest with Asner?'

'You mean why was Peter playing with billionaires?' said Julia tightly. 'It's a question I asked him many times, believe me.'

She took a tiny sip of tea which seemed to barely touch her lips. 'Peter and Michael were good friends at Oxford. Michael Asner was a Fulbright scholar, would you believe? Furiously bright, but a horrid little man, if you ask me.'

'So you knew him?'

'I met him a handful of times in the early days of our marriage. I never really liked him; always so full of his own cleverness, as if he was doing us a favour letting us talk to him, even before he became super-successful.'

'Had you seen him recently?'

She shook her head. 'Peter and Michael drifted apart once Michael began to move in those powerful Wall Street circles. The last contact I was aware of was about fifteen years ago, when he left the firm of investment brokers he had been working for and set up his own wealth management business. He couldn't be bothered with us in the years running up to that, but when he was fishing around for investments, suddenly we were good enough. Or at least our life savings were.'

Julia looked up. 'You heard he died in prison, of course?' she said. 'I can't say I was sorry. How could anyone do that to a friend? Peter was a quiet man. He kept everything bottled up inside him,' she said, clutching her hand to her chest. 'When the scheme collapsed and we lost the money, he seemed to be coping well, but then he had a heart attack on that little boat of his. We thought he was going to pull through, but he had another sudden cardiac arrest in hospital a few days later.'

Ruth glanced at her watch again. Fox would be here any minute, and she couldn't imagine he would be pleased to see her again.

'You said Sophie hadn't been herself recently. How did her father's death affect her?'

'They were very close,' Julia said quietly. 'If I'm honest, I was rather envious of their relationship. It's been tough for all of us, of course, but Sophie . . . We had to sell her flat in Chelsea, her boyfriend finished with her, and her other friends? Well, she was dropped like a stone. Do you know, only three of her friends came to the funeral? *Three!*'

'People can be very judgemental,' said Ruth.

'People can be bastards, Miss Boden,' said Julia, bitterly. 'And you can quote me on that. We paid through the nose for Sophie's education; she is a beautiful, refined young woman, and yet when it comes down to it, you realise what ultimately matters to people: money. They only care about money.'

She produced a tissue and dabbed at her eyes.

'Sorry. This is all very difficult. I'll have to sell the house, of course. We remortgaged to liquidate some cash, and now . . .' She looked around at the devastation of the burglary. 'I knew we should have kept paying for the alarm system,' she said, shaking her head. 'But Peter said it was an unnecessary expense. At least I took the Chanel on holiday with me,' she added, clasping her handbag to her side protectively.

Ruth paused, wondering how to phrase her next question.

'Sophie must have been very upset about losing the family home, too.'

Julia's shrewd grey eyes locked on to Ruth's.

'Don't start imagining motives where there are none, Miss Boden,' she said, steel in her voice. 'I read the papers, I know how the press can spin things: a young girl fallen on hard times tries to trap a rich man and it goes tragically wrong. That did not happen with my daughter, do you understand me?'

'Honestly, Mrs Ellis,' said Ruth quickly, 'I'm really on your side. I just want to see justice done.'

'Justice?' she spat. 'I don't believe in justice any more. Not when Michael Asner's wife is still sitting in some big house in upstate New York. Where's the justice in that?'

Ruth looked up at the kitchen clock. Twelve on the dot – time was up.

'I'd better be going,' she said, stuffing her notebook into her handbag. 'I'm sure Sophie will be in touch very soon. Perhaps the police will have more news.'

Julia went with her to the front door.

'Do you have a photograph of Sophie I could take?' she asked quickly.

Julia nodded. She went into the study and returned with a family snapshot.

'You will help her, won't you?' she said. 'Sophie's a good

girl and she's already been through so much. I don't know what's happened with this man in the hotel, but she wouldn't hurt a fly, you do believe that, don't you?'

'Yes, I do,' said Ruth truthfully. Just then, there was the sound of a car turning into the drive and her heart sank. *Shit.*

She walked down the drive as Fox was getting out of his saloon.

'We must stop meeting like this,' she said, lifting one eyebrow.

Fox didn't smile. 'Why are you here, Ruth?'

'Just doing my job, unlike you.'

'What's that supposed to mean?' he frowned, slamming his door.

'Mrs Ellis has been burgled, Inspector.'

Fox looked up at the house, concern on his face.

'Bit of a coincidence, isn't it, both mother and daughter burgled within a day of each other?'

'I'll let you know when I've examined the evidence,' he said, clearly annoyed to be arriving at the scene after a reporter.

'So any more details on Nick Beddingfield?'

He moved to walk past her. 'As you say, I've got a job to do.'

'Come on, Fox,' said Ruth, invading his personal space. Fox sighed and took a step back from her.

'We've tracked down his mother in LA. She's distraught, understandably. She's on a flight out to London, not that she can collect the body just yet.'

'Where's she staying?'

'Oh, give me a break, Boden.'

'You know I'll find out, so there's no point in not telling me.' She batted her eyelashes at him. 'For me, Ian?'

Fox gave a hint of a smile.

'That's the first time you've called me by my Christian name.'

'I'll do it again if you tell me where Mrs Beddingfield is staying.'

'The Horizon Hotel, Paddington. Now get out of here before I accuse you of tampering with evidence. Again.'

She watched him walk up to the house, feeling a moment's sympathy – for Fox, who had to deliver so much bad news; for Mrs Beddingfield having to fly twelve hours to see her son's dead body; for Julia Ellis, who was all alone in a house full of ghosts. But as she turned and walked back towards her car, her thoughts were for Sophie Ellis, who had been dragged into this mess through, she suspected, no fault of her own.

'You will help her, won't you?' her mother had said. And she would. Not only was this going to help Sophie, Ruth knew it was the story to help herself.

21

'Get your bag, princess,' said Josh, wiping his mouth with a napkin. 'We're off.'

'Where are we going now?' said Sophie. She had been enjoying their room service picnic – a club sandwich, fruit salad and a bottle of Badoit water. Lounging on the bed, eating off a silver tray, it all seemed decadent and slightly naughty, and she was in no rush to leave the relative safety of the suite.

'We're here to find out about Nick, remember?' said Josh, picking up his jacket. 'And the obvious place to start will be at his apartment.'

Sophie reluctantly stood and brushed the crumbs off her white 'Jil Sander' shirt – another of the fakes from the lock-up he'd brought along. It was a size too small and the buttons were straining slightly, but Sophie still liked the Parisian air it gave her.

'Aren't the police going to be there? Surely that's the first place they are going to check.'

Josh pulled a face. 'No, because the flat wasn't his.'

'Whose was it?'

Josh sighed and opened the door. 'I'll tell you on the way.'

They took a cab from the front of the hotel, turning down the Rue du Faubourg Saint-Honoré with its smart boutiques and cafés. She saw a flower stall doing a brisk trade in sunflowers and a baker's with an art deco frontage and a queue snaking out of the shop. She wound down the window and let the warm air roll over her as Paris passed before her. The honking traffic on the Place de la Concorde, the stateliness of the Tuileries Gardens, the waters of the Seine glinting and flashing as if she were in some Technicolor-drenched movie set.

'Having fun?'

'It's better than wading through the Thames, yes,' she replied, wishing she were in Paris under different circumstances.

Her companion looked cynical. 'Just because we've crossed the Channel, don't start thinking we're safe, okay?' he warned.

'Don't you think I know that? I know we're in trouble, Josh. I was there, remember? I have a bullet hole in my bag to prove it, and for all we know, those Russians might be waiting for us at any point in this city. So yes, I wish we were on a minibreak, but we're not, so I just want to find out what Nick was up to, report it back to Fox and go home.'

Josh turned away from her, relaxing back into his seat; she watched him stifle a smile. Did he really appreciate the danger they were in, or was this just an everyday occurrence for a man like Josh? He certainly didn't seem to be as ruffled as she was.

They travelled in silence until they passed a Monoprix store. Josh told the driver to stop, and ran inside the shop, leaving Sophie in the cab. Watching the street scene, she noticed that Paris seemed unsettlingly quiet.

'*Les vacances*,' explained the cab driver when she asked him in her schoolgirl French.

She was glad when Josh returned, carrying a small black rucksack.

'What's in there?' she asked.

'Toothpaste,' he said flatly, sitting down next to her as the taxi took off.

'Why don't I believe you?'

Josh raised an eyebrow.

'I'd say that was a common theme of our acquaintance.'

He was maddening, she thought, edging away from him on the black plastic taxi seat. Why couldn't he converse with her for five minutes without tormenting her? Leave her to enjoy the view and forget about the last two terrible days, just for one moment?

'So tell me about Nick's mysterious apartment.'

'I don't want this to be difficult for you,' said Josh, looking straight ahead.

'Tell me,' she pressed. 'It can't be any worse than everything else I've heard over the past couple of days.'

'Okay,' said Josh, letting out a long breath. 'I guess you've grasped by now that Nick lived off women?'

Sophie felt her stomach turn over again. In her head, she knew it was true, but she supposed her heart hadn't quite caught up yet. She gave a tight nod.

'Last year, he spent the summer in Monte Carlo, where he met a woman. She was a countess, an older lady. Nick told me she lived in a suite in the Hôtel de Paris – that's in Monaco – and had properties around the world.'

'She was "older"?' Sophie asked, noticing his emphasis on that word. 'How much older?'

'Older,' repeated Josh.

'*How* old, Josh?'

He shrugged. 'He showed me a photograph of her on his phone. She was well preserved. Sixties, maybe more.'

Sophie felt sick. Could it be true? It had to be.

'You men,' she said, her mouth turned down. 'If a woman is rich, it doesn't matter what she looks like, does it?'

'Oh yes, and I suppose you're telling me that women are so different? What do all your Chelsea girlfriends do for a career? They hang around nightclubs hoping to snag a banker or a minor royal. You saw them at the Chariot party:

all those long-legged model types with their Birkin bags and their eyeball-sized diamonds. You think they care what their husbands *look* like?'

Sophie thought of beautiful Francesca and her tubby, red-faced fiancé. Josh was right, of course. He was always right.

'Doesn't make it okay, though, does it?' she said.

Josh put a hand on her arm.

'I know this is hard for you,' he said quietly.

'Thank you,' she conceded.

There was a few seconds' pause.

'Were you in love with him?'

Sophie gave a half-laugh.

'Can you really be in love with someone after a few days? I liked Nick a lot, I know that much. I liked being with him. I liked the way he made me feel. Happy, special, worthwhile. I hadn't felt that in some time.'

She looked back at Josh.

'But now I know that's what he *did*. He made women feel special, that was his job. So now I feel pretty shitty and stupid.'

She saw the cab driver glance at them in his rear-view mirror. Did he speak English? Was he listening to them? Sophie found she didn't really care; she wanted to know everything, however idiotic it made her look.

'So what about this countess?'

'She let Nick live in her apartment in Paris. I don't think she's been here for years.'

'That was nice of her,' Sophie said tartly.

'Don't be like that, Sophie.'

'How am I *supposed* to be, Josh? Am I supposed to accept all this? Just shrug and think, "Ah well, so I've been taken in by a con man, *c'est la vie*"? Well I can't. I'm sorry, but I just can't.'

She turned back to the passing scenery, watching through misty eyes the crowds milling around the Louvre's glass pyramid, the Seine with its long black barges and the island in the middle of the river. From a distance it looked like a fortress rearing up from the water with steep walls that plunged into the Seine.

'Look at that,' she said, her mood mellowing.

'That's where we're going,' replied Josh.

On the island itself, it was like stepping back in time. She saw a juggler and a mime artist, fishmongers serving crabs on beds of ice, cafés advertising *chocolat et digestifs*, bakeries displaying pastries and tarts loaded with redcurrants and blackberries, each shop window making her drool more than the one before.

'This is fantastic,' she said, desperate to step out of the cab and soak it all in.

'This is Île Saint-Louis,' said Josh. 'Not many tourists come here; they all pile on to the Île de la Cité and Notre-Dame cathedral instead.'

He signalled to the driver to pull over at the kerb.

'Final stop,' he said, as the cab moved away. It was a small, traditional-looking café restaurant with a zinc-topped counter and bare floorboards. They took a table on the pavement, sitting in rickety rattan chairs, and Josh ordered '*deux cafés*' while Sophie nervously glanced at the other patrons of the café. There was a couple hunched together, both wearing matching Ray-Bans, and a young man with uncombed hair scribbling into a notebook.

'We're surrounded by poets,' whispered Sophie.

'We're surrounded by people who *look* like poets,' corrected Josh as the waiter brought their drinks.

'So what are we doing here?' said Sophie, wincing at the strength of her espresso.

'We're looking for Nick's apartment.'

'The countess's apartment, you mean.'

Josh ignored her.

'When I was in Paris, Nick and I agreed to meet at this

café because it was across the road from *la comtesse*'s place.'

Shielding her eyes from the sun, Sophie looked up at the smart grey building in front of them. It had a long row of balconies and shutters at the windows.

'You don't know which one? That's an awful lot of apartments over there,' she said.

'Île Saint-Louis is like a little village. We might have some luck,' said Josh, waving the waiter over. He was a short man, perhaps in his sixties, with grey hair and a white apron.

'*L'addition*,' said Josh, handing him a twenty euro note and waving away the change. '*Puis-je vous poser une question?*'

'Of course. I speak English, monsieur.'

'Excellent,' said Josh, smiling, 'I wonder if you know my friend, *la comtesse*. I know she used to come to this café; she said it was her favourite.'

The man's chest visibly puffed out.

'*Oui, la comtesse*, she lives across the street there,' he said, pointing up to the corner balcony on the top floor of the building. 'She would wave to me in the mornings. Always the same order: *tart tatin et chocolat chaud*, even in summer.'

His smile dimmed a little.

'But she has not been to visit for many years. She is not ill, I hope?'

'No, she is in fine health,' said Josh. 'And she asked me to send her regards.'

They finished their coffee and crossed the street.

'I think you made his day,' said Sophie, waving to the waiter.

'I do try,' said Josh. 'I'm all about the public relations.'

'But how are we going to get . . .' she began, but Josh made a silencing motion as he craned his neck to look up at the building's balconies.

'Shh!' he said. 'I'm counting.'

He stopped at the building's wooden door, where there

was a line of buzzers. 'Now, if I've got this right . . .' he said, pressing the intercom button for Apartment 3. They waited, but there was no reply. He tried again: still nothing.

'No one's home.' He smiled.

'What did you expect?' said Sophie cynically. 'We know where Nick is.'

'Yes, but who knows if *la comtesse* has other gentlemen friends?'

Just then, the door opened and a well-dressed woman stepped out of the building. Josh didn't hesitate.

'Oh, *scusi moi*,' he said to the woman in terrible French. 'Is this Le Juno apartments? *Nous* . . . erm, we rent an apartment here?' He pulled a piece of paper from his inside pocket and waved it at her. '*Pour les vacances?*'

The woman was about forty, with glossy brown hair streaked with blonde, and she wore a plain blue shirt in the way only a stylish French woman can.

'No,' she said, slightly bemused. 'There is no rental apartment in this building,' she added in perfect English.

Josh pretended to consult his paper.

Sophie looked at him in bewilderment. What was he playing at? Where had his fluent French gone?

'But this is Avenue Michel?' he said, holding up a hand.

'No, Avenue Michel is two streets that way,' said the woman patiently.

'Ah, *bien sûr, merci beaucoup*,' said Josh. Sophie noticed the little smile the woman flashed him as she walked off. Did every woman in the world fall under his spell, even the terribly chic Parisian ones who really ought to know better? Then she noticed that Josh hadn't moved and realised what his lost tourist act had been for.

'Is your foot keeping the door open?'

'Not big, not clever, but it works.' He smiled.

They waited a minute until the woman had disappeared and the waiter across the road was back inside the café, then walked into the cool lobby, unsurprisingly empty at that time of day.

Sophie felt nervous as they went inside. She could still hear the crack of the bullet and never wanted to experience anything like that again. If Josh knew where Nick's secret apartment was, then maybe the Russians did too. After all, they had tracked him down to the Riverton.

There was an old-fashioned cage-style lift at the end of the hall, but Josh turned towards the stairs. 'Less likely to meet anyone this way,' he said. 'Can you make it to the top?'

Sophie rolled her eyes.

'Oh, I think I'll manage.'

'That's right, I've seen you run,' he smiled. 'Right, why don't you go and wait by the door to apartment three,' he said when they had reached the top floor.

'Where are you going?'

He pointed up a further narrow flight of stairs.

'The roof.'

He opened the black rucksack and took out a screwdriver and a short crowbar.

'What are they for?'

'Look,' he said, indicating the glass dome illuminating the stairwell. 'If they have skylights here, they've probably got them over the apartments too.'

'Josh, no,' she said, shaking her head. 'I'm serious. You'll break your neck.'

'I'm more nimble than you think,' he said sarcastically.

'But what if it's alarmed?'

'Then we're fucked,' he replied with a straight face. 'I'll only be a few minutes. Just wait by the door.'

'No,' said Sophie fiercely. 'I'm coming with you.'

She could see he was about to object, but then he changed his mind.

'All right,' he said, handing her the rucksack. 'You can carry the bag, then.'

189

The roof was gently pitched, but hidden from the street by a parapet that ran all the way around the building.

'Just be careful,' hissed Sophie as Josh set off towards the far end. She allowed herself a peek over the edge and felt sick. The block backed straight on to the Seine, and it was at least a two-hundred-foot drop down into the water. She quickly pulled her head back in.

'Josh, wait for me,' she called, tiptoeing along a foot-wide pathway, both arms spread out for balance. She found him at the far end of the building, leaning over a two-foot-square window that was set into the sloping tile roof.

'Assuming we're got the right apartment, this goes down into the *comtesse*'s living room,' he said, pulling out the screwdriver. 'I think I can lever this open.'

'Josh, this is trespassing. This is *burglary*.'

'Look, Sophie, if you've got any better ideas, I'm all ears,' he said. 'As far as I know, this was Nick's main base for the past six months, so it's our best chance of finding any clues about what he was up to or who he was dealing with.'

'Who had him killed, you mean.'

He wedged the crowbar into the gap between the window and the frame and heaved, but instead of popping the skylight open, the iron bar slipped and trapped Josh's hand, making him drop it with a clang.

'Shit!' he hissed, waggling his hand in pain.

'Well, maybe that's because it's locked,' Sophie said.

'I *know* it's locked,' he said irritably.

'Can't you just pick the lock?' she asked, her voice getting lost in the wind.

Josh gave a laugh.

'I know you think I'm some sort of criminal mastermind, but I sell watches for a living, remember?'

'You mean you've never done this before?'

'No, Sophie, I haven't. Have you?'

Sophie bent to look closer at the skylight's fastening. It

had a hefty iron padlock, but the latch was badly rusted and the wood around it hadn't been painted in decades.

'Hand me the screwdriver,' she said.

Reluctantly, Josh gave it to her and watched as she slotted it behind the hinge and pulled. With a creak, the wood splintered and the hinge swung free.

He raised his brows in surprise.

'Who's the criminal mastermind now? Try the other one.'

With a little waggling and yanking, the second hinge also cracked and Josh was able to lift the whole window free. Sophie peered down; it seemed a long drop.

'How are we going to do this?' she said, but Josh was already in motion, swinging his legs over the edge and letting himself down slowly.

'Go back to the front door,' he ordered. 'I'll be there in a minute.'

When Josh opened the apartment door, he was grimacing.

'Are you okay?' she asked, stepping inside.

'Not exactly a soft landing,' he grumbled.

'Do you want me to fetch a stretcher?' She grinned.

He swatted her on the arm as she looked around the apartment. It was exquisite, all gold leaf, velvet and polished wood – even the dust sent swirling up from the antique rug from Josh's fall seemed to dance and sparkle in the sunlight coming in through the floor-to-ceiling windows.

'Wow, what a place.'

At once elegant and relaxed, it was tastefully and expensively furnished with antiques – matched Chinese vases sat on a walnut bombe chest painted with gold roses, and a white marble fireplace dominated the room. There were intricate parquet floors and gilt-framed carved mirrors on the white walls, making it seem even bigger than it was. Sophie walked over to a pair of double doors that opened on to a balcony overlooking Paris.

'Oh my goodness, look at the view!' she gasped. She could

see the Quai d'Orléans and the two towers of Notre Dame stretching into the powder-blue sky and a bateau-mouche chugging along the moss-green waters of the Seine. She could picture Nick having his morning coffee on the terrace, watching the world go by, smiling at his luck. It suited Nick, this place, she thought sadly, it really did.

'This isn't an open-house viewing, princess,' said Josh. 'And there's a decent chance someone heard the racket of us breaking in, so I think we'd better do what we came to do, don't you?'

She knew he was right. 'So what are we supposed to be looking for, exactly?'

'Anything that might tell us what Nick was up to, why someone might be after him and what they think you know.'

'Not much, then,' said Sophie, pulling a face.

'Do your best.'

She moved over to a writing desk covered with an old-fashioned blotter and opened a drawer. It was filled with papers: bills, letters, a bank statement. Sophie's eyes widened.

'Look at this,' she said. '*La comtesse*'s bank account.' She had never seen so many figures on a statement.

'Come on, Sophie, focus,' said Josh impatiently, putting the sheet back in the drawer. 'We're not here to snoop, we're here to find out about Nick.'

'Well there's nothing about him in this desk,' said Sophie defiantly. She looked down at the empty space where a laptop might have sat. 'Wouldn't he have had a computer?'

Josh shook his head. 'Yes, but most likely he took it to London.'

'So why are we here, then?'

'Because we're not trying to find evidence, we're trying to find traces of his life. The places he went, the people he spoke to.'

He looked around the apartment thoughtfully.

'Just look around,' he said. 'There's wine on the side in

the kitchen, there are clothes hanging in the wardrobe; Nick didn't leave in a hurry and he was clearly planning on coming back. So he'll have left something – somewhere – which can point us in the right direction.'

Sophie walked over to the mantelpiece and picked up a lacquered photo frame.

'Is this her?' she said.

It was an old picture, in colour, but that oversaturated and slightly faded colour you saw in photographs from the sixties and seventies. The woman in the picture was undeniably beautiful. But more than that, proud and upright, somehow. Sophie didn't need Josh to tell her this was the countess.

'Hey,' said Josh softly, taking the picture from her. 'Make it easy on yourself, okay? It was just a transaction for him, believe me.'

'Not exactly reassuring,' she said sadly. 'I'm sure he'd have said the same about me if you'd asked.'

They went back to work, Josh taking the bedroom, Sophie going through the bookshelves in the living room and the bathroom cabinets. She found nothing; in fact, beyond a razor sitting by the sink, there was little to show that Nick had ever been here.

'Come through to the bedroom,' called Josh. 'I've got a job for you.'

He was standing at the open wardrobe going through Nick's suits.

'Can you sort through those?' he said, nodding towards the bed. It was covered with receipts, business cards, random bits of paper Josh had found in the pockets of Nick's clothes.

Sophie sat cross-legged on the bed and went through them. There were ticket stubs, restaurant bills, scribbled notes; she read each one out loud.

'One from Monte Carlo, Avignon, Beaulieu-sur-Mer, Cannes . . .' she read. 'A load from Paris. Look, there's even an invoice for a "diamond necklace, 2,400 euros".'

'Obviously trying to keep the countess sweet,' said Josh, looking up.

'Or someone else,' said Sophie.

There was nothing specific, but Josh was right, it did begin to paint a picture of where Nick had been over the past few months, the sort of places he had been visiting.

'So we know he's been to the South of France a lot, and not just to visit the countess in Monaco,' said Josh. 'And we can tell he's had money. A lot of Michelin stars in those restaurants, no McDonald's Happy Meals for Nick.'

'But isn't that the way he always operated? I mean, he had the nicest clothes, the suite at the Riverton, he didn't live in a tent.'

Josh shook his head.

'It's boom or bust in the con game. Sometimes you're up, sometimes you're down. Yes, he had to maintain the appearance of being a wealthy oil trader, that's true. But according to these receipts, it looks like he actually was flush.'

'So?'

'So whatever he was doing was working. Maybe he didn't need your money after all . . . Or I could be completely wrong, I really don't know.'

He rubbed his eyes.

'Well, I don't know about you, but I could do with a drink.'

'I saw some wine in the wardrobe.' Sophie smiled.

'In the wardrobe?' queried Josh.

He went to take a look. Sure enough, there were two bottles on the shelf and a further box of the stuff by Nick's shoes.

'I know next to nothing about wine, but as our friend Nick was not a man to scrimp on the luxuries, I'm guessing this will be half-decent.'

'It is,' confirmed Sophie, taking the bottle off him. 'This is a Romanée-Conti, one of the best red wines money can buy.'

Josh looked up in surprise. 'You know about that stuff?'

'Chelsea girls can't afford to look stupid at dinner parties,' she said tartly.

She bent down and opened the brown box on the floor. It was full of bottles with the same mottled label.

'That's strange,' she said, picking up another bottle. 'More Romanée-Conti. Loads of it.'

Josh shrugged.

'As you say, he always liked the finer things in life.'

'But this wine is vintage and very rare. You'd be lucky to find one bottle, let alone twelve.'

She twisted the bottle round to show him the label.

'Look what it says here.'

'Appellation Romanée-Conti Contrôlee?' read Josh, a confused look on his face. 'It's all Greek to me.'

'The AOC is just a standard phrase to show where the bottle originated. In this case, it's Romanée-Conti in Burgundy.'

'You do know your stuff,' said Josh, but Sophie shook her head.

'Actually it doesn't really matter what it means; what's funny is the word "contrôlee" – look. It's missing the accent on the first "e".'

'So?'

'Well, it's wrong. It should be contrôlée. A top vineyard like this wouldn't get something like that wrong.' She picked up the first bottle Josh had found in the wardrobe. 'Look, this one's right. It's got the accent in the right place.'

'The ones in the box are fake,' said Josh slowly.

'Fake?' She'd heard mention of counterfeit wine on her wine-tasting course but wasn't sure it actually existed.

Josh nodded. 'It's big business. Extremely profitable and relatively low-risk if you sell to the right people. There's a lot of rich, gullible folk out there who have heard of the big, impressive vineyards but know nothing about their taste.'

'So how does it work?'

Josh puffed out his cheeks.

'I don't know a great deal about it. One way is to find empty bottles that once held expensive vintage wine. There's a brisk black market in empty Château Margaux and Château Pétrus bottles. You could find a corrupt sommelier in a restaurant to sell you their empties. Or buy or steal from private individuals. You pour any old crap inside them. Cork them up. Sell them on as *an investment* and hope they don't open one for a few years, by which point you've scarpered.'

He examined Nick's bottles more closely.

'Or you do a wholesale fake. The bottle, the label, cork, the wine inside. I think that is what has happened here. Nick said he had a big job in France. Plus it explains why he was in London at some flashy party.'

'He was drumming up business?'

Josh nodded.

'He wanted to offload his wine on the nouveau riche who wouldn't know a Romanée-Conti from Ribena.'

Sophie looked at him.

'And presumably that's why you bought a ticket too. Drumming up business.'

'Well . . . I didn't exactly *have* a ticket,' said Josh.

'You gatecrashed?'

'Gatecrashing sounds so vulgar. I like to think I was just missed off the guest list – at least that's what I told the girls on the door.'

Sophie recalled how nervous she had felt walking up to those clipboard Nazis at Waterloo with their icy stares. But that hadn't stopped Josh; nothing seemed to stop Josh, did it? She had to remind herself that she hadn't exactly had an invitation either – not one with her real name on it, anyway.

'Nick had bought his ticket, though,' said Josh, pushing a

corkscrew into one of the fake bottles. 'I checked on the seating plan; he was on one of the best tables. Someone could have bought it for him, of course, but it's still ten thousand quid a ticket. He obviously thought it was a good investment.'

He took a glug of the wine, straight out of the bottle.

'Well, one thing's for sure. He can't have done this alone. You'd need someone to source the bottles, someone to print up the labels and put them on the bottles; it'd be a logistical nightmare, especially when you're trying to do it all under the radar.'

'But how do we find these people?' said Sophie. 'Look them up in the Yellow Pages under C for Criminals?'

Josh raised an eyebrow.

'Maybe that's not such a bad idea,' he said, walking through to the living room. 'Look for a diary, an address book, a business card, anything.'

'I've checked,' replied Sophie. 'There's nothing in those drawers or on the bookcase. I didn't even see a telephone directory, come to think of it.'

She followed him through to the study.

'Did you go through this?' Josh picked up a writing pad from the desk. It had obviously been left there for jotting down telephone messages.

'There's nothing in it,' said Sophie. 'Well, nothing we can use. Just numbers, no names or addresses or anything.'

Josh picked up the telephone.

'Well, let's see where it leads us.'

He dialled the first number and waited. '*Bonjour. Est-ce qu'il serait possible de parler avec Nick, s'il vous plaît?*' he said. A pause. '*Oh, d'accord. Je m'excuse.*'

He looked over at Sophie. 'Dry-cleaners.'

The next one was a reservation line for Air France, the next a taxi service. There were at least a dozen numbers scribbled down on various pages, and Josh dialled them all. His expression changed as he was connected to one on the back page of the pad. He immediately put the phone down without speaking.

'Who was it?'

He looked down at the telephone, not speaking.

'Josh! Tell me!'

'Maurice,' he said quietly. 'Or at least, that's who he was calling. The number was for Le Cellar, a nightclub in Montmartre. That's where Maurice hangs out.'

'Who on earth is Maurice?'

'Maurice Balbi,' said Josh with a look of distaste. 'He's a fence, a fixer. A middleman with ideas above his station.'

'You know him?'

'Barely. I've only met him a couple of times, but he's the go-to man in Paris for that sideline I was telling you about.'

'The fake stuff?' said Sophie, looking down at her shirt. 'I thought you said it wasn't your business.'

'It *was* my business. I'm into watches now.'

'So Maurice makes counterfeit goods?'

'Never did anything like that himself, but he always knew a man who could.'

'So let's go see him,' said Sophie, hoping to sound more enthusiastic than she felt.

'No,' said Josh, shaking his head. 'I don't want you going there and meeting these people. They're dangerous.'

'I'm not fifteen, Josh,' she smiled. 'And in case you hadn't noticed, we're already involved with dangerous people whether I like it or not.'

'Sophie, you don't understand . . .'

'I *do*, Josh. Believe me, I do. People want to kill me, or get information from me or whatever the hell is going on. But sitting around waiting for them to sneak up behind me doesn't seem like much of an option. So thanks for the warning, but I'd rather face this head on.'

He looked at her for a long moment.

'I was wrong about you.'

'Wrong?'

'You can be a feisty little something.'

'You're a bad influence,' she said, putting the Cellar number in her pocket.

'But you like it.' He grinned.

She felt her cheeks begin to prickle. 'Let's go,' she said, turning away and not looking back at him until they were on the street.

22

Ruth didn't think she would ever sleep again. Her eyes were wide open and her foot was constantly jiggling. *That's what happens when you drink five cups of coffee in quick succession*, she thought. But she'd had to do something, she'd needed an alibi. She'd been sitting in the same scratchy armchair in the nondescript lobby – dusty potted palms, broken vending machine – of the Horizon Hotel in Paddington for two hours, trying to look inconspicuous, which wasn't easy. It wasn't the sort of hotel where you'd linger in the foyer admiring the architecture.

Still, despite a few odd looks from the duty manager, no one had asked her why she was sitting there in the one chair that put her in eavesdropping distance of both the front desk and the concierge. And Ruth had finally been rewarded for her patience. A little after three o'clock, an attractive woman carrying a small suitcase announced herself as Barbara Beddingfield, superior room for one.

Ruth had swivelled slightly to take a good look at Nick's mother. Although she was at least sixty, she looked good. The ash-blond hair piled up on top of her head, with the stray wisps falling carelessly over her face, gave her a sexy, bohemian air. Her jeans were fitted and her dark blue peasant blouse was something that Ruth would quite happily have had in her own wardrobe. It was the off-duty look of someone two decades younger, but she had that quiet confidence of an attractive woman who had once been truly beautiful.

You can see where lover boy got it from, thought Ruth as Mrs Beddingfield wheeled her case into the lift.

Ruth counted to a hundred, her caffeine-wired foot still tapping away impatiently. She desperately wanted to follow the woman, but she had to give her a little time to settle in. Who wanted a journalist knocking on the door the moment you arrived in the country? Barbara could well bolt, and Ruth couldn't risk losing this interview, which could well make all the difference to a story that was frankly Swiss cheese at the moment. If she was honest with herself, Ruth knew she had nothing she could take to Jim Keane, let alone Isaac Grey just yet. An American businessman had been killed in a posh hotel, the girlfriend had been burgled then shot at . . . and that was about it. The Michael Asner angle was intriguing – she had asked Chuck Dean in the office to research Asner's connection with Peter Ellis in more depth – but right now this was just a short news item, not the big splash that Isaac was after. Still, there it was in her head, her dad whispering, 'Instinct, Ruthie, instinct' – and Ruth's instinct was telling her that this was a good story, a big story, one worth pursuing, even if the facts so far did little to support her gut feeling.

She looked back towards the lift doors, weighing up her options, but then her mind was abruptly made up for her. Detective Inspector Ian Fox and DC Dan Davis walked into the lobby. Ruth froze, but they didn't see her. Instead, they walked up to the front desk, showed their warrant cards and asked for Mrs Beddingfield's room. Ruth held her breath until they were both in the lift, then let it out in one long stream. *Damn*. If Fox had turned to the left instead of the right for the lifts, he would literally have stumbled over her.

Of course they would come here to see Barbara Beddingfield instead of the other way around, she thought, mentally kicking herself. As a source of potential information,

Nick's mother would have been jumpy enough having to come to officially identify the body, so dragging her into the police station would certainly not have helped them in their enquiries. Besides, Paddington Green was only a short walk away for Fox and Davis.

Ruth quickly paid for her coffee and walked out into the sunshine; she couldn't risk them seeing her on the way out. Crossing the road, she went into a burger joint and grabbed the cheapest thing on the illuminated menu, then took a plastic booth by the window, giving her a commanding view of the hotel's entrance. Fox and Davis emerged thirty minutes later, heading back towards Paddington Green without so much as a glance in her direction. Ruth was just gathering her things when she saw Barbara Beddingfield walk out, turning in the opposite direction.

'Shit,' muttered Ruth, leaving her tray on the table and pushing out through the door as fast as she could. Her heart jumped as she searched the crowd. She *couldn't* lose her now. Then she spotted her: already a few hundred yards ahead of her down the Bayswater Road. Ruth had to trot to catch up, her heels click-clacking on the pavement. Panting and hot, she finally caught sight of Nick's mother as she entered Patisserie Valerie behind Selfridges. Ruth didn't pause this time: she followed her straight in. The café was packed, full of chattering tourists and mothers with pushchairs. Barbara sat at a table for two by the window, and Ruth walked over.

'You don't mind if I sit here, do you?'

Barbara looked as if she minded a great deal but was too polite to say so.

'Sorry, but it's the only seat left,' said Ruth.

'Hey, be my guest,' said Barbara, her tanned face crinkling like leather as she smiled. Up close, her skin gave away her true age, dry and lined from years in the sun, with deep scoring around the mouth that told of a lifetime of heavy smoking.

'You're American?' said Ruth as she ordered a mint tea from the waitress: no more caffeine today. 'Are you on holiday?'

Barbara shook her head sadly as the waitress brought their drinks.

'I only wish they served something stronger here,' she said, stirring three packets of sugar into her drink.

'Are you okay?' Ruth asked.

Barbara Beddingfield puffed out her cheeks as her eyes welled with tears.

'It's my son. He was in London on business for a few days and he got killed yesterday. I've just had to fly out from LA to deal with things. Why, I wouldn't mind some liqor,' she said with a shrug.

Ruth looked at this woman, this grieving mother, and realised she couldn't keep up her deception. She knew she was supposed to be a hard-nosed news-hound whose job it was to get information by any means necessary – God knew she'd intruded on people's grief plenty of times in the past. But this time, she just couldn't do it.

'I know,' she said, feeling her cheeks colour.

'You . . . you know?' said Barbara, looking up, confusion on her face. Ruth knew she had to tell her the unvarnished truth.

'I'm a journalist,' she said quickly. 'My name is Ruth Boden. I work for the *Washington Tribune*.'

Ruth saw Barbara Beddingfield's expression change from bewilderment to anger and finally contempt.

'You followed me here?'

'Yes, and I can imagine what you think of me, but I have been covering Nick's story and I thought I might be able to help.'

'Don't insult my intelligence, Miss Boden,' said Barbara. 'Helping me is the last thing on your mind.'

'I can see you have no reason to believe me, I understand

that. But I do want to get this story out there and I do want to help catch whoever did this to Nick. Whatever you think about the press, we can sometimes be useful in cases like this.'

'This is not "a case",' said Barbara, her eyes flashing. 'This is my son.'

'I know, Mrs Beddingfield, and believe me, you have my deepest sympathies, but if I'm right, this is bigger than Nick's death. I think other people could get hurt too.'

Ruth expected Barbara Beddingfield to laugh at her, or at the very least stand up and walk away. But instead, she stared down at her coffee cup, her hands trembling.

'Tell me what you know,' she said quietly.

'The girl who found Nick? Her name is Sophie Ellis,' said Ruth. 'She has been questioned in connection with the murder, but I don't believe she did it. In fact, I think this girl is now in serious danger.'

Barbara looked up at her, her eyes red.

'I met with Inspector Fox, and he mentioned her.'

'What did he tell you?' asked Ruth, fishing around.

'Not much. I don't think they know much. He seemed impressive enough, but we both know that people literally get away with murder.'

Ruth nodded.

'Fox is a good detective,' she said. 'But he's a busy man and it's my job to know everything. And I always get my story.'

She could tell from her expression that Barbara understood exactly what she was saying. Perhaps Ian Fox and his team would have this wrapped up by tomorrow, but what if they didn't? It was just another case to them, another question mark in the unsolved file. And tomorrow, they would certainly be swamped by new crimes to solve and the difficult and dead-end mysteries would be pushed to the side. Ruth, on the other hand, could keep investigating the story for as long as necessary – some scandals took months, even years of dogged and painstaking research and determination before they were revealed. If Barbara wanted to know what had happened to her son, she needed Ruth on her side. Their eyes met and Nick's mother gave her a nod.

'So tell me about Nick,' said Ruth gently.

Barbara gave a laugh. 'Where do I start? He was a good boy, always ate his greens? Star of the high school baseball team?'

'Start with the last time you spoke.'

'We didn't speak every day like some families; in fact I might not hear from him for weeks at a time. So if you're asking why he was killed, I don't know.' She looked down at her coffee again. 'But I can guess it was to do with money.'

Ruth sensed a story here, but she was experienced enough to know when to ask questions and when to let a subject speak, and Barbara Beddingfield seemed like a woman who wanted, needed to talk.

'I'm just a normal mom, I guess,' she continued. 'All I wanted was for Nick to get a regular job, meet a nice girl, settle down and bring the grandkids over on a Sunday. But I guess we weren't the sort of family you see in TV ads. We weren't really a family at all, when it came down to it.'

'But Mrs Beddingfield—'

'Ah, that's just it,' she smiled sadly. 'I'm not a "Mrs". I never married Nick's father – I couldn't.'

'Why not?'

'He was already married, Ruth,' she said. 'I guess you'd call me a mistress. Nick's dad was a wealthy guy, powerful, but he was never going to leave his wife. For a while that didn't matter to me, because I was happy to take whatever he could give. And he was good to us – for a few years, anyway. But then I guess he found a younger model and he stopped coming around so much. And then the money stopped coming too. I think that was why Nick wanted to make money so much, and why he didn't care how he did it, what rules he had to bend.'

Ruth's inner instinct was tingling again.

'Are you saying Nick was involved in criminal activity?' she said, trying to hide her excitement. This could be an interesting twist. She had assumed the line about Nick being a wealthy businessman was straight up – had Fox been holding something back?

'I'm saying I'm his mother and I didn't like to ask too many questions, but I'm not stupid. I see things, hear things, even out in LA.'

'You didn't see him much?'

'Whoever knew where Nick would be? He had his apartment in Houston, but you'd get a postcard from Maui or an email saying he was in France, then suddenly he'd pop up needing to stay for a week. I never expected him for Thanksgiving, put it that way.'

'So what do you think he was involved in?' Ruth asked gently. 'Drugs?'

Barbara shook her head, her tanned face creased with disappointment.

'Maybe that would have been better in a way; at least then I could con myself that he was hooked. No, Nick was arrested four years ago for fraud. Something to do with trying to get money from a woman by deception. He had a good attorney and got off, but I'm not sure he learnt his lesson.'

She looked at Ruth again.

'I'm sorry, I really don't know any more than that. I'd be the last person Nick confided in if he was doing anything illegal. Maybe you should try asking his girlfriend.'

'Sophie Ellis? The girl from the Riverton?'

'No, her name's Jeanne Parsons,' said Barbara wearily. 'Nick was always very vague about her, but I went to visit him in Houston once and I saw post addressed to her.'

Ruth quickly wrote down the name.

'Maybe this will help too,' said Barbara, opening her handbag. She handed Ruth a photograph of Nick as a younger man. 'You can keep it, I had some copies done for the police.'

He was in his early twenties, Ruth guessed, and was leaning proudly against a motorbike, a semi-ironic gesture of rebellion. *The Wild One indeed*, thought Ruth. Nicholas Beddingfield had certainly been handsome, and even in this static picture he exuded a certain something: charisma probably. Maybe even sexiness, although Ruth felt uncomfortable thinking of him in that way. After all, the only time she had seen him in the flesh was when he was lying dead on the floor of the bathroom in the Riverton.

Barbara snapped the bag closed and stood up. As she did so, she clutched Ruth's hand. 'You will try to find out, won't you?' she said, a look of pain on her face. 'I know he wasn't perfect, but he was my little boy. That's how I'll always think of him. I know you can't bring him back, but no one should be allowed to get away with what they did.'

'I'll do all I can, Mrs Beddingfield,' said Ruth.

'Promise me,' she said urgently. 'Please.'

'I will. I promise.'

Ruth watched the woman walk out, her shoulders hunched with grief, wondering if she herself would ever feel such pain. Then she pulled out her mobile and scrolled to the *Tribune*'s office number.

'Chuck, it's Ruth. Get on to the Washington office. I've got a name and I need them to track someone down.'

23

Montmartre was every bit as beautiful as Sophie had imagined it would be. The sinking sun cast long shadows down the narrow cobbled streets, bathing everything in a warm orange glow. She gazed at the windows of the boulangeries and patisseries with the painted signs hanging over their doors, like a fragment of old Paris, the Paris of Renoir, Lautrec and Manet, when gentlemen would doff their top hats to ladies with muffs and bustles.

'It makes you just want to drink pastis,' said Josh as they walked across a small square with a cute little stationery shop on one side, an ironmonger's on the other, its old fashioned brushes and shovels all piled out on the pavement.

'I could do with a stiff drink,' she said, wanting to get their visit to Le Cellar over and done with. She thought of their hotel suite at the Bristol and wished they were back there.

'Well, Le Cellar is famous for it. You could even go the whole French hog and try absinthe.'

Josh had given her the impression that the club was packed with cut-throats and pimps, and despite her brave speech about taking things head on, she had no desire to spend any more time in a dark thieves' den than was strictly essential.

'We're not there to try out the cocktail menu. I want to be in and out before it gets dangerous.'

'It's not that bad,' smiled Josh. 'It might not be one of those tourist traps that plays dinner jazz and charges for the nuts, but this early in the evening it will be quiet. Stay close and we'll be fine, okay?'

Josh led her away from the main drag and into a maze of tiny side streets, finally stopping at a small doorway with an art deco-style sign reading 'Le Cellar'.

'Wait here,' he said as he pulled open the heavy black door. 'I'll be two minutes, tops.'

Sophie looked around at this dank alleyway. That glorious sinking sun she had seen falling on the hill had left this part of Montmartre hours ago, if indeed it ever made it this far. She eyed the large industrial skip at the far end of the lane, imagining dog-sized rats and casually dumped bodies inside. She didn't realise she had been holding her breath the whole time, until Josh reappeared moments later.

'Maurice will be back in "*cinq minutes*",' he said. 'That's Parisian for "at least an hour". Let's go and get fleeced with the rest of the tourists while we're waiting, eh?'

Sophie followed him back the way they had come, stopping in a busy square with shutters and window boxes. A white picket fence marked the centre, inside which was the chic French equivalent of the shopping-mall food court. Tables, chairs and umbrellas were arranged in vague formation around a dozen or more cute little wooden food stalls. Sophie was immediately enveloped by a delicious combination of smells drifting from the booths: sizzling sausages, gamey stews and buttery crêpes. With the famous bulbous spires of the Sacré-Cœur behind it, Sophie felt she was on a film set.

'Welcome to La Place du Tertre,' said Josh. 'It's a total tourist trap, so be careful, there are people out to scam you at every street corner.'

Sophie almost laughed out loud. Only two minutes earlier, she had been standing alone in a dark alleyway next to a club frequented by gangsters, and here was Josh warning her about getting drawn in by the street artists with their overpriced views of Paris.

'So why bring me somewhere so dodgy?' she asked, as he led her towards a café at the far end of the square.

'It's worth the risk – this place does amazing soup.'

They sat at a table for two with a view of the square and all the trimmings: red and white checked tablecloth, wine bottle with melted-down candle, laminated menu with pictures and descriptions in four languages. Josh didn't even glance at it, ordering *soupe à l'oignon* for both of them.

'This stuff will change the way you feel about onions, I promise you,' he said.

'So tell me about Maurice,' said Sophie.

'I've told you all you need to know,' he said quickly. 'He's a rat and a leech and you shouldn't trust a word he says.'

'Why are we going there to ask him questions, then?'

'Because he's all we have.'

Sophie nodded. Josh was never one to sugar the pill, but at least you got a straight answer with him.

'So tell me about you, Sophie Ellis,' he said finally, slugging at the beer the waitress had just brought over.

She felt suddenly on the spot. Josh hadn't shown the slightest interest in her before now, and all of a sudden he was observing her as if she was the most fascinating creature on earth.

She shrugged quickly. 'There's nothing to tell.'

'Come on, don't be modest,' he grinned. His face looked quite different when he smiled. Mischievous rather than brooding. 'I'm sure you won a few rosettes at gymkhanas when you were a cute ten-year-old.'

Sophie shook her head slowly.

'Nope, nothing that interesting.'

'Really?'

'Seriously,' she lamented. 'If the last couple of days have any positives, it's that I have come to realise that I haven't really done anything with my life. I'm twenty-seven next month and I don't have anything interesting to talk about, I haven't really been anywhere off the beaten track, unless you include off-piste at Klosters. I don't even do anything worth mentioning.'

She laughed ruefully. The truth was, Sophie was a nothing. She had led such a predictable middle-class life, she didn't really know who she was.

'You must do something,' said Josh, his grey eyes glistening. 'Catalogue modelling? International assassin?'

'When I met Nick, I had just started a personal training business.'

'There you go,' said Josh. 'And did you enjoy it?'

'It was good to have a project and to start making some money.'

'I asked if you *enjoyed* it?'

She reflected on it for a moment. It all seemed so long ago. She had enjoyed doing something she was good at and she had felt she was helping people – even if it was only getting pampered women into smaller and smaller bikinis.

'I suppose it's not exactly what I would choose to do in an ideal world.'

'So what is?'

The waiter put two bowls of French onion soup in front of them. It had a thick crust of bread and stringy cheese floating across the oily surface. It smelled absolutely delicious.

Sophie stuck her spoon through the cheese, and smiled slowly. 'You know, I'd love to live somewhere like this. Maybe not this place exactly but the place it's pretending to be. A pretty village where I'm surrounded by creative people.'

'And what would you do there? Make them all do squat thrusts?'

Sophie laughed.

'No, I'd paint or write, I suppose. Or at least try to.'

Josh cocked his head.

'So why don't you?'

'Well I did, sort of. I spent six months in Florence once. It was wonderful.' She almost sighed at the memory. Maybe she was looking at it with rose-tinted spectacles, but it represented the one time in Sophie's life when she had really felt alive. But that had been her old life, back when she had money. She hadn't realised it at the time, but it wasn't the money she'd liked. She had liked the experiences, the things money had allowed her to do: a really cold glass of wine at a beautiful beach café, a view over a stunning snowy mountain range, a ride in a speedboat over the bluest waters imaginable.

'But you need money for those sorts of things. In the past year I haven't had a whole lot of it.'

Josh gave a short laugh.

'Bollocks,' he said. 'You could get a cheap flight to Pisa, catch a bus to Florence, then find a room somewhere. Maybe not a smart little apartment by Il Duomo, but just a cute place where some warm sunlight comes through your window. And if you like it? Stay. Find a job, be a waitress, bar-tend. Someone as beautiful as you could easily find work.'

Sophie felt herself blush. If anyone else had said it, she knew she would have thought it sounded foolish, even irresponsible, but Josh made it sound like a real adventure. When she had been dating Will or hanging out with Francesca – even that long week with Nick, if she was honest – she had always felt that you needed money for anything worthwhile: that idea that you got what you paid for. But Josh was different. In his version, it was as if having money could make you lose sight of what was really important, the things that really made you happy.

As if he had read her thoughts, he put down his spoon. 'It's a good feeling finding something you love,' he said. 'Especially if you might even be able to make a little money out of it. Like me. I really do love watches. I love finding an old Omega at an antique fair and getting it repaired, polished, brought back to life. And along the way, I get to talk to interesting, successful people, but mainly I just love the elegance and the minute intricacy of a timepiece, that's what gets me up in the morning.' He smiled, that cheeky, naughty smile. 'Well, that and the chance of making a big profit without working too hard.'

Sophie bent over her soup, suddenly aware that Josh was watching her. What was he thinking? What did he see when he looked at her? Did he *really* think she was beautiful? Her blush deepened as she realised she wanted him to, because the truth was he was very sexy. Not good-looking in a smooth, movie-star kind of way like Nick, but everything about Josh crackled with naughtiness. And there was something else, a vulnerability beneath that brash facade that was maddeningly elusive.

'We should go,' said Sophie quickly, but Josh didn't move.

'Did you do it?' he asked quietly.

'Did I do what?' She felt the colour drain from her face. 'You mean Nick?' It upset her that he could even ask the question.

He didn't take his eyes off hers.

'No, I did not kill Nick,' she said, holding his gaze. Josh looked back at her for a long moment.

'Okay,' he said finally.

'*Okay?* That's it?'

'I believe you,' he said frankly. 'I just had to ask.'

He stood up, placing some euros under his plate.

'Now let's go and meet Maurice. Clearly you've got a life

213

out there that you need to be living. And you can't start until we find out who really did kill Nick.'

Le Cellar was not actually in a cellar at all, but on the first floor.

'French sense of humour,' said Josh as they went up a rickety wooden staircase. At the top, a fat man in a T-shirt emblazoned with the words 'So What?' was sprawled in a chair cleaning his nails with what looked like a knife. If he was supposed to be Le Cellar's security, they needed to have an urgent review, thought Sophie. He didn't even look up as they walked into the bar.

As Josh had predicted, the place was virtually empty: two men on stools, deep in conversation at the counter, and an old man and a very thin young woman slowly dancing to an old Sinatra tune. Sophie immediately guessed which one was Maurice; he was the very dark, short man at the counter with the slicked-back hair, who looked like a rat.

She was about to ask Josh, but when she turned to him, he had gone. Without a word he walked straight over to Maurice and kicked his chair. Immediately, the two men began shouting at each other and waving their hands in a threatening manner, while the dancers swayed on oblivious to it all. Sophie glanced over at the fat man by the door; he appeared to have dozed off. But then, just as she felt sure they were going to come to blows, Maurice's mean face split into a grin and he threw his arms open.

'Joshua,' he cried, hugging him. Josh also embraced the other man, who looked like a Maltese Popeye, with tattooed ham-hock arms and a navy fisherman's cap.

'You should have given me more notice, my friend. I could have arranged a homecoming, got some of the old crowd down.'

So much for Josh's claim of having only met Maurice a couple of times, thought Sophie, just as Maurice looked her way, his black eyes sizing her up. He immediately began talking to Nick in French; Sophie could not pick up any recognisable words except 'bastard'. She hoped that was good. Josh beckoned to her.

'Sophie, come and meet my friends Maurice and Panda.'

'*Bonjour*,' she said awkwardly. She didn't like to see Josh so friendly with someone who was clearly as dodgy as hell.

'*Ah, tu parle Français aussi?*' said Maurice.

'No, not really,' said Sophie, flushing. 'That's about it, actually.'

Everyone laughed and Sophie relaxed a little.

'Well, any friend of this old rogue is a friend of mine,' said Maurice, grasping Josh's arm, then banging the bar.

'Johan, bring us all pastis,' he called to the barman. 'You remember Josh. A friend of Nicholas.'

Sophie watched nervously as the barman served the liquid into four glasses and Maurice added water from a jug on the bar, turning the drink milky.

'Down ze 'atch, as you say in London, no?' said Maurice, knocking his back. Sophie did the same and immediately began coughing. Gosh, it was strong.

'I see your companion is more used to our champagne, huh, Joshua?' laughed Maurice as Josh slapped her on the back.

'Went down the wrong way,' managed Sophie between gasps.

Maurice fixed her with that searching gaze again, nodding to himself. 'Let's go to my office where we can talk, yes?'

He raised his eyebrows to Panda, then led Sophie and Josh through a door behind the bar. Maurice's office was no more an office than Le Cellar was underground; more like a cramped storage room with an old sofa and three chairs around a wonky table.

'So tell me,' he said, closing the door behind them. 'What trouble are you in this time, my friend?'

'No trouble of mine,' said Josh, nodding towards Sophie.

'Ah, so it is as I thought. You are the damsel in distress, no?'

'Yes, I suppose so. It's just that . . .'

Josh flashed her a warning look and Sophie trailed off, embarrassed.

'Sophie is in trouble, yes,' he said, 'but it's Nick who has got her there.'

Maurice's face clouded over.

'Nick?' he said. 'What has that old gigolo been up to this time?'

'You tell me.'

Maurice shrugged. 'I have not seen Nick for months.'

'Why do I think you are lying?' said Josh with a nasty smile. 'And I suppose you know nothing about his wine scam, either?'

'Wine? What wine?' said Maurice, taking a step backwards. 'Why don't you call him up and ask him? Nick will tell you the same thing.'

'I would,' said Josh, backing him into a corner. 'Except he's dead, Maurice.'

'Dead?' He frowned as he absorbed the information.

'Murdered yesterday in London. And of course you wouldn't know about that.'

Maurice held up a hand. 'That is nothing to do with me, I swear. I loved him like a brother, you know that.'

'Well, I want to find out who killed him,' said Josh, bringing his face just inches away from Maurice's. 'He told me that you and he had worked together recently, so I want you to tell me everything you know. And if you don't tell me, don't bet against Scotland Yard knocking on your door. They sure want to find out who killed him too.'

Maurice's expression changed.

'You come here to my bar and threaten me with the police?' he said angrily. 'Fuck you, *rosbif*.'

Josh grabbed him by the front of his shirt.

'I'm not sure I'm making myself clear here.'

Maurice didn't flinch.

Sophie watched Josh tighten his grip on the man's shirt.

'Okay,' spat Maurice finally, pushing him away. He straightened his back and smoothed down his shirt. 'Nick needed some labels making for the wine bottles, so I put him in touch with a counterfeiter in Montparnasse. The best. Apparently he was very satisfied with the work he produced, and he paid me well for the contact. That was the beginning and end of my involvement.'

'Who is the counterfeiter?'

Maurice looked shifty. He was a terrible liar, thought Sophie. Even she could tell when he was dodging the truth.

'The printer has returned to Tunisia. I do not have a number for him any longer.'

'Then tell me who else was involved,' said Josh impatiently. 'Give me a name, Maurice. A contact.'

'And what will you give me in return?' said Maurice, his black eyes glistening with greed. 'I run a business here. I give you something, you give me something. It makes the world go round, no?'

He turned to Sophie, undressing her with a long, lascivious stare. 'Nick has good taste in women,' he said softly, then turned back to Josh.

'How about you go and have another pastis, *mon ami*. Maybe leave me here with Sophie.'

'Leave her out of this,' said Josh.

Maurice stepped towards Sophie and stroked her cheek, making her flinch back.

'Why?' He smiled, showing small, yellowing teeth. 'She would like it. All Nick's girls like a good fuck, don't they?'

Josh moved like lightning, pushing Maurice up against

the wall with his hand around the man's thick throat before Sophie could even blink. The door burst open and Panda stood there holding a club.

'Let's not make this more difficult than it has to be, eh, Maurice?' said Josh in a low, threatening voice. He had almost lifted the Frenchman off the ground, but Sophie didn't fancy his chances against the more robust Panda.

Maurice spat in his face.

'Fuck you,' he hissed.

Josh drew his left fist back to throw a punch.

'Don't,' screamed Sophie as Panda came up behind her and put his arm around her throat.

Josh glanced round. His teeth bared as he saw Panda, then he slammed Maurice harder against the wall.

'A name, Maurice. Just give me a name and we'll be out of here.'

Panda's thick biceps were pushing down on Sophie's throat and she could barely breathe. Finally Maurice said something in rapid-fire French and Panda let her go. As Josh released his grip on Maurice, the tension slowly dissipated.

Maurice pushed Josh away. 'I can give you the name of the drop point, a wine wholesaler in Cannes. But I swear that's all I know,' he said tersely.

'What's it called?'

'He is a wine merchant called Jacques Durand. He has a shopfront in the old town, not far from the harbour. He took supplies from Nick and sold them on to rich Russians on the Riviera.'

'Russians?' queried Josh. Sophie knew he was thinking the same thing as she was.

'Yes, Russians,' repeated Maurice. 'You know that's who has all the money now.'

'Thanks, Maurice, you've been very helpful,' sneered Josh, leading Sophie towards the door.

'Don't ever come back here,' said Maurice in a low, threatening voice. 'If you come back, I will kill you.'

Josh turned back, his coolness returning.

'That's what I like about you, Maurice,' he smiled. 'You always did think big.'

He held Sophie's hand in a firm, protective gesture and all she could do was squeeze back gratefully.

24

They arrived at Gare d'Austerlitz on the left bank of the Seine at a little after nine p.m. It was still busy with commuters heading home to the suburbs and the towns to the south.

'What are we doing here?' asked Sophie, puzzled.

'The sleeper train leaves for Nice in thirty minutes. If we're quick, we can make it.'

'What about Le Bristol?' she asked, dreaming of that comfortable emperor-sized bed.

'Another time,' he said, not looking at her.

'Stay here,' said Josh, at the entrance to the ticket office. 'I'm going to buy the tickets. You go to that kiosk and get some water and food,' he added, thrusting a fifty-euro note at her.

She nodded, thinking she would also buy a strong coffee. She could still taste the aniseed from the pastis in Le Cellar and didn't want any reminders of that place.

Sophie bought what they needed from the small station shop and walked back out on to the concourse. Josh was still in the ticket queue. She looked at him for a moment, realising this was the first time they had been apart in over twenty-four hours. She still didn't really know who this man was, but she did know he had defended her from that rat-faced pimp Maurice. Her face flushed as she thought of it. What if Josh hadn't been there? *Well, you wouldn't have been in that godawful club for a start*, said a voice in her head. But the thing was, she had to stay with Josh. Without him, she would be lost. She would almost certainly be in London, possibly in a police cell, maybe even dead.

She shivered, despite the heat. With a desperate need to hear a familiar voice, she realised she hadn't yet contacted her mother, who would be back in London from Denmark. She would be frantic with worry and Sophie didn't blame her. Her daughter had been questioned in connection with a high-profile murder and now she had disappeared without letting anybody know where she was, or what she was doing.

Defiantly, she went back into the kiosk and bought a five-euro phone card, then crossed to the bank of payphones near the ticket office. She felt a stab of guilt as she lifted the receiver. Josh would certainly be angry if he knew what she was doing; he'd drummed into her the need to stay off the phones and that the only way to contact the outside world was email – and even then, only from a public computer. But how was she supposed to find a bloody internet café in the middle of Paris while being chased by the police, hit men and now, probably, Maurice and his cronies? She would call her mother for just a few seconds. Just to let her know she was safe. And anyway, if by some miracle someone did trace the call, they'd be miles away from Paris.

'Hello, Julia Ellis,' said the voice at the other end of the line.

Sophie felt a sudden wave of relief and homesickness. She wanted to burst into tears, but she knew she had to hold it in for her mother's sake.

'Mum, it's me.'

'Darling!' cried Julia. 'Where *are* you?'

'Don't worry, I'm safe.' At least Josh would be happy she kept it vague.

'Come home, Sophie, please. The police are worried about you.'

'Worried?' said Sophie. 'They want to arrest me.'

'Well, you're not making things any easier for yourself by disappearing. You have nothing to hide, so why don't you come in and speak to them again? Mr Gould will go with you.'

'I can't. I need to find out who killed Nick first.'

'Sophie, don't be ridiculous,' hissed her mother. 'That's the police's job, not yours. I had some officers round here this morning actually, taking fingerprints and whatnot.'

'Fingerprints? For me? But they've already got my finger-prints.'

She could feel the clock ticking and knew she had to get off the phone.

'The burglary, darling,' gasped Julia. 'I came back from Denmark and – oh! It was horrible, Sophie. They'd turned the place upside down, torn the curtains, it's incredible what these thugs will do. High on drugs, I shouldn't wonder.'

Wade House had been burgled? Sophie immediately felt unsettled. Had they been after her? Had they been looking for something? Presumably whatever it was they had been after at her flat.

'Nothing appears to have been taken,' Julia was saying, 'but they left it in a terrible mess and the TV is in pieces. I hope it's insured; you know how your father loved cutting corners.'

In the distance Sophie could hear a tannoy announcement; she didn't understand it, but she recognised the word 'Nice'.

'Mum, I have to go,' she said.

'Sophie, please, we need to talk. Are you sure you're all right? I'm at my wits' end.'

People were moving towards the platforms now. She couldn't be on the phone when Josh came looking for her.

'Sorry, Mum. I love you.'

She put down the receiver and hurried back to the kiosk just as Josh came striding towards her.

'Everything set?' he said, tapping two train tickets against the palm of his hand. 'They've announced the platform, we'd better get moving.'

Sophie forced a smile and picked up her bag.

'Let's go.'

They climbed on board just as the guard blew his whistle, and moved through the gently swaying train to find their allocated sleeper cabin. It was tiny. Two bunk beds on top of each other with just about enough room to sit and a metal sink of the type you'd get in a lavatory.

'Cosy,' said Josh, locking the door behind them.

'You can go on top,' said Sophie, putting her bag on the bottom bunk.

'Just how I like it,' he quipped, but Sophie ignored him.

'Well, I don't think they have a disco on the train, so I guess we'd better get some sleep,' added Josh, climbing into the top bunk. 'Early start tomorrow.'

Sophie got into her bunk and, making sure she was out of his line of view, undressed and slipped into the lightweight sleeping bag.

Josh turned off the light and pulled down the window blind. For a while they were both silent, listening to the train click over the points, feeling the gentle rock of the carriage, hearing people talking quietly as they passed in the corridor outside.

'What time are we going to be in the south?' said Sophie, unable to sleep.

'Seven-ish. The train only goes to Nice, so we'll have to double back on ourselves to get to Cannes.'

She wriggled around the sleeping bag, staring up at the base of Josh's bunk, trying to picture him up there. *Stop it, Sophie*, she thought. She supposed it was the romance of being in a sleeper train, feeling a little like Eva Marie Saint in that Hitchcock film she was in with Cary Grant. *North by Northwest*? It had been years since she'd seen it, but she was sure they'd shared a sleeper train cabin. Or was it Audrey Hepburn?

'It's not quite Le Bristol,' she said.

'You have very expensive tastes, Miss Ellis,' said Josh and she could hear the smile in his voice. 'D'you know, this used to be the most glamorous way to travel a hundred years ago? It was called the Blue Train and it ferried all the wealthy people from London and Paris to the Côte d'Azur. It was all first class. Coco Chanel, Churchill, royalty – they've all been on it.'

'You know a lot about a lot of things,' said Sophie candidly.

'I know a little bit about a lot,' he responded. 'I left school at sixteen, so everything I've learnt has been from books, people I've met, TV programmes I've watched. I suppose I keep my ears and my eyes open.'

'So how did you get into this?'

'What, selling watches?'

'Josh, you know what I mean. The lock-up, Maurice, all that.'

There was something about talking to but not seeing someone, not looking them in the face, that made it possible to ask anything. She wasn't sure what she wanted him to say, of course, except that she wanted to hear something good. Josh might be a thief or a con man, she didn't really know, but back at Le Cellar he had been – what? *My hero*, she thought, feeling embarrassed and, if she was honest, turned on at the same time.

'After school I was jobless, aimless, kicking around the arse-end of Edinburgh. There were a lot of drugs and gangs, and I was terrified by all that. So instead I got in with a crowd that used to sell fake stuff around pubs and on street corners. I was that cocky little bleeder you'd see on the high street surrounded by a crowd, selling cheap perfume: "gen-u-ine Armani, ladies, a tenner for two".'

His impression made her giggle. She'd never have bought anything from a rogue street trader like the one he was describing – but then she'd never seen Josh, had she?

'How did you meet Nick?'

'That was when I moved from Scotland to London in my early twenties. I think in the back of my mind I really believed the streets might be paved with gold. Of course they weren't, but then you *could* charge twice as much for knock-off Blue Stratos on Oxford Street. Anyway, I bumped into Nick in some nightclub in Soho. I tried to sell him a Rolex and you know what he said? "Don't waste your time." I thought he was telling me to sod off because he could see the watch was a fake, but he wasn't. He told me I had a gift.'

'A gift?'

'Charm, patter, I don't know. I never found it hard to sell the watches, however ropy they were, put it that way. I suppose I should have got on a training scheme and become a salesman, sold washing machines or insurance. Anyway, Nick brought me into a couple of scams he was running. And the rest, as they say, is history.'

'What kind of scams, Josh?'

He was quiet for a moment.

'Nothing I'm proud of. But I was grateful to Nick. He taught me a lot and gave me focus, made me see that I didn't have to spend the rest of my life standing on street corners selling vinegar in fancy bottles. He did me a huge favour.'

'He led you astray, more like,' said Sophie softly. She wondered if that was how it worked for all criminals. She didn't suppose that people started out bad, but somewhere along the line they met the wrong person, fell in with the wrong crowd and were tempted onto another path.

'Don't be too down on Nick,' said Josh. 'Everyone assumes he was this morally bankrupt monster destroying innocent women's lives, but let me tell you, most of those women were playing some sort of game with him too. They all wanted something from Nick. Those women' – he whistled – 'they can be ruthless.'

Sophie was surprised how readily Josh was defending Nick.

'I got the impression that the two of you didn't like each other that much,' she said. 'Or was all that stuff at the Chariot party an act too?'

'No, we did fall out,' said Josh in the darkness. 'Nick seemed to think that because he'd helped me out in the past, whenever he called I would come running. There was a job in Monaco last summer.' He paused. 'I didn't want to be involved.'

'Why not?'

She heard him snort.

'You *are* nosy, aren't you?'

'Come on, Josh. It might be something to do with his death.'

'It involved duping old ladies in Monte Carlo, if you must know. Somehow I doubt a member of the blue-rinse brigade killed Nick.'

Sophie didn't know why she was so glad Josh had turned down Nick's scheme, but she was. She supposed she wanted to hear that Josh McCormack wasn't all bad, that he had a heart and it wasn't hidden too far below the surface.

'So why didn't you do it?' she asked.

'Look, I just couldn't. That was the reason I started the watch consultancy business, selling real watches this time. I suppose I just didn't want to end up like Nick, hopping from one hotel room to the next, skipping out on the bill at the end of the week. Anyway, he never really forgave me. Couldn't understand why I wanted a regular life.'

'I have to say, you don't strike me as the regular-life kind of guy either,' said Sophie, teasing gently.

'I don't want to be looking out of the window wondering if my kids are going to see a squad car turning up at the house,' he said, his voice serious, maybe even a little angry.

Sophie frowned.

'You have kids?'

She heard the snort again.

'One day.'

'Well, you'd have to get married first,' she said.

'I'd have to find a wife first.'

'What about the girl in Camden?' she asked, remembering the alibi he had given her on the *Nancy Blue*. *What are you doing bringing* her *up like some jealous girlfriend?* she scolded herself.

'Oh her,' chuckled Josh. 'I never did call her back. Some pretty Chelsea posh girl popped up and took up all my time.'

'Do you want to? Call her back, I mean?'

She surprised herself, not just by asking the question, but at how bothered she was over what his response might be.

Josh paused for a long moment.

'Probably not. She was some crazy musician chick and I think there's enough excitement in my life right now.'

Sophie closed her eyes, wondering if that was Josh's type; a boho beauty with a guitar and lots of piercings. She'd smell of exotic perfume, give him an expert blow job, then sing him to sleep. If she had been more awake, she might have recognised a brief flutter of envy about the unknown Camden musician, but her eyes were closing, heavy now, so heavy, and she couldn't think about anything else except the gentle lull of the carriage rocking from side to side.

When she opened her eyes again, she could see Josh standing in the cramped space next to the bunks, his perfectly round bum pointing towards her as he bent over to pull up his trousers.

'Sorry,' she said, failing to avert her eyes from his naked back as he pulled on a new T-shirt.

'Morning,' he grinned playfully. 'Thought I'd better

smarten up my image if we're going to do the Riviera properly.'

'Where are we?' she asked sleepily as he pulled up the blind.

'Just past Antibes, so we should be there soon. You should wash, clean up. The toilets are just at the end of the carriage. They're not great, but there's water and I've got a spare toothbrush and some paste in my holdall.'

'I don't suppose you have any spare clothes in there?'

'Nothing suitable for walking through Nice in broad daylight. Anyway, stop complaining. Those jeans suit you.'

She was still smiling to herself as she swayed down the corridor, bumping from side to side. She stopped to peer out of the window, squinting at the too-bright blue sky. It couldn't be much past seven, but already the cloudless sky and the rising orange sun promised a glorious day. *As it should be for my glamorous time in the South of France*, she thought, before reminding herself that they were here to do a job. For now, though, she allowed herself to soak up the sights and sounds, enjoying the sensation of the ice-cold water she splashed on her face in the toilet, feeling her energy rise as they approached Nice station. She had no idea what the day held, but there was an excitement, an anticipation of the unknown she was beginning to enjoy.

'Let's go,' said Josh, picking up Sophie's bag as she returned to the cabin, just as they pulled into the platform. 'We could get the train to Cannes, but a cab should be quicker.'

They joined the rest of the passengers streaming from the train and through the barriers to the concourse, which was crowded with people waiting to get on the train for the return journey to Paris. Sophie was just looking for the sign for the taxi rank – at least 'taxi' was 'taxi', whatever country you were in – when Josh took her hand, gripping it tight.

'Keep moving,' he whispered.

Sophie did as she was told, matching his pace as they moved towards the exit.

'What's up?'

'I think we're being followed,' he said under his breath. 'Big guy, muscular, short black hair. Don't look.'

But Sophie couldn't help herself, glancing behind to see the man – unmistakable in an unseasonable black coat – pushing through the crowd while talking on his mobile phone.

She felt herself stiffen.

'This way,' said Josh, pulling her towards an exit sign to the left.

Suddenly Sophie felt someone grab her in a vice-like grip. Pain seared up her arm.

'Josh!' she screamed, meeting the second assailant eye to eye. Instinctively she swivelled around and kicked the man as hard as she could in the shin. He lost his grip, cursing in a language she didn't recognise as Sophie sprinted for her life.

Josh caught up with her, grabbing her hand and pulling her out into the street, body-swerving a crate and dodging a crowd of teenagers standing at a bus stop. Out of the station, Sophie was immediately buffeted by noise and movement on all sides. The roar of traffic on the road, the blare of car horns, mopeds zipping in front of them, people everywhere. She didn't have time to process it all, had to treat them all as objects to be avoided, to get past, to get away from.

'Keep going,' yelled Josh as they reached the other side of the road. Sophie didn't need to look to know that the crop-haired man and his friend with the sore shin were close behind them. She could almost feel their feet pounding through the pavement. Fear and adrenalin made her run faster.

'Down here!' They plunged into a warren of back streets; hotels and cheap restaurants – *plenty of internet cafés around here*, Sophie thought crazily – with doorways and back entrances providing a wealth of places to hide, but they couldn't stop; one blind alley and they could be trapped. They sprinted out of a narrow street and on to another main road.

'Look out!' Sophie screamed as Josh was almost tossed over the bonnet of a white taxi with a squeal of brakes.

'*Monsieur! Monsieur!*' he cried, waving to the driver. '*Arrêtez!*'

He yanked the cab's door open and they both fell inside.

'*Allez, tout de suite, s'il vous plaît!*' he shouted. '*Vite, vite!*'

Mercifully, the driver did as he was told and they jerked into motion. But their relief was short-lived. Through the rear window, Sophie could see the two men jumping into a car just behind them.

'That's not a taxi behind,' panted Josh. 'There's more of them.'

Josh turned to the driver and told him to take a quick left, then a right. As soon as they were around a corner, he yelled for the cab to stop. Pushing a fifty-euro note into the cabbie's hand, they jumped out and Josh slammed his hand on the roof of the car.

'Drive!' he yelled, pointing down the road. The man didn't need telling twice, and squealed off, leaving twin rubber burns on the tarmac.

'In here,' said Josh, diving through the open door of a hotel to their left. Moving quickly, but casually enough not to draw attention to themselves, they walked through the lobby and followed the sign to '*La Piscine*'.

'Keep moving,' panted Josh. 'They'll spot we're not in that taxi any minute.'

Sophie squinted as they stepped out into the bright sun again, shards of light glinting off the blue water of the pool. There were people laying out their towels for sunbathing and the happy noise of children splashing in the shallow end; it seemed so strange, incongruous when they were running for their lives.

'There,' she said, spotting a gate at the back of the hotel grounds. Quickly checking that the lane behind it was clear, they ducked through and found themselves in a loading area for a restaurant; the kitchen doors were open at the back and the driver of a delivery van was wheeling a crate inside.

Josh pointed at the rear doors of the van, still open with the ramp down.

'Come on, inside,' he said.

The back of the van was piled high with boxes and crates, but there was just enough space to squeeze behind them. Sophie froze as there was a clank, then a thud – and darkness as the driver closed the doors. She held her breath, only relaxing slightly when the diesel engine growled into life and they began to move. As they turned a corner, the boxes began to shift, and Sophie had to grab on to the side of the van, feeling Josh's knee stabbing into her ribcage.

'How long do you think we're going to be stuck in here?' she whispered.

'Until he makes his next pit stop, I guess.'

That could be hours, thought Sophie. He could be going to Turkey for all they knew. She could feel the van take a left turn, then a right. It picked up speed, and from the change of gear and the rev of the engine, she could tell that they were going uphill. It was pitch black and hot in the back, and the dust from the floor was tickling her nose, but with every moment she felt a growing sense of relief; they had escaped again – but it had been close, very close.

'How the hell did they find us?' Josh hissed in the dark. 'Damn Maurice; he was the only person who knew we were coming down here. You can bet he would have squealed if the Russians offered him some roubles.'

'Russians?' whispered Sophie. She remembered the man swearing as she had kicked him; it hadn't been French, that was for sure. Had it been the same men as that night by the river? Had they followed them all this way? Somehow that

231

was all the more terrifying – whatever they thought she had, they must really want it badly.

'Russians, Germans, I don't bloody know who they are,' growled Josh. 'All I know is they were waiting for us – they must have known we were on the train.'

Sophie felt a sudden wave of guilt.

'It could have been me,' she said quietly.

She waited for Josh to reply, but he didn't say anything.

'I'm so sorry, Josh,' she whispered. 'When you were buying the tickets, I phoned my mother. I thought it would be okay because we were leaving the city,' she said, her words quickening as she tried to explain herself. 'As I was talking, there was a tannoy announcement about the departure to Nice and I said "I've got to go". So stupid, it must have been obvious.'

'But that would mean they've been bugging your mum's phone,' said Josh.

'She did say she had been burgled. Maybe—'

'You stupid bloody idiot,' he growled, his voice rising. 'You could have got us both killed, do you realise that? In fact you still might – why can't you do anything I ask?'

'Shh!' she hissed. 'Calm down, the driver will hear us.'

'Fuck the driver!' he snapped.

'Look, it was a mistake, Josh. I'm sorry.'

'The mistake was getting involved with you in the first place,' he barked. 'I could have been sitting on my boat right now, drinking a beer, enjoying the sunshine. But no, I got sucked in by a damsel in distress. I took pity on you and look where it's got me! In the back of a bloody van hiding from an entire team of well-organised goons who all seem to want to kill you. I'm starting to think they've got a bloody point!'

'Josh, please! None of this is my fault . . .'

'Yeah? Well, those Russians or whatever they are seem to think differently. What is it they want from you, Sophie? You've clearly got something if they're going to the effort of bugging your mother and following you to France. What do you know? Because I'm starting to think there's something you're not telling me.'

'I don't know anything!' she shouted, but then was thrown backwards against the side of the van as it screeched to a halt. They heard footsteps on the pavement and then the back of the van opened, blinding them with the sudden light.

'*Mon Dieu!*'

Calmly Josh stood up, ducking his head under the roof of the van.

'*Bonjour,*' he said to the flabbergasted driver. '*Excusez-moi. Je pense que nous sommes perdus.*'

Sophie crawled out from under the boxes and sheepishly followed Josh on to the street. The driver just stood there, his mouth open, watching as they walked away.

They were in a high part of the city, looking down over the terracotta rooftops of Nice, and beyond that the glistening silver of the Mediterranean. If she squinted, Sophie could just about make out the station and the train tracks that snaked out east and west. There was a bang behind them and they turned to see the van pull away.

'There goes our ride,' said Josh. He didn't look angry any more, just shaken and resigned.

'What did you say to him?' asked Sophie.

'I'm sorry, I think we are lost.'

Sophie couldn't help it: she burst out laughing.

25

It hadn't been a productive day at the *Washington Tribune*'s London bureau. Ruth rubbed her eyes and gave her piece one last read before submitting it. *Looking radiant in a scarlet Issa dress, Kate held her husband's hand and waved to the small crowd* . . . She smiled ruefully; a story on the Duke and Duchess of Cambridge visiting the American Embassy for a tea party wasn't exactly Watergate, was it? Normally Ruth would have passed something like this on to Jim's PA Rebecca – she seemed to love these kind of assignments – but as Rebecca had called in sick with a bout of menstrual cramps, Ruth had been forced to bite the bullet. Jim wanted 750 upbeat, smiley words about the royals meeting the ambassador, and Ruth needed to keep him sweet while she worked on the Riverton murder.

Clicking the 'send' button on her computer, she pulled out her earplugs, sat back in her chair and took a swig of her coffee. *Eww – stone cold*. She desperately needed a caffeine hit if she was going to make it to the end of the day; she'd been pulling too many late nights recently.

'Hey, Chuck,' she said, waving her paper cup at her colleague across the office. 'Any chance of doing a coffee run?'

Chuck smiled and held up his own cup.

'I went ten minutes ago,' he said. 'I did ask, but you had

your headphones on and I didn't want to disturb the master at work.'

Dammit. She dropped her coffee cup into the trash bin and looked across to Jim's office; the lights were off. Chuck was right, Ruth had been 'in the zone', bent over her computer writing her royals story for the last hour – she hadn't even noticed the bureau chief leave.

'Where's the boss man got to?' she asked Chuck.

'Pub, round of golf, shopping for shoes? Who knows – he never shares his plans with me.'

Ruth laughed. She liked Chuck. He was far too much of a company man to ever question Jim in an editorial meeting, but get him on his own and he could be sarcastic and funny.

'Maybe he's gone to help Rebecca with her women's problems,' he said with a knowing smile.

'My money's on that one,' said Ruth playfully. Perhaps it wasn't strictly professional to gossip about your boss behind his back, but it made the working day a little more fun. Jim's relationship with his PA had been a running joke between the rest of the staff. It was pure speculation, and especially considering they were all hard news journalists, no one had a shred of evidence to back it up, but the two of them did seem particularly pally. Anyway, if it was true, Ruth could certainly have understood it. It was an occupational hazard of being a foreign correspondent that it was difficult to maintain relationships. There was a high turnover of staff and the particular stresses of the job tended to mean you were either absent, overworked or both; not ideal traits in a potential Mr or Miss Right – she knew that from personal experience. She was pulled from her thoughts by the insistent ringing of her desk phone. She grabbed it.

'Miss Boden?'

The voice was American: Texan, Ruth guessed. Low slung and treacly.

'Yes, this is Ruth Boden,' she said.

'This is Jeanne Parsons. I got a message from my housekeeper to call you urgently.'

Ruth was surprised the woman had called back so promptly. Overnight, the Washington office had assisted in tracking down Nick Beddingfield's girlfriend, providing her with a number first thing that morning. Ruth had indeed spoken to the housekeeper, who had rather tersely told her that 'Mizz Jeanne is sleeping.'

'Thank you for calling me back,' said Ruth. 'I'm phoning about your friend Nick Beddingfield.'

There was a pause, and Ruth could hear a door being closed.

'Yes, Nick,' said the woman finally. 'How is he?'

'I'm afraid I have some bad news. Nick Beddingfield is dead.'

Ruth clicked on to her computer and pulled up the photograph of Jeanne Parsons that the Washington office had sent over. It had clearly been taken at some sort of society function; she was wearing an off-the-shoulder ball gown and holding a flute of champagne. She was a perky, smiling forty-something blonde, with a tiny body and big breasts; the sort Ruth imagined to be the life and soul of any party, except she certainly wasn't smiling now.

'Oh no,' she said, her voice trembling. Ruth heard the click and hiss of a cigarette being lit and imagined the hazy blue smoke being blown at the ceiling. *God, I could do with one right now*, she thought.

'How did it happen?' asked Jeanne.

'He was found dead in a hotel room in London, the Riverton. The police are treating it as suspicious.'

'And who are you, Miss Boden? Are you not a police officer?'

'No, I'm a journalist.'

'Ah, that figures,' said the woman. 'So if you're a reporter, I guess you'll know Nick was more than my friend.'

'Yes. And I'm so sorry to have to tell you this.'

There was another pause.

'So what do you want to know?'

Ruth flipped her notebook open.

'I want to know who might have wanted to kill him. Did he have any enemies? Had any business deals gone wrong?'

'That boy ticked off a ton of people over the years, honey. He was always hustling people.'

'Hustling people? How exactly?'

'Whichever way he could. Let's just say he could charm the birds down from the trees – and he often did.'

'So you're saying Nick was a con man?' asked Ruth, her pencil poised over her pad.

'Well that depends on your point of view, doesn't it? Nick was a salesman, he could sell anyone anything – does that make him a con man? He was a businessman, I guess, but he sailed pretty close to the wind sometimes.'

'Like what?'

'One time we went to Dallas and he talked a Ferrari showroom into letting him "borrow" some bright red quarter-of-a-mil monster for the week while he decided if it was "up to his standards". I had to send someone to take it back because I knew *he* was never going to.'

She gave a gentle, affectionate laugh.

'But he was such fun. He made life fun and you don't realise how seductive that can be. When I was with him, I felt we were like Bonnie and Clyde. Little old me, boring society wife.'

'You're married?' said Ruth with surprise, then felt foolish. *Of course* she was married.

'And not to Nicky,' laughed Jeanne. 'Although sometimes I wished I was.'

'How long were you in a relationship for?'

'About two years on and off. I gave Nicky the keys to my

bachelorette flat in Houston and he stayed there when he wasn't flying off around the world.'

'When was the last time you saw him?'

'About a month ago, I guess. I live in Dallas with my husband and only saw Nicky about every month or so for a night at a time – I think you can guess how it all worked. But lately he'd been spending a lot of time in Europe. I did hear things, though.'

'You heard things? About Nick?'

Jeanne sighed.

'What we had was barely an affair, we were both too busy for that. But in my world, people like to talk. This life, this society as they call it, it's a tiny place. Each one of us, we live our lives in a fishbowl, everyone knows everything about everyone. So yes, people knew about me and Nick and they would go out of their way to tell me how they'd seen him in Megève with an American heiress or in Monte Carlo with some old countess. People are vicious, Miss Boden. Quite vicious.'

'And do you know why he was in London?'

'Not exactly, but I spoke to him a couple of weeks ago and he told me he was going to be in England for a big business thing. He said if I heard on the grapevine that he'd been seen in London with a young, beautiful woman, I was not to worry because it was just work.' She laughed again, but this time it sounded sad. 'That was Nick; so sweet. He thought I didn't know about the other women, wanted to spare my feelings.'

'I'm so sorry, Jeanne.'

'So am I,' she whispered, her voice finally breaking. 'So am I.'

26

Cannes was having one of its hottest days of the summer. In the harbour, the gleaming white yachts gently bumped together while the Mediterranean twinkled in approval, as if a thousand diamonds from one of the smarter jewellers on the quayside had been sprinkled over the tide. Sophie wound down the window of their taxi and closed her eyes, feeling the breeze in her hair, the taste of the sea on her tongue – she felt as if she was coming awake after a very long sleep. It was a day that made you feel glad to be alive, but for Sophie that feeling took on a quite literal meaning. She was still shell-shocked from their brush with the Russians and absolutely furious with herself for putting them both in danger.

Josh was obviously unhappy too. He had been silent for most of the forty-minute journey from the outskirts of Nice – still fuming from her revelation in the back of the van – and not even the sight of the bright Riviera streets, hemmed in by happy holidaymakers and chic residents on both sides, was enough to make him smile.

The taxi stopped at a crossing to allow a tall, beautiful woman in a leopard-print bikini to pass. She was wearing five-inch heels and was carrying a tiny dog in a Louis Vuitton holdall.

'I'm not sure Cannes has heard about the global recession,' said Sophie, trying to lighten the mood.

'Russians,' said Josh flatly as an image of the stony-faced

hitmen jumped into her mind. 'The West might be in a recession, but for lots of countries these are boom times. Ten years ago this place was full of the wealthy French and a sprinkling of the Euro elite; now they call the Riviera "Moscow on Sea".'

His expression softened as he pointed to the swish shops and hotels all along the Croisette. 'I bet you every one of those places has someone who speaks Russian these days. They can't afford not to.'

At the harbour, the taxi turned away from the sea and into the old town, stopping on a narrow lane lined on both sides by little boutiques and cafés, a high-rent area for wealthy patrons with sports cars and Range Rovers parked at the meters.

'Are you sure this is the place?' Sophie asked Josh as they paused across the road from a wine shop with an arty display of fine champagne in the window. It had an ornate wooden frontage with carved stone pillars either side of the door; there was even scrolled gold lettering on the glass: *M. Durand, Wine Merchant*. It looked formal, 'establishment' – the last place, in fact, you would expect to be a front for criminal activity.

'A lot of things are not all they appear on the surface,' said Josh, 'I thought you would have worked that out by now.'

Sophie began to object, but then bit her lip. She really had no wish to provoke an argument, especially as she was still feeling so guilty about what had happened in Nice. But still, she felt nervous – intimidated, even – about going inside such a grand-looking shop.

'What are we going to say in there?' she asked.

'*You* aren't going to say anything,' said Josh.

'Of course, *I'm* not allowed to do anything,' she said tartly. 'But what are *you* going to say to him?'

'Give me your purse.'

Sophie frowned. 'Josh, I asked you a question.'

'Give me your purse,' he repeated. Reluctantly she handed it over and watched as he took something out and put it in his pocket.

'What are you doing?' she asked, but he was already crossing the road and Sophie could only follow.

If the exterior of M. Durand's establishment had looked exclusive, the inside was forbidding. There was a pyramid of Cristal champagne at one end of the shop, signs – as Josh had predicted – written in Russian, and a whole wall devoted to the finest red wines, their labels proudly pointing outwards for inspection. Not that you were actually supposed to touch anything, that much was clear. These wines were presented as if they were artworks, their green bottles sculptures in a museum.

'May I help you?' said a pinched forty-something man in heavily accented English. His black eyebrows rose as if to signify that he found the idea extremely unlikely.

Josh took the business card that had been in Sophie's purse moments earlier and deliberately put it on the counter, facing the man.

'Detective Inspector Ian Fox,' he said. 'From Scotland Yard in London. I imagine you've heard of it?'

Sophie saw the man's manner immediately change. His initial self-possession melted away and he became instantly more compliant and eager to please. She imagined that a Russian wielding a chequebook would have had a similar effect.

'Please, give me one moment,' he said, walking behind them to lock the door and turn the 'Ouvert' sign to 'Fermé' before pulling down the blinds.

'We can talk more privately now,' he said slowly. 'I am Monsieur Durand, the proprietor of this establishment. How can I help you?'

Josh cut straight to the chase.

'I'm investigating the death of Nick Beddingfield,' he said. 'You *do* know Mr Beddingfield?'

There was a brief, telling pause as if Monsieur Durand did not know which way to jump.

'Yes, I know him. Not well, but our paths have crossed through my business.'

'Well not any more,' said Josh. 'He was murdered in London on Monday.'

Monsieur Durand made a tutting sound.

'Terrible,' he said. 'Do you know who killed him?'

'Someone violent, ruthless.'

Josh let the words hang in the air. Sophie couldn't help but admire his performance. Forget the knock-off perfume and the vintage watches; Josh McCormack could easily have had a successful career as an actor – he had that chameleon-like ability to inhabit a part, so you completely believed what he was saying.

'That is a shame,' said Monsieur Durand, regaining his composure. 'But I don't understand why you are telling me this.'

'We are looking into every aspect of Mr Beddingfield's life, monsieur. His personal life, his business affairs, everything. You dealt with him as a supplier of fine wines, I assume?'

Monsieur Durand shrugged.

'I get my stock from multiple sources. Auction houses, private cellars, other retailers, but yes, I occasionally dealt with Monsieur Beddingfield.'

Josh leant forward on the counter, meeting Monsieur Durand's eye.

'I'll come straight to the point, monsieur. We have evidence that Mr Beddingfield was supplying you with counterfeit wine.'

'Counterfeit wine?' The Frenchman's eyes opened as wide as an owl's. 'That's impossible!'

'Impossible?' repeated Josh, casually turning his gaze towards the wall of lovingly displayed wine. 'Really? So I take it you can personally vouch for every single bottle on these shelves?'

'I run a respectable business . . .' spluttered the proprietor. 'And I resent the implication.'

Sophie was no expert in non-verbal communication or the 'tells' that signified lying, but she was fascinated to see two small triangles of colour appear on Monsieur Durand's cheeks even as he protested his innocence.

'Let me tell you what I know about the counterfeit wine business,' said Josh, slowly. 'I know it's booming. I know that some collectors who suspect bottles in their cellar to be fake would rather quietly offload the wine to unscrupulous dealers than make a song and dance about it and frighten the market. I think you are such a dealer, Monsieur Durand, and that you also accepted supplies from Mr Beddingfield without asking too much about their provenance.'

Durand's face was now bright red with anger.

'What do you want, Inspector?' he snapped. 'Are you suggesting that I am in some way involved in his death?'

Josh smiled and shook his head.

'Here's the good news, Monsieur Durand. I'm not investigating wine fraud. I'm part of Scotland Yard's murder squad and all I care about is finding who killed Mr Beddingfield.' He narrowed his eyes. 'However, I do have a friend at Interpol who might be very interested in examining your stock. I understand they can get a court order allowing them to open every bottle in your warehouse, should the mood take them.'

Sophie knew that Josh was bluffing, but Durand looked stricken, his face pale.

'We know Nick Beddingfield had a business partner,' said Josh. 'Now all I need from you is a name.'

'I really don't know—'

Josh slammed his hand down on the counter, causing Durand to jerk backwards as if he had been slapped.

'A name,' he repeated.

Durand hesitated for a moment, then his shoulders sagged.

'Sandrine Bouvier.'

From the way the little man said the name, it was obvious they were supposed to recognise it. He looked from Josh to Sophie and back again.

'She is one of the greatest living winemakers,' he frowned. 'Do you not know this?'

'I'm more of a beer man myself,' said Josh. 'Although Officer Ellis here enjoys a tipple, don't you?'

'Have you ever sampled a glass of Pétrus or a Romanée-Conti?' asked Durand.

'A bit out of my price range,' said Sophie, imagining herself as a police constable who'd buy her Chardonnay in Sainsbury's rather than dabble in a £1,500 bottle of Burgundy.

Durand walked over to a case and picked up a bottle, cradling it like a precious jewel.

'Wines like this are so expensive because they are so difficult to produce. The soil, the weather, the winemaker's technique, that's what separates the *premier grand cru* from an ordinary village wine. Which is why I was not sure that Monsieur Nick's wines were counterfeit.'

Josh frowned.

'They were real?'

Durand carefully placed the bottle on the counter.

'One day Nick brought me the most exquisite Cheval Blanc. If he had brought me only one bottle, I would have been convinced. But he had a dozen bottles of a very rare vintage, Inspector – so I asked him where he got them.'

'And?'

'He refused to tell me,' said Durand bitterly, as if reliving the moment. 'But I could not rest. I needed to know where they had come from; it became an obsession. *Oui, bien sûr*, this winemaker was a criminal, but they were also a genius. So I started to follow him.'

He looked up, his eyes glistening. 'And I found my answer: Sandrine Bouvier was his lover.'

Sophie struggled to keep her face expressionless. She was beyond feeling betrayed, but even so, no woman wanted to hear that she was just another conquest, just one of an endless procession of lovers dotted around Europe like pins in a map.

'And Sandrine Bouvier is a renowned winemaker?'

A look of dismay and contempt passed across Durand's face.

'The best. She and her husband own a respected vineyard in the Châteauneuf-du-Pape area.'

'Okay, so this Sandrine was having an affair with Nick Beddingfield,' said Josh, 'but that doesn't mean she was involved in the counterfeit business.'

Durand wagged his finger impatiently.

'No, no, Inspector,' he said. 'It is the only explanation. Nick's wine could only have been made by someone great, an expert blender. Sandrine is such a person, trained in Saint-Émilion, in one of the great estates. She is a wonderful winemaker, a genius, one of the few who could blend such a delicious nectar.'

He took a business card from a holder on the counter and wrote an address on the back with a flourish. 'That is the name of her estate. It's in Provence, perhaps an hour's drive.'

He paused as he handed over the card.

'Please do not mention my name, Inspector. The estate is a good client of mine. A *legitimate* client.'

Josh grunted non-committally, as if he was thinking of something else.

'So tell me, if these wines are so convincing, how can you tell the difference?'

Durand smiled smugly.

'Only a man with a sophisticated palate like mine, with years of experience in the trade, would know.'

He touched the bottle on the counter.

'Believe me, Inspector, this is an exquisite wine, counterfeit or not.'

'This one?' said Josh, picking it up and examining the label. 'How much?'

'Five thousand euros,' smiled Durand. 'That is beyond the salary of a policeman, no?'

'Perhaps, Monsieur Durand,' said Josh flatly. 'But it is also illegal.'

Nodding to Sophie, he turned towards the door, still carrying the bottle.

'But . . . you can't take that, monsieur!' protested Durand. 'It is my livelihood.'

'Sorry, sir,' said Josh, flipping the sign back to '*Ouvert*'. 'Evidence. You have a nice day.'

And they walked out into the sunshine.

27

It wasn't until Ruth was halfway to the tube that she realised she didn't know where she was going. After the telephone call with Jeanne, she had packed up her stuff, waved to Chuck and told him she was heading home – but which home exactly? Her cosy one-bedroom flat in Islington with its uneven floors, messy bookcases and heating turned up full blast? Or David's sterile, pin-neat bachelor pad? She hadn't spoken to David since she had stormed out the previous morning; she couldn't even really remember what that argument had been about. Maybe they had moved in together too quickly, she thought. But then they *had* been dating for two years; wasn't that long enough to know if you wanted to be with someone?

Oh, this is ridiculous, she scolded herself as she ran down the station steps and clunked through the barrier. *You're forty-one years old. Extend the olive branch, be the bigger person.*

She glanced at her watch; it was only four thirty, plenty of time to stop off at the supermarket. She'd buy some steak, good wine and something sweet and sinful, have it all ready for when David got back at eight. That'd give her a couple of hours to work on the Riverton story, then they could kiss and make out. She found herself smiling as she rode the Jubilee line to Docklands. She was in that weird lull when the tubes were eerily quiet before the post-work exodus, so she easily got a seat. She stared out at the blackness of the tunnel, the gentle sway of the train almost hypnotic. However much she tried to think of other things, her mind kept jumping back to Nick Beddingfield; her hazy picture of him was finally starting to feel more distinct, more solid. Far from being a wealthy businessman, he was possibly – no, *probably* – a fraudster and, as a criminal, even a white-collar criminal operating in the upper echelons of society, he was likely to have countless unsavoury people with a beef against him. That was good news for Sophie Ellis, of course, as it was looking less and less likely that she was his killer. But if not Sophie, who? Ruth thought back to her conversation with Jeanne Parsons and the comment Nick had made to her; something along the lines of, 'If anyone sees me in London with a beautiful woman, don't worry, it's only business.'

Was the woman he was referring to Sophie Ellis? She certainly fitted the description. But would he think of her as 'business'? Had Nick been trying to con Sophie? Maybe get her to invest in a bogus Texan oil well? Ruth wondered if Inspector Fox had any of this information; probably. Barbara Beddingfield had told her that Nick had been charged four years ago; that would have been on his record. It was irritating how closely Fox played his cards to his chest. For a moment Ruth considered calling Dan Davis – he was always more than happy to leak information on the vague promise of a reward – but then she rejected the idea. She had enough complications with men at the moment.

She got off the tube and headed for the Marks and Spencer at Canary Wharf plaza for her made-up feast, then popped into Hotel Chocolat for a cute little box of expensive truffles, although she couldn't resist breaking into them on the short walk to David's apartment. He wouldn't notice a couple were missing, she thought.

She frowned as she opened the door of the flat. She could immediately smell the distinctive aroma of her Jo Malone

Pomegranate Noir candle – she'd bought it for herself as a moving-in gift only last week. Strange: it wasn't like David to even notice a scented candle, let alone light one. Then she heard the sound. A splash, dripping water, coming from the bathroom. Involuntarily, Ruth's mind leapt back to that Riverton Hotel room, to Nick Beddingfield's lifeless toes pointing at the ceiling. But that was stupid: what was she thinking? That there was some crazed bathroom killer on the loose who had now murdered her lover? Much more likely David had come home early and was washing off the grime of the city. She smiled to herself: she could surprise him, maybe wash his back, that'd be a good way to make up. She tiptoed towards the bathroom and, with one finger, pushed open the door.

The floor was covered with clothes: David's boxer shorts, David's blue shirt, but also a tiny lace bra and a barely-worth-it thong, all tangled on top of each other. Bile rose in her throat, but she couldn't help looking. In the low candlelight there was David, swathed in bubbles, and in front of him – *of course, of course* – was the blonde PR Ruth had seen him with in the bar the other night. The girl's head was resting tenderly on David's chest, her breasts peeking out just above the water as David played lazily with her nipples. For a moment the scene was frozen, suspended in time. Then Ruth dropped the bag of shopping with a clatter.

'Fuck, Ruth!'

David sat bolt upright, spilling sudsy water all over the floor. The blonde, whose name Ruth couldn't even remember, leapt out of the water, grabbed a towel and pushed past her without making eye contact.

Ruth bent down, grabbed the pile of clothes from the floor and threw them after her.

'Here. You'll be needing these,' she said.

David was standing now, his flaccid cock covered with bubbles. Pathetic, ridiculous.

'I'm so sorry, Ruth,' he stuttered. 'I never meant for you to see this.'

'Of course you didn't,' she spat. 'That's why you brought that slut back here at five o'clock when you thought I would be at work.'

David's expression changed.

'Susie's not a slut,' he said.

Ruth almost laughed. Her boyfriend was standing there, bubbles sliding down his legs, trying to defend another woman. How gallant.

'Oh no? So what is she then?' said Ruth, whipping a towel at David, suddenly disgusted by his nakedness.

'She's . . . I like her,' he said simply.

His words felt like being slapped. She would have preferred it if David had gone for the standard 'it's all been a terrible mistake, she meant nothing' defence. But it hadn't been a mistake, had it? The only mistake had been letting Ruth find out about it.

'Well if you liked her so much, perhaps you should have thought about that before you asked me to move in with you,' she said.

A look of shame and discomfort crossed David's face.

'I don't know why I did that,' he said.

'No, neither do I, David,' said Ruth.

She heard a bang – the front door closing. At least the girl was gone. For now, anyway. With sudden clarity, Ruth knew she would be back. David would be forced to make a choice, and Ruth knew deep down he would go for the younger, perkier blonde who flattered him and made him feel important. Well, she wasn't going to hang around for him to inflict that final wound. She walked through into the bedroom and grabbed a bag, shoving clothes inside.

'Please, Ruth,' said David, following her in. 'Don't go off like this, we need to talk.'

'What is there to talk about?' she shouted. 'You've fucked

some airhead bimbo and now I'm leaving. That all seems pretty straightforward to me.'

She yanked open a drawer and grabbed a handful of her underwear – comfortable, everyday underwear, she thought, not like Susie's lacy wisps.

'No, actually,' she said, turning to face him. 'Actually I would like to ask something. How long has this been going on?' Ever the journalist, suddenly Ruth wanted to know every fact, every detail.

David shrugged, the towel clasped in one hand at his waist.

'Just a handful of times,' he said.

Then it hit her. *That* night, the night they'd come back here and had amazing sex, the night he'd asked her to move in – he'd been seeing Susie then. In fact, was that why they had had sex in the first place? Because he had been canoodling with his new girlfriend in the bar, got all horny and didn't know what to do with it? Ruth felt filthy and violated.

He reached out for her but she flinched backwards.

'Don't touch me,' she hissed.

'Fine,' he said, suddenly truculent. 'Do it your way. You always do.'

'And what's that supposed to mean?' Ruth could hear her voice rising. 'That this is all my fault?'

'No, Ruth, nothing is ever your fault, is it?' he said bitterly. 'It's fine for *you* to be late, it's fine for *you* to be worried about your career, but when have you ever paid any attention to me or what I need?'

Ruth just gaped at him. 'Unbelievable,' she said. 'You really are trying to make this my fault, aren't you?'

'Ruth, I'm not saying—'

'Yes, you bloody are! If you'd wanted to tell me about your work or your bruised fucking feelings, why didn't you try talking to me? How many times have I asked you,

"Honey, what's wrong? How can I help?" But no, it was always, "Nothing, I'm fine."'

'Well, maybe if you'd tried a little harder—'

'Fuck off, David,' snapped Ruth. 'This is *nothing* to do with me. Maybe we were having problems, maybe we could have worked it out, maybe not. But instead of fixing things, you chose to screw someone else. Someone who will laugh at your jokes, feed you stories, feed your ego.'

'Susie isn't—'

'Spare me, David,' said Ruth. 'I'm sure she's wonderful. And I'm sure you'll be very happy together. Oh, until she gets bored waiting for you to finish your phone call to Tokyo and screws someone else she thinks can help her career.'

He began to object, but Ruth wasn't listening. She grabbed her bag and walked to the door.

'Oh, and by the way,' she said, holding up the key to the front door David had only given her a week ago. 'If I see one word of that escort story in your shitty little paper, I will come back here and cut your balls off.'

She opened the door, closed it carefully behind her, then burst into tears.

28

If Sophie closed her eyes, she could imagine she was on holiday. With the car's window open, she could feel the warm continental breeze on her face and for a moment she could convince herself that it was two, three summers earlier, she was just jumping in a cute little Jeep and pootling down to the beach in some gorgeous corner of Italy or Spain. It was only when she opened her eyes that she saw the inside of the cramped hire car and realised where she really was. Bumping along the back roads of Provence with someone she barely knew, trying to unearth the past of a dead man. Not how she'd planned to spend the summer, that was for sure. At least the countryside was gorgeous and distracting: endless rolling hills of green or sun-scorched orange and narrow winding roads lined by cloud-scraping poplar trees. And then there was Josh. Moody and maddening, sarcastic and confrontational, but there were worse people to get lost with, she thought, watching him with the crumpled map on his knees, his brow furrowed, his eyes focused on the pothole-strewn roads.

'There it is,' he announced, craning his neck to read a passing road sign. He twisted the steering wheel suddenly to the right and shoved the map at Sophie. 'Bois du Lac, five kilometres, see if you can find it. We must be close to the road for Château Cavail by now.'

Sophie looked at the map, tracing their journey from

Cannes up into the foothills of Provence towards Avignon. They hadn't taken the most direct route, partly due to missed turnings and the rather laissez-faire attitude of the French towards road signs, and partly because it made sense. The more they could make their movements random and unpredictable, the less likely it was anyone could catch up with them. Not that she was in any particular hurry to get to Château Cavail, anyway. As far as Sophie was concerned, all she would find there were more questions and more heartache. She knew by now that what she had imagined she had with Nick was just that – imagined. And she was fairly sure there were dozens of women around Europe who had shared the same delusion, possibly at the same time. But she had no desire to meet any of Nick's ex-lovers, especially a glamorous winemaker Monsieur Durand had described as a genius. If she'd had her choice, Sophie would have simply stopped the car and walked through the fields until she found a stream, then bathed her feet and felt the sinking sun on her face. But she couldn't do that, could she? The freedom, the liberation she had felt arriving in Paris had turned into another kind of trap – she felt herself being forced down a path. She didn't know what she'd find at the end, but she was fairly sure it wasn't going to be a sunny meadow full of butterflies.

'Well this is the Bois du Lac, though I can't see the *lac*,' said Josh.

The village Josh had spotted on the map was really just one dusty road with a few boxy cottages straggling either side; the population couldn't be pushing much past two hundred. Still, there was a butcher's, a baker's and a chemist, plus a garage that obviously doubled as the propane outlet and farm shop.

'There!' said Sophie, pointing to a sign. It was peeling and half hidden by an overgrown hedge, but she could still read: 'Château Cavail, 1 km'.

'At least it's a decent road,' said Josh. 'They must have to drive trucks up and down here with deliveries all the time.'

They drove up into the estate, hemmed in on both sides by line after line of crocodile-green vines set out in shaggy rows that undulated with the curves of the hills. Finally they came over a rise and saw the house: a shimmering white château with turrets at each corner and a long drive with yews either side.

'Nice place,' said Josh as they pulled up by the wide stone steps at the front of the house. 'No wonder Nick wanted a piece of this.'

'Josh, please,' said Sophie quietly.

'Sorry,' he said, looking genuinely apologetic.

'I'm not exactly looking forward to meeting this Sandrine, even if it does seem as though we have a lot in common.'

'Yeah, I can see that. Well, think of yourself as Constable Ellis again. We're just here to get information, remember? Because the more we know about what Nick was doing, the quicker we can get you back home, okay?'

Sophie gave him a weak smile. 'Okay.'

As they got out of the car, a tall woman with long black hair was walking towards them from the side of the house. She was beautiful; chiselled features and pale-brown skin and dressed in a loose smock that couldn't disguise her slender figure. Sophie knew this was Sandrine Bouvier before she even spoke; she just had to be. She was everything Sophie was not: exotic, assured, with an air of experience and, yes, sexiness that so many French women seemed to possess.

'You are the people who called?' the woman asked in perfect English.

'Yes,' said Josh, shaking her hand. 'Mrs Bouvier?'

She nodded. 'And you say you want to talk to me for a newspaper article?'

Josh shook his head slowly.

'I'm afraid I wasn't entirely truthful with you on the

255

telephone, Mrs Bouvier. I'm afraid we have some bad news.'

She looked from Josh to Sophie, then back again.

'Bad news?' she asked, the flicker of panic visible in her hazel eyes. 'Then you had better come inside.'

The chateau was cool and surprisingly dark – *built to keep the sun out*, thought Sophie as they walked across stone-flagged floors, past simple rustic furniture with tapestry cushions and cut flowers in terracotta pots. Sophie guessed that most of the women on her fitness client list would pay a small fortune to have their multi-million-pound Georgian town houses transformed into a pale imitation of something this tasteful and understated.

Sandrine led them out on to a wide terrace at the back of the house with a fine view of the vineyards stretching away in their endless rows. A thatched pergola shaded them from the sun as they sat down around a wooden table.

'It's Nick, isn't it?' said Sandrine finally.

Josh nodded. 'My name is Josh, this is Sophie. Nick was a friend of ours, Mrs Bouvier.'

'Call me Sandrine, please.'

'Nick is dead, Sandrine,' he said. 'He was killed in London a few days ago.'

She looked away, nodding, silent for several seconds.

'Do you know? I was almost expecting this,' she said, inhaling through her teeth. 'Not today, of course, you never know when something like this will come, but Nick was . . . He lived that way, you know? He burned too brightly.'

Sophie saw tears in the woman's eyes and felt wretched. On the drive from Cannes, she had imagined this meeting, imagined what Sandrine Bouvier was like, how she would react to the news of Nick's death. But now she was here, face to face with this woman's grief, it was a more difficult meeting than she had thought. Sandrine had loved Nick Beddingfield, she could see that. He wasn't hard to love, after all.

A young woman in an apron appeared carrying a tray, and Sandrine quickly stood up and walked over to the edge of the terrace, staring out at the vineyards, hiding her tears.

'*Sur la table, merci, Hélène*,' she said, and the girl left a bottle of wine and three glasses, then disappeared.

'You must excuse me,' said Sandrine, as she returned, dabbing her eyes. 'As you will appreciate, my relationship with Nick was a secret. If my husband ever found out . . . Let us say it is best the staff have nothing to gossip about, no?'

She poured them each a glass of the deep red wine, concentrating intently on the bottle.

'You made this here, on the estate?' said Sophie, smelling the wine's heavy bouquet.

'I blended it myself,' she said, taking a long, steadying sip.

'Really?' said Sophie. 'This is excellent. Truly.'

Monsieur Durand had been right; if Sandrine really had created this wine, it was very impressive. Rich, but not over-powering, it was as if ripe grapes were bursting on your tongue.

Sandrine shrugged. 'It is the only thing I was ever good at. Actually, it is why I am here,' she said, raising a hand to indicate the house. 'I travelled all over the world studying winemaking techniques: Napa, the Hunter Valley, Chile. But then I met my husband and' – she shrugged – 'back *en France*.'

'Do you make wine for your husband's estate?'

She snorted. 'The wine industry is dominated by men. As a woman, no one took me seriously; even my husband sidelined me to the role of *femme au foyer*. I think you say "housewife". He just wanted me to make babies.'

She looked away again. The sadness in her eyes was replaced by something else – fear.

'How was he killed?' she asked softly.

Josh exchanged a look with Sophie.

'He was found dead in his hotel room on Monday morning.'

'He hadn't returned my calls in several days,' said Sandrine, thinking out loud.

Sophie felt another wave of guilt, working out that he had probably been avoiding Sandrine's calls when he had been with her.

'It was a wound to the head,' continued Josh. 'He was probably hit by an intruder.'

'Someone he knew?' she asked tensely.

'The police don't know,' said Sophie, feeling suddenly more courageous in the company of Sandrine.

'Who found him?'

'I did,' said Sophie, feeling awkward.

Sandrine nodded.

'I see.'

Sophie watched the Frenchwoman's mouth sour with hurt. She hoped she was too discreet to ask any more about the circumstances in which she had discovered Nick's body.

The woman rubbed her eyes and turned back.

'Then we must celebrate his life, no?' she said, raising her glass. '*Bonne chance, mon chéri*,' she said, looking up to the blue sky.

They sat that way for a long minute, Sophie sipping her wine and wondering if Sandrine had any idea about Nick's other women. Perhaps not; he was very good at making you feel you were the only one who mattered to him. Maybe even a sophisticated, worldly woman like Sandrine Bouvier could be taken in.

'How did you get involved with Nick?' Sophie asked finally.

'You know how easy that is,' quipped the Frenchwoman.

It was a few moments before she spoke again.

'My marriage is not happy,' she said. 'But we are Catholic. Pierre, my husband, won't divorce me, but he is happy to have mistresses all over the world. In fact, he is in Avignon with his girlfriend right now,' she said, curling her lip. 'Two years ago, I took a lover – no one important, a man from the village; I just needed to feel wanted again. But Pierre found out and he beat me until I was blue.'

She looked up at them, her green eyes sparkling defiantly.

'Oh, you say, why not leave him, yes? Of course I would have, but I had no money. Pierre controls everything, including my bank account.'

Sandrine paused, a half-smile coming on to her face.

'I met Nick at a party thrown by the wine merchant Jean Polieux in Antibes. Nick was different, funny – exciting. And we began an affair. I was so scared that Pierre might find out, but I couldn't help myself.' She turned to look at Sophie. 'I fell in love.'

'But you never left your husband,' said Sophie.

'I told Nick I wanted to leave Pierre. We had a plan to make enough money so I could start a new life.'

'The counterfeiting,' said Josh. Sandrine looked at him sharply, but he just raised his eyebrows.

'Nick was my friend, madame. He told me everything; that is why we are here. I knew he would want you to hear of his passing from a friend.'

'That is kind,' she said, her voice cracking. 'Thank you.'

Josh glanced at Sophie again.

'But that's not all. Nick was murdered. We need your help to find out who killed him. What you were doing here, well, it could be important.'

Sandrine gazed at Josh for a moment, then nodded.

'Come,' she said, standing and leading them down from the terrace, along a gravel path and through a green wooden door. Sophie immediately felt goose bumps rise on her bare arms as the temperature dropped. They were inside a large stone warehouse with concrete floors and a grey steel gantry running down one side. The rest of the space was taken up by hundreds of wooden barrels, all stacked on top of each other. Sandrine unlocked a door and they stepped into a large room dominated by a long table cluttered with dozens of bottles, flasks, even a small stove. It was like a cross between a chemistry lab and a farmhouse kitchen.

'My sanctuary,' she said with a smile. 'This is where I come to create my wines, such as the one you tasted at the house and . . . the others.'

She chose two bottles from a shelf and gave one to Sophie to examine.

'Pétrus 2003,' Sophie said, reading the label. 'This is a two-thousand-euro bottle of wine.'

Sandrine put the bottle into a machine and pulled a lever to remove the cork, then poured the dark liquid into a wine balloon and handed it to a wide-eyed Sophie.

'Try it, I think you'll enjoy it.'

Sophie swirled it around for a minute or so to oxidise the liquid, mesmerised for a moment by the deep purple colour. Then she raised it to her nose to take in the aroma and quickly sucked in a mouthful, letting it wash over her tongue to absorb the flavours.

'What can you taste?' asked Sandrine.

'Blackberry, roasted coffee, maybe even vanilla?'

'Exceptional, isn't it?' she smiled. 'Now try this.'

She opened a second bottle, this time without a label, and poured the plum-coloured wine into another glass. With a glance at Josh, Sophie repeated the process.

'It's Pétrus,' she said. 'It's the same wine. Isn't it?'

'No, it is something I created.' Sandrine shrugged. 'I made twenty bottles of it. I will give you one to take back to London.'

'But this is amazing,' said Sophie. 'You're so talented, why isn't your chateau more famous?'

'Because I am not the winemaker. Sure, I help out with blending, tasting, finalising the wines, but not officially. Even if I was appointed as head winemaker tomorrow, it takes years, even decades for a winery to establish itself to the point where it can charge more than a hundred euros a bottle. Even then, you need the nod from influential critics like Robert Parker.'

She opened her hands to indicate her blending lab.

'So this remains my hobby: to create the best wine I can, perhaps to match the masters.'

'Does your husband know?'

She laughed mirthlessly.

'Of course not. He is never here. On business, in bed with his mistresses. And none of the staff dares ask questions about the wife's little hobby.'

'And it was your hobby which Nick suggested as a way out for you?' asked Josh.

Sandrine nodded.

'Come, let's walk back to the house,' she said. She locked the warehouse and led them along another path which wound through the vineyards.

'I knew about counterfeit wines, of course, they have always been part of the industry,' said Sandrine as they walked. 'But the way Nick talked about it, he didn't make it sound like it would be something illegal. He said it was a way to use my talents – and if the wine we put in our bottles was as good as the real thing, who would ever know? He made it sound like my escape.'

'What wines did you make for sale?'

'Older ones generally.'

'Why?' asked Josh, clearly interested.

'There was no point making more modern vintages. Many of them are still in the cellars of the wine producers, and nowadays the estates use sophisticated anti-fraud devices: proof-tagging, microchipping. But old wines are different. Before 1960, many of the top producers sold barrels to private clients or dealers, who bottled the wine themselves.'

She turned to look at them.

'How many people have tasted a 1947 Cheval Blanc or even know what one looks like? These people who buy wines, they have no knowledge of wine,' she said with distaste. 'They only care that it is rare and valuable.'

She stretched up to pull a handful of grapes from a vine and passed them to Sophie to try. They were sweet and juicy.

'I made the wine here on the estate from these grapes, plus other varieties of grape I buy wholesale,' she explained. 'Nick took the bottles from the chateau to a cellar near Avignon. We have about ten thousand bottles of blended wine we pass off as three-hundred-euro burgundy. Then a few hundred bottles of really good *grand cru* that he sells for fifteen hundred euros or more. Nick handled the entire sales operation.'

Sophie did a quick mental calculation. This was millions of euros' worth of counterfeit wine. She looked at Josh and saw that he had reached a similar conclusion. Two million euros was certainly enough of a motive for someone to kill Nick.

They turned back towards the chateau, the sun slanting through the vines, striping the red earth.

'Do you think Nick could have fallen out with a customer?' asked Josh. 'Maybe annoyed someone?'

'It's possible, but Nick was careful. We mainly sold to wealthy professionals, lawyers, bankers who wanted to impress clients at dinner parties, or small boutique wine merchants like Monsieur Durand, who don't ask too many questions about provenance. There were also a few sales directly to rich Russian and Chinese clients he met on the Euro party circuit. That was why he had gone to London, to collect more business. That is what he told me,' she said, her voice falling more quiet. 'The truth is that he was getting ready to leave me.'

'How do you know?'

'There was another lover.'

'The countess?' said Sophie.

'The old woman with the Paris apartment?' Sandrine

snorted. 'I know all about her. She was rich and lonely. They weren't lovers. They were friends. Nick saw her occasionally; he made her life feel exciting. In return she let him use the apartment.'

'So who are you talking about?'

'I thought it might be you,' she said quietly. 'In the last weeks, before he left for London, he was distant. I kept catching him on the phone to someone, talking in a low voice. And when he called me, I had the sense that someone else was in the room.'

'It can't be me,' said Sophie fiercely. 'I only met Nick just over a week ago. We bumped into each other at a party. I had never seen or spoken to him before that.'

'So you are not "A"?'

'"A"?' replied Sophie.

'I am a woman.' Sandrine smiled. 'I know how love works. So of course I went through his phone. There were dozens of texts from someone called "A". The last text I saw said "Meet at Jean's party on 10th", which I took to be Jean Polieux's annual party.'

'So you have no idea who A is?'

Sandrine shrugged. 'As much idea as you do, *ma chérie*.'

'Did you take down the number?' asked Josh.

The Frenchwoman nodded.

'Did you call it?' asked Sophie.

Sandrine smiled.

'This is a woman's instinct, is it not? You want to know who your rival is, so you know how to fight them.'

Her face turned sad.

'No, in the end, I could not. I suppose I didn't think I would like what I was going to hear.'

They had reached the front entrance of the chateau now.

'Could you give me the number?' said Josh. 'It might be the link we're looking for.'

They followed Sandrine into a study. She crossed to a

writing desk just inside the door and pulled out a hardback address book, writing down the number on a Post-it note in her loopy Gallic writing.

'Here, I have something else for you too,' she said, opening a drawer and handing Josh a stiff white card. 'This is the invitation to Polieux's party. You should go. Perhaps you will find something there too.'

Thanking her, they walked back out into the sunshine. At the top of the stone steps, Sophie turned back to Sandrine.

'What will you do now?' she asked.

Sandrine gave her a half-smile. 'Do not worry, I will be all right. Making the wine with Nick, it gave me confidence in what I do. I think I will try to sell my own wines – and if Pierre doesn't like it, well . . . as I say, I will be okay.'

Sophie nodded, about to follow Josh down to the car, but Sandrine touched her arm.

'Today, my heart aches, tomorrow too, I think,' she said, holding Sophie's gaze. 'But a little piece of him will always be there.'

'I know,' said Sophie, reaching across to hug her goodbye. 'I know just how you feel.'

29

Ruth stood in the darkening street, staring up at the windows of the *Tribune*'s office, two or three of them glowing orange even though it was past seven. *Is this it?* she thought. *Is this really home?* When she had tearfully run out of David's building and grabbed a cab, there had been no hesitation when the driver asked 'Where to?'

She had come straight to the one place she felt safe and valued, the place where she could lose herself in words and facts and stories. The place she could hide.

She allowed herself a wry smile as she walked inside, because that was the truth. All her life she had used work as a shield, throwing herself into her job when her parents had split up, burying herself in more and more assignments when her dad had died. She had blamed work for relationships that had gone awry, friendships that had petered out, the motherhood that had never happened, because, well, it was easier than looking inside herself for the real reason.

Waving to the security guard and swiping her card to activate the lift, Ruth thought back to a relationship she had once had with a South African photographer when she had been stationed in Cape Town. Jonathon. He had been so handsome – sharp, too. In fact, now she thought about it, Jon had been pretty damn perfect. So what had gone wrong? Isaac Grey, that was what. He had called wondering whether Ruth was interested in a post in Cairo. She had taken it on the spot, explaining to her heartbroken lover that it was a career opportunity she simply couldn't miss. Of course that had been a lie, like all the others. Work was simply an excuse not to let anyone get close. Not for the first time, Ruth wondered if decisions were made in life not because of what you really wanted, but because of what you were afraid of.

As the lift took her up to the office floor, she closed her eyes and immediately she could see them together, as clearly as if it had just happened.

Her mum and Robert, the publisher of her dad's paper. Together on the kitchen table, her mother's long cotton skirt hiked up around her waist, his black leather briefcase propped up next to the radio blasting out the country and western songs she loved to listen to when she made meatloaf. And now it had happened to Ruth. Twenty-odd years later, the second she had let someone get close to her, she had been betrayed.

'I thought you were going home.'

Ruth jumped as Chuck's face appeared above the partition. She clutched at her chest and let out a long breath.

'Don't do that,' she said. 'My life flashed before me.'

'How was it?' smiled Chuck.

'Not as exciting as I'd have liked. Anyway, what are you doing here?'

'Finishing up your research about Michael Asner. All is about to be revealed.'

'Well I'm glad someone is working hard today,' she said, her mind involuntarily jumping back to the image of David standing in the bath.

'Is there a problem?' frowned Chuck.

Ruth sighed. 'Do you fancy a drink?'

The Frontline Club, just a stone's throw from Paddington station, was Ruth's favourite London watering hole. Over the years she had become a permanent fixture at the bar, and she couldn't remember a time when she didn't have a good night out there. It was not a trendy media social watering hole like Soho or Shoreditch House, but in Ruth's eyes, it was infinitely more interesting: a members' club whose *raison d'être* was to champion independent journalism. She loved the gung-ho adventurers she might meet there: the war correspondents just back from the Sudan, the photographers who spent more time in Jeeps than on the tube. She loved mixing with them, partly because they had shared experiences and friends, but partly because they reminded her why she had gone into journalism in the first place.

Ruth got a bottle of wine from the bar and found a table, while Chuck slid in opposite her and took a file out of his man bag. *Gay?* wondered Ruth idly. Choice of bag did not define your sexuality, of course, but then she couldn't remember Chuck ever talking about any girlfriends, and he *could* be pretty bitchy. It would be a shame if he did swing the other way: he was good-looking in a clean-cut pretty-boy sort of way. *Stop thinking like that, Ruth*, she scolded herself. *It's only been about an hour since you became single.* She closed her eyes to push the thought from her head – to push all thoughts from her head – and concentrated on the wine. She poured two generous glasses, then pushed one to Chuck.

'Okay, tell me what you got.'

'So you wanted to know about Michael Asner,' said Chuck, opening his file.

'Yes,' she said, knocking back her wine. 'Come on, blow my socks off.'

Chuck fumbled with his papers, and Ruth had to remind herself that it was probably quite intimidating for this green new boy to be interrogated by his de facto boss. She remembered what it was like those first few months in the Washington office, how terrified she had been of Isaac Grey and all the other grizzled old-school print guys. Chuck obviously had a sharp mind – he had graduated *summa cum laude* from Yale – but that didn't mean he was good under pressure. Still, she liked him, and you didn't see many academic high-flyers scrambling to get into the inkies these days. With so many tempting openings on Wall Street or in Silicon Valley, who in their right mind would jump onto the sinking ship of print journalism?

'Take your time,' she said kindly. 'It's not an exam.'

Chuck looked up from his notes and gave her a weak smile. 'Sorry, just a little disorganised.'

'Well, let's skip the back story,' she said. 'We all know that Asner basically promised the punters a huge return on their money, but he didn't bother to invest any of it.'

Chuck nodded. 'Yes, it was a pyramid scheme: he'd use the money from new investors to pay supposed "profits" to people further up the scheme, and seeing the big returns, the original people invested again. And so it went, round and round.'

'Well the thing I'm interested in is the *who*, not the *how*,' said Ruth, pouring more wine into her glass. 'I spoke to a woman in Surrey, the wife of an ordinary accountant, who lost everything in the Asner scam. Is that common?'

'Yes, almost a quarter of the victims were what you'd call ordinary investors,' said Chuck, flipping through his notes. 'Asner made his investment seem incredibly exclusive, but he allowed a lot of feeder funds from London, Paris, Madrid to join in, and that's how mom and pop investors got caught. They were caught up in the hype, flattered to be allowed in – the headlines make you think it's all billionaires who can afford it, but I think a lot of people will lose everything because of Asner.'

Ruth nodded thoughtfully.

'Which brings me to the big question: how was Asner killed?'

'It was a prison fight about three months ago,' said Chuck, pulling out another sheet of notes. 'The official account is that two Russian thugs were having a brawl and Asner was simply in the wrong place at the wrong time – got stabbed in the neck with a shiv: a makeshift prison knife.'

Ruth leant forward on her elbows.

'And what do you think, Chuck? Do you think that's what happened?'

Chuck shrugged and sipped his wine. 'If you're asking for my gut reaction, I'd say that sounds very convenient. A lot of very rich, very powerful people lost money with him. Moguls, oligarchs, some even say organised crime syndicates used the scheme as a way of laundering cash. None of these people are the kind who like to lose money.'

'So you think someone had him killed? For revenge or punishment, maybe?'

Ruth didn't expect an answer, of course, she was simply talking it through, weighing up the facts, but she also respected Chuck's opinion. She knew the pages and pages of notes spread out in front of him were the result of hours of diligent research: telephone calls, first-hand interviews, digging out documents and court reports – the proper way, not just half an hour surfing the net.

'I think it's highly likely someone *wanted* Asner dead,' said Chuck. 'And it's the easiest thing in the world to have somebody killed in an American prison.'

'Who's been watching too many episodes of *The Sopranos*?' said Ruth.

'A bit before my time,' said Chuck.

God, he must have been in junior high when that started, thought Ruth, feeling horribly old.

'No, a life sentence means life in the States,' continued Chuck, 'so what's to stop some guy who is already serving a hundred years from stabbing some fat old banker? It's no skin off his nose and he could probably get a few cartons of cigarettes out of it.'

'So the money,' said Ruth. 'Where did it all go?'

Chuck tapped the table with one finger.

'That's the billion-dollar question – literally, as it happens. Of course, a huge chunk of it funded Asner's lifestyle. He had homes around the globe, a fleet of vintage cars, a private jet, a multimillion-dollar art collection, all the usual stuff.'

'Nice for some,' said Ruth.

'Yes,' agreed Chuck, his confidence growing as he warmed to the subject. 'But here's where it gets interesting. No one knows how much went into the Asner fund exactly, but it almost certainly ran into the billions. When Asner was finally caught by the SEC, he was extremely helpful with the authorities, telling them all about his bank accounts and properties around the world, but the Securities and Exchange Commission says they only recovered something like four hundred million.'

'So where did the rest go?'

'Exactly. There are endless conspiracy theories about it; it's like Blackbeard's treasure. But it's logical that a cunning, manipulative crook like Asner would have planned for the possibility of getting caught. He would definitely have buried some gold somewhere.'

Ruth was drawn in by Chuck's enthusiasm. She usually found financial news quite dull – God knows she'd had to listen to enough of it with David – but the Asner scandal was like a blockbuster thriller: wealthy victims, pantomime villains, jets and limos, even the tantalising hint of pirate treasure. But juicy though it was, Ruth had a story to put together. This was a murder case, not a profile of a financial meltdown. Peter Ellis's involvement with Asner was little more than a footnote, just another layer of the tragedy and bad luck that the Ellis family – specifically Sophie Ellis – had been forced to endure. Unless she could find something more, of course.

'Okay, so let's get back on track with the Riverton case,' she said, turning to signal to Hayden, the Welsh barman, for another bottle. 'How deep is the connection between Asner and Peter Ellis?'

Chuck pouted and pulled out a black and white picture of some young men in mortar boards and gowns.

'They both went to St John's College, Oxford,' he said. 'Asner had graduated from Columbia University and had gone there on a Fulbright scholarship. Peter and Michael met through the university yacht club and became best friends, according to most of the people I spoke to there. What's also interesting is that Edward Gould, Sophie Ellis's solicitor, was at Oxford then too.'

'Gould knew Asner?' she said. That seemed more than a little convenient. 'Did you speak to him about it?' she asked.

Chuck nodded.

'Typical lawyer, very slippery. He just said Asner and Peter were thick as thieves. He remembers they started a company together selling sailing gear. As you might imagine, Asner was a brilliant salesman: loud, outgoing, pushy. Gould remembers buying a waterproof jacket from him which leaked. I don't think he's ever really forgiven him.' Chuck smiled.

'But did Asner get in touch with Ellis after the scandal? That would be some nice colour for the story.'

Chuck pulled a face.

'I tried Julia Ellis, but she was less help than the lawyer. If I had to guess, I'd say that if Peter did speak to Asner, he wouldn't have shared it with his wife. There's no question that Julia hates Asner with a passion. Again, this is a hunch, but I got the sense her hostility wasn't just because they lost all their money through the investment. I think she was resentful that Asner had gone on to be so successful while they were stuck in Surrey. Apparently Peter had asked Asner to be Sophie's godfather, but he was "too grand" – Julia's words – to bother replying to them.'

Ruth smiled; this was good. No answers as such, but then

she hadn't really expected that, but there was plenty of solid information that she could build on.

'Excellent work, Chuck,' she said, squeezing his arm. 'Seriously, it's very useful.'

Chuck shut his file and shrugged. 'If I had longer . . .'

'Listen, the FBI and the SEC couldn't get to the bottom of it, I didn't think you'd crack the case, but it's brought the picture into focus.'

She felt a pang of guilt as the boy put his file back in his bag. He probably had no idea that the writing was on the wall for the bureau, and if Isaac did close it down, then where would he go? Degree from Yale, contacts in the media world; he'd probably be fine, maybe even fare better than Ruth herself. At least he was young and relatively cheap – on a résumé, that could count for a lot these days.

'Let's get drunk,' she said, lifting her glass defiantly.

By eleven thirty, Ruth was absolutely hammered. She was faintly aware that she had been loud and opinionated, rather than witty and entertaining. She felt a wave of tiredness but had no intention of going back to her flat, with its empty wardrobes and fridge with its single jar of half-eaten olives.

'Let's hit a club, Chuck,' she slurred. 'I haven't been out dancing in years.'

'How about I get you a taxi home?' said Chuck.

'Ooh, a young man offering to take me home,' she giggled, tipping her wine glass back to get at the last dribble of Chablis. 'My lucky night.'

His face was indistinct, but Ruth didn't think Chuck was buying her seduction technique.

'All right,' she sighed, clambering to her feet. 'I can take a hint.'

Chuck held up Ruth's coat, but she missed the sleeve and staggered against him.

'Sorry. Too much to drink,' she said in a theatrical stage

whisper. 'It's just that I found my boyfriend in the bath with a woman fifteen years younger than me this afternoon. Is that bad?'

Chuck gave a sympathetic smile. 'I always thought you deserved better than him,' he said quietly.

'Now you tell me!' she said, slapping him on the arm. 'I could have saved myself all that bother!'

Chuck steered her through the bar and out on to the street. For a moment, the pavement felt unsteady beneath her and she grabbed Chuck's shoulder.

'See? You're always there for me, aren't you?' she mumbled, pushing her face close, but missing her aim and cracking her head against his.

'Oww!' she cried, sinking down on to the steps of the club, clutching at her brow, although she was too anaesthetised to feel much pain. 'Sorry, Chuck, sorry, sorry, sorry,' she said, as he sat down next to her. 'You should stay away from me, I'm a walking disaster area.'

'Don't be silly,' said Chuck.

'Look at me! I'm just some broken-down old hack.'

'Ruth, you are the reason I got a transfer to London,' said Chuck seriously. 'I'd read your pieces in the *Tribune* and hoped I'd get to work with you.'

Ruth squinted at him, trying to absorb this information.

'Really?' was all she could manage.

'Yes, Ruth. You're brilliant, you must know that.'

'But I'm drunk,' she whispered. 'And I'm a fraud.'

'You're drunk all right,' said Chuck with a smirk. 'But you're not a fraud. You're one of the best journalists in the business.'

'Was,' said Ruth, holding up one finger. '*Was* one of the best. When I was young like you, I had ideals, principles. Freedom of the press!' she shouted towards the street. 'Democracy! Liberty! I'd go out of my way to seek out the truth, no stone unturned. True, very true.'

'So what's changed?' said Chuck.

'Now, I slip a police officer five hundred bucks in a brown envelope under the table in some horrid coppers' pub. I follow people, I doorstep them when a daughter is missing or a son is murdered. I intrude on their grief and their misery. I'm a disgrace, Chuck. I'm the worst sort of traitor; a traitor to myself.'

She was feeling totally wretched; tears began to spill down her cheeks.

'Come on, Ruth, that's just the job,' said Chuck.

'No! No, it's not,' she said. 'It didn't used to be like this. *I* didn't used to be like this.' She twisted around to face him. 'Do you know, I've failed to hold down one successful relationship in twenty years? Not one! And who'd want me? Look at me, crying, drunk in the street.'

Chuck smiled.

'One day you will find a guy who deserves you,' he said kindly. 'Not a dork like David who doesn't appreciate what he's got; a real man, a man who knows that Ruth Boden is the best thing that's ever happened to him.'

His words were so soothing, so flattering. She wasn't entirely sure they were right, but she'd take whatever reassurance she could get right now. She had never noticed what long lashes Chuck had. Dark and thick, like a girl's. Before she could even think about what she was doing, she moved in and pressed her lips against his, tasting the wine on his mouth. Gently Chuck pushed her away.

'God, I'm so sorry, Chuck,' she said, her hand over her mouth. 'See? I can't even get that right.'

'Ruth, you're wonderful and beautiful and maybe if you hadn't had two bottles of wine to drink, I'd be doing cartwheels that you tried to kiss me. But . . .' He stood up and, taking her hands, pulled her to her feet. '. . . I think it's time you went home to bed. Alone.'

He raised an arm and a taxi puttered to the kerb.

'Here,' he said, helping her inside and handing her the research file. 'Take this, it's sobering reading if nothing else.'

'Thank you,' said Ruth simply. 'I don't deserve a friend like you.'

'Yes you *do*, Ruth Boden,' smiled Chuck kindly. 'And the sooner you realise it, the better.'

30

Loud knocking woke Sophie with a start. She had had a rather fitful sleep, laced with dreams about being chased by faceless monsters, and it took a moment to realise where she was. La Luna Motel was a two-star hotel on a back street in the Le Cannet district of Cannes. Le Bristol it was not, looking more like the sort of establishment you could hire by the hour, sheets extra. But it was cheap, it was anonymous and most important, it'd had rooms available when Josh and Sophie had rolled in from their jaunt to the wine country at almost midnight.

Not that Sophie had really wanted the day to end. Despite the simmering danger of the past few days, she had enjoyed going out into the warm green vineyards, and despite their awkward shared history, she had liked Sandrine, with her quiet dignity and her undiminished love for Nick, although she knew that he was planning to leave her. Best of all, after the chateau they had stopped at a tiny bistro in Bois du Lac. At the mention of Sandrine's name, they had been welcomed with open arms by the patron, a red-faced, jolly woman named Madame Babette, who had plucked the menus from their hands and insisted on bringing out 'only the best'. As they sat on a terrace overlooking one of Sandrine's vineyards, course after course was placed before them, each more delicious than the last: bean soup with fresh parmesan, pasta parcels of mushroom and shallots, giant shrimps; there was even a plate of Parma ham and some of the juiciest grapes Sophie had ever tasted. As they ate, Josh poured a wonderful local wine and told her stories about his adventures. Hiking in the Scottish Highlands, a tour to Brazil with an amateur football team, motorbiking from coast to coast in America. He had once even dated the actress and model Summer Sinclair. Sophie knew he was cleaning it up for her, presenting himself as a lovable rogue with an interesting past, but she didn't mind that; she was in no particular hurry to have reality intrude on what had been a magical night.

Now she rubbed the sleep from her eyes and peered through the peephole in the door. Josh's face bulged up at her, looking impatient.

'Who did you think it was, princess? Prince Albert?' he asked as she undid the safety chain and let him in. He looked around at the tiny single bed and the 'en suite', a cupboard-sized toilet-cum-shower with a tiny sink.

'Not bad,' he said. 'I think you got the better deal. My room looks like a prison cell.'

Sophie thought back to when they had checked in, how the Chinese night porter with the missing front tooth had smiled when he had said they had 'velly nice' doubles. Light-headed from the wine and conversation, she had hesitated for a moment then asked for two singles, whilst giving Josh a sidelong glance almost willing him to object. But this morning, the haze of the wine faded, she was glad they had not put themselves in a compromising situation.

Josh pulled a passport out of his back pocket.

'Look what arrived this morning.'

'Yours?' said Sophie, raising a brow. 'Or another dodgy friend's?'

'Mine,' he said crossly. 'Christopher went to the boat and retrieved it. He sent it to a friend in Paris who couriered it here overnight.'

'Was the boat safe?'

'There was no one there. No blue tape, no police, no Russians.'

Sophie widened her eyes.

'So we can go home!'

Josh frowned.

'When we've come this far? Sophie, I think this wine scam is the thing that got Nick killed. But do you trust the police to pursue it? I don't.'

She knew he was right.

'So have you phoned that number Sandrine gave you?' she asked officiously, perching on the bed. Josh shook his head, obviously disappointed.

'Been trying since eight this morning, but for some reason it won't connect. I keep getting that annoying French voice telling me the number is not recognised.'

'Can I try?'

'I don't see why you'd have any more luck,' he said, but he still handed her Sandrine's note and his mobile phone.

Sophie carefully keyed in the number written on the paper, but Josh was right, it didn't seem to be connecting. She looked down at the phone for a moment, thinking.

'Do you think maybe Nick's new girlfriend is having the same problems as us?' she said.

'What do you mean?'

'Well, we've been assuming they're chasing us for some information Nick gave me about this wine thing, right? If that's true and Nick had multiple women on the go, then it follows that the bad guys will have been chasing them too. Maybe they found this mysterious "A" woman and burgled her flat too. If I was her, I would definitely have changed my number.'

Josh nodded.

'That would explain why we can't get through,' he sighed. 'We should have known it wouldn't be that simple.'

He put the note back in his pocket.

'Anyway, enough of that, Columbo,' he said, 'better make use of that shower, 'cos I'm taking you out.'

'Where?'

He smiled mysteriously.

'You'll have to come with me to find out. It's a surprise.'

Sophie raised her eyebrows sceptically.

'Josh, the last two times you "surprised" me, we ended up breaking and entering and playing fisticuffs with Maurice the fence.'

A smile played at his lips.

'You will like this. I promise.'

Sophie stood in the street, giggling nervously.

'What is it, Josh? Tell me, please!'

'Stop struggling, it's a nice thing, remember?'

He was standing behind her, his hands over her eyes. Their taxi from the hotel had dropped them near the harbour, then Josh had led Sophie through the streets of Cannes, past the bustling Forville market and the majestic Carlton hotel with its steel-domed turrets, and finally up past the exclusive shops of Rue Mace. He'd stopped her at a corner, then covered her face and turned her around. Sophie was feeling the flutter of butterflies as if she was on a first date.

'*Et voilà*!' said Josh, dramatically pulling his hands away

For a moment, Sophie just blinked, not sure what she was looking at. She cast her gaze up and down the street which was filled with high-end fashion boutiques and expensive knick-knack shops. Then she saw the name painted on the door right in front of them.

'Cameron?' she said, turning to look at him.

'If we're going out to a swanky party tonight, we've got to look the part,' he grinned.

'But this place costs a fortune!'

Sophie had read about Cameron in *Vogue*; he was one of the world's most in-demand hairdressers. His main salon was in Paris, with outposts in New York and Moscow – and now Cannes, apparently. She had seen the Cameron hair products for sale in Harvey Nichols – thirty pounds for a bottle of shampoo alone.

'Listen, we are here to investigate Nick's life, right?' said Josh. 'So we need to fit into his world; we can't just turn up to that party in jeans and trainers.'

'But how did you get an appointment?'

'Ah, that'll be my concierge friend at the Bristol. He knows one of the stylists at the Paris branch personally.'

Now it all made sense: that was why Josh had insisted they stay at a hotel with a world-class concierge. Even Josh's charm wouldn't have got them into Cameron; the salon was exclusive in the purest sense: unless you knew how to get inside, you were excluded.

'Come on, princess, you *shall* go to the ball,' said Josh, ringing the bell and waiting as a security guard opened the door. *A security guard for a hairdresser's?* Maybe this was the Russian influence too.

'I'll see you back at the hotel,' said Josh as he announced Sophie to the receptionist.

'You can't *leave* me,' Sophie hissed, glancing around.

'Don't worry,' he mouthed. 'It's all paid for.'

Sophie wanted to grab his arm, but a flamboyant stylist with an octopus tattoo peeping out from his skimpy vest appeared and led her to her chair. He introduced himself as George and flipped his hands through her hair, announcing in creaky English that he must lift the colour.

In the end, Sophie thoroughly enjoyed herself. In fact, she couldn't remember when she'd had more fun. George was camp as Christmas and hilariously indiscreet, telling scandalous stories about his wealthy clients and their husbands, men he swore were queuing round the block to get into his pants. She was brought cute little baby cappuccinos, a bowl of fruit salad and a pile of edgy magazines to flick through while the colourist got to work. She even had a visit from a manicurist, who transformed her chipped fingernails and gave her a soft hand massage. When her hair was finally washed and set, George spun her chair around so she could see the transformation.

'You like?'

She gasped. It was like magic: buttery blonde highlights had been woven through a darker honey base; she looked sunkissed and radiant, her hair falling in elegant waves.

'Is that really me?' she whispered.

'*Non*,' said George. 'It is the *new* you. And about time too, no?'

Josh's key wasn't behind the desk when Sophie got back to the hotel, and the gap-toothed Chinese man seemed pleased to confirm 'man no here', making her good mood instantly disappear. These last two days – the meeting with Sandrine, her afternoon of pampering – it had been all too easy for Sophie to fool herself that she was on a slightly offbeat minibreak. But always at the back of her mind was that nagging unease that she was in danger. She had no idea how the police investigation into Nick's death was going, and while she was desperate to call her mother for an update, the last time she had done that they had almost been snatched at Nice station. It could have been a coincidence, of course, but Sophie didn't want to take the risk. No, the visit to Cameron's salon had been a much-needed distraction, but it had only been that: a distraction from the chaos which she neither understood, nor had any idea when – or if – it would end.

By the time she let herself into her room, Sophie was anxious and agitated again.

'Josh?' she called nervously, but it was empty. It was then that she noticed the two large cardboard bags sitting on the bed.

There was a note pinned to one: 'Been shopping, had to guess size. Hope it's okay, call for you at six, J.'

Sophie reached inside and pulled out a tissue-paper parcel. She unwrapped it carefully and gasped as layers of ivory fabric slid out. She held it up: it was a floor-length gown with a deep-scooped neck, made from beautiful silk crêpe trimmed with seed pearls. It was exquisite.

'Where on earth did he get this?' she whispered to herself. She picked up the bag to read the address and as she did, she noticed there was something written on the back of Josh's note. 'Oh, and try not to pull the tags off, because it has to go back tomorrow. Sorry.'

She laughed out loud. *Typical*, she thought. But still, it was a nice gesture. Josh McCormack *could* do lovely things when he tried. She looked in the other bag: a long white cashmere wrap and a pair of five-inch heels, which would cripple her but look fantastic.

Sophie laughed to herself as she ran a shower, filling the room up with steam. She was just wrapping her hair in a towel – she didn't want it to get wet after George's loving attention – when she noticed that Josh had also left a small bag of toiletries on the sink. His choice was tasteful and accurate. Almond Provençal soap, razors, avocado body cream, some clear lip gloss and peach-coloured blush. As she stepped into the shower – mercifully hot – and began soaping herself, she was struck by how intimate it felt using the products he had bought for her. Perhaps they were a reflection of how he might like her to smell and feel, and she was surprised at how much that thought excited her.

It took her no time to dress. The gown slithered over her curves, a perfect fit. Either Josh was psychic or he had been paying close attention to her body – she didn't know which thought unsettled her the most. The cut was very low around her breasts, but she was tanned and toned enough to carry it off. Her hair fell soft and loose on to her shoulders.

Josh stopped and looked at her as he entered the room.

'Wow,' he said finally.

'You don't look too bad yourself,' she said.

That's an understatement, she smiled to herself, unable to take her eyes off him. She knew from the Chariot party that Josh looked good in a suit, but tonight he looked like a matinée idol: clean-shaven, square-jawed, gorgeous.

'So tell me, how did you manage this?' she asked, feeling flustered. 'I can't imagine the boutiques on the Croisette lend thousand-euro gowns every day of the week.'

'Well, we're only technically borrowing it.'

'Technically? Josh, you didn't steal it, did you?'

Josh looked hurt.

'You underestimate me,' he said, smiling. 'Look, I chatted up some bird with a Ferrari on the Croisette. Got her to drop me off at the boutique. I went in, bought the dress. You can wear it tonight and we'll take it back tomorrow.'

She tried not to think about him chatting up a wealthy bimbo.

'They're going to know it's been worn.'

'As long as you don't spill claret down it they won't. I'm just going to take it back to the boutique's manager and tell her you – or rather the girl in the Ferrari – dumped me. She isn't going to quibble with Rudolfo.'

'Rudolfo?'

Josh put on a hammy Russian accent.

'I am Rudolfo, son of the oligarch Alexander who has one of the big, big yachts in the harbour,' he laughed.

'You didn't,' Sophie giggled.

'I did.'

'You are terrible.'

'And you are beautiful,' said Josh simply.

Blushing, she pulled the pashmina around her shoulders.

'By the way, the scarf doesn't have to be returned. Or the shoes – they're for you.'

'I can pay you back when we get back to London,' she said quickly. 'For the haircut, the shoes . . .'

He shook his head.

'I said they're for you.'

She stepped across and kissed him lightly on the cheek. 'Thank you,' she said, watching him looking uncharacteristically off guard.

She caught a glimpse of them in the mirror behind the door, and even she had to admit what a great-looking couple they made. Their eyes met in the reflection and she looked away.

'I think we should go,' she said quickly.

'There's no rush,' said Josh, glancing at his watch.

'There *is*, Josh,' she said. 'I just want to get this over with. If Nick was supposed to be meeting this A at the party tonight, I just want to find her and then leave.'

She noted his momentary disappointment. Had he been thinking of tonight as a real date?

'Don't pin too much on tonight,' he said quietly. 'We don't know if we're going to find any answers. We don't know if this woman will even be there . . .'

'You're right, we don't know anything,' said Sophie, surprised at her own passion. 'But I want to find out. I want to get to this party and start putting the pieces together, because I want my life back, Josh. I just want to go home.'

31

The somewhat ordinary address on the invitation – 134 Rue de Rivoli – hadn't prepared Sophie for what she saw as the taxi drove through the iron gates.

'Bloody hell,' she gasped, looking towards the end of the palm-tree-lined drive where the Villa Polieux stood like a glorious neoclassical full stop. 'It's like something out of *Tender is the Night*.'

'I think that was set at the Hotel du Cap down the road,' smiled Josh. 'But you're right. It's pretty incredible.'

Painted a shimmering white, with wings either side of the main house, the villa had pale grey shutters at every window and was surrounded by sculpted hedges and neatly trimmed flower beds.

'Who owns a place like this?'

'It belongs to the Polieux family; it's their summer retreat,' said Josh. 'They're one of the oldest and most prestigious wine merchants in France, and I'm not talking about selling a few bottles of plonk to rich Russians here. I mean these guys are into wholesale distribution, wine bottling and retail; they've got a grape merchant division as well as owning some of the top estates in Bordeaux. If you drink a bottle of wine in France, there's a decent chance the Polieuxs have had something to do with it.'

'You seem to know a lot about them,' said Sophie, giving Josh a sidelong glance.

'You have a suspicious nature, Sophie Ellis,' said Josh. 'I haven't been sunbathing while you were getting your hair done. It pays to know where you're going and who you're likely to bump into.'

'Sorry,' she said. 'I just thought . . .'

'I know what you thought. Anyway, you can see why Nick got involved with this world, can't you?'

They were met at their car by a uniformed waiter who handed them flutes of champagne and wordlessly led them into the house. The high entrance hall was lit by dozens of the tallest candles Sophie had ever seen. Even in the flickering light, she could see that the floor was intricately patterned with marble and the furniture was gold and ornate. As the waiter turned to the left, they could hear music and excited chatter. They walked out into a ballroom that made Sophie gasp, despite herself. It was the size of a tennis court and was brilliantly lit by three dazzling chandeliers. As she looked up in wonder, she saw that the entire ceiling was painted in one vast depiction of the heavens: the Holy Mother surrounded by angels, and at the centre, a half-clothed figure she suspected was Marie Antoinette.

'Try to close your mouth,' said Josh with a smirk. 'Sophisticated people like us aren't impressed by things like that, remember?'

'Sorry,' she hissed, and tried to look more regal. It wasn't easy when she was clearly surrounded by some of the most elegant people in France. The ladies were all wearing flowing gowns – every colour from shimmering silver to peacock blue – the men, beautifully cut dinner suits. Sophie was glad Josh had been shopping; if she had worn her day dress purloined from Josh's garage, people would have been handing her their empty glasses.

But the more she looked at the women here, the more Sophie began to despair of ever finding the elusive A. If everything she had been hearing about Nick was true, it could be any one of them: young, old, glamorous or even elderly and wizened. Nick's modus operandi suggested he went wherever the money was; and this party was dripping in money.

'How the hell are we going to find this woman, Josh?' she whispered.

Josh looked irritated.

'I'm working on it, okay?' he hissed.

'Seriously, we don't know anything about her except she's been invited to this party and her name begins with A,' pressed Sophie. 'It's not exactly much to go on, is it? What are we going to do, get our clipboards out and question everyone here if they've seen or heard of Nick Beddingfield, otherwise known as Nick Cooper, or maybe even something else?'

'I'll think of something, stop worrying.'

They followed the flow of the party out on to the terrace overlooking the lights of Antibes harbour. The sky was mottled pink and purple, and the Mediterranean shimmered like mercury in the dusk. It was as if they were in their own private world, just the two of them, where everything was good and safe and happy.

'Can you smell that?' she said, touching Josh's arm. 'It's roses and pine trees. Oh Josh, I could live here.'

'I thought you wanted to find Nick's mystery woman and then leave immediately,' said Josh sharply. Sophie glanced at him, desperately wishing she could read his mind. He was definitely pissed off about something. Was he simply being his usual moody self, or was he really upset because she wanted to go home? Did he want to stay with her in this state of limbo for ever? She could ask herself the same question. Of course she wanted all this to be over; she hated the constant anxiety of not knowing what was happening, the prospect of prison, while the idea that someone might want to kill her was alien and terrifying. And yet despite the danger, the threats and the fear, there had been something quite exhilarating about the past few days.

'Thank you,' she said quietly.

He looked at her in surprise.

'Thank you? For what?'

She gestured around the terrace.

'All this, Josh. Not just for the dress and the shoes and the hair, which by the way are all absolutely amazing, but thank you for helping me. I don't know where I'd be without you; in a jail cell or at the bottom of the Thames most likely. You've saved my life, you helped me when you really didn't have to, and I've been such a thoughtless cow to not stop and tell you how grateful I am. There's no excuse, so I don't blame you for being in such a bad mood with me.'

'I know you haven't got a very high opinion of me, but I just did what any decent bloke would do. I wasn't going to stand back and let you get killed. Besides, I'm not in a bad mood with you,' he said, avoiding her eyes.

'You are. I can tell. You're all sniffy and huffy and your brows knit together a bit like this,' she said, doing an impression of a grumpy person.

She wanted to make him laugh, but instead he remained serious. His eyes locked with hers, and she felt a charge run between them so that she could almost see the sparks on the night air.

'Listen, Sophie, I know this has all been a nightmare for you and that you'd rather be anywhere else – with anyone else.'

She was about to object, but he held up a hand to stop her.

'No one wants to be on the run from the police and whoever the hell else is after us,' he continued softly. 'But look around, look where we are. We're in one of the most amazing houses in one of the most beautiful parts of the whole world. No matter what happens tomorrow, or the next day, we're here now. Why not enjoy it? Why not pretend to be a real princess? Why not drink the champagne and dance the polka? For one night, let's have fun, just me and you, okay?'

They were only inches apart. It wasn't just the warm, scented gardens she could smell now, but Josh; the soft suggestion of soap and aftershave on his skin, the hint of champagne on his lips.

The tension between them was so electric it almost made her tremble. For the last three days – had it really only been three days? – she and Josh had barely been apart. And yet if they discovered who had killed Nick and returned to their lives in London, would she ever see him again? And would he care if she walked out of his life?

'Well, if we're planning to dance the night away, I'm going to put this scarf in the cloakroom,' she said, forcing a smile. 'We wouldn't want to lose it.'

She walked away from him towards the house, and when she glanced back, she saw that he was still watching her. She puffed out her cheeks, uncertain of the emotions she was experiencing, aware that there was more at stake from the evening than just discovering the identity of A.

The cloakroom had been roped off and was being manned by two beautiful young women dressed as cigarette girls. In their little hats and tiny scarlet uniforms they were clearly struggling with the volume of furs, capelets and jackets.

'Could I leave this scarf?' asked Sophie, gesticulating to make up for her lack of French.

One of the girls flashed her a helpless expression.

'*Je regrette, mademoiselle*, we have no tickets left.'

'Oh,' said Sophie. She really didn't want to lose it, not when it was a gift from Josh. The girl saw her disappointed expression and held up a finger.

'*Un moment, s'il vous plaît*,' she said, taking Sophie's pashmina. Sophie watched as the girl pulled two white stickers from a roll and wrote the same number on each, handing one to Sophie. 'We improvise, I think,' she smiled.

'Thank you,' said Sophie, 'But what number is this?' She held up the ticket.

'Seven zero one,' said the cloakroom girl, pointing to each numeral.

'*Merci*,' grinned Sophie. '*Merci beaucoup*.'

Josh was not out on the terrace, so Sophie rushed back inside, searching the ballroom for his face. She spotted him on the far side, talking to a pretty girl in a violet gown. Catching his eye, she clumsily signalled to meet her on the terrace. Josh's expression was concerned as he walked out.

'What's the matter?' he said, glancing around. 'Trouble?'

'No, no, the opposite actually. Do you have the number that Sandrine gave you? The number of Nick's other lover.'

'Sure, but why?' he said, pulling out his wallet to retrieve the Post-it note.

'Look at this,' said Sophie, pointing at the number the cloakroom girl had written. 'How did you read the last four digits of Sandrine's number?'

'0627,' said Josh, holding up the Post-it.

'Me too. That's what I dialled in the hotel this morning – and that's why we couldn't get through.'

She could see he wasn't getting it.

'It's not a seven, Josh. It's a *one*; the French write it differently, with a long sweep at the front so it looks like a seven – and they cross their sevens to make the distinction.'

'Shit. We've been phoning the wrong number,' muttered Josh.

'Yes, but that's good, don't you see?' she said, her eyes sparkling. 'Let's call it now. If Nick's girlfriend is here, she will pick it up and we can identify her.'

Josh smiled and pulled out his mobile.

'I'll take the ballroom; you wait out here and listen for

anyone answering their phone. I'll keep ringing. If I get them, I'll ask them to meet me by the terrace steps.'

Sophie walked to the edge of the terrace, her pulse quickening. It was a long shot, of course. Maybe Nick's lover hadn't brought her phone; maybe she wouldn't hear it ring. But there was always a chance, wasn't there? And by Sophie's reckoning, they were due a little bit of luck. She weaved through the crowd, her ears peeled, willing herself to pick up a noise, but all she could hear was the clinking of glasses and the gentle hum of conversation and laughter. And then she heard it; the faint but persistent chirp of a mobile phone. There were dozens of people out on the terrace, even more milling around the gardens below; it could be anywhere. Sophie looked from left to right, desperately watching for movement, someone lifting a mobile to their ear.

There, she thought. It was coming from the area down by the infinity pool, she was sure of it. She moved across to the stone steps and, gathering up her dress to expose her silver shoes, followed the sound as quickly as she could. The pool was surrounded by dark slate, and its clear turquoise water was shimmering in the darkness. As she walked around it, Sophie could see a group of three women, evidently come down here to smoke. The one with her back to Sophie reached for her clutch – the ringing was definitely coming from there. It could be a coincidence, of course, so Sophie hung back in the shadows. She could not see the woman's face, just her graceful neck, her long dark hair, and the full skirt of what was obviously a very beautiful gown.

Sophie turned and looked back towards the house, where she could make out Josh's tall silhouette against the double doors.

She beckoned to him and then walked towards the woman, who was pulling the phone away from her ear. Her heart was thumping loudly as the woman turned, her profile illuminated by the silvery moonlight.

'*Allô?*' said the woman into her phone. There was a pause, then she turned again – towards the terrace steps.

'You?' whispered Sophie, her hand going to her mouth. 'Lana?'

There was no mistake: the woman's face was illuminated by the yellow light from the house. Lana Goddard-Price, the woman who had asked her to house-sit, the woman who had told her to help herself to anything in her Knightsbridge home: the woman who had set everything in motion.

'Sophie,' said Lana, moving away from her friends. There was no surprise in her voice, only a matter-of-fact statement, as if she had just bumped into a vague acquaintance she didn't see all that often. 'I didn't expect to see you here.'

'So I take it you two know each other?' said Josh, walking up behind them. Sophie kept her gaze on Lana. She couldn't think of anything to say except the obvious truth.

'Nick's dead, Lana,' she said in the most level voice she could manage.

If Sophie had expected the woman to crumble, to weep, to betray her distress, then she was disappointed. Lana simply closed her eyes and nodded sadly.

'Collect your coat, then we should leave. I think we had better find somewhere quieter to talk.'

32

Lana's house was a thirty-minute drive away in Cap Ferrat, an exclusive wooded peninsula beyond Nice, sandwiched between the understated but extremely expensive villages of Villefranche and Beaulieu-sur-Mer. Josh and Sophie sat in silence, unable to talk in front of Lana or her driver, each wrapped in their own unspoken questions as the car drove past the crowded restaurants and pretty terracotta houses of Saint-Jean, then out on to the headland, the pine forest closing in around the impressively discreet properties on the winding sea road, each one protected by high walls and security cameras. The Goddard-Prices' home was smaller but no less impressive than Villa Polieux, with its pale pink exterior and neat garden bursting with bougainvillea.

Not that Sophie was in any mood to appreciate it. The journey had given her plenty of time to imagine almost every possible scenario to do with Nick and Lana, but one thing seemed obvious: whatever Lana Goddard-Price's motivations were, it was no coincidence that she had chosen Sophie to house-sit for her. And that meant that Sophie had been duped. Why? She had no idea. But the very idea that she had been sucked into this chaotic and dangerous plot on purpose made her almost sick with anger. Josh clearly felt the fury coming from her, and as the car pulled to a stop, he took her hand and gave it a reassuring squeeze. That was something, she supposed.

Stepping out into the balmy night air, Sophie could hear the shrill rasp of crickets in the bushes and feel the breeze blowing through the umbrella pines. For one moment she had the urge to run off into the dark forest, leave all her burning questions unanswered, leave the whole sorry mess behind. But she had to know. She had come too far to turn back now.

The house was in darkness as they stepped inside. Josh and Sophie followed Lana down cool stone corridors and into a wood-panelled study. Lana went behind the desk and switched on a lamp, then indicated a pair of sofas.

'Please, sit.'

She took a cigarette from a case on the desk, lighting it with a slim gold lighter.

'Terrible habit, I know,' she said, blowing a long stream of smoke at the ceiling. 'When my personal trainer isn't around, I fall back into terrible habits.'

'If your name is Lana, then who is A?' asked Josh, settling back in his seat.

'My full name is Alannah. Most people call me Lana.'

Sophie glared at her. 'Well, what do you want from me, *Alannah*? We know you were Nick's lover. I somehow doubt it was an accident your house-sitter was involved with him too.'

'Nick had many *amours*, but I wasn't one of them,' said Lana, pouring herself a brandy from a decanter on the desk, then sitting down opposite Sophie and Josh. 'Our relationship was of a professional nature. I was paying him to do a job, which was to get involved with you.'

'But why? Why on earth—'

'Hang on,' interrupted Josh. 'Can someone fill me in, please? So it was your place in Knightsbridge Sophie was house-sitting?'

Lana nodded. 'And she put me through my paces at the gym.'

'So it *was* a set-up,' said Sophie bitterly. 'You put those invitations on the mantelpiece deliberately.'

Lana smiled. 'I knew you wouldn't be able to resist going to the parties, although I was surprised you went the very first night. Still, it meant Nick could get to work as quickly as possible.'

'To work?' yelled Sophie, all her frustrations spilling over. 'I'm not some bloody dog to be trained! What the hell do you want from me, Lana?'

'You really don't know, do you?' said Lana, her voice as soft as the evening breeze. 'Sophie Ellis, you are the key to a fortune.'

Sophie felt goose bumps prickle up her arms.

'But I don't have any money,' she said. 'You *knew* that. That was why I started the personal training.'

Lana stubbed her cigarette out in an onyx ashtray.

'How much do you know about your father's professional life, Sophie?'

'I'm not here to answer your damn questions,' shouted Sophie. 'You should be answering mine!'

Josh touched her arm.

'It's okay,' he said. 'Let her talk.'

'No, Josh!' said Sophie, her voice cracking. 'She lied to me from the very start; why should I listen to her now?'

'Because it's the only way we'll find out what's going on.'

'Your friend Josh is right, Sophie,' said Lana. 'I know you have no reason to trust me, but believe me, I do want to help.'

Sophie looked at Josh again, then sighed.

'My dad was a good accountant, is that what you want to know? He made one bad investment, but he was clever, he'd have made it back . . . Look, what's he got to do with any of this?'

Lana was nodding.

'You're right about that, Sophie. Peter Ellis *was* a clever accountant, very clever indeed. So clever in fact that no one, not even those closest to him, suspected that he was involved in one of the biggest financial scams of all time.'

'*Involved* in a scam? Are you talking about Michael Asner here?' demanded Sophie.

'Michael Asner, the Ponzi scheme fraudster?' said Josh, sitting forward. 'But I thought your dad lost all your money to that guy.'

'He did. Our family was ruined because of Asner. My dad invested everything with him and lost it when the scheme collapsed.'

Lana gave a small tinkling laugh.

'That's what your father wanted people to believe, but in fact Peter was very much involved in the scheme. He was the bag man.'

'Bag man?' asked Sophie.

'Someone who collects dirty money,' explained Josh softly. 'I think she's suggesting that your father buried the cash for Asner so that if the pyramid scheme went down, there was still some squirrelled away.'

'Very good,' said Lana, giving Josh a thin smile. 'Your friend is shrewd as well as good looking.'

Sophie looked at Josh desperately, hoping he would tell her it was all a lie, but his expression told her otherwise. She put her head in her hands, rubbing her temples. It was all so fantastic, her head was starting to pound. *Could* it be true? She had known her dad and Asner had been at uni together, but why would Peter Ellis let his family suffer such hardship and humiliation if he had access to the missing Asner millions?

'I just can't believe it,' she said quietly. 'He was a small-time City accountant. He did people's taxes and sorted out their pensions.'

'That's why he was perfect, Sophie,' said Lana, sipping her brandy. 'I don't know whether he was involved from the start, or whether Asner approached him when things started to get hot and he had to make a contingency plan, but it was a stroke of genius to choose your father. Asner knew that the SEC would investigate his close Wall Street colleagues, but a small-time British accountant who had lost all this money in the scheme? He'd be completely off their radar.'

'How do you know all this?' asked Josh.

Lana stood up and pulled a thick manila file from a drawer in the desk.

'I have spent nine months and hundreds of thousands of dollars looking into Asner's affairs. Private investigators, forensic accountants, they've collected every last scrap of information on him and sifted through it. I think I know more about him than the FBI.'

'But why?' asked Sophie, shaking her head. 'Why go to all that trouble?'

'Because my family lost everything too,' said Lana. Her eyes were bright and fierce.

'Your family?' said Sophie.

'My family are based in Madrid. They were wealthy, but not super-rich. Like yours, they invested everything they had in Asner's scheme, hoping for a glorious return for their pension. Like your parents, like hundreds of others, they lost everything. I support them financially now, but that's not the point. No one should be allowed to get away with what Asner did.'

She walked over to pour herself another brandy, and Sophie noticed that her hands were shaking.

'I knew from the start we were unlikely to get anything back. The Securities and Exchange Commission has been trying to trace the money, of course, but it's like looking for a needle in a haystack, and besides, it has limited resources like any governmental department. So I recruited my own team to look into it. They did a very good job, even if I do say so myself.'

'So where is the money?' said Josh.

'I don't know.'

'You don't know? Why not?'

'Because the trail ends here.' Lana looked at Sophie.

'With me? That's crazy!'

'Is it?' said Lana. 'Everyone involved with the Asner investigation believes he must have stashed the money somewhere, but I'm convinced your father was the one who hid it.'

'I don't believe it,' said Sophie. 'If he had all that money, why would he have made us suffer like that?'

'Suffer?' laughed Lana. 'You hardly suffered, Sophie. You had to come down a few pegs in life, that's all. And your father would have thought the discomfort was worth it for the rewards he knew were to follow. My guess is that he would have waited two or three years for the scandal to die down, then quietly distributed the money back to Asner's wife and inner circle, and of course kept a big chunk for himself – he would have set you up for life.'

A sickening thought suddenly occurred to Sophie.

'Was my father killed?'

Lana shook her head sadly. 'I don't know. But either way, the trail ends with you. With such a large fortune at stake, your father would have made his own contingency plan; he would have told someone else where the money was hidden in the event that anything happened to him or Asner.'

'And you think that person was me?'

'Of course. He loved you, he trusted you. Who else would he turn to?'

Sophie looked at Josh, her eyes pleading.

'But he didn't tell me anything.'

'So let's get this straight,' Josh said to Lana, narrowing his eyes. 'You engineered it so that Sophie would come and house-sit for you, presumably so she would bring all her personal possessions with her? Then you hired Nick to

298

seduce her, to work his way into her life and find out everything he could about it?'

Lana nodded.

'You're a cold bitch, aren't you?' he said.

'I thought it was the best way,' said Lana uncertainly, her composure slipping.

'The best way?' snarled Josh, banging his fist down on the desktop. 'You got Sophie wrapped up in all this, you got Nick *killed*, all for nothing.'

'I did not get Nick killed!' shouted Lana.

'Well, who did?' said Josh. 'If you hadn't roped him into your dirty little scheme, he'd still be alive!'

'Why do you think his death was anything to do with this?' said Lana defensively.

'You want us to believe it was his little wine scam?' sneered Josh. 'Don't make me bloody laugh! There are *billions* involved in this!'

'STOP! Both of you!' yelled Sophie, holding her hands over her ears. 'Please, I can't stand it!'

Silence descended on the room.

'Whoever killed Nick is now after Sophie,' said Josh, still glaring at Lana. 'In London two Russians tried to shoot her. They turned up again in Nice. We don't know who they are, but they are armed, connected and resourceful.' He tapped a finger against the thick file. 'So who are they?'

Lana bit her lip and looked thoughtful. 'Russians?'

'Eastern European of some description. Although I suppose they could just be guns for hire.'

'If my team managed to trace Asner's involvement with Peter Ellis, it's possible other investors made the same connection,' said Lana. 'A lot of rich people gave a lot of money to Asner, and no doubt they want it back just as much as me. There's a list of the probables in my file. Ukrainian oligarchs, Chinese business fronts, maybe even the Russian Mafia.'

'Jesus,' said Josh.

'Could I have a drink?' croaked Sophie.

Lana poured her a large brandy and Sophie put the cool glass to her cheek. *Could* it be true? It was insane, but in some funny way, it did provide an explanation for what had happened. Peter and Michael Asner *were* old friends, and her dad was also experienced in offshore financial planning, Sophie knew that from her work at his firm. Dad didn't really have any close friends, only the old duffers at the sailing club, and if he'd had a secret to keep, he certainly wouldn't have shared it with her mother. Julia Ellis was not the sort of woman you'd tell anything important, not unless you were happy for everyone in the butcher's and the post office to know every detail by the end of the day. She knocked back the cognac, wincing as it burned her throat.

'What do you know, Sophie?' asked Josh.

'I don't know anything,' she said, looking down at her empty glass. 'Really, I don't.'

Lana came across and sat down beside her.

'Sophie, you *must*. Maybe Nick *did* get killed because of it.'

'You think he found something?' asked Josh.

Lana looked at him.

'Perhaps. Nick's brief was to talk to Sophie about her father, see if he had told you anything, maybe mentioned a bank account or some tax haven you used to go to on holiday. So yes, maybe he did discover something.'

'And you think he tried to use that information to his own advantage?'

'That might explain the Russians,' said Lana sadly. 'Nick was smart, he could have worked out that selling the information to the highest bidder was more lucrative than the money I was paying him. And perhaps they killed him when he was no longer useful.'

Josh shook his head.

'That doesn't add up. If Nick had given them the information, then why go after Sophie?'

Lana lit another cigarette and stood up.

'Maybe he changed his mind, refused to tell them? I haven't got all the answers,' she said, taking a long drag. 'That's why I need you.'

'Us?' said Sophie warily. 'What for?'

'She wants us to find the money,' said Josh. 'Right?'

Lana nodded, blowing out smoke. 'If we find it and return it to the proper authorities, then you're free.' She shrugged. 'There is no point in anybody chasing you.'

The silence in the room indicated that everybody agreed with the statement.

'And by "return it to the proper authorities", you mean after you've taken a big slice,' said Josh with a twisted smile.

'I only want what's mine!' snapped Lana. 'I only want justice.'

Josh and Lana began bickering between themselves, but their voices faded into the background as a vague thought sharpened into focus.

'My book,' said Sophie quietly.

Josh and Lana both looked at her.

'What book?' said Lana.

She looked over at Josh for reassurance.

'Lana, you said that Nick's brief was to find out if my father had given me any information, maybe a bank account number or something? Dad gave me a book for my birthday, this second-hand copy of *I Capture the Castle* – it was an in-joke between us.'

'I don't understand,' said Lana. 'How does this get us the bank details?'

'This book, it's old, a bit worn, and the name of the previous owner is written in it. There's a number in it too. I assumed it was a phone number or a date of birth, but . . . You think it could be an account number?'

'Why didn't you mention this before?' snapped Josh. 'We've been running around all this time risking our necks, and all along we had the bloody thing with us? Sophie, why didn't you say anything?'

'I didn't know it was relevant!' she shouted back. 'And *you* said I was in danger because of something Nick gave to me, not my dad.'

'I'm not bloody psychic!' he replied.

'All right, all right,' said Lana, holding up her hands. 'Where is this book now? Do you have it with you?'

'It's in my bag, back at the hotel in Cannes.'

'In the least secure hotel in France,' scoffed Josh.

'Then we must go there immediately.'

Lana stood up, grabbed the manila file and headed for the door. 'Well?' she said, turning back, her hand on the doorknob. 'What are you waiting for?'

33

'So do you *really* think Sophie killed this American?' asked Francesca Manning, peering over the top of her skinny macchiato. 'I tried to get it out of that dishy police inspector, but he wouldn't tell me anything.'

'I kind of wanted to know what you thought,' said Ruth, glancing at her wristwatch. It was four o'clock in the afternoon and she was still feeling terrible. Her blood felt like glue, she had a thumping headache, and she was trapped in Starbucks with the Sloane from hell. This morning, she had been quite pleased with herself that she had tracked down Sophie Ellis's best friend through Facebook, but ten minutes in Francesca's company and Ruth was beginning to wonder how good a friend she actually was. Instead of concern for her missing friend, Francesca seemed to be revelling in the drama of Sophie's misfortune, as if she was watching some soap opera with ringside seats.

'Twelve months ago I'd have said there was absolutely no way she could do something like that,' continued Francesca, spooning the froth off her drink. 'But after the year that Sophie's had, you know, losing all her money, well, you just don't know how that sort of stress affects people, do you? Take the night she met Nick. Left me high and dry to make my own way to my boyfriend Charlie's apartment, just so she could stay and pull one of the Chariot party guest list. Very selfish,' she said, shaking her head. '*Entre nous*, I think she's just totes jealous that I'm getting married to someone as successful as Charlie. For all we know, perhaps this Nick character told Soph he wasn't interested in anything more than a shag and then she killed him.'

Ruth turned on her Dictaphone, sensing something interesting.

'So what's the Chariot party?'

'The party where she met Nick,' said Francesca, rolling her eyes. She flicked her hair over one shoulder and leant into the tape-recording device. 'Basically she was house-sitting for some woman at the gym who said that Sophie could have all of her party invitations for the season. The Chariot party was a real high-rollers' shindig at Waterloo station the other day.'

'Who was the woman who owned the house? Do you know?'

'Lana Goddard-Price,' said Francesca confidently. 'I googled her; she's married to a *Sunday Times* Rich-List banker – you would not believe the labels in that woman's wardrobe.'

'So you've been to the house?' asked Ruth, her interest going up another notch.

Francesca nodded. 'It's this amazing place just off Brompton Road. I was telling Charlie only yesterday that he'd better start getting some bigger bonuses, because I want a place just like it when we're married.'

Ruth pulled out her notebook. 'You wouldn't happen to have the address, would you?'

'It's about a twenty-minute walk from here,' said Francesca, writing down the Egerton Row address. 'And don't forget, if you ever need any financial experts for the *Tribune*'s business section, my Charlie is the man for the job. He's going to have to raise his profile internationally if he's ever going to get a promotion.'

* * *

Ruth was glad to get out of the café and breathe in some fresh air. She took a paracetamol out of her bag and washed it down with a vitamin C drink the bottle insisted would 'get you feeling your old self'. Ruth had drunk two bottles of the stuff already and was prepared to swear in court that it wasn't true. She still felt as bad as she did when she crawled out of bed that morning, although there was something other than alcohol poisoning that was making her feel unwell. She grimaced at the memory of her predatory lunge at poor Chuck Dean outside the Frontline Club. What an ass she'd made of herself, she thought, wondering if she could avoid the *Tribune* office for the rest of the day.

She shook her head and powered down Pelham Street, mulling over the Nick Beddingfield story in her head. Despite her hangover, Ruth was never happier than when she was chasing down leads, putting clues together. The past few months she had felt quite frustrated on the job, but the truth was, she couldn't imagine herself doing anything else. Trapped in some dingy office thinking up marketing slogans for breakfast cereal? Ringing up strangers persuading them to take out life insurance? The very idea gave her the shivers. She loved being out there alone, left to her own devices. You could disappear for weeks on end and your editor would understand, your friends wouldn't get pissy – because that was your job. You *were* the job.

Of course, that was the old days, back when spending the night in a bombed-out house or watching mortars fly over your head still felt romantic. Here in London, buzzing and energetic though the city was, there were precious few stories that made Ruth feel as engaged, as excited as this one. Which was why she *had* to crack it – she couldn't let Nick Beddingfield get away from her.

Ruth looked up, realising she was at her destination. *Nice place*, she thought at she studied the glorious white stucco-fronted house in front of her. Francesca had been right when she had described it, rather enviously, as one of the most beautiful houses in London. Ruth took a second to imagine herself as its owner, and quickly decided she had no desire to ever live in something this grand. *A girl could get lost just going to the bathroom*, she smiled to herself.

She went up the front steps and pressed the bell, knocking on the door for good measure. Finally, the door opened a crack and a housekeeper in a black and white uniform peered out, her expression one of faint irritation.

'I'm looking for Lana Goddard-Price,' said Ruth, trying to see past the woman into the house.

'No here. South of France,' the woman said, beginning to shut the door.

Ruth made a guess that the housekeeper was Filipino. She had no command of the Tagalog language, but she knew of one currency that was understood the world over. She rooted around in her purse, drew out three twenty-pound notes and held them through the gap like a fan.

'Could I ask you a couple of questions?' she said with a winning smile. 'Five minutes of your time. Please?'

The housekeeper hesitated for a moment, then opened the door just enough for Ruth to slip through.

'Thank you,' said Ruth as the woman folded the money into her pocket. 'What's your name?'

'Cherry,' she said warily.

'Okay, Cherry, nothing to worry about,' she said soothingly. 'No one's in trouble. I just wanted to asked about the girl who stayed here. Sophie Ellis? She house-sat for Mrs Goddard-Price.'

'I see her only one time. Thursday. I let her in, then leave for holiday.'

'So she arrived last Thursday?' said Ruth, glancing around the entrance hall, craning her head into the living room, trying to take in as much as she could.

'Girl gone. She bad girl. She go in Mrs G's wardrobe.'

Ruth nodded sympathetically. Francesca had told her, without any apparent remorse, how she and Sophie had borrowed 'a few nice things' for the Chariot party.

'Did she leave any of her own things?'

Cherry shook her head.

'Can I just look at Sophie's room, where she slept, where she kept her belongings?'

'Police take everything,' said Cherry. She clearly hadn't enjoyed their visit. Ruth wondered if the woman had a proper work permit.

'Well could I at least speak to Mrs Goddard-Price?'

'I say, she in France.'

'And who is she in France with? Mr Goddard-Price?'

There was a glint in Cherry's eye.

'Husband in Switzerland,' she said with a hint of smile. 'Maybe she with other man.'

'Other man?' frowned Ruth. 'What other man?'

The maid's mouth opened and closed like a fish and she began backing Ruth towards the door.

'No more questions; I know nothing,' she said.

'Cherry, please. Who is Mrs G with?' But she could see that the housekeeper would say nothing else.

'All right, okay. But couldn't you at least give me Mrs Goddard-Price's number so that if I have any more questions later, I can call her?'

She smoothly produced another crisp twenty, which immediately disappeared into Cherry's pocket. Sucking her teeth, the housekeeper walked over to a closet in the hallway. It was full of brushes and cleaning products, and was where Cherry apparently stored her coat and her handbag.

She took a blue plastic pen out of a pen pot, scribbled down the number and handed it to Ruth.

'You go now.'

Ruth was bundled out on to the steps and heard the front

307

door being locked behind her. She looked down at the number in her hand.

'What *have* you been up to, Mrs G?' she wondered to herself.

Ruth sighed. There were so many missing parts of the puzzle, she didn't know where to start. If only she had access to the information Detective Inspector Fox and his team had. They would be investigating Nick's movements and business transactions, maybe getting access to his bank accounts. And if Nick had 'form', as they said in the force, then there was a good chance Fox knew about his potential enemies. If Sophie Ellis was still a suspect, they'd have built up a profile of her too by now.

'All right, Ian Fox,' said Ruth, pulling her mobile out of her pocket. 'Let's see what you know.'

She quickly tapped in a text message:

Fox, it's Ruth. Can you call me? We need to meet. Important.

She looked down at it for a moment, then added an '*x*' at the end. Not very professional, perhaps, but hey, she was a woman in a man's world – she had to use whatever weapons were to hand.

Feeling a spot of rain, she pulled up the collar of her jacket and hurried to her next meeting.

34

It was hard to see anything out of the windows of Lana's Gulfstream; they were tiny. Presumably the passengers on the sleek private jets weren't that interested in sightseeing. All Sophie could see was a long expanse of tarmac and a stationary baggage cart with no driver. *Welcome to America,* she thought. Lana's private jet had landed at Teterboro airport, an aviation facility in New Jersey popular with private and corporate aircraft. It was small, yes, but it was a 'landing rights' airport and, as such, an approved point of entry into the United States for people who weren't American citizens. Sophie felt anxious as they waited for the plane to be inspected by the Customs and Border Protection agency.

At least Josh had his proper passport and had been able to hastily arrange his ESTA – the document required for US travel – at Nice airport. Sophie already had one from a previous trip to the States, but for all she knew, Inspector Fox could have American airports on red alert for a Sophie Ellis entering the country. If an alarm was going to go off, it would happen any minute.

'Can you see anyone?' whispered Josh. He sounded uncharacteristically nervous. Despite Lana's reassurances, they had spent the entire seven-hour journey from Nice paranoid that they would be met by a SWAT team and two truckloads of FBI agents in black suits and wraparound shades.

'Please relax,' said Lana. 'I assure you, the United States authorities have no interest in either of you. We simply have to wait for the landing officials to scan our fingerprints, then we can leave.'

Sophie looked back at the woman, sitting calmly in her armchair. How could she seriously expect them to relax? From the moment of meeting Lana by the pool at Villa Polieux, Sophie had been off-balance, feeling as if she was teetering on the edge of a cliff. The jaw-dropping revelation that she had been set up by Lana and Nick would have been enough, but now Sophie was being asked to accept that her father, the one man she had trusted and idolised in this world, was in fact a crook and had deliberately lost her family's life savings. It was enough to mess with anyone's head.

'Let me see your book again,' said Josh. 'If we're going to have to sit here, I might as well try and crack the code.'

Sophie opened her copy of *I Capture the Castle*, which had been safely retrieved from La Luna hotel.

In the centre of the title page was Peter Ellis's handwriting: *To my dearest S, read this and think of our castle. Happy birthday. All my love always, Daddy.* But in the top right-hand corner, above the title, the words 'Benedict Grear' had been written, in the small cursive writing of a teenager perhaps, alongside the date '22 12 56'. Sophie had seen it there before, of course, but the paperback had been old and a little worn and she had simply assumed it was the name of its previous owner. How many times had she inscribed her own name in her treasured novels as a way of claiming ownership of a story she had loved? It wasn't uncommon to see something similar in any second-hand book.

But suddenly these few words had taken on huge significance. They had spent at least an hour in Sophie's cramped Cannes hotel room thinking up ever more outlandish – and desperate – explanations for the words. When Google had thrown up nothing, Josh had tried breaking them down into anagrams, tried assigning letters to the numbers in the hope of forming words; Lana had even translated them into Spanish and back. Nothing made any sense. Finally Lana had suggested the Gulfstream.

'If you don't know what it means, then there's really only one person who might: Michael Asner's widow Miriam. And even if she doesn't, perhaps she'll tell you something she wouldn't tell the investigators.'

It made sense, and as Lana had the means of flying them to the US, it seemed ridiculously simple. Simple, that was, until they were actually there, sitting on the tarmac, waiting for a siren to sound. Sophie felt her nerves might snap at any moment.

'You do realise we don't even know if it is a code?' she said. 'It could genuinely be just something the previous owner wrote in there.'

'I have no idea of its relevance,' said Lana, fixing her with her cool stare. 'But I do know it is the only thing your father gave to you, and until we exhaust every possibility, we have to assume it does have some hidden message.'

'We have exhausted every possibility!' said Sophie. 'I don't know what you expect—'

There was a cough, and they looked up to see the pilot at the door.

'Sorry to interrupt, but the immigration team are here.'

Their immigration ordeal took just a few minutes; a few questions and some fingerprinting and they were through.

'Is that it?' breathed Sophie.

'I told you,' said Lana. 'You have no convictions, you've committed no crime on American soil and the British police are hardly going to bother their American cousins about a missing witness who for all they know is probably still somewhere in Chelsea.'

Sophie let out a long breath.

'So where next? A diner for burgers and shakes?'

'Not quite,' said Lana officiously. 'I have a car waiting which will take you to Pleasantville. The driver knows Miriam's address.'

'You're not coming with us?' said Josh, surprised.

'No, I'm going to the city,' said Lana, handing Sophie a card. 'This is my address in New York. Find out what you can and I'll meet you there. We'll have dinner this evening.'

'So what's to stop us finding the money and running off with it?' said Sophie, only half joking.

Lana didn't smile. When she spoke, her tone was light but her dark eyes were deadly serious.

'I found you once, Sophie,' she said. 'I can find you again.'

Sophie sat in the back seat of the town car and craned her neck to watch the buildings of the airport terminal disappear behind them. She could barely believe it. They were in America.

'Do you trust her?' she said, turning to Josh.

'Sophie, she tricked you into her house, set you up with Nick, lied about who she was. No – I don't trust her an inch.'

'Neither do I,' said Sophie, still feeling duped and angry and humiliated.

He paused, looking towards the driver. The sliding glass panel between him and the passenger area was closed, but Sophie could tell Josh didn't trust that either.

'But what choice do we have?' he said finally. 'She's given us use of a private jet, a car, all the resources we need to find out who killed Nick and to set the record straight. The brutal truth is we can't fix this on our own, Soph. Much as I'd like us to.'

'I always got the feeling you could do anything,' she said softly. She looked down at his hand on the seat beside her, and was suddenly desperate to reach out and touch it, desperate to tell him how she felt when she was with him:

safe, stronger, complete. But instead she turned away, watching the New Jersey streets as they turned on to the freeway, feeling deathly tired.

She'd had a short nap on the plane, but when was the last time she had slept properly? she asked herself, wondering if she would ever sleep like that again. Careless, innocent, untroubled. Was her innocence really gone for ever? Her eyelids were heavy, but when they closed, all she could see was Josh. She had wondered whether the swell of feeling she'd had for him at the Villa Polieux had just been the balmy summer air and the fact that he'd looked so handsome in a suit. But she was self-aware enough to know that her feelings for him were getting stronger rather than fading. On the one hand, it made her feel fickle and ridiculous. Only a week ago she had been strolling along the Thames with Nick Beddingfield, although she knew now that all those emotions had been based on a lie. Her relationship with Josh was something else. They had shared so much together, been through so much. During those long nights in the garage, in the tiny sleeper carriage of the train, even at the motel, he had made no move on her, hadn't tried to touch her. But still, she was sure he had felt that electricity between them at the villa. She was *sure* of it. Finally Sophie dozed, vaguely aware of the sway of the car, the feel of Josh's leg against hers, nothing else.

Not long after – or had it been hours? She really couldn't tell – Josh nudged her awake.

'Almost there, sleepy,' he said gently. She rubbed her eyes and looked out at the changed landscape of Westchester County: the single-storey clapboard houses with well-tended and shady lawns surrounded by that great American staple, the picket fence, the golden sunshine slanting through oaks and pines. Miriam Asner's house was on the outskirts of town, its mower-striped grass edged by a silver pond.

'Not bad,' said Sophie sarcastically, as they stepped out of the town car and stretched. It wasn't quite the Fifth Avenue luxury of Miriam's old life, but it was close. Looking at the widow's lovely property, you'd say that crime definitely did pay.

'I Googled her,' said Josh, holding up his mobile. 'As part of an agreement with the US prosecutors, Miriam Asner was allowed to keep a million dollars.'

'She must be devastated.'

Josh smiled. 'It's all relative, I suppose. If you're used to the Royal Suite at the Waldorf, this is probably torture.'

Sophie looked towards the shuttered windows with their neat curtains.

'Well I hope she's in. It's a long way to come if she's spending the summer in the Bahamas.'

'Lana says she is a recluse, gone slightly loopy since Asner popped off. I don't think hermits go out much.' He shrugged and picked up Sophie's bag. 'Let's go and see, eh?'

As they walked along the gravel drive, the town car reversed back on to the road and Sophie turned to wave goodbye.

'What time's he coming back?' she asked.

'What time's who . . . ? Oh sh—!' Josh dropped the bag and sprinted after the car, waving his arms. 'WAIT!' he shouted, but it had already turned on to the road.

Josh came back panting, his face flushed.

'Why didn't you bloody stop him?'

'I've been asleep, Josh. I assumed you'd arranged for him to wait or come back later.'

'Well now we're stranded here. If only you'd thought instead of waving at him—'

'*Me?* Now this is my fault . . . ?'

There was a cough behind them.

'Can I help you?'

A tall, slender woman with a dark auburn bob was standing in the doorway of the house. Sophie recognised

Miriam Asner at once from the newspaper photographs of her sitting dignified and impassive throughout her husband's court case. Long grey palazzo pants and a crisp white shirt showed off her willowy figure, and she was holding a Paulo Coelho novel, as if their shouting had disturbed her from a snooze in the garden. Perhaps it had.

'Sorry,' said Josh, immediately switching on his lady-killer smile. 'We didn't mean to startle you. My name is Joshua McCormack and this,' he said, with a slight pause, 'is Sophie Ellis. Her father Peter was an old friend of Michael's.'

'What's this about?' asked Miriam, frowning.

'It might take a while to tell you that. Can we come in?' Sophie smiled awkwardly.

Miriam hesitated and then nodded, turning along a path that skirted the house.

'There's no air-conditioning, unfortunately,' she said over her shoulder. 'We should sit by the pond.' She gestured towards a group of four Adirondack chairs at the foot of the lawn and went back into the house.

When the Asner scandal hit her family, Sophie had read a great deal about Michael and Miriam, seeking out newspapers and magazine articles on the internet as if it would help make sense of what had happened. Miriam was from good New England stock, the sort of woman who was raised to support her wealthy husband and entertain on his behalf, with an occasional charitable project to fill the emptiness of her days. Her aloof manner and perceived 'airs' hadn't gone down well with the press, who had demonised her for the way she had steadfastly refused to condemn her husband. But today Sophie thought she looked like the elegant, sixty-ish widow she was. She didn't come across as wicked or arrogant, just sad and rather tired. Miriam Asner had always claimed that she knew nothing about her husband's Ponzi scheme. If that were true, it struck Sophie that she was also a victim, along with the rest of Michael's investors.

Miriam returned with three tumblers of iced tea served on a silver tray. She passed them to her guests, each with a neatly folded white napkin wrapped around the base. Sophie wondered if the older woman still imagined herself as the social grande dame, or whether it was simply good manners that refused to be blunted by circumstance.

'Do you want to tell me why you are here?' said Miriam, her voice as crisp as her shirt. Sophie looked at Josh and he gave her a reassuring smile.

'I suppose you know my father and your husband Michael were friends,' began Sophie uncertainly.

'Were, past tense,' said Miriam, her mouth pursed.

'Yes, well, either way, my family lost a great deal of money with your husband's scheme; everything they had, in fact.'

'And you want the money back?'

'Well, yes, of course, but—'

'My dear woman, look around you,' said Miriam. 'All I have is here, believe me. If you are seeking these spurious missing millions, well all I can say is good luck.'

'Don't you believe your husband had hidden anything else, perhaps for you?'

Miriam shook her head vigorously.

'The authorities have been over this,' she sighed. 'They have found nothing. That is because there is nothing to find.'

'Well, if you'll forgive me, Mrs Asner, we believe there is.'

Miriam waved a hand in front of her face, her eyes welling up with tears. 'My husband is barely cold in the ground,' she said quietly. 'Can't you people just leave me alone?'

'I'm sorry, Mrs Asner, but—'

'Do you think I like living this life?' she cried suddenly. 'Do you think I enjoy being too scared to go to town? If there was money, I'd take it and find a new life on some far-flung desert island, believe me. My life has been ruined. My friends have gone. Everything's gone: the beach house, the boats, the jet, even my golf clubs. The US marshals changed the locks on the house I'd been living in for thirty years.'

She took a drink of her tea and Sophie saw her hands were shaking.

'They're still watching me, you know that? Waiting in cars on every corner, following me, listening on the phone.'

'Who?' asked Sophie, glancing at Josh. 'Who's following you?'

'FBI, SEC, Donald Trump, who knows? But I'm sure of one thing: they all think I know where the money is.'

'And you don't?' asked Sophie, her heart sinking.

'No. No, I don't.'

She took a ragged breath and blew her nose.

'The irony is no one comes here, no one calls.' She looked at them fiercely. 'Not unless they want this buried treasure you all seem to think exists. Crackpots, con artists, they all send letters. And the lawyers, of course. Always the lawyers. No doubt you've seen this creature Andrea Sayer on Fox News?'

'The lawyer trying to bring the class action?' said Josh. 'I read about that on the internet.'

Miriam nodded. 'Yes. Her,' she said, her voice dripping with disgust. 'She plagues me almost daily, threatening to take even this,' she said, gesturing towards the house, 'unless I turn over the secret about this money. But I'm sorry to have to tell you this: it does not exist.'

Josh sat forward.

'I think you misunderstand us, Mrs Asner. We're not here to ask you about the missing money; we're here to *tell* you about it.'

Sophie looked at him and he nodded.

'Someone has tried to kill me, Mrs Asner,' she said. 'They think I have some of Michael's money, a secret stash that he – or rather my father – siphoned off before the scheme collapsed.'

Miriam's clear green eyes widened and she looked from Sophie to Josh and back.

'Is this a joke?' she whispered.

'I wish it was,' said Sophie, and taking a deep breath, she gave the woman a brief outline of the events since Nick's death. The burglaries at her flat and at Wade House, the chase along the river, the near-miss in Nice and Lana's revelation about Peter Ellis's father's involvement.

'You've had quite an adventure, haven't you?' said Miriam when she had finished. 'And I was sorry to hear about your father,' she added quietly. 'I know they hadn't always seen eye to eye, but Michael spoke highly of Peter. I think he believed Peter was the only man who really understood him.'

'And do you think it's possible my father was involved in your husband's investment scheme?' asked Sophie.

Miriam gave a weary smile.

'It's possible, of course, but you're really asking the wrong person. As I said to the police – and the FBI, the SEC and the lawyers – my husband did not discuss his business dealings with me.'

Sophie had to admit that would make sense, in the same way her own father would never tell Julia Ellis what he did in the office. Here, in polite American society, where divorce was just a career move, it would have been even less likely. Whatever else he was, Asner was a smart cookie, and he would never have given his wife – however close they were – ammunition to either blackmail him or take him to the cleaners should she take a shine to the golf pro.

'Well I wonder if you could take a look at this?' she said, reaching into her bag for her copy of *I Capture the Castle*. She knelt down next to Miriam and opened the title page to show her Peter's inscription and the name of the previous owner – perhaps.

'This name, Benedict Grear,' she said. 'We think this is

the name of someone connected with Michael, perhaps a friend or an attorney who might be the key to where the money is. Does it ring any bells?'

Miriam shook her head. 'Never heard of him, sorry.'

'What about the number?' said Josh. 'A date of birth, perhaps? It could even be a bank account number.'

Miriam was beginning to look irritated. 'It's not familiar, I'm sorry. It's not my birthday, or Michael's, or anyone I know. And it seems a little short for a bank account number or routing code, doesn't it?'

Josh nodded. They had of course noticed that, but they were hoping Asner's wife would see some significance not obvious to them. Sophie put the book away, feeling a flutter of despair. Surely they couldn't have come all this way for nothing?

'Think, Miriam, please,' she said. 'Perhaps Michael left something behind, a journal or a notebook?'

'Really, I can't help,' she said firmly. 'I don't have any diaries or notebooks. When the Ponzi scheme was discovered by the authorities, the investigators took the files, the computers, even the cell phones. They took everything.'

Dismay had spread across Miriam's face, and Sophie's heart sank. *Oh God, she really doesn't know anything,* she thought.

'I'm sorry, Mrs Asner, we didn't mean to upset you. It's just . . . well, I hoped you might have the answer.'

'No, don't apologise,' said Miriam. 'I can see you're desperate, and why wouldn't you be when people on all sides seem to be out to get you? I can certainly identify with that feeling.'

She stood up, gathering the empty glasses on to her tray.

'Why don't you come up to the house?' she said. 'I don't have the answer you're looking for, but I do have something you might like to see.'

They followed her up the lawn and into the cool darkness

of the house. It was modestly furnished – mismatched furniture and whitewashed walls – with a distinctive nautical Cape Cod feel to it: gingham drapes with rope tie-backs, a stripped dresser with carved wader-bird ornaments. Leaving her tray on a table, she led them through into a comfortable living room dominated by two leather sofas facing a media centre.

'It's in here somewhere,' she said, opening a glass-fronted display case and looking inside.

While she was waiting, Sophie walked over to a bookshelf, fascinated to see what kind of reading matter Michael Asner might have gone in for. There were the usual suspects – Stephen King, James Patterson, Michael Crighton – and a surprising number of sailing books, just like her father. She was about to comment on it when she heard the TV clicking on.

'Here it is,' said Miriam, bending over the DVD player. 'Now, if I can just...' Then, to Sophie's amazement, suddenly there was her father on the screen in front of her. Only it wasn't the Peter Ellis she remembered. He was younger, much more handsome and happy. For a moment, she couldn't breathe. The colours were oversaturated and the picture was grainy, but there was no mistaking her dad, in his tweed jacket and flared jeans. His hair was longer – well, he *had* hair! – but the glasses were the same and the slightly stooped way he stood made something in her chest hurt.

'He's so... young,' she said, feeling a pang of sadness, and yet this connection back to her father gave her a strange reassurance that everything would be okay.

'Home movies,' said Miriam, smiling at Sophie's reaction. 'Super 8, I think. Michael had them all converted on to DVD about five years ago. I'd forgotten we still had them. This was when Mike and Peter were at Oxford, of course.'

On the TV, Peter Ellis was standing by a river waving at the camera.

'Bring it closer!' Sophie heard him say. The picture cut to a boat sitting in the water, the name clearly visible on the bow.

'*Iona*?' she gasped. It was her dad's beloved sailing boat.

On the TV, she could now see Michael Asner – younger, and actually quite handsome – sitting at the back of *Iona*, his hand against the tiller, a cricket jumper tied around his shoulders.

'I think they were all fixated with *Brideshead Revisited* and *Chariots of Fire* back then, some stupid imagined ideal of Englishness. Michael told me he tried, but he didn't fit in.'

'Weren't there other Americans at Oxford then?' asked Josh.

'Oh yes, but old money: New England, Ivy League types who rowed and swanked about in their school scarves. Mike was from Sacramento, he had long hair and listened to all that horrible rock music.'

Sophie gave a sad smile. Julia had never approved of her father's taste in music, but he would play Pink Floyd and Deep Purple at full blast when they were in the car together. It was one of their little shared things.

'The two of them were thrown together out of necessity,' continued Miriam. 'I believe your father was a grammar school boy, wasn't he? From a blue-collar background? He didn't fit in with the stuck-up private school guys any more than Michael got on with the jocks, so they scraped the money together for the boat. That way they could join the sailing society and fit in with the money crowd, but I don't think it worked too well.'

The film finished and switched to another scene: a birthday party for someone Sophie had never seen before. Miriam stepped across and ejected the DVD.

'Thank you,' said Sophie. 'It was kind of you to show me that.'

'Not at all.' Miriam smiled and crossed to the bookshelf,

taking down a leather-bound album. 'Here, I think I've got one you can keep.'

She opened the book; it was full of photographs stuck to the page with old-fashioned photo corners. She turned the pages until she got to a spread of snaps presumably taken at the same time as the Super 8 film: pictures of Michael Asner standing proudly by the *Iona*. She pulled out one of Sophie's father standing with his arm around his friend, the boat's sail visible in the background. 'There you go; I've got plenty of these as you can see. Something to remember your visit by.'

Sophie's eyes filled with tears. 'Thank you so much, I'll treasure it.'

'Could I just ask,' said Josh. 'Peter and Michael were obviously very close at Oxford. Why did they fall out?'

Miriam glanced at Sophie warily.

'They always said it was over the boat. Peter bought out Michael's share, and later regretted it. But it could have been something else. Mike said he and Peter used to make plans together, cooking up get-rich schemes to show all those toffee-nosed stuck-ups. They were going to move out to New York, take on Manhattan. But then . . .' She looked at Sophie again. 'But then Peter got married . . .'

Sophie nodded.

'It's okay, I know my mother wouldn't have let him run off to America. Dad used to make a big thing about family being important, keeping the family firm going, but he was always looking at his sailing charts, always planning his big getaway. In some ways, I wish he had.'

'Well, if what we've been told is true, perhaps they did come up with a get-rich scheme in the end,' said Josh.

Sophie looked at the picture of *Iona* again. Up until this moment, she hadn't been able to believe that her dad, this staid, boring accountant from Surrey, had been involved with a scheme which had swindled millions – billions, perhaps – from wealthy investors on both sides of the

Atlantic. But now? Well, it was still hard for her to imagine, but at least now Peter Ellis had a motive. Perhaps it had all been a way of getting even for something that had happened at university. Had it just been revenge? She turned to Miriam.

'Did Michael and my dad make up? I mean, could this story be true, that Peter and Michael cooked up the scheme together?'

Miriam shook her head.

'If they did, I didn't hear about it. Peter never came to dinner, I can tell you that. But then, I guess if his part in it was to hide the money, they would have kept their friendship a secret, wouldn't they? Perhaps we'll never know.'

Sophie looked at Miriam.

'But I have to, Mrs Asner, I have to find out. I'm in danger, and I'm scared.' To admit it out loud made the situation more real.

Miriam's face softened.

'You should speak to Andrea Sayer,' she said quietly.

'The lawyer you hate?' Sophie asked, raising a brow.

Miriam nodded. 'She's spent long enough demanding things from me; now maybe it's time she gave a little back. Andrea Sayer is always crowing about how she knows more about my husband's case than anyone alive, so if anyone might know who this Benedict guy is, she will.'

'And you're thinking that it will annoy her having to speak to us?' said Josh.

'Maybe a little,' laughed Miriam. 'That woman's so self-important, I'd love to see the look on her face when she meets someone who knows things about Michael Asner she doesn't.'

The smile faded.

'She's based in Manhattan,' she said, pulling a letter from a drawer and handing it to Josh. 'Her address and phone number are on there. If you're quick, you'll be able to catch her before she leaves the office for the weekend. Although that woman is constantly on the job.'

'What's the quickest way to get to the city?'

'Trains from Pleasantville station go all the way to Grand Central,' replied Miriam. 'My car's in the garage being serviced or I'd run you to town.'

'How far is the station?' asked Josh.

'Five miles west of here. There's a bus stop just opposite the house. Or you could give ten dollars to Jim Bryant at the gas station and he'll take you.'

They walked away from the house and out on to the road, looking for the bus stop. Josh tried to make banter but Sophie was deep in thought. It was strange: she'd gone to Miriam Asner's expecting to hate her; she had been so angry that she had managed to ride out the waves of her husband's maelstrom, escaping virtually unscathed whilst Sophie's family, and hundreds like them, had lost everything. But now she only felt sorry for her. Miriam Asner was a woman who knew nothing except how to hold the perfect tea party or organise a wonderful dinner for her husband's clients. Now she was alone, friendless and trapped in a little cottage on the edge of nowhere, where no one ever called. It was as if someone had chosen the perfect punishment for her.

They crossed the road and looked at the bus timetable. Sophie groaned: one hour until the next connection.

'I can run five miles in about forty minutes,' she said seriously.

'You run. I'll pay Jim Bryant my ten bucks,' grinned Josh, hefting Sophie's bag over his shoulder.

After they had been walking a few minutes, he glanced across at her.

'So how are you feeling?'

Sophie shrugged.

'Strange. I didn't believe it, you know? About my dad, I mean. But now it feels real, like I can understand how it happened.'

'You think what Miriam said was true? That they did it to

get even with the posh kids who made them feel small?'

'I don't think we'll ever know. If my dad was involved, I don't believe he just did it for the money.'

'Well, maybe . . .'

Josh trailed off and Sophie looked up at him.

'What's wrong?'

She noticed it as soon as the words came out of her mouth. Up ahead, a car had slowed to a stop and was sitting in the road. It hadn't pulled over into a lay-by; it had just stopped dead, gunning its engine.

'You know what? I think we'll go the other way,' said Josh, taking Sophie's hand. But there wasn't time. With a screech of tyre rubber on asphalt, the car leapt into motion, driving straight at them.

'This way!' shouted Josh, throwing the bag into a field to their right and bundling Sophie over the fence just as the car rushed by, missing him by millimetres and sending him pinwheeling into the dirt.

'Josh!' shouted Sophie, but he scrambled to his feet, swearing.

At the side of the road was a line of trees that marked the start of some woodland.

'Grab the bag and make for the trees,' he said through gritted teeth. He was limping, but he was moving, and that was all that mattered at that moment. Frantically she wondered if they could use his mobile to call the police. But how crazy would that phone call sound? 'Can you help us, we're being chased by hit men who are after a billion dollars of stolen loot. Yes, I know I put "vacation" on my customs form. No, I'm not on medication.' There was no time to worry about that now, though, only time to act. She helped Josh squeeze through a gate, then felt her heart jump. Glancing back, she could see two men gaining on them. There were two tracks – one that led deep into the wood, and another that skirted around the perimeter.

'This way,' she hissed, taking the perimeter path. Josh stopped as if he was about to argue. She could see why he wanted to go into the trees. It was dark, with more places to hide. And yet there would be no one to see or help them. They would be murdered and the next people to find their bodies would be walkers in about two weeks' time. She felt a surge of determination to escape.

'Come on!' she shouted.

They were both fast runners but they could not outrun a bullet. Expecting a shot at any moment, she willed her legs to move even quicker until her muscles throbbed and her lungs ached.

'It's the gas station,' she panted, noticing some buildings up ahead.

They began running as fast as they could, Josh hampered by his injured knee but still managing to keep up with Sophie, her bag slamming against her legs. The gas station was in full view, a little two-pump affair with a wooden shack behind it.

'Oh no,' she gasped and skidded to a halt, Josh almost falling over her in the process.

'What the hell are you doing?' he panted.

'There,' she said, pointing. Driving slowly out from behind the house was another SUV with blacked-out windows.

'Shit,' said Josh, swivelling around the other way. 'We're trapped. The others have doubled back.'

Sophie looked behind him and could see the first car coming towards them at speed.

'Which way?' she said, her hands on her knees. They clearly wouldn't get far cross-country, and their way back to Miriam's was blocked. As they watched, the SUV at the garage began to power towards them, its wheels kicking up dust.

'Grab my hand,' said Josh. 'When I say jump, go left.'

'What?' said Sophie, but Josh was already up and pulling her along with him – straight towards the gas station and the oncoming car.

'What the hell are you doing?' yelled Sophie.

'Playing chicken!' shouted Josh. 'One . . . two . . . jump!'

He yanked her to the left and they leapt together, landing on a grassy embankment, rolling over and over, finally coming to rest with Josh lying full-length on top of her, the bag jammed painfully between them. Looking over Josh's shoulder, she could see the SUV skidding to a halt diagonally across the road, blocking it. The doors opened.

'They're coming,' she gasped as they scrambled to their feet.

An old red pick-up truck was pulling into the garage.

'Help us!' screamed Sophie.

The driver had white hair and a startled expression.

'What's going on?' Sophie glanced at the name embroidered over the man's shirt pocket.

'You. You're Jim Bryant? We're friends of Miriam Asner. She said you'd help us. Please. Those men are after us.'

'Get in,' he growled.

They ran round to the passenger door of the truck and jumped into the big bucket seat inside.

'You folks didn't kill no one, did yer?' said Jim as he fired the engine.

'No, but it's a long story. Please, just trust us and get us out of here,' pleaded Josh.

'She-it, boy,' smiled Jim, revealing a missing canine. 'In that case, think we'd better go the quiet way.'

He slammed the truck into drive, twisting the wheel away from the road and jerking off down a farm track hidden behind the line of trees. Sophie turned in her seat to look out of the back window: she couldn't see either SUV or the men, but she still didn't feel safe, even though Jim was putting distance between them with every skidding turn, cutting across fields and skirting farmhouses, almost completely avoiding the roads.

'You might want to watch your heads,' he shouted as they thunked into a pothole and bounced straight out again, flying out of their seats and bumping against the roof. He wrenched the wheel to the right and the truck skidded through a gap in some trees and careered up through a dry river bed, sending stones flying in their wake.

Who was after them? wondered Sophie, confident that they had left them behind. The Russians? The FBI? It could have been anyone. All that counted right now was getting away. They could worry about all the rest later.

'Thanks for helping us, Mr Bryant,' she said, raising her voice to be heard over the thrumming engine.

'Call me Jim, sweetness. And you're welcome. Don't agree with what her scumbag husband did to all his investors, but Miriam is a pretty foxy lady.'

He paused to downshift as they turned on to a road, a single-lane blacktop that wound down into a grove of red oaks, the sunshine only leaking through in shafts of brilliant yellow.

Josh looked at him. 'Could that have been the FBI back there?'

Jim shrugged. 'Why? You something to do with her husband?'

'My father was an old friend of Michael Asner,' explained Sophie.

'Her house is being watched, that's for sure. Mine's the only gas station in three miles, they got to get their reg'lar and their Twinkies somewhere. They been sitting there for months with those wires in their ears.'

'We need to get to Manhattan,' said Sophie, desperate to get away from Pleasantville.

'If you pay for the gas, I'll take you all the way. If you're trying to avoid some folks, that's the best way to get to the city. No, ol' Jim knows all the back roads from here to Hazzard County.'

He winked, and Sophie leant over to kiss his leathery cheek.

'You're a very kind man,' she said as Jim blushed.

He turned to Josh.

'You've got a good girl,' he smiled. 'You look after her, y'hear? My Martha passed not two years since, and ain't a day goes by I don't think of her. Woman couldn't cook for shit, but she was a good one. You find yourself a good one, you hold on to her, okay?'

Sophie glanced at Josh, but he turned and looked out of the window, small spots of colour in the centre of his cheeks.

'I'll try, Mr Bryant,' he said quietly. 'I'll certainly try.'

35

Ruth couldn't quite believe that there were people working out at the gym at eight o'clock on a Friday night. *Haven't these people heard of pubs?* she thought as she peered through the glass partition of the Red Heart at a dozen people still working the machines. She looked at her watch, eager to get this over with. Ian Fox had texted her back, clearly intrigued, and they were due to meet when his shift finished at nine p.m.

'Can I help you?'

Ruth turned to see a cute, ruddy-faced young man wearing the club uniform – a red T-shirt and black jogging bottoms with the logo of a heart doing press-ups. His plastic name badge read 'Hi, I'm Mike'.

'I certainly hope you can help me,' said Ruth, flashing him a smile. *Steady, Ruth*, she reminded herself. *Remember what happened last night.*

Reaching into her bag, she introduced herself and handed him a business card.

'I wanted to ask a few questions about Sophie Ellis. I'm sure you've heard she's got mixed up in something?'

'I guessed as much,' he said hesitantly. 'The police were here yesterday, going through her locker and everything.'

He began to look uncomfortable.

'I'm only the assistant junior manager.' He gave a nervous

330

laugh. 'Kind of a glorified receptionist, really. Sharif – he's the owner – is out at a meeting at the moment.'

'That's okay. It was you I wanted to talk to anyway,' lied Ruth. Make them feel important, they'll give you more. Another one of her dad's maxims. 'I understand you're a good friend of Sophie's?'

She was amused to see that Mike's face instantly flushed pink.

'Well, yes. Not close, which is a shame, because she's lovely.' Another nervous laugh. 'I probably shouldn't have said that, should I? Now you're going to think I doffed that bloke at the Riverton out of unrequited love.'

'Don't be silly,' smiled Ruth, although that exact thought had indeed passed through her head.

'You don't really think Sophie had anything to do with it, do you? She isn't a suspect, is she?' Mike's expression suggested that he might burst into tears if that was the case.

'Witness, yes. Suspect, no.'

'That's what the police officer said.'

'Inspector Fox?' asked Ruth.

'No, someone called Davis, I think.'

'So how was she the last time you spoke to her?' asked Ruth. 'Was anything bothering her? I hear she had money troubles.'

Mike shook his head.

'No, Sophie wasn't the type to let anything like that get her down. The first time she came in, I thought she was going to be another of those stuck-up Chelsea girls, but she wasn't like that at all. She got stuck in, never complained about picking up the sweaty towels the customers drop on the floor, nothing like that. She was great.'

I think someone has a big crush on Little Miss Sophie, thought Ruth, suppressing a smile.

'Actually, for the last few weeks she's been really upbeat,' said Mike. He walked over to the gym notice board and pulled off the flyer for 'Ellis Training' that Sophie had pinned there. 'She'd set up this personal training business and had landed some wealthy housewives as clients. And she was house-sitting at that rich Spanish chick's place, which must have been amazing.'

'That was Lana Goddard-Price? She came to this gym, didn't she?' said Ruth, remembering what Francesca Manning had told her.

'Yes,' said Mike, frowning. 'It was all a bit weird, though.'

'In what way?'

'Well, I was pleased for Soph, of course, but I never really got why that Lana woman asked her to become her trainer. Sophie wasn't working on the day they met, so it wasn't like she mistook her for a Red Heart trainer.'

'So Sophie isn't a qualified trainer here?' asked Ruth, her interest piqued.

'Nope,' said Mike. 'She's really fit, and we all had to do a two-day training course when we started working at the gym, learning about the equipment, that sort of thing. But that's about it. Which is why I thought it was odd. I mean, these rich birds always want the very best people, like some film star's personal trainer or a massage therapist who's been name-checked in *Tatler*. Not a nobody they meet on the weights.'

Interesting, thought Ruth.

'Yeah, and there was another thing I checked too.' He rattled a few keys on his computer and swivelled the monitor around so Ruth could see. It was the member's account page for Lana Goddard-Price.

'What am I looking at?' she asked.

'Look at the date,' said Mike. 'This Lana Goddard-Price had only been a member of the gym for a week when she met Sophie, and see here' – he pointed at a box with an 'X' in it – 'that means she had been offered a discounted trial session with our best trainer when she joined. It's standard procedure when you sign up. But she turned it down. Why would she do that, then ask Sophie to train her a few days later?'

Ruth shrugged. 'Maybe she was cheaper.'

Mike shook his head.

'Soph said Lana was paying her a fortune. I wasn't surprised. This woman used to bring a Chanel handbag into the gym to carry her water bottle.'

'So why do *you* think Lana Goddard-Price asked Sophie to be her trainer?'

Mike looked at her thoughtfully, as if he was weighing up whether he could confide in her. 'To be honest, I thought she was after her.'

'After her?'

'You know,' he replied, looking awkward. 'I thought Lana might be a lesbian. Believe me, I've seen a few things in the changing rooms. It doesn't matter if these rich housewives are married. They get bored, ignored by their husbands, they want a bit of a thrill.'

'And you think that's what happened with Sophie?'

Mike shrugged, his face pinking a little. 'I thought it was a bit full-on to be anything else. Getting Sophie to train with her, inviting her to live at her house all in the space of a fortnight . . . It was a bit odd unless there was an ulterior motive.'

He looked at Ruth, his eyes wide.

'Hey, I haven't got her into any trouble, have I? I mean, it's only a guess.'

'Not at all,' said Ruth. 'And you've been very helpful.'

Mike smiled proudly, as if Ruth had just handed him a certificate for first prize in the obstacle race.

'Have I really?'

Yes, thought Ruth truthfully. *And if nothing else, you've given me something to talk about with Detective Inspector Fox later.*

* * *

He was late, of course. Very late. Ruth looked up at the clock above the bar: less than an hour till last orders. She wasn't surprised; she had spent enough time with coppers to know that they rarely punched out on the dot like factory workers. If they had been unlucky enough to stumble on an international terrorist cell at ten minutes to the end of their shift, they couldn't very well wave them on their way with a cheery 'mind how you go, sir'. Plus she had chosen her local – a quiet pub in the back streets of Barnsbury – as the venue for their 'date', and even with the lack of traffic, it would take Fox a good half hour to get there from Paddington. But Ruth didn't mind; it gave her time to think over the information Mike at the Red Heart gym had given her. Not his theory about Lana Goddard-Price's seduction tactics, but his point of 'why Sophie?' It was a question that had been bothering Ruth too. So what would make Lana Goddard-Price welcome Sophie into her life with such open arms? Had she taken pity on her? These women *did* like to be seen to be involved with charity. But Sophie Ellis was hardly a starving African baby. Was Lana an old friend of the family? No, Sophie would have mentioned a detail like that to Mike and her mother. Mike was right, there *had* to be an ulterior motive. The question was what?

'Someone's deep in thought.'

She looked up and saw Fox. She felt a flutter of surprise – or was it pleasure? – and smiled.

'Sorry, miles away,' she said, slightly flustered. 'I was thinking about the case. You know me, I find it hard to switch off.'

'In which case, I think you need another drink,' said Fox, taking the chair opposite and pushing a glass of red wine across to her. 'The barman told me you were on Rioja.'

'Thanks. To switching off,' said Ruth, raising her glass, chinking it against the policeman's pint. Fox looked around at the pub's cosy interior and unbuttoned his suit jacket.

'So I take it this is your local? I sort of imagined you hanging out in sophisticated nightclubs with lots of neon and expensive cocktails,' he said, his narrow eyes glinting under heavy brows.

'Well, Elton John did call me, begging me to come out. But I said I was meeting my friend Ian who's much more important.'

'Oh it's Ian again, is it?' smiled Fox, taking a sip of his pint. 'You must want something. I thought you were going to give *me* information.'

She searched his face, trying to guess what was going on in his mind. He had come out to meet her, after all – that must mean something. In her experience, police only co-operated with a journalist when they wanted something: some detail on the case, even a name-check on an article to boost their profile. And then there were officers like Dan Davis who were in it for the money or bragging rights in the canteen after they'd got into a reporter's panties. She was sure Ian Fox was not one of those detectives . . . or was he?

'Just making conversation,' she said. 'Not that it would do any harm to compare notes.'

'I'm not sure how well that would go down with the Met Commissioner,' he smiled.

'So I assume you've not heard from Sophie?'

Fox shook his head. 'I've got to make a decision on that one this weekend.'

'You mean list her as missing?'

He nodded.

'The longer she goes without making contact with anyone, even her mother, the more we have to worry about her. My guess is that she's just scared. According to Julia Ellis, she phoned up two days ago and said she wanted to work out who killed Nick.'

'So she's gone underground to play Nancy Drew.'

'It seems that way.'

'What do you know about Lana Goddard-Price?'

'Who Sophie was house-sitting for?'

Ruth held up her hand. 'You don't have to tell me anything if you don't want to, but can I just think out loud here? It's just that I can't work out why Lana would ask Sophie to house-sit for her. It's the one thing about this story I can't get my head around.'

'The *one* thing?' said Fox wearily. 'Most days I think this thing's like a box of snakes, can't make head nor tail of it.'

'I take it you've tried ringing Lana's phone? I couldn't get through.'

'Yes, Ruth,' he said gruffly. 'I'm a police inspector, not an idiot. We tracked down Simon Goddard-Price in Geneva, who gave me the landline of their house in Cap Ferrat.'

'So you've spoken to her.'

'Yes.'

'And what did she say? Come on, Fox, give me something!'

Fox took another drink and shrugged.

'She was shocked, upset, as you'd expect. Although I suspect she was more worried about the scandal of having a house-sitter who was mixed up in a murder than she was about Sophie's well-being. The husband was more bothered about the house. In fact, he made the housekeeper come back from holiday to do an inventory of the property to check for theft.

'And was anything taken?'

'No. Unless you count the unauthorised use of some rather expensive dresses.'

Ruth saw an opening.

'Burglary wasn't Nick's style anyway,' she said casually, giving him a sideways glance. 'How much do you know about the fraud operation he was involved in?' She was fishing of course; all she knew about Nick's past was what Barbara Beddingfield had told her in the café.

'You mean the wine scam?' said Fox.

Bingo.

'That was why he was in London, wasn't it?' said Ruth smoothly.

Fox nodded.

'Our information is that Nick was touting bottles of expensive vintage wine at the Chariot party for twenty per cent under the market value. The Serious Fraud Squad seem to think it might have been counterfeit.'

'So you think there was enough money in the scam to warrant murder?'

'Ruth!'

'All right, all right!' she said, holding up her hands. 'Sorry. It's just . . .'

'Just what?'

She looked at Fox, hesitating. *Ah, what the hell*, she thought. She was feeling a little giddy from the red wine she'd drunk waiting for him. Plus if anyone would understand, it was him.

'Look, I know this sounds mad and probably a little bit sad, but I don't really have anything much in my life right now apart from this job.'

She blushed. *Does he think I'm mental? Probably*. Still, she ploughed on.

'So when I get a story like this one, a story my gut's telling me is something special, I can't seem to leave it alone. I keep picking at it, pick, pick, pick. In fact, this morning I actually called in sick so I could sit at home drawing a big flow chart on my living room wall, trying to fit all the pieces of the story together.'

She thought it best not to tell him about poor Chuck Dean. She wasn't that close to Ian Fox, yet. Besides, avoiding the office all day *had* given her the chance to brainstorm at home.

'You think I'm a saddo,' she added, looking up.

'Yes, I do,' said Fox. 'But you're only describing the

average copper. Well, perhaps not the average copper, but there are plenty of us who eat, sleep and dream their cases.'

She looked down at his left hand for a wedding ring and he caught her.

'Forty-three and never married,' he smiled. 'Beats being a divorced, alcoholic police cliché.'

He paused. 'Do you want to show me?'

'Show you what?' she asked distractedly.

'Your flow chart,' said Fox.

She started to laugh nervously.

'Listen, I'm not Dan Davis,' he replied quickly. 'You said you wanted to compare notes, so here's your chance.'

'Is that allowed?' she teased, aware that she was being flirty.

'I'm not offering to log you on to the police database, Ruth,' said Fox with irritation.

Oh crap, she thought. *He was offering to do exactly what I wanted and now I've scared him off.*

Fox took a deep breath. 'Sorry, long day,' he said. 'Look, quid pro quo here. You've told me about your life, here's mine: being a detective really isn't like it is on the telly. Whenever you see a cop drama, they have a murder or whatever and they spend weeks working on that one case. In real life, we'd have that case and a dozen others heaped on us all at once. And even if we don't, we've got piles of paperwork or court appearances from stuff we worked on a year before, then there's our superiors hassling us about targets and budgets . . .' He gave a wry smile. 'It's like having a real job. So actually, it'd be nice to just focus on one thing.' He raised his eyebrows. 'If the offer's still on, of course.'

Ruth stood up.

'I'll get some bottles from the bar.'

As Ruth turned the key in the lock to her Islington apartment, she offered up a prayer of thanks. At least the flat was tidy.

Well, tidy-ish. Given that she so rarely had visitors and only had herself to please, she had spent the past few years living in happy disarray: she had a place for everything, and that place was often on the floor or draped over a chair. But as she had so recently moved much of her stuff over to David's, her little flat was unusually free of clutter. As long as Fox didn't look in the kitchen, she might just get away with it.

'Where shall I put these?' He held up the bottles of beer they had bought at the pub.

'I'll take them,' said Ruth. 'Why don't you go into the living room, make yourself at home.'

She winced. Did that sound like a come-on? *Was* it a come-on? The truth was the three large glasses of wine she'd consumed on top of the alcohol still in her system from the previous night's binge had made her a little tipsy. She slipped into the bathroom and checked her make-up. *It's not a date, Ruth*, she scolded herself. But a girl had to look her best at all times, didn't she? There was no harm checking your hair wasn't sticking up like a gonk, especially when you had an attractive police detective in the house.

Satisfied, she went back into the kitchen and poured some nachos into a bowl – ah, the domestic goddess – and took them through with the beer and her wine.

Fox was standing at the window looking down at the street.

'Nice place, this, must have cost a packet.'

'I wish,' said Ruth. 'It's rented, but I still love it.'

The Victorian conversion was on the very fringes of gentrified Islington, where the pretty Georgian squares were just beginning to melt into council estates and all-night minimarts. Still, it had that desirable N1 postcode and Ruth rarely felt intimidated walking home from the tube at night. Or maybe that was something to do with having spent time in Sarajevo and Belfast.

'So this is the famous flow chart?' said Fox, walking up to the whiteboard.

She stuffed some nachos into her mouth.

'It came with the flat,' she said. 'It's owned by an investigative journalist friend at the *Observer*. He went to live in New York and when I became his tenant I got custody of the whiteboard. It's fabulous for games of dinner-party Pictionary. You should come to the next one.'

Fox was only half listening, being absorbed in the hasty notes that Ruth had scribbled on the board that morning.

'I was a bit hung-over, so I didn't get very far. My problem is too little real information about any of the players.'

Fox pointed to the word 'Nick'.

'You didn't know there was a wine fraud, did you?'

Ruth pulled a face.

'Not a wine fraud as such,' she said, 'but I knew he'd been charged with fraud. It was reasonable to assume that was how he made a living; he certainly wasn't the wealthy businessman he'd pretended he was to Sophie.'

She sat down in an armchair, tucking her feet under her. 'That's the thing with all of them – I'm not sure anyone on that chart is exactly what they seem on the surface.'

Fox pushed his hand through his short brown hair.

'That's the way I've been thinking too. Everyone's got something to hide.'

He turned and smiled. Ruth looked at him. He really was quite good-looking, she thought. Shame he spent most of his life scowling. Not that she was one to criticise; she'd been pretty gloomy these past few days, but then who could blame her? She glanced around the half-empty apartment and made a vague note to contact David that weekend. She had no desire to speak to him, but every intention of getting her belongings back as quickly as possible; if he thought he could use her good linens, her nice candles to feather his pleasure den for PR Susie, then he was very much mistaken.

'So let's fill in the blanks,' said Fox. He picked up the marker and scrawled the words 'wine fraud' next to Nick's name. He looked at Ruth. 'To answer your question, it was certainly motive enough for murder,' he said. 'A single bottle of vintage wine can go for twenty grand.'

Ruth looked down at her glass. 'Really? I'd better start paying more attention when I'm in Waitrose.'

Fox shook his head.

'It's not always the wine itself – at least that's what the fraud squad guys were telling me. Wine fraud can have links to wider organised crime. It's as if these bottles are made of solid gold, like little recession-proof trading units. And obviously that makes them very attractive for people who might want to hide where their money's come from.'

'Money laundering?'

'Yes, drugs, prostitution, anything really. And a bottle of fake wine's much easier to get through customs than a suitcase of money or a few kilos of heroin. The crooks sell it on legitimately and turn that cash back into smack, whores or whatever, on the other side of the border.'

Fox drew a line from 'wine scam' to the word 'money', then back to Nick.

'So if Nick had been pushing his phoney claret on the Russian Mafia or the Triads or whoever, and they discovered it wasn't the real deal, they could well have got pretty upset.'

Fox pulled a face. 'It's a nice theory, of course,' he said, putting the lid back on the pen. 'But we have zero evidence to prove that's what's going on.'

'What about those guys shooting at Sophie down by the river?'

'One, we don't know they were gangsters,' he said, ticking the points off on his fingers. 'Two, we don't know for sure who the possible other guy was – yes, we checked the owner of the boat, Joshua McCormack. But that's not necessarily the man that Sophie ran off into the night with.'

'I checked out McCormack. Does he have a criminal record?'

Fox shook his head. 'No. Apparently he's a watch salesman. He's no relation to Sophie. Her friends have never heard of him.'

'Maybe he's part of the wine fraud.'

'Perhaps,' said Fox. 'Although there's no hard evidence that Nick was involved in a wine fraud.'

He held up the almost empty bowl of nachos.

'I don't suppose you've got anything else to eat, have you? I came straight from my shift and I'm starving.'

Ruth didn't need to look to know that the fridge was empty except for a green-haired garlic bulb and a withered lemon.

'Give me two minutes and I'll order Chinese,' she said, heading for the phone in the hall. Coming back through, she saw that Fox had been busy at the whiteboard, adding a spider's web of links to Nick's central hub: 'Chariot party', 'Wine fraud?', 'Womaniser – con man?', 'Russian connection?' and so on.

'What's this one?' he asked, tapping a word Ruth had written that morning: 'Asner'.

For a moment she hesitated. Did she really want to reveal everything to him? But then what exactly was she hiding? She felt certain Fox knew that the Ellis family had lost money recently. Besides, she wasn't getting anywhere on her own: that was the uncomfortable truth. She needed Fox's input, even if it was just as a sympathetic sounding board.

'Michael Asner,' she said, picking up her glass.

'The Ponzi scheme guy?' asked Fox.

Ruth nodded. 'Peter Ellis was an investor and basically lost everything the family had.'

'That gives Sophie a motive,' said Fox slowly. 'If she thought Nick was going to be the answer to her financial troubles and found out he had nothing, she'd be pissed off.'

'But you don't believe that, do you?'

'If she was some hardcore gold-digger who'd invested years in their relationship, maybe. But they'd been dating what? A week? And Sophie Ellis is a ditzy posh girl, not a social player.'

'So you think she's innocent?'

'I don't think she killed him, but I still think she's the key to it all. Look at your whiteboard – everything leads back to her.'

They talked a while longer until the doorbell rang and Ruth ran down to collect the food, laying it out on her coffee table: ribs, dumplings, noodles and beef in satay sauce. She and Fox picked them from their cartons as they talked.

'Have you spoken to Jeanne Parsons?'

Fox nodded. 'Nick's girlfriend in Texas.'

'What did she tell you?'

'Not much.'

'When I spoke to her, she said that Nick had said that if he was seen in London with a beautiful woman it was just work.'

'Really?'

Ruth felt a flush of pride at having tracked down information the police had missed.

'Nick and Sophie were apparently inseparable from the minute they met. If we assume that Sophie was that beautiful woman, then she was the work,' said Fox thoughtfully.

'And if Nick was a con man then it makes Sophie a victim. She was a *mark*. All day I've been asking myself what Sophie Ellis had that Nick – and possibly other men with guns – wanted.'

'Money and sex,' said Fox, picking up a dumpling and dunking it in chilli sauce. 'Money and sex are always the motive.'

'Have you checked the CCTV cameras around Nick's suite?'

Fox raised an eyebrow. 'Hotels aren't like banks with cameras everywhere. The biggest crime they can expect is someone walking off with a monogrammed robe.'

'So you couldn't tell who'd been to his room?'

Fox suppressed a burp and shook his head.

'No, we had a look at some security footage of the lobby which confirmed Sophie's story of running for the taxi and returning at the time she did. That was about it.'

'What about other forensic evidence from the hotel suite?'

'We found prints on some shards of glass on the bathroom floor. They must have come from the smashed champagne bottle used to whack him over the head. There were also hair samples. Six different types, but they could be from the maid, other guests, Nick and Sophie. Unless we have something specific to match it with, then I'm not sure how useful that is. We could go down the DNA testing route only to find it's the maid's.'

Ruth began to pace the room.

'How did Nick think he was going to make money from Sophie? A couple of phone calls and he'd find out her family had lost everything.'

They lapsed into silence as they ate, Ruth running the options over in her mind.

'Did you get any leads from Nick's phone or laptop?'

'That's part of the problem. There was nothing like that in his suite. I doubt a man like Nick wouldn't have had those things. So they must have been taken by his killer.'

'Again, it gets Sophie off the hook. A crime of passion is one thing. A meticulous clean-up operation is another.'

It didn't bring her any closer to answers, but her brainstorm with Fox had certainly had the desired effect: she had more questions.

'Thanks, Ian,' she said as she collected up the now empty plates and cartons.

'What for?' he said. 'I should be thanking you for all this.'

'For coming here and letting me talk it through. I know you didn't have to – in fact, probably shouldn't have.'

She met his gaze and felt . . . what? A connection, something she really hadn't felt with a man for a long time. It was there for one shimmering moment, then he looked away and it was gone.

'Well, I'd better go,' he said, getting up.

He lingered, and for second Ruth thought about asking him to stay, but that was madness, wasn't it? Besides, they'd both got what they wanted – just another of those little transactions between the press and the police.

She saw him to the door.

'Thanks again,' she said. 'And sorry for dragging you so far north.'

'My pleasure,' he said. 'Really.'

And then he was gone and Ruth was left standing in her hallway, wondering if she was ever going to be able to get to sleep.

36

The bus approached Manhattan from the north, passing down through the Bronx and across the Triborough Bridge. Manhattan was magnificent whichever way you came at it, and the sight of the Chrysler Building glinting in the lazy early evening sun made everything, even Sophie's problems, pale into insignificance just for one glorious moment.

Jim had dropped them at a bus stop outside a Duane Reade where Josh and Sophie could just blend in among the shoppers. 'Who pays any attention to some working stiff at a bus stop?' Jim had said as he held open the pick-up's door and Sophie had kissed him goodbye.

They made the final part of the journey to Andrea Sayer's office by bus, calling her en route to tell her to expect them.

Sophie wasn't sure if they should telegraph their presence, not when they had been so close to getting caught. What if this lawyer had called the authorities? So now with each jerking stop, each hiss of the bus doors, she felt herself tense, expecting to be swarmed by men in Kevlar or burly assassins. But each time, it was just more tired, sullen New Yorkers slowly going downtown.

Still, it was impossible not to feel a shiver of excitement. She was in New York. Everything about the streets was familiar from a million cop shows: the fire hydrants, the yellow cabs, even the shape of the delivery trucks. It was as if someone had created a huge film set just for her.

'Next stop,' said Josh, craning his neck to look up at the skyscraper to their left.

They stepped out of the air-conditioned bus on to the sidewalk right in front of the famous Miller Building, a soaring white-fronted 1920s façade dominated by a Frank Gehry sculpture of a bird in flight. The notoriously dense New York summer heat hit Sophie immediately; it was almost palpable, like being squeezed in a giant hand. It was only twenty paces from the sidewalk to the lobby, but she could already feel the cotton dress she'd picked up in Cannes sticking to her.

Josh announced them to the receptionist, then moved purposefully towards the lifts, but Sophie grabbed his arm and pulled him to one side.

'What exactly are we going to tell this lawyer?'

Josh glanced around to make sure they weren't overheard.

'Not everything. Just enough.'

'How much is enough, Josh? Shouldn't we tell her everything? She could help us.'

'If Asner siphoned off some of the fund into a secret stash, then *we* need to find this money. Us. Not Andrea Sayer. Not any of the US government agencies.'

Sophie felt a flutter of panic.

'Us? Why?' she hissed. 'We're not going to keep the money . . . are we?'

'Sophie, don't be so bloody naïve. If Asner's secret stash exists and the Feds get the money before we do, then we're screwed. We'll have zero leverage and that could be very bad for us.'

'Leverage? What do we need leverage for?'

Josh looked impatient.

'I hate to remind you, Sophie, but you're a possible suspect in a murder inquiry. For all we know, you are the *only* suspect. We need to use whatever we've got to take the heat off you. The second the Feds have Asner's booty, I guarantee they won't give a shit about helping you or me, even if Nick's death is linked to the Asner money. And once the press find out that your dad hid Asner's siphoned cash, you and your family are going to be hung out to dry. Now come on, we've got to catch her before she leaves.'

Sophie followed Josh into the lift and watched as he pressed the button for the twenty-fifth floor. She could see the sense in what he said, but she still felt anxious and out of control.

Josh saw her biting her lip and gently touched her mouth with his thumb.

'Don't do that,' he said softly. 'You'll ruin those lovely lips of yours.'

'I wish I had your gift of the gab, Josh, but I don't,' she snapped, pushing his hand away. 'And I don't know what to say in there.'

Josh smiled. 'Have confidence in yourself, princess. You'll know what to say when we get up there because you always do. You're a natural.' She looked at him.

'A natural con woman?'

'No, Sophie,' he laughed. 'Just a natural.'

Sophie felt her stomach turn as the lift doors hissed open. For a moment she thought they must have stopped at the wrong floor. She had been expecting glass and chrome and big garish modern art on white walls, something befitting a media-friendly trial lawyer. This office looked like a dentist's waiting room: slightly shabby carpet, an off-the-peg sofa and a wilting pot plant next to the tiny – and empty – receptionist's desk.

'Mr McCormack?' said a woman walking out of an office towards them, her hand extended. 'I'm Andrea Sayer.'

She was small and dark with a mass of curly hair and big tortoiseshell glasses. There was something vaguely chaotic about her, not the sort of person you would expect to be a trial lawyer in one of the biggest fraud operations of all time, thought Sophie.

'It's a good job I'm not the type to disappear to the

Hamptons over the weekend,' she said with a strong New York accent, showing them into her office. 'Even my secretary's gone for the weekend, so I can't offer coffee, but at least we can talk undisturbed.'

They sat down and Sophie looked at Josh, but he just raised his eyebrows and inclined his head towards the lawyer. Sophie took a deep breath.

'My name is Sophie Ellis,' she said. To her surprise, the woman did not react.

Okay, thought Sophie, so maybe she wasn't as wanted as she had thought.

'Miriam Asner suggested we spoke to you.'

That got Sayer's attention. The attorney sat forward, peering over the top of her glasses.

'She did?'

'Yes, we've just come from her house in Pleasantville.'

'And she spoke to you? May I ask why? No offence, but I've been trying for a year. I can barely get her to answer the phone.'

'My father was an investor in the Asner scam. His name was Peter Ellis.'

Sayer nodded, but with a slight 'so what?' shrug.

'My dad knew Asner at university; maybe that's why she spoke to us.'

'And she recommended you come to *me*?' smiled Sayer. 'Forgive my amusement, but I get the impression she believes I'm part of a huge conspiracy to ruin her life and trash her name.'

'She did rather give us that impression too,' said Josh.

'So what did she think I can help you with?'

'Well I'd like to get my family's money back. We weren't exactly rich, and we lost everything.'

Andrea laughed.

'Perhaps you should be asking Miriam. It's a more direct route.'

'We did,' said Josh. 'Miriam claims she knows nothing about the money and says she has nothing left to give.'

'Well, that's technically true at the moment. She doesn't have access to any money beyond what she negotiated with the Feds. The question is whether she knows where the missing money has gone.'

'And you think she does?'

'Someone does, Ms Ellis,' said Sayer, looking at Sophie.

'But if you don't know where it is, how are you planning on getting it back?'

She shook her head, her curls bouncing. 'We're not.'

'Sorry?' said Sophie. 'I thought you were trying to trace the billions Asner hid.'

'A common misconception, although there is a grain of truth to it. A court-appointed trustee is recovering the money in conjunction with the SEC. I am simply acting for some of the victims of Asner's scheme. Essentially I'm fighting to get my clients pushed up to the front of the queue when it comes to handing out compensation – if there ever is any, of course. I assume that's why you're here.'

Sophie glanced over at Josh again.

'Well, yes, my father received no compensation after the scam collapsed.'

'Not many people did,' Sayer said sympathetically. 'A few hundred million dollars were recovered – most has gone in fees to the trustee and to the investors with the biggest lawyers. Hence our class action suit against Asner – we don't think it's fair that the smaller investors should get such a raw deal, so clubbing together gives us more muscle.'

Josh sat forward.

'You said there was a grain of truth about finding the money?'

Sayer gave a small smile.

'Well I'm not the sort to hang around and wait for the government to sort it out.'

'But *is* there any money?'

'I spent two hours in a jail cell interviewing Michael Asner myself. He pretty much told me everything – how much money there was, where it came from and how the scheme worked. He was a vain man and he was boasting about it. He didn't admit to me that there was any hidden money, but it was something he apparently crowed about to inmates in the slammer.'

'Could that just have been jail talk?' asked Josh.

Andrea shrugged.

'A crook as clever, as ruthless as Asner wouldn't pull a scam like that and not keep something aside for a rainy day. There's at least one hundred million dollars in my opinion, maybe three or four times that much. Asner never thought he was going to get the length of sentence that he did. He was sixty-five. He would have assumed ten years inside, a non-violent white-collar criminal; they would have quietly paroled him after five and he would have disappeared to some island somewhere to live out his retirement on the hidden cash.'

Josh gave a low whistle.

'One hundred million bucks. He'd need a warehouse for that much cash.'

'Oh, it wouldn't be in real money,' said Sayer. 'He could have converted it into diamonds, gold or bearer bonds and hidden them away in some anonymous vault somewhere.'

'Not in a bank?' asked Sophie.

'Could be in an offshore account, yes, although most traditional tax havens like Switzerland and Liechtenstein are cooperating with the authorities these days.'

'Can't you trace all the transactions that Asner made over the years?'

Sayer laughed. 'Don't you think the authorities have tried that? No, the money went into Asner's account, then was probably withdrawn as cash – and simply disappeared. Our best guess is that he was using a second player to hide the money for him.'

Sophie felt her scalp prickle.

'But you don't know who?'

'We've checked his phone records, emails, diary logs, financial statements, but it's a tiny needle in a very big haystack. Unless we have a name, we have no idea where to start. But we have to find a way. Asner was a sociopath. His scam was like a game to him, but he was playing with countless lives with his little scheme. Some of his investors were public funds; that means public amenities lost their funding – community centres, day care, outreach programmes – and thousands of people will lose their pensions. And that's the tip of the iceberg. No, Miss Ellis, believe me when I say I'm motivated to find that money and get it back to the right people.'

Sophie looked at her, feeling torn. Andrea Sayer was one of the good guys, she could feel it, and if she told the lawyer the truth, then maybe she could help. But Josh was right too. Once they gave the authorities everything they had, they were vulnerable, dispensable. Sophie found herself at the crossroads – and she had to choose a path.

'Does the name Benedict Grear mean anything to you?' she said suddenly

'No. Should it?' replied Sayer, her clever eyes piercing.

'I don't know,' stuttered Sophie. 'Maybe someone connected to the Asner scheme? A lawyer he used, or an investor?'

Sayer shook her head. 'What is this about?'

Sophie knew she had to word this carefully.

'When my father lost his – our – money, he came to the same conclusion as you: that he'd be at the back of the queue, so he decided to do some of his own investigating.'

'Good for him,' said Sayer. 'So why's he not here?'

'He's dead, Miss Sayer.'

'Oh I'm sorry. And call me Andrea.'

'After he died, we found that name written down in a file he'd collected on Asner. We wondered if it might be something he'd discovered during his research.'

Sophie hoped her expression hadn't betrayed her lies.

The attorney looked at her; her face said she was unconvinced by what Sophie was saying. After a pause, however, she turned to her computer and rattled at the keyboard.

'We have interviewed everyone in Asner's inner circle,' she said. 'We've built up a pretty big database about the scheme – we managed to get the SEC to pool their resources too.'

She clicked away.

'No . . . nothing on Benedict Grear. But then we don't have the time or resources to speak to everyone Asner ever met.'

She sat back in her chair.

'Why do I get the feeling you're not telling me everything, Ms Ellis?'

'Because we . . .' Josh began to speak, but Sophie put her hand on his knee. He had been right in the lift; she needed to start taking control. This was her problem, her life, and it was about time she grabbed the steering wheel.

'You say you want to find Asner's hidden booty. Well so do I. We were British investors, Miss Sayer. You think your clients are at the bottom of a very long list for compensation; believe me, my family is bumping along the seabed. I want to help. My dad and Michael Asner were old friends. Perhaps someone they both knew knows something, anything that might help us find the truth.'

Andrea looked thoughtful.

'You could talk to Tyler Connor.'

'Who's he?' asked Josh.

'A biker. Small-time hood, big-time meth dealer. This man shared a ten-by-ten cell with Michael Asner for months.

You spend that much time together, you're going to get close. If you want to find out who Benedict Grear is, maybe Ty got to hear about him.'

'How do we speak to an inmate?' asked Sophie.

'Ty was released six weeks ago.'

'Do you have contact details for him?'

Sayer sighed and flipped her Rolodex.

'He's living in Fort Lauderdale. I warn you, though, he's intimidating. Not a nice man.'

She scribbled down the details and held out the note. As Sophie reached for it, Sayer pulled it back, fluttering in mid-air.

'If you find out anything, anything at all, you have to tell me,' she said, holding Sophie's gaze. 'That's the deal, Ms Ellis.'

'Yes, of course,' said Sophie, feeling the top of her neck begin to flush.

'This is serious, Sophie. The SEC, the FBI – they don't fuck around. And if they find out you've been withholding information from a major fraud inquiry, believe me, they will find a way to hurt you.'

37

Robert 'Squirrel' Sykes, society editor of *Class* magazine, looked at Ruth with a sly smile.

'So tell me again,' he said, leaning forward. 'You're there in the hallway, your hair perfectly back-lit by the bathroom cabinet, and the sexy policeman says in a deep voice, "My pleasure"? Why didn't you just grab him and take him right there?'

Ruth slapped his arm.

'I only split up with David three days ago. What sort of girl do you take me for?'

'The sort who should be gagging for a bit of saucy rebound sex, that's who.'

She flipped her napkin at him and tried not to smile. Ostensibly, her Saturday afternoon lunch with Robbie at Scott's was to pick his brains about Lana Goddard-Price, but they'd spent the first twenty minutes huddled at their corner table talking about Fox, or 'your dirty detective' as Squirrel insisted on referring to him. The truth was, since their intimate night brainstorming over Chinese, Ruth hadn't been able to get him out of her head, and in a way that wasn't a million miles from what Robert was suggesting.

Fox was infuriatingly bullish and patronising and he clearly didn't trust her enough to give her the information she needed, although she had to admit she reciprocated on that score. But there was something aloof and elusive about him that was as sexy as hell. However, the last thing she needed right now was any more inappropriate liaisons; the prospect of having to face poor Chuck Dean was embarrassing enough, and she and Fox had a potentially useful working relationship.

'Anyway, I didn't come here to talk about my non-existent love life,' said Ruth. 'I've got a story to write, remember?'

'Oh, I know and it sounds so exciting. Honestly, you're wasted on the *Trib*. You should *so* come over to *Class*. You know Cate Balcon loves you.'

The idea of approaching *Class*'s glamorous editor had of course crossed Ruth's mind more than once. *Class* was a respected stylish glossy and one of the few magazines left which actually ran in-depth features on crime, political intrigue and the back-stabbing antics of the upper classes. Plus it would be a joy to spend the day in the energetic slipstream of Robbie Sykes. But Ruth wasn't quite ready to leave the cut-and-thrust deadline hell of newspapers, especially when the prospect of bureau chief was still on the table.

'It's flattering to be considered,' she said, 'but I'm gunning for a Pulitzer, which isn't going to happen unless I finish this story.'

She smiled at the thought of American journalism's highest accolade; the prize she had always dreamed of winning. Two friends from college now had them and she had been a more promising journalist than both of them. But so far she had never really got the killer break. Never had that right-place-at-the-right-time story. She knew she had not yet fulfilled her potential.

'Well it's your loss,' said Robbie with mock affront. 'You're missing out on some fabulous parties.'

He poured her some more wine and looked around the restaurant with its chic twenties decor and crisp white tablecloths, the diners a mix of edgy media types and old money.

'Although I could do with coming here more often,' said

Robbie. 'Darling, this is a treat. I only hope I can earn it.'

'So come on then, tell me what you know about Lana Goddard-Price.'

Since her visits to the gym and Lana's house, Ruth had become convinced there was more to Mrs Goddard-Price than met the eye. She was particularly intrigued by Mike's suggestion that Lana had somehow targeted Sophie. She wasn't entirely sure how it would help her solve Nick Beddingfield's murder, but she had been a journalist long enough to know that random leads often led you in interesting directions.

And who better to find out a little bit more about Lana Goddard-Price than Mr Social Intrigue himself, the Squirrel? Even if a quick glance at the wine list had told her that she'd be paying for it for months to come.

'Okay, our friend Lana is late thirties, though she claims thirty-four,' said Robbie, buttering a roll. 'Spanish, former model – although not a very successful one from what I can gather. She'd been knocking around London for years, hanging around with the club crowd rather than the country set: traders rather than investment bankers, footballers and the like.'

He crinkled his nose in distaste.

'Anyway, there were whispers she was a bit of a gold-digger, but she was never a player until she met Simon Goddard-Price and married him about a year ago.'

'And who's this lucky man?'

'Hedge fund manager, chairman of GP Capital. Absolutely loaded; we're talking net worth of about four hundred million. Rich list, private jet and so on, works out of Geneva now, I think.'

'You *think*?' teased Ruth.

'Darling, it's not my fault if these people choose to hide themselves away. Simon doesn't dabble in the society circuit very much. You're lucky I got this much.'

'So the bottom line is that Lana struck gold after all?'

Robbie pursed his lips. 'I don't know about that. Rumour has it that Simon wants a divorce. That grand house in Knightsbridge is in hubby's name, and word is Lana signed a pre-nup; five years ago they weren't worth the paper they were written on, but the law is changing. My guess is the house won't be part of the pay-off. She'll probably be left with six months' housekeeper wages as severance.'

Ruth scribbled it all down. Lana was on the skids and presumably knew it, so it was reasonable to assume that she would be looking for an exit strategy. But what had that got to do with Sophie Ellis?

Robbie suddenly looked more animated.

'Darling, Simon Cowell is over there. I just want to pop over and say hi. Order two coffees. Irish.' He winked.

Ruth craned her neck to see Cowell, but she had the wrong seat to be in eyeshot. Sighing, she ordered the warm pistachio cake and two Irish coffees and began doodling on the notebook in front of her.

She wrote three words in the middle of the page. Lana. Sophie. Nick. She circled the word Lana. She was definitely linked to Sophie. She was 'after her', according to Mike from the gym; targeting her, befriending her, drawing her into her world. If she wasn't after Sophie in a sexual sense, then it meant she wanted something else from her. Money? Contacts? Information?

A penny suddenly dropped. Another person had been after Sophie too – Nick. He had romanced her, become attached to her world, and Jeanne Parsons had made Ruth question his motives. If Nick and Lana were both targeting Sophie, then it made *them* connected. And Ruth was sure that Nick's murderer was linked to him somehow.

She felt giddy with excitement. She grabbed her bag and went out of the restaurant. Stabbing numbers into her phone, she called Chuck Dean.

She took a deep breath; mumbling some contrite apology about her behaviour at the Frontline Club would only make things worse.

'Chuck, I need you to do something for me. Don't worry, it's not of a sexual nature,' she said brazenly.

For one moment, she thought he had taken it the wrong way, but his low baritone laugh reassured her that their friendship was back on track.

'CCTV footage from the Riverton lobby. I need you to get hold of it. Not just on the morning of Nick's murder, but during his entire stay.'

'Okay,' he replied, not even flinching about the big ask. Every journalist in town would be after the footage. She supposed some night-shift security guard would be making a nice little earner selling copies.

'Do you want me to sift through it frame by frame?'

There was a reason Ruth hadn't tried to get hold of the footage before. Fox had already intimated that it hadn't been that useful. It had shown Sophie leaving and entering the Riverton at exactly the times she had told the police inspector. Ruth also did not have the resources to identify every person caught on film; there would be so many guests milling around the lobby in the hour before and after Nick's death that it would be a lengthy and ultimately pointless exercise going through the CCTV frame by frame, unless you were looking out for a specific someone.

She lowered her voice and glanced around Mount Street.

'I want you to check the footage and see if you can identify Lana Goddard-Price. I'll send you some links to photographs of her. I want to know if at any time she visited Nick Beddingfield in his hotel, all right? Can you get that done as quickly as possible?'

'On it already,' said Chuck as she ended the call.

She heard the sound of a throat being cleared loudly and pointedly behind her.

'There you are,' said Robert dramatically. 'I was just thinking you'd invited me for lunch and then run off without paying the bill.'

38

If Montmartre had been everything Sophie had expected, Fort Lauderdale was nothing like the place she had imagined. She had pictured a quiet, family-friendly tourist town with a sugar-white beach, a jigsaw of Creole cottages and board-walks, shopping malls and fun parks. Instead it was a bust-ling city complete with a downtown financial district and out-of-town commuter belt. There was barely an inflatable dolphin to be seen. Certainly not in Sistrunk, the run-down neighbourhood their taxi was crawling through. Sophie was feeling more uncomfortable by the minute as they pulled up at a red light. On both sides were pawn shops and pizza joints, along with a liqor store that had a grille instead of a door, presumably to discourage hold-ups. A group of kids – no more than nine or ten – sat on BMX-style bicycles outside the store, openly smoking a joint; Sophie could smell the sickly-sweet herb through the open window. The light turned green and they moved off, past a down-and-out pushing a shopping trolley full of cans, past a red-brick church with a hoarding reading 'Thou Shalt Not KILL', past a single palm tree jutting out of a vacant lot, waving like a flag of surrender for the American Dream.

'You sure you guys want this address?' said the driver, glancing at them in his mirror, as they turned into a side street and pulled up outside a crumbling apartment complex.

Sophie looked up at the graffiti-scarred walls and wished

she was back in the comfort of Lana's Gulfstream that had brought them from New York.

In the last twenty-four hours she'd clocked up more air miles than your average pilot. After their meeting with Andrea Sayer, they had checked into an anonymous two-star hotel on the Lower East Side and called Lana. She had told them to get some sleep, then meet her – and the jet – at Teterboro at seven a.m. From there they flew straight to Fort Lauderdale executive airport, then drove into town to meet Tyler Connor. Lana had gone south to Miami, where she apparently had some friends.

I'm not surprised she didn't want to hang around here, thought Sophie, looking at the building's barred windows. It was exactly how she imagined a drug dealer's house to look.

'Can you wait for us?' said Josh, slipping the driver a twenty-dollar tip.

'Sure, but don't be too long, huh?' he said, his gold tooth winking at them in the sunshine.

Michael Asner's biker cellmate lived in a complex called Shoreside Villas, a run-down block arranged around a pool long since drained of water and, despite its name, without any glimpse of shoreline.

'Shouldn't we have met him by the beach or in a diner or somewhere?' whispered Sophie to Josh as they walked around to apartment 2B. Josh's glance told her he agreed with her.

'We won't be long. Just a few questions, then we're out of here, okay?'

Josh knocked twice. Inside, they could hear the thump of rock music. He slammed his fist against the door instead; it immediately opened a crack. 'Yeah?' said a deep voice.

'You Ty?' said Josh. 'I'm the dumb-ass Limey who called earlier.'

There was a pause, then a gale of booming laughter and the door swung open.

'Come on in, funny guy,' said the man-mountain standing just inside. 'And bring your bitch with you.'

Despite six weeks of Miami sunshine, Tyler Connor's skin was still jail-cell white and covered in the smudged spidery tattoos of the correctional system. He was at least six foot five, with a fifty-inch chest, Sophie estimated. He was not fat, just bulky from prison yard weights, his arms bulging under a T-shirt that read 'No Wuckin' Furries'. His beard was scrappy and his face narrow, but the one thing you noticed were his eyes – they were so dark, they looked like the ends of expired matches. He was quite terrifying – as was his apartment. It was dingy and cluttered, lit only by a lamp with a red bandanna draped over it and the glare of the TV, currently showing a porn video. There was a half-assembled motorcycle in the hallway and the low coffee table was covered in what looked like drug paraphernalia.

'So who do we have here?' purred Ty as Sophie shuffled inside. 'A fancy bit of Euro-pussy, huh? So you lost all your money with Mikey, baby-doll?' he said, leering at her. 'You want Ty to make it all better, huh?'

Josh took a protective step in front of Sophie, but she turned to face the big man.

'No, Mr Connor,' she said. 'Someone is trying to kill me and I need your help to work out who.'

The lecherous smile faded from his face.

'And what's in that for me, sugar?'

Josh pulled out a roll of dollar bills and tossed it to the biker. He gave it an uninterested glance, then pushed it into his pocket.

'You got any smokes?'

Josh took a packet of Marlboro reds from his jacket and shook one out. Sophie was once again impressed. Josh was not a smoker – he'd come prepared. Ty lit the cigarette from a Zippo lighter, then spread himself across a creaking armchair, gesturing to the sofa next to the table.

He had the courtesy to switch off the porn video.

'So who d'you piss off, English girl?' he said, blowing smoke at Sophie.

She shrugged, determined not to show how much Tyler Connor intimidated her.

'That's what we want you to tell us. You shared a cell with Michael Asner for over six months. Did he ever mention a Benedict Grear to you?'

Ty blew a smoke ring into the air, then let his mouth open and close with a popping sound.

'Never heard of him. Who is he?'

'We think he helped Asner hide a hundred million dollars before his Ponzi scheme collapsed.'

'Yeah? And who told you that?'

Sophie met his gaze.

'A little bird.'

'Fuck that little bird, bitch. Gimme names.'

Sophie shook her head slowly.

'You're the one who needs to provide the names, Mr Connor. Or would you prefer to return our money?'

Ty grinned at her, showing a gap where a canine should have been.

'You want to come and get it back?' he said, pushing his crotch up.

Josh sat forward, his Scottish accent suddenly more pronounced.

'No, pal,' he said. 'I'll come and take it. Nay fuckin' bother.'

Ty looked at him with surprise, then sat up slightly straighter.

'I thought you Limeys had a sense of humour.'

'No more jokes, Ty,' said Josh evenly. 'Tell us what you know about Asner's hidden money. We know he talked to you about it.'

'Yeah, he did.'

Sophie felt a flicker of hope.

'What did he say?' she asked.

Ty shrugged.

'Mikey said too much in jail, that was his problem. But then it was his currency.'

'Currency?' asked Sophie.

'I bet a pretty little lady like yourself has never been in the slammer,' said Ty, recovering his swagger.

'Really? You'd be surprised,' said Sophie.

Ty looked up and gave her a half-smile. 'Then you'll know it's not an easy place for someone like Michael.'

She thought of Michael Asner and his Brioni suits, his John Lobb shoes, his $500 haircut, every inch of him wiped clean of his poor Sacramento background.

'Because he was rich?' she asked.

Ty laughed.

'Fuck, no. Half of those kids inside loved Asner, worshipped him because of his money. He made *billions*, man. He was like the king to those guys, a big-time thief who said fuck you to all that Wall Street bullshit. Asner wasn't some small-time con – he pulled off the scam everyone inside dreams of but no one has the balls or the brains to do.'

'So why wasn't it easy for him?' asked Sophie.

'Because the other half hated him. They thought he was an arrogant sonofabitch, which I guess he was, strutting around the yard like Tom fucking Cruise.' Ty stubbed his cigarette out on the top of a beer can. 'Cried like a baby the first night, though. He was scared to death, man.'

'Scared of what?' asked Josh.

Ty shrugged.

'What you think? Getting fucked in the ass, getting shanked in the yard. So I told him: it's an economy inside – supply and demand. Mikey had to give the animals something, so he gave them stories. Shit about all the famous guys he met at parties: all those rappers and TV actors. And he

365

told them all about his houses and cars and jets. Man, they ate that shit up.' He laughed. 'They even came to him for advice about making money. I mean, sure, some of them laughed at him, asked him how, if he was such a smart-ass, he'd ended up inside. So he told them he'd beat the system, told them about his little stash of cash.'

'He boasted about the millions he had hidden?'

Ty's face twisted into a sneer.

'He couldn't keep his dumb-ass mouth shut – that's what got him killed.'

Sophie opened her eyes a little wider.

'What do you mean?'

'There was a guy inside called Uri Kaskov – they call him Uri the Bear. Russian.' Ty gave a little shiver. 'Man, those goddamn Russians scare the shit out of me.'

'Russians,' repeated Josh quietly to himself, and Sophie imagined he was thinking the same thing as her. Were these the same Russians who had been chasing them halfway across the world?

'Uri heads up one of the Russian gangs based in Miami,' continued Ty, clearly enjoying having them hanging on his every word. 'They run drugs, whores, credit card shit, you name it. He went down a year ago for extortion, a little bit before Mike. Uri moved in on Mikey and offered to protect him.'

'What did Uri want in return?' asked Josh.

'Shee-it, dawg, what you think?' said Ty. 'The money, of course. Everyone heard Mikey talking about hidden loot, so Uri would have offered to protect him for a cut of it.'

'And Asner agreed?'

Ty laughed again. 'Hey, maybe Mike suggested it. He told me he knew of at least a dozen people who wanted him dead: rich, powerful people, just the sort who could get to you in jail. Protection from someone like Uri was just what he wanted.'

The biker shrugged.

'Besides, he had no fucking choice. Irony was, Uri was the one who cut his throat in the end.'

Josh and Sophie exchanged a look.

'Why?'

'Uri started piling on the pressure; he didn't want to wait no more for the money.'

Sophie frowned.

'So Asner didn't have access to any money?'

'Mikey told me he hid it with a friend, said he'd try to contact him. The morning he died, he was going for a meeting with Uri to stall him. I guess it turned sour – next thing I heard, I was getting a new cellie.'

'So was Uri punished for it?'

Ty shook his head. 'Two guys were sent to the hole, but they were Uri's guys, lifers doin' like three hundred years back to back. Whatcha gonna do to those guys?'

Sophie felt a curious mix of fear and relief. Fear because Uri the Bear was the kind of man who might cut your throat if he became impatient, but there was also a strange sense of relief that at last she knew who had been chasing her. Somehow it wasn't so bad if you could put a name to the bogeyman.

'Do you know who Asner's friend was?' asked Josh. 'The one who was hiding the money?'

Ty shook his head. 'Never gave me no name.' He looked directly at Sophie. 'But maybe he told Uri before he opened his neck.'

That was exactly what Sophie had been thinking. And another terrible thought had just occurred to her. If Asner had indeed given Uri Kaskov her father's name, perhaps the Russian or his friends on the outside had contacted Peter Ellis – and perhaps that extra stress had contributed to his heart attack.

'What else can you tell us about Uri?' she asked.

Ty yawned and scratched his balls. It looked as if his patience was beginning to wear thin.

'He's a mobster. Moved down from Brighton Beach about fifteen years ago. He's got a nightclub in South Beach, some strip joints, a couple of steak restaurants in Sunny Isles, all money-laundering fronts for other stuff. His son Sergei runs the operation now Uri's inside.'

Ty wiggled his fingers at Josh.

'Hey, funny man, gimme another butt before you go, huh? Story time's over.'

Josh stood up and threw him the packet.

'Here, you knock yourself out,' he said. 'We'll find our own way out.'

Sophie found she was trembling as they stepped back out on to the street. Squinting in the sudden sunshine after the dimness of Ty's flat, she peered up and down the road. They'd been chased by Uri's men in London, the South of France, New York state. And now they had run straight into their back yard. She might as well have painted a target on her back, she thought as she looked around anxiously for the taxi.

'The cabbie didn't bloody wait,' she cursed out loud.

'Can't say I blame him,' said Josh. 'Come on. No loitering, start walking. I'm not going to let anything happen to you.'

A white cab approached, and Josh dived into the road to hail it. He took Sophie's hand and led her to the taxi, putting his arm protectively around her shoulders as they sat in the back seat and she rested her head against him.

'So now we know who's after me. But this is only going to stop when we find the money, and we've got nowhere else to go. This is the end of the trail.' A tear trickled down her cheek and she wiped it away with the back of her thumb.

'That's not the Sophie Ellis I know,' said Josh reassuringly. 'Sophie Ellis doesn't just give up. You're a fighter. You're not going to let these gangsters beat you, are you?'

'But what can we do?' she said, turning to him. 'You can't reason with these people, Josh. When they find out we don't have the money, they'll cut our throats too.'

'They're not going to touch a hair on your head.'

The way he said it – tender yet fierce, protective and strong – she almost believed it, and she was grateful for his words. But what good was one man against an army of Russian gangsters?

They lapsed into silence as they drove away from Ty's neighbourhood and out on to the highway, the shops and offices giving way to motels, drive-thrus and Jiffy Lubes, whatever they were. When they had put enough distance between them and the ghetto, Josh leant over to the driver and asked him to pull into the lot of a diner.

'Come on, we need to eat before we can plan our next move,' he said. It was only when they pushed inside and smelled the sweet aroma of fresh waffles and bacon and coffee that Sophie realised how ravenous she was.

They sat in a booth at the end of the diner, with a view of the highway and the silvery gulf beyond, and quickly ordered an omelette for Sophie, and eggs over easy for Josh. The music was loud, old fifties rock 'n' roll on the jukebox, and as she sipped at the black coffee the waitress had brought over, the normality of the situation made Sophie think more clearly.

'If Uri killed Mike Asner, then maybe he killed Nick too.'

'It's possible,' said Josh.

'*Probable*,' insisted Sophie. 'You can see what's happened here, can't you? Uri's men came to get me at the hotel and killed Nick when he wouldn't tell them where I was.'

Josh gave a light, cynical snort.

'What's wrong with that theory?'

He looked unimpressed. 'You're still giving Nick the benefit of the doubt, aren't you?'

'*Benefit of the doubt?*'

'A bit of distance, and now he's this perfect romantic ideal of cheekbones and chivalry, giving up his life to save you.'

'I didn't mean that.'

'Sophie, this is a man who took money to seduce you and extract information so he and Lana could run off with a fortune. He's dead, and that's sad, but you shouldn't be dreaming up these heroic scenarios for him.'

Sophie was about to object, but there was some truth in what he was saying. She didn't want to accept that Nick was a cold-hearted con man who had willingly and brutally torn her life apart.

'All I'm saying is it's one version of events that could have happened. And because of that, we should call Inspector Fox and tell him. Remember, I don't want to be the only suspect in Nick's murder, Josh.'

Looking up, she saw that Josh was tensed, his eyes darting around, on full alert.

'What's wrong?' she asked quietly.

'I think we should leave,' he said in a low voice, pulling a twenty-dollar bill out of his pocket and putting it calmly on the table. 'There's a fire exit to our left,' he whispered. 'When I say go, run for it.'

Sophie grabbed her bag in one hand and the glass sugar shaker in the other, ready to throw it. It was a pathetic, pointless defence, but if Uri's men were coming for her, she was going to go down fighting.

'Don't get up on our account,' said a voice. Sophie whirled around and found her exit blocked by a stern-looking man in his thirties. He had a regulation haircut and was wearing a dark sports jacket over a polo shirt. He didn't *look* Russian.

Over his shoulder, she could see men in similar clothes standing by the door and the fire exit Josh had pointed out.

'Miss Ellis, do you think you could put the sugar down?' said the first man. 'I would like to speak to both of you.'

She looked over at Josh, who let out a long breath and

shrugged, sitting back down in the booth. Sophie followed his lead, placing her makeshift weapon back on the Formica tabletop.

'Who are you?' she said as the man squeezed in next to her.

'My name is Hal Stanton. I'm a regional officer for the Securities and Exchange Commission.'

'The SEC?' Relief flooded her body; he wasn't Russian, he wasn't going to cut her throat, that was all she cared about in that moment.

'You've heard of us then?' said Stanton, holding up a finger to get a coffee from the waitress.

'Can we see some identification?' said Josh. The man pulled an ID card from his inside pocket and slid it across. Sophie looked down.

'That's not a good photo,' she said.

Stanton gave a half-smile. 'I guess some of us just aren't photogenic.'

The waitress brought Stanton his coffee and he sipped it. He didn't seem in much of a hurry.

'So I take it you're in charge of tracking down the Michael Asner money?' said Sophie.

'Not exactly,' said Stanton. 'I'm just one cog in the machine. A man named Thomas Fallon is the court-appointed trustee; he's in charge of hunting down and allocating funds to the victims. Your family has probably heard from him. But we're involved, yes.'

'What do you know about my family?' said Sophie.

'Enough,' said Stanton, looking at her over his coffee.

'How did you find us here?'

Hal Stanton gave a soft snort. 'Do you think it's coincidence that Ty Connor was released from prison four weeks after Asner got killed?'

'You've been tracking him,' said Josh, shaking his head, as if he should have worked it out sooner. 'You wanted to see if Asner told him anything, see if he tried to dig up the buried treasure. And then you saw us walk into his apartment.'

'Something like that,' said Stanton. 'But as it happens, I was also tipped off by Andrea Sayer. She reckoned we should meet.'

Sophie had guessed the lawyer would have called the authorities. If Andrea had told Stanton about their visit, she'd presumably told them everything else.

'Have you found Benedict Grear yet?' she asked.

Stanton shook his head. 'I was hoping *you* had.'

'No,' said Josh. 'Ty Connor was our only lead – and he says he's never heard of Grear.' He gave a cynical smile. 'But then you already know that, don't you?'

'We know everything, Mr McCormack,' smirked Stanton. 'That's our job.'

'Oh yeah? So where's the money, then?'

The smile drained from the agent's face.

'This is one of the biggest fraud inquiries in US history, not some free-for-all Easter egg hunt.'

'Some of that money belongs to my family, Mr Stanton,' said Sophie evenly.

'You sure about that?' he replied.

Sophie swallowed. Was Stanton telling her he knew about her father's involvement in the scam? No, he couldn't – if the federal agencies knew about Peter Ellis's role as the 'bag man', as Josh put it, they would have shut down Sophie and her mother just as they had done with Miriam Asner. They would have seized assets, frozen accounts, gone through their homes with sniffer dogs and X-ray machines. What Stanton was doing was warning them off.

'Is that a threat?' she said.

Stanton shrugged.

'Take it any way you like, Miss Ellis. All I'm saying is that the stakes are high in this case. If you want to have any hope of going back to London and living a quiet life, I suggest you cooperate with us in every way possible.'

'That does sound like a threat,' said Josh.

'So sue us,' said Stanton with a twisted smile. 'In the meantime, perhaps you could tell us everything else Mr Ellis found out about the Asner case.'

Sophie repeated the version of the story she had given to Andrea Sayer, the one where her father was playing amateur detective in the slim hope of recovering some of his investment, all the time becoming more and more convinced that Josh was right: she had to keep going, had to get to that money before the authorities, before the Russians, because without it they had nothing.

'So you're sure that's all you know?' said Stanton when she had finished. 'Just a random name your father had written down in a file?'

'My father was an accountant, not a policeman, Mr Stanton,' said Sophie. 'He had no real idea if Asner had hidden that money, it was probably just a hunch.'

'A hunch,' repeated Stanton.

'Yes. I know it sounds stupid,' said Sophie, 'but we lost everything to that man. My mother is having to sell our family home. I thought my children would play on the garden swing just like I did, but Michael Asner took that from us. So excuse my father if he was clutching at straws – he was just trying to get back what was ours.'

She could hear the words coming out of her mouth but she could barely believe it was her. Was she morphing into Josh, she asked herself, able to weave a line, a story at the drop of a hat? What was it that Andrea Sayer had said back in New York? *If they find out you have been withholding information, they will find a way to hurt you.*

But she couldn't stop now. She met Stanton's gaze directly.

'Please, Hal. Find the money. I can't speak for the rest of

Asner's victims, but it killed my father and now it's broken my mother.'

Hal Stanton nodded and handed her a business card. 'Do you have a number I can reach you on?'

She wrote her own mobile number on a napkin, knowing her phone was sitting waterlogged in Josh's lock-up.

'I'll be in touch,' he said, getting up. 'And kids? Please stop with the Scooby-Doo shit, okay? If we catch you on our turf again, we won't be so nice.'

They watched as he left, followed by the other anonymously dressed men, and got into the black town car in the parking lot.

'I don't believe that,' said Sophie, cupping her hands around her cheeks. Josh put his finger to his lips. 'Don't speak,' he mouthed. 'Let's go.'

They walked outside into the hot, humid air. The town car had gone. Josh led her away from the diner into the car park, where the noise from the highway would stop anyone from overhearing them.

Her heart was pounding. 'Oh my God, Josh, what have I done?' she said, struggling for breath. 'I've just spent the last ten minutes lying to a government agent.'

'You did well,' said Josh.

'Well?' she stammered. 'The Commission has resources. How difficult is it going to be for him to find out I'm not poor Miss Innocent-Michael-Asner-Victim and that I've been questioned in connection with the death of a high-profile American in London?'

She looked at him with wide eyes. 'What if he arrests me? In Florida? I could end up in jail like Michael Asner, and Ty and Uri the Bear.'

Josh turned to face her.

'Pull yourself together,' he ordered, gripping her arms. 'You did what you had to do.'

'This isn't a game, Josh,' she croaked, a sob swelling in

her chest. 'You heard what Andrea Sayer said. When they find out we're lying, they will screw us.'

'*If* they find out we're lying,' corrected Josh. 'He didn't know squat about your dad, that much I could tell.'

His mouth curled into a grin.

'You gave him your old phone number, eh? You're learning, princess.'

'I'm learning to be a con,' she said miserably.

'You're learning to stand on your own two feet, Sophie,' he said. 'And by the way, I loved the bit about the garden swing. Like I said, you're a natural.'

Despite herself, Sophie couldn't help laughing.

'Oh Josh, what are we going to do?'

He puffed out his cheeks.

'You're right about one thing. Now we're in the picture, they're going to do a full background check on you. It won't be long before they know about Nick, your dad, everything. And then word will get back to Inspector Fox about where you are and what you've been doing. I can't imagine you're going to be the Met or the SEC's favourite person.'

'Thanks for the reassurance.'

'The point is we've got to move fast,' said Josh. 'I reckon we've got forty-eight hours tops to find the money.'

'That's if we don't get killed by Uri the Bear first,' said Sophie grimly.

'Well, that's one thing we won't have to worry about,' said Josh, walking back to the taxi.

'What do you mean?'

'We're not going to hang around and wait for the Russians,' he said, opening the door. 'We're going to go and find them.'

39

That fence looked pretty high. Ruth looked down at her knee-length dress and her wholly impractical heels. *Not exactly ideal mountaineering gear*, she thought, slipping off her shoes and hitching up her skirt.

'Here goes nothing,' she muttered to herself, wedging a stockinged foot in the crossbar of the fence and hoisting herself up. She had tried ringing Lana's bell, of course; she wasn't entirely crazy. She'd knocked on the door and shouted through the letterbox too. She hadn't really expected the woman to be in, but then it wasn't the lovely Mrs Goddard-Price she wanted to talk to today. Stepping back into the street, Ruth had happened to look up toward the second floor – and had seen a curtain twitch.

That – and a certain amount of desperation, if she was honest – was what had led her to be climbing over the Goddard-Prices' fence and into their back garden.

'Dammit!' she hissed as her tights snagged on an overhanging bush. They came away with a small ripping sound. *Great, that'll look professional*, she thought. Not that scrambling over six-foot railings and a thorny bush was something they taught at journalism school along with shorthand and interview technique.

Scratched and grazed, Ruth finally thumped down on the patio on the other side, tugging her bag to get it free.

After all that, this better work, she thought. Back at Scott's restaurant, her theory about Lana being connected to Nick Beddingfield had felt watertight. But, trespassing on Lana Goddard-Price's property, she realised how spurious her thinking actually was. There was only one person she was going to end up putting in jail the way she was carrying on, and that person was going to be herself.

Ruth looked up at the windows with their drawn curtains. The whole place looked quiet and shut up, neglected almost. Presumably Lana Goddard-Price was in no rush to leave the South of France; why would she? If she really was mixed up with Nick Beddingfield, she would have wanted as much distance between them as possible. And Fox had told her that Simon was still in Geneva. But Ruth wanted to speak to Cherry, the housekeeper.

She walked across the patio, skirting around some large terracotta planters, and peered in through the French windows, cupping her hands around her face to get a better view. It looked like a posh living room with white sofas and . . .

She stepped back with a cry as a face loomed up in front of her. She turned her ankle over and stumbled backwards, landing painfully on one knee. She was busy swearing and rubbing her injured parts when the door opened and Lana's Filipino maid appeared, waving a broom.

'Cherry. Just who I wanted to talk to . . .'

The woman replied with a stream of rapid-fire Tagalog, most of which Ruth suspected was swearing.

'You get out,' she finished, jabbing at Ruth with the broom. 'I call the police.'

'No,' said Ruth, staggering to her feet. 'I came here to speak to you, ask you a few more questions.'

'No speak,' Cherry said angrily. 'You go! Now!'

Behind Cherry, Ruth could see another figure enter the room. A man, about forty; he had his shirt open and was holding a wine glass. The housekeeper followed her gaze and tried to close the door, but it was too late.

'I see,' smiled Ruth. 'Using your employer's house as a love nest when she's out of the country? She won't like that.'

Cherry looked trapped.

'Is my boyfriend,' she said.

'It doesn't make it right,' quipped Ruth. 'I think Mrs Goddard-Price will probably agree with me.'

'You not tell her, please!' said Cherry, knowing she was beaten.

'Not if you answer a few more questions,' said Ruth, pushing past her into the house.

The housekeeper looked pained.

'Mrs G, she tell me not to speak to no one.'

I bet she did, thought Ruth, opening her bag.

'All I want to do is show you a couple of pictures,' she said, pulling out a file. 'That's all, then I'll go.'

Dammit, why didn't I prepare for this? thought Ruth, fumbling with the pile of photographs. She'd just grabbed her research folder on the way out, and hadn't sorted out the picture she needed. She put them on the tabletop and flicked through them until she found the right one. It was the head-and-shoulders shot of Nick Beddingfield the police had released when the Riverton murder was first announced.

'Remember when I was here before and you said another man used to visit Mrs Goddard-Price? Is this the man?'

The maid took the photo and examined it, then handed it back. 'No,' she said.

'Are you sure?' pressed Ruth. 'He isn't the one who used to come when Mr Goddard-Price was away on business?'

'No.'

Ruth felt her heart sinking. She had felt sure this was the connection she had been looking for.

'It was him,' said Cherry, pointing down at the table. Ruth's eyes opened wide. The housekeeper's finger was on a picture of Peter Ellis, from the Ellis family snapshot that Julia had given her that day she had visited her at Wade House.

'This man? You're certain?'

Ruth felt goose pimples run up her arms. Could it be true? Lana was having an affair with Peter Ellis?

'Yes, certain. Once, twice, he come here.' She made a circle with her thumb and forefinger and pushed her other forefinger through the hole, in and out to signify sex.

Ruth stifled a frown. It was another connection. But still she was no closer to putting Lana with Nick.

'Sophie's room. Could I just have one quick look?'

'Top floor. Two minutes,' frowned Cherry, knowing that Ruth had leverage.

Ruth ran up the sweeping staircase, two stairs at a time. Instead of going all the way to the top, she darted into the master suite.

This had to be Lana's, she thought, admiring the sumptuous bedroom with white drapes and walnut furniture. She opened both bedside cabinets and the dressing table drawer, looking for a diary, a notebook, anything that might connect Lana to Nick, but there was nothing; only boxes of thank-you cards, and glossy magazines and piles of cosmetics.

She turned as she heard a noise behind her. Cherry was standing in the doorway looking furious. Ruth cursed silently.

'You go now,' hissed Cherry.

Ruth acted as if there was nothing wrong with finding a random journalist ferreting around the mistress of the house's bedroom.

'If Mrs G comes back home, I want you to contact me immediately.' She rooted around her purse, but she had given her last business card to Mike at the gym. There was a biro on the cabinet top. She took it and scribbled her contact details on a page she ripped out of her notebook.

Cherry looked wary.

'I promise I won't tell Lana about your boyfriend being here, but you must cooperate with me, okay?'

'Please, go,' said the housekeeper, almost wailing.

Ruth nodded. She knew she was beaten. For now. But she wasn't finished looking into Lana Goddard-Price.

40

Sunny Isles, a barrier island just off the coast of Miami, had the right name, thought Sophie as their car crossed the long bridge from the mainland. The late afternoon sky was bright blue, the air rushing in through the window tasted tropical and the beach circling the island was like a golden halo. But around Miami, Sunny Isles had another name: Little Moscow, and as they turned into the maze of pastel-painted condominiums, hotels and shops crowded around the foot of the bridge, Sophie could see why: Eastern European delis and restaurants advertising borscht and blinis, some even written in the angular Cyrillic script. But there were signs too of the modern Russia in the expensive fashion boutiques, the low rumbling sports cars and the body-beautiful women strolling the streets in tiny shorts and bikini tops. She caught Josh watching two model-grade beauties cross the street and nudged his arm. He turned to look at her, and gave her a surprised smile.

'What's up?' he grinned as the cab pulled up outside the Steppes steak restaurant.

'Are you sure this is the right place?'

'Not exactly, no. But it's a good guess.'

Arriving in Miami from Fort Lauderdale, they had checked into a cheap motel in the touristy Coconut Grove area and split up. Sophie's job was to go shopping: a razor for Josh, some clean underwear and new shoes – hers had been ruined in their off-road chase two days ago. Josh meanwhile went to an internet café, where he had found a *Miami Herald* story documenting the rise of the Russian mob in the south Florida area. In the story, the Steppes steakhouse in Sunny Isles had been linked to 'noted Russian mobster' Uri Kaskov, which was why they were sitting outside it now. The Steppes was where they were hoping to find Uri's son, Sergei.

'Look, if our boy's not here, we'll just share a Chateaubriand and soak up the sun.' He smiled, but she could see the nervousness in his eyes.

'It's not too late to turn back,' she said quietly.

'Do you trust me?' he asked.

Sophie didn't have to think; she simply nodded.

'Then let's go in.'

They walked up the steps and on to a large open-air terrace overlooking the ocean. The waiters wore the embroidered waistcoats and high leather boots of traditional Russian dress, but the menu was typical Florida: steaks, seafood and elaborate cocktails.

Sophie had been expecting the place to be full of Tony Soprano lookalikes in silk suits and chunky gold jewellery, but she was relieved to find it was packed by well-heeled tourists and smart-looking business people, all chatting and laughing. Josh seemed in the mood to join in, because when their waiter came by, he immediately ordered champagne and lobster for two.

'What's this? The Last Supper?' said Sophie.

'Come on, princess, lighten up,' said Josh. 'This is Miami – you're supposed to get a tan, but you look absolutely white.'

'Is it any wonder?' she muttered. 'I feel like I'm staring down the barrel of a gun.'

'Hey, for all we know, this Little Moscow thing could be something they cooked up for the tourists. Have a cocktail and relax.'

But Sophie couldn't relax. In the taxi outside Ty's place, she had said it was the end of the trail, and she still felt that way. They had started on this journey as a way of finding out who had killed her boyfriend and to clear her name. But along the way, she had discovered that nothing – her boyfriend, her life, even her father – was as it seemed. And now they knew who was chasing them, it seemed they were giving up, surrendering themselves to whatever fate the Russians chose for them: for the first time since they had started running, on that cold back street by the Thames a lifetime ago, it felt as if it was out of their hands.

'Is this really such a good idea?' said Sophie.

'The lobster?'

'No, Josh,' she said. 'Handing ourselves in to this Sergei, Uri's son.'

Josh let out a long breath.

'Sophie, we just don't have a choice,' he said, lowering his voice. 'Yes, we could keep running, keep looking for the money, but what then? What if we found it?'

'We could go away, disappear,' she said urgently. 'Just you and me, somewhere they'd never find us.' She blushed as the words came out of her mouth. She paused, holding her breath, but if Josh had caught her intention, he didn't react.

'Sophie, listen to me,' he said quietly. 'There is nowhere we could go that these people wouldn't find us. Right or wrong, they think that money is theirs, and if we take it from them, they will keep hunting us – for ever. Do you want that?'

'No,' she said simply.

'Then we have to go see the top man, tell him what we know – and hope that's enough.'

'And what if it isn't?'

Josh gave her a smile. 'Then we'd better hope this lobster is pretty bloody good.'

Right on cue, two waiters appeared bearing a silver tray

laden with food, with two enormous lobsters centre stage.

'You crack on,' said Josh as they laid the feast out on the table. 'Just got to see a man about a dog. See if you can dig the good stuff out for me, I'm rubbish with those nutcrackers. I'll only be a few minutes.'

Sophie watched him thread his way through the tables, then glanced down at the lobster, staring back at her with blank eyes. Curiously, it made her think of a boy named Charlie Simmons. Sophie guessed she must have been fourteen and head over heels in unrequited love with the floppy-haired boy from the school down the road. Her mother had clearly decided it was time for a talk about the birds and the bees, so she took Sophie to a posh restaurant in London, ordered lobster and announced that if she was ever to stand a chance with any man, she had to learn to be a lady – and for Julia Ellis, being a lady involved knowing how to behave in polite society. Being able to crack a lobster without losing your dignity was just one of the things on her checklist.

Sophie smiled as she began the ritual of opening the hard coral shell and pulling out the sweet snow-white meat. Her mother meant well, of course, it was just that Julia's idea of what constituted an ideal husband – the one with the biggest pile of gold – seemed ridiculously naïve now. Sophie could barely believe the hours she had spent smiling politely as red-faced boys called Rupert or Alexander boasted about their small achievements at endless Chelsea dinner parties or slumped against the bar in too-loud, too-smug nightclubs. But her mother had been wrong. Just because a man had money didn't make him right for you. A good marriage was never going to make you happy if there was no love, no chemistry with the man you were marrying. She looked out at the sea, now bruising orange and purple as the sun dipped closer and closer to the waves, and wondered how she could have missed out on all this. Not this swanky restaurant, but feeling like this. As if life was one big adventure, even if right now it meant being in quite a lot of danger. And sharing that adventure with one person who made you feel alive, special, just by the way he looked at you.

You've fallen for him, whispered a voice in her head as she plunged her fingers into the lemon water.

Suddenly she just wanted to see Josh. Lost in her thoughts, she wasn't exactly sure how long he'd been gone, but she was sure he should be back by now. She scanned the room nervously.

Where *was* he? The noise seemed to swell around her, the laughter from the next table taking on a malicious, sinister air. She didn't even have enough money to pay for the meal. She stood up, fighting down the urge to panic, and stopped a waiter.

'My friend from this table?' she said. 'Have you seen him?'

The waiter shook his head and Sophie moved through the tables towards the rest rooms. Knocking on the door of the men's, she called Josh's name, but there was no response. Pushing all those ingrained ideas of social niceties to one side, she opened the door and ducked inside. 'Josh? Are you in here?'

But there was nothing except two urinals and an empty stall.

'Josh, where are you?' she whispered urgently, moving back towards the kitchen – could he have gone to speak to the chef? And then there he was, coming out of a door marked 'Office'.

Her heart swelled with relief. 'Where have you been? I've been stuck at the table . . .' His handsome face looked so serious, she stopped.

'What's going on, Josh?'

'The manager has arranged a meeting,' he said, taking her arm and leading her through the steamy kitchen, ignoring the glances of the staff in their whites. Sophie felt her pulse quicken. She knew this was the plan, but now it was actually happening, she wasn't at all sure it was the right thing to do. 'Do you trust me?' – that was what Josh had asked her when they'd arrived at the Steppes. Nothing had changed, the answer was still yes, so when a black SUV pulled up at the kitchen's rear door, she got inside after Josh without a word, even though it felt as if they had just walked into the lion's den.

The car crossed the bridge from the island and drove south, on to Collins Avenue and along the Miami seashore. Sophie wished she had seen South Beach in different circumstances, because it truly was glamorous. The sorbet-coloured hotels, the art deco lines, the hot Latin sounds pumping out of the bars; it was like a neon-lit party town. Now they were passing the waterfront mansions and sleek motor yachts moored in Biscayne Bay. This was multi-millionaire central, the playground of some of America's richest citizens. An iron gate swung inwards and the car turned off the road, past an armed guard and into a circular drive. The house behind was a Spanish hacienda-style with whitewashed walls and a rippled terracotta roof, and beyond it Sophie could just glimpse the sea. Whatever illegal activities the Kaskov family were up to, they were certainly lucrative. Properties of this size weren't bought with the proceeds of surf 'n' turf restaurants, no matter how popular they might be.

A squat man in a black suit opened the car's door and beckoned them out. Then wordlessly he turned and walked around the side of the house. Josh and Sophie could only follow, across a sloping emerald lawn to where a man in riding gear was standing next to a horse, brushing its glossy chestnut coat. Despite her fear, Sophie couldn't resist reaching out to stroke the horse's neck.

'Beautiful, yes?' said the man, turning towards her. Sophie was caught off guard. She had been expecting a stable-boy type, but the man holding the reins was strikingly handsome, with chiselled features and dark hair that gleamed. In fact, he looked exactly like the many gorgeous South American polo players she and her friends had giggled over on their summer trips to the Guards or Cowdray Park polo clubs.

'She's a polo pony, isn't she?' said Sophie.

The man nodded appreciatively.

'She's a Criollo/Arabian cross, from Argentina, which makes her one of the best breeds of polo ponies in the world. Now I just have to decide if I want to buy her. What do you think?'

He looked Sophie up and down, his dark eyes running over her as if he were feeling her haunches and checking her teeth.

'I'd say you have already made your decision,' said Sophie, looking away from his blue-eyed stare.

'So you are Sophie Ellis,' he said matter-of-factly.

'Yes. We're here to see Sergei Kaskov.'

He turned and offered a hand.

'Then I am pleased to meet you, Sophie Ellis.'

Sophie was stunned. On the drive from the Steppes, she had imagined what Uri the Bear's son would be like and had pictured a crop-haired thug with a scarred face. The real Sergei Kaskov looked like a model in a Ralph Lauren advert and sounded like the product of an English prep school. He motioned to a security guard to take the horse away.

'Let's sit by the water,' he said, walking down the lawn. 'It's a much more pleasant place to talk.'

The grass ended in a tiled area surrounding a beautiful infinity pool which seemed to flow straight into the ocean beyond the compound. Sergei gestured towards a pair of white sofas separated by a low table. 'Please, make yourselves comfortable,' he said. 'Can I get you anything to drink? Some food perhaps?'

'Thank you, no,' said Sophie as they sat across from him.

Despite the Russian's smooth manner, she was on edge and her appetite had completely deserted her. It didn't help that the squat man and two others were standing at a discreet distance watching their every move. She didn't want to turn, but she suspected there were others behind them too.

'Well now,' said Sergei. 'It's a pleasure to finally meet you. I'm sure you're aware we've been looking for you for quite some time.'

'Looking for her? That's one way of putting it,' said Josh.

Sophie willed him to be quiet. Sergei might look like a gentleman, but they had both heard about his father's impatience with Michael Asner; she sensed confrontation was not the best approach.

'I have not been seeking Miss Ellis personally, Mr McCormack,' said Sergei calmly. 'Although having now met her, perhaps I should have done. Sadly, these days it is often necessary to outsource certain tasks. I apologise if one of my contractors has been a little heavy-handed.'

'We've been shot at, chased, run off the road,' said Josh. 'You could have killed her.'

'I don't want to kill you, Miss Ellis,' said Sergei, leaving a slight emphasis on the word 'want'. Sophie looked into those glacial blue eyes and got the message loud and clear. He didn't *want* to, but he would if he had to.

'Whatever you may have heard about me, I am simply a businessman. My father conducted a transaction with Michael Asner and we expect that contract to be honoured. It's quite simple.'

A maid came and placed a tray on the table, and handed them all a cold glass of pale liquid.

'This is kvass, a traditional Russian drink. Try it,' said Sergei. It wasn't a request. Sophie sipped it and suppressed a cough as it burned down her throat.

'It's good, isn't it?' smiled Sergei.

'What do you want from us, Mr Kaskov?'

He wiped a small fingerprint smear from the top of his glass.

'I rather thought that was obvious,' he said. 'My father protected Michael Asner in prison. In return, Michael offered him a large amount of money. My father called in his investment, but Asner began to drag his feet. Understandably my father was angry.'

'And he killed him,' said Josh.

'That was unfortunate,' said Sergei, as if it was of no consequence. 'Personally I would have waited until Mr Asner had told us how to locate the money. As it was, we only had the first name of the man who was the guardian of the funds. It was weeks before we discovered that "Peter" was your father, Miss Ellis. And then we discovered that he too had passed on.'

'Did you kill him as well?'

It wasn't until Josh had asked the question that Sophie realised she desperately wanted to hear the answer. She felt sure you could make a murder look like a heart attack. But Sergei was shaking his head.

'We are not barbaric, Mr McCormack. And we are not stupid; we don't make the same mistake twice.'

He looked at them as he sipped his drink slowly.

'So,' he said finally. 'I simply wish to know where the money is. Give it to us and I promise you will never see or hear from us again.'

Sophie suddenly pictured Uri's men – or had they been Sergei's? – in her apartment, tearing it apart to find what they wanted; then she saw them in Wade House, beside the river in Chelsea, at the station in Nice, and she knew Josh had been right. These men were ruthless. They would never rest until they had what they wanted.

'She doesn't know where the money is,' said Josh.

'You'll excuse me,' said Sergei, 'but I don't believe that.'

'Well why do you think we're here?' said Josh.

Sergei gave a short laugh. 'I was rather wondering.'

'We haven't got a death wish, Mr Kaskov,' said Josh. 'The truth is, until we spoke to Ty Connor this morning, we genuinely had no idea who you were. All we knew was that someone was chasing us.'

'Someone killed my friend,' said Sophie. 'I thought they were trying to kill me too.'

Sergei did not react, merely raised his eyebrows slightly, indicating that they should continue.

'So when we heard who you were and what you wanted,' said Josh, 'we thought we would come and tell you what we know. Or in this case, don't know.'

'Very sporting of you,' said Sergei.

'I don't want this money, Mr Kaskov,' said Sophie fiercely. 'I just want my life back.'

'So what do you know?' he asked, steepling his fingers in front of his soft pink lips.

Josh took Sophie's bag and, unzipping the plastic make-up pouch, pulled out her copy of *I Capture the Castle*. He passed it to Sergei.

Sophie's heart jumped. *What was he doing?* That was her dad's gift to her! She wanted to reach out and snatch it back, but she knew that wouldn't help their situation, so she stayed still.

'This is all we have,' said Josh. 'You've searched Sophie's flat; we presume it was you who searched her mother's house too. This is the only thing that Peter Ellis gave Sophie that has any possible reference to the money. Look on the front page.'

Sergei opened the book.

'Benedict Grear?' He frowned. 'Who is he?'

'We don't know,' said Josh. 'Neither does Asner's widow and neither does the SEC apparently. But you found Peter Ellis and you found us, so you obviously have the resources to work this out.'

Sergei gave him the ghost of a smile, as if he was flattered by Josh's observation.

'And this is all?'

'Yes,' said Sophie and Josh in unison.

'I hope so,' said Sergei. He waved the book in the air and the squat guy stepped forward and took it.

'No!' cried Sophie, unable to stop herself. 'That's mine! My father gave it to me!'

Sergei shook his head, the smile gone.

'No, Miss Ellis, it is mine.'

He waved his hand again and Sophie screamed as she and Josh were both seized from behind and pulled to their feet.

'Please, you've got the book,' shouted Josh, 'We've told you everything we know.'

Sergei looked at him coldly.

'Ah, now that is exactly what we're going to find out.'

The squat man stepped forward and punched Josh in the mouth. Sophie tried to scream again, but a huge hand clamped around her face, pinning her jaw shut. She could only watch as Josh was held by two big Russians, while the squat man hit him again and again: to the body, to the head.

'No!' she screamed.

Sergei stepped in front of her, grabbing her hair and twisting it painfully.

'You care about this man, I take it?' he said. His voice was soft, almost feminine. Sophie nodded.

'Then tell us where your father hid the money.'

The hand was removed long enough for her to gasp: 'I promise you, I don't know.'

The squat man brought his knee up into Josh's stomach, then backhanded him across the face, sending an arc of blood flying on to the tile.

'Josh!' she shouted.

'Last chance, Miss Ellis,' said Sergei.

'You have to believe me,' she pleaded. 'I would tell you if

I knew, but I really, really have no idea, he didn't ever tell me—'

The hand covered her mouth again and she struggled in desperation, but whoever was holding her had an iron grip.

'Very well, bring him,' said Sergei.

Sophie watched in horror as two of the Russians picked up Josh and carried him to the edge of the pool. At a signal from Sergei, they plunged his head and shoulders under the water. He kicked his legs, thrashing his head from side to side, but his arms were pinned behind him.

Sophie was screaming hysterically.

'Josh! Josh! Please stop, I'll do whatever you want, please!'

Sergei raised a hand and Josh was pulled out, coughing and retching.

'Speak to me, Miss Ellis,' he said.

She felt weak and delirious.

'Maybe it's at my parents' house,' she sobbed. 'He had an office but that was cleared out when he retired. Everything was brought back home.'

The Russian pushed his face close to hers. 'Do you take me for a simpleton?' he hissed. 'Do you wish to insult me? Of course we searched there, you stupid little girl. There was nothing.'

His blue eyes held hers as he said, 'Again.'

Josh was pushed back into the pool. He fought harder this time, churning the blue water into a white froth, but gradually his movements became slower, less urgent.

'You're killing him!' yelled Sophie. 'Let him up!'

'Tell me what I want to know,' said Sergei.

'I *can't*,' she said, tears streaming down her face. 'I wish I could, but I can't. We've told you everything we know. You *have* to believe me.'

Sergei gazed at her for a moment longer, then gave the slightest shake of his head.

'Get rid of them,' he said.

Suddenly it went dark. For a moment Sophie was disorientated, then she felt the material on her face and realised a bag had been put over her head. Her arms were forced behind her back and her wrists bound with thin rope.

'Please, don't!' she cried.

Then she heard a voice very close to her ear, deep and accented.

'Speak or struggle again, I will cut your throat. Nod if you understand.'

She nodded.

Helpless and terrified, Sophie was roughly lifted, half carried, half marched, along a path. She had no idea where Josh was, or whether he was being taken to a similar fate. Frozen with terror, her mind sought out a happier, calmer place and she found herself thinking of her father, the last time he had taken her out on *Iona*, just before he died. Although it had been a sad time for her dad, Sophie had loved that day out on the river, just the two of them, laughing and talking. Even then, Peter had still been full of his plans to get away, dreaming of that castle on a desert island just like he always had. *I hope you're there now, Daddy*, she thought, her tears soaking into the rough fabric covering her face.

Suddenly there was a thunk and a sliding noise, then Sophie felt herself lifted and pushed down as an engine kicked into life. Of course, she was in the back of a van: she could smell the oil and feel the vibrations through the floor.

'Hello?' she said tentatively, remembering the threat about speaking. 'Is anyone—' She cried out as something heavy was thrown on top of her. It rolled and slithered to one side, then she heard a gasp and a cough: Josh! Her heart leapt – he was alive! She felt a small sliver of hope as she heard the van doors slam and the vehicle began to move. Perhaps they were being taken somewhere else for questioning. *Don't be so bloody stupid*, she scolded herself. They were taking them somewhere else, yes. But for disposal, not questioning. Sergei wasn't so stupid that he'd kill someone on his own property, but then he wouldn't want them running to the police screaming about torture either. *If it were me, I'd dump us in the sea*, her mind thought crazily. But another, more steady voice also spoke in her head. *Fight back, Sophie*, it said. *Don't let them win.*

'Josh,' she whispered. 'Josh, can you hear me?'

She was rewarded with a spate of coughing and she moved towards the sound.

'Where are you?' she said desperately.

'Where do you' – *cough, cough* – 'think I am?'

She shook the bag off her head. In the dim light of the van, she could see Josh lying curled on his side, shivering uncontrollably. He was wet and cold and probably in shock. A black bag was over his head and his hands were tied in front of him.

She crawled over, gripped the bag between her teeth and pulled it over his hair.

'Finally,' coughed Josh.

Sophie smiled in the dark, despite herself.

'What do you think they're going to do with us?' she asked.

Josh stiffened as another wave of coughing seized him.

'I dunno,' he said at length. 'But I doubt they're taking us to the movies.'

They lay there on the floor, listening to the engine. They weren't making many turns: were they on the highway? Heading out of town? Sophie couldn't even tell if they had been driving for five minutes or twenty. All she could do was lie there watching yellow lights from the crack in the door sweep across the roof of the van.

A single tear rolled down her cheek and Josh shuffled up closer to her.

'Don't cry,' he said softly. 'We'll get through this.'

'It's slowing,' she said, her body tensing again. 'We're turning off the road. What are they doing?'

Suddenly the rear doors opened and Sophie was grabbed by the arm by one of Sergei's men and yanked out of the van. She was sent sprawling on to a dirt road, scraping her knees and the palms of her hands, still bound with rope. There was another thud and a groan as Josh landed next to her.

Her stomach clenched with fear. *This is it*, she thought, feeling faint with terror. They were going to kill them. She looked at Josh and knew she just wanted to be held by him, to die with him. The Russian towered over them. She closed her eyes, her heart hammering, a faint groan escaping from her lips. Then she heard footsteps walking away from them, and the slam of a door. She opened her eyes and saw the van skid off, its wheels sending a shower of gravel into her eyes.

'Josh!' she yelled, scrambling to her feet and blinking in the setting sunlight as she watched the tail lights of the van disappear towards the horizon. Relief almost knocked her to the ground again.

She wriggled her wrists around. The binding had not been put on tightly and she managed to get one hand free, then the other. She ran over to Josh and unfastened the rope around his wrists.

He took her in his arms and she started weeping.

Josh held her like that for a long time as she cried, stroking her hair, murmuring softly, 'It's okay, we're safe, we're safe now.'

Right then, she only cared that she was alive and in Josh's arms.

Finally she pulled away from him and looked around. They were in swampland, possibly not too far away from the sea, as she could still smell the salt in the air and gulls circled overhead.

Up ahead, they could see the yellow street lights of what

looked like a main road. Josh stumbled and groaned, holding his side, and Sophie put her arm around him, supporting him.

'So what now?' she said.

Josh nodded towards the road. 'We should get back to Miami,' he said firmly. 'I wouldn't want to be around here when it gets dark. It would be pretty lame if we survived Sergei and then got mauled by the gators.'

41

She could barely remember how they got back to the motel in Coconut Grove. Unable to reach Lana by phone, they had stumbled along the road, getting more and more anxious as the sun began to set, until finally a pick-up truck had stopped when Sophie stuck her thumb out to hitch a lift.

She had never been more glad to see a hotel room. She double-locked the door, smiling grimly at the futility of it, and went to get some towels from the bathroom. Soaking one in warm water, she wiped the blood from Josh's face, then carefully pulled off his still wet shirt, wrapped another towel around his shoulders and dried his hair.

'TLC,' she whispered.

'I need to get beaten up more often,' he chuckled, then winced, holding his side.

'Should I call a doctor?' she said, hating to see him in so much pain.

'Nah, I've been roughed up worse than that back in Edinburgh.' He smiled.

She sat down on the bed next to him.

'I don't understand. Why did they let us go?'

Josh shrugged.

'If they saw us at Miriam Asner's, maybe they assumed we were being tracked. I bet Sergei and Uri are in enough trouble without having the SEC seeing us going into the Kaskov compound alive, then turning up dead the next day.

Besides, they probably think they might still need us.'

Dead. Sophie's mind jumped back to that scene by the pool and she reached for his hand.

'Josh, I thought they were going to kill you,' she said, her voice cracking.

'Hey, come on,' he said. 'I'm tough as old boots.'

'We shouldn't have gone to see Sergei; it was so stupid.'

'We had to, Soph,' said Josh. 'Those guys would have kept coming after us until they got what they wanted. Now they have it, we're safer than we were.'

'I guess. But now they can find the money and none of Asner's victims will ever see a penny of it. It's all going to go on Sergei Kaskov's polo ponies and manicures.'

Josh gave a weary laugh.

'Sorry,' he said more seriously. 'I've let you down.'

She shook her head.

'No you haven't.'

'But you wanted the money.'

'Not for myself,' she said firmly. 'I wanted the money for the old guy who lost his life savings. I wanted it for the family who lost their children's college fees, I wanted it for all those people who worked really, really hard and thought they were doing the right thing to safeguard it by investing it. I didn't even want it for my dad. He shouldn't have hidden it, whatever reasons he had.'

Sophie paused for a moment.

'You know,' she said softly, 'when we lost everything, I really thought my world had fallen apart. I actually cried when the Mulberry bags went to the dress agency and I was almost inconsolable when I had to leave my Chelsea flat. I was a spoilt little bitch.' She gave an embarrassed grin.

'I can't say that the Asner scam was the best thing that ever happened to me, but having money made me think I was happy when really I wasn't. People think money is security, it's freedom, and for many people I guess it is. But for me, it was just insulation. I was drifting. I didn't know who I was. I didn't think I was good at anything – I can see that now. If you need designer bags and exotic holidays to be happy, then I'm not sure that counts as really being happy.'

Josh looked at her for a long moment.

'So what does make you happy?' he asked.

'You.'

The word hung in the air between them, but Josh didn't move. *What's stopping you?* she pleaded silently, wondering whether she had read the signals completely wrong. *But I couldn't have, could I?* And then he reached for her, his hand brushing her cheek, his fingertips barely touching her skin, the most tender thing she had ever felt. He moved closer, and she began to babble.

'We should phone the SEC,' she said. His lips brushed hers and then pulled away teasingly. 'Tell them everything we know,' she added, her voice trailing off into a moan. And suddenly he was kissing her – urgently, passionately. She could taste blood on the corner of his lip and wanted to be gentle with him, but her desire was as strong as his. Her whole body ached for him. Unable to wait any longer, she lifted her dress over her head as he snaked his arms around her back to unfasten her bra. Her breasts sprang free, and he pressed himself against her, taking her head in his hands, planting soft kisses on her lips as if he were drinking her in like sweet nectar he had been long denied.

'You are so beautiful,' he growled, his voice full of desire, and Sophie pulled him in to her harder, smiling. She felt on fire, every nerve ending alight, every sense, taste, touch, smell heightened, her lust making her dizzy. She reached down to unbuckle his belt, impatiently tugging his trousers down and off, wanting, caring for nothing but to feel him inside her.

Josh couldn't wait either. They fell on to the bed and he spread her thighs, pulling her sheer panties to one side and then sliding into her in one movement. She gasped, moaned, exquisitely full of him. Clenching herself around him, she rotated her hips as they found their rhythm. In and out, hard, soft, quick, slow. Kissing her throat, her earlobes, her nipples, his stubble rough, his lips soft, the extremes of sensation driving her wild.

She had never felt more intimately connected to anyone. He was passionate and yet tender, maddeningly sexy and yet gentle and loving. They had known one another barely a week and yet he found her sweet spots with such accuracy it was as if they had been romantically involved for years.

She could think of nothing except the absolute pleasure of him being inside her, moving as one, her whole body shivering on the edge of climax until finally she cried out, biting his shoulder with such force that it surprised her when he moaned with contentment rather than pain. White-hot ripples of lust radiated from her belly down to the tips of her toes, wave after wave of glorious, pulsating pleasure. He came moments after her, and they lay in silence, calm, exhausted, slowing their breathing together, overwhelmed by the intensity of what had just happened.

They made love again a little while later; slower, less frantic the second time around, with more time taken to explore and enjoy each other's bodies. She took him in her mouth, savouring his taste, bringing him to the edge of pleasure, astonishing herself that she could make one man so wild with desire.

She had no idea what time they fell asleep. So when she woke up in the middle of the night, she felt completely displaced. It was perfectly quiet. No ceiling fan, no noise of traffic on the street outside, just the faint sound of crickets and bullfrogs in the distance. For a second she tensed, before the blissful recollection of falling asleep in Josh's arms came to her. She reached for him, but the other side of the bed was empty. Still drowsy, she sat up and pulled the white sheet around her naked body. Josh was sitting in a chair in his T-shirt and boxer shorts, bent over a reading lamp.

'Josh?'

He looked up, and when he didn't smile, Sophie immediately felt a stab of pain: she didn't regret what had happened for one second – did he?

'Everything okay?' she asked.

He looked at her for a moment.

'I think I know where the money is,' he said.

'What?' she said, suddenly feeling wide awake.

He held up a battered paperback book, and Sophie's heart gave a jump – I Capture the Castle; she would have recognised that green cover anywhere.

'How the hell have you got that?' she gasped. 'Sergei took it from us.'

'Sleight of hand,' smiled Josh. 'When I was out doing my research on the Russians, I found a little second-hand bookshop. They had about five copies of I Capture the Castle, so I bought one and copied the name and the numbers into it. I knew the Russians wouldn't know the difference.'

She got up and walked over, wrapping a towel around herself.

'Josh, why didn't you tell me?'

'Because I knew you wouldn't have reacted in the same way. Sergei had to believe he was getting the real thing. I'm sorry.'

He handed it to her. 'And I thought you'd probably want to hang on to the original.'

She looked down at the desk. Josh's smartphone was sitting there, and he had been writing something on a notepad.

'So what's all this about?'

'You were right, Sophie,' he said, excitement in his voice. 'The book is the key to it.'

'You know who Benedict Grear is?' she said incredulously.

'Not who, where,' said Josh. Sophie sat on the arm of his

chair as he turned to the front page. 'We always wondered who Benedict Grear was, rather than *what* it was. You know why I thought of it? Walking into the restaurant yesterday, seeing all those tourists, thinking they probably thought the Steppes was named after the stairs at the front of the restaurant. Stupid, I know, but it triggered something in my mind: what if Benedict Grear isn't a name?'

Sophie frowned.

'But it *is* a name . . .'

'Yes, a name of a place, not a person,' replied Josh, running his finger under the text. 'Benedict Grear is Ben Grear,' he said. 'Ben is Gaelic for mountain. I did a search; there's a Ben Grear in Scotland. And this number here?' he said, pointing at the faint pencil numerals in the corner of the page. 'Again, we were making wrong assumptions. We thought it was a date of birth or a sort code or account number. But it's Ordnance Survey coordinates.'

Josh picked up his phone.

'There's an OS Explorer map of the Ben Grear area and you can download digital copies.'

He played around with the phone until he showed her a map page.

'Look, here's the mountain, and if you read off the numbers from the book, it gets you here.' He tapped his finger on the screen, just below the mountain. 'It's a building, on an outcrop of land in this small loch. You said your dad always told you he'd get you your own castle one day, didn't he? I bet that's it. And I bet Asner's money is hidden somewhere there.'

He looked up at her, a wide grin on his face.

'All we have to do is go and get it.'

Sophie knew she should feel excited, she knew she should whoop for joy; after all, that was what they had been looking for all this time – the pot of gold at the end of the rainbow. But she didn't, she just felt flat. The one thing this journey had taught her was that money only brought heartache.

'It's stolen money, Josh,' she whispered. 'I don't want stolen money. My dad would know that.'

'Would he?' said Josh.

'What do you mean?' said Sophie, pulling the towel higher.

'Listen, your dad loved you, right?'

'Of course!'

'And he knew you liked the good life. He would have wanted you to be comfortable, to give you everything you'd always wanted. Nice house, nice car, all that.'

He shook his head. 'I've met a lot of rich people in my time. Gangsters. Corrupt businessmen. You look at their wives, their grown-up kids, do you think any of them stop to question how Daddy is paying for it?'

'I'm not like that!'

'I know that, Sophie. But did he?'

She suddenly felt terribly sad, because she knew there was a grain of truth in what Josh was saying – more than a grain, in fact. She *had* been fixated on material things: the shoes, the postcode, the boyfriend with a big engagement ring. And now she realised how little all that meant, but her dad had never met – *would* never meet – his new daughter and that was a tragedy. Maybe there was some way of making amends, maybe she could still fix it – but to do that, they had to get to the money before the Russians or anyone else.

'We have to go to Scotland,' she said quickly.

'I'll call Lana. Maybe we can get out of Miami this morning. We have to get there before Sergei works out what we have.'

'Why didn't you give him the false co-ordinates in the book?'

'He's not the sort of man you want to lie to. You just have to out-smart him.'

She looked at him, doubt creeping in.

'Are we going to call Hal Stanton?'

'No.'

She frowned. 'Why not?'

'Because we're almost there, Soph.'

She felt a cold shiver somewhere deep inside her. It was a moment before she recognised what it was. Doubt.

She looked at Josh playing with a route map on his iPhone. There was a definite reluctance to get the authorities involved. Was that because he had an inherent distrust for the establishment? This was a man who skirted around the law, not worked with it. Or was it something else?

An unwelcome thought began to present itself in her brain. A thought that made her pull her towel a little tighter round her body. Josh couldn't have an ulterior motive for wanting to keep the authorities out of this, could he?

As she tried to rid herself of the notion, Josh curled one strong arm around her waist. Pressed up against him, she could feel him harden beneath his boxer shorts.

'This wasn't exactly what I had in mind for a first date,' he said, stroking her hair. She felt herself relax in his arms. She was wrong to question Josh. She trusted him implicitly. He'd had so many opportunities to abandon her, and yet he'd stuck by her side from the moment she'd left his houseboat and been chased by the Russians.

'When this is over, we'll go somewhere hot and sunny and wonderful. Brazil, Bali, the Maldives. We can stay there six months, a year, longer. You can write books or poems or paint pictures, or we can just sell coconuts and spend the rest of our time doing what we did last night. Doing what I wanted to do to you since the moment I saw you. But first we have to find the money.'

She pulled away from him. 'You wanted to have sex with me at the Chariot party?' she grinned.

'I was as jealous as hell that Nick had got his paws on you first.'

'Maybe you should have tried a bit harder,' she replied, circling his T-shirt with her fingertip and feeling the coarse scrub of chest hair underneath. As she looked up at him, she wondered how things might have panned out had she met Josh before, rather than after Nick. Or if Josh had tried harder, hung around a little longer to talk to her. Would he have charmed her away from Nick? If he had succeeded, where would they be now? On his houseboat, enjoying the English summer, or in her tiny Battersea studio, which seemed so remote it was as if it belonged in another lifetime? Or would she not even have given him a chance? Josh was the antithesis of her usual type, but it had taken this week, this journey to realise that he was exactly what she wanted.

He smiled, and the corners of his soft grey eyes creased into fine lines. It was a hell of a sexy smile.

'Much as I would like to make up for lost time, we should get moving.'

Sophie unfolded herself from his embrace and began to dress. She splashed some water on her face, brushed her teeth and threw all their belongings in their two small nylon bags. She was ready to finish this.

It was almost four a.m. and the sky was still black.

They shut their room door quietly and dropped the key off in a drop box, leaving two fifty-dollar bills behind the reception desk.

'Stop,' said Josh, putting his hand in front of Sophie.

He peeped through the front window shutters.

'See there?' he whispered. 'Blue saloon car across the street. There's someone in it.'

'Not Sergei's men again?' said Sophie, her heart starting to hammer.

'I'm guessing the SEC or the FBI. Come on. There must be a back exit somewhere around here.'

They went through the small courtyard behind the motel and scrambled over the back wall. A dustbin clattered over as Sophie fell on top of it, which set off a dog barking.

Josh phoned Lana, who told them to get to her hotel as soon as they could. They wandered the streets for ten minutes for a taxi, and only when they had reached Lana's hotel – South Beach's art deco jewel, the Raleigh – did Sophie even start to feel safe.

42

The insistent ring of her mobile phone woke her. Peeling open one eye, Ruth squinted at her alarm clock and groaned; it was three thirty in the afternoon. It had been a long time since she had slept this late. True, she had always been a night owl – working through till the early hours, when her brain seemed to function better. Perhaps it was sensory deprivation like a blinkered horse; having the world cloaked in darkness and quiet allowed her to concentrate. But the truth was this time she had just overslept, exhausted from long hours and too much stress.

'Dammit,' she hissed, stretching to grab her phone.

'Hello,' she croaked, swinging one leg out of bed, then the other, feeling for her slippers with her toes.

'Ruth, it's Isaac. We need to talk.'

His voice made her stand up, wide awake.

'Isaac. It's Sunday.' She sounded foggy, but her mind was already up and running, trying to second-guess why her editor-in-chief might be calling on a Sunday afternoon. Was he about to tell her that the bureau was closing down, effective immediately: don't bother to come in tomorrow because the doors will be bolted and your pink slips will be in the post?

'So what if it's Sunday?' snapped Isaac. 'I'm working seven days a week trying to keep this paper from sinking to the bottom of the goddamn Potomac, and I expect my employees to do the same.'

'I *am* working, Isaac,' said Ruth calmly. 'You know me, I never switch off. I'm famous for it.'

She went over to the kitchen sink and poured herself a big tumbler of cold water.

'I'm assuming you've seen the *Chronicle* this morning?'

'Sure, not read it yet,' she said. 'Been too busy, had an interview to transcribe. Saw the front page, though, obviously.'

She tiptoed to the front door and snatched up the bundle of papers which had been delivered many hours earlier.

'What I want to know,' Isaac was saying, 'is why we're not getting scoops like these guys are. Was I not clear last week when I said we needed grade A exclusives? The *Chronicle*'s lead is exactly the sort of item I'm talking about. You should congratulate your boyfriend; maybe we should think about getting him over to the *Trib*, whatdaya think?'

Boyfriend? She felt a cold, creeping sense of horror. Cradling the phone between her ear and her shoulder, she laid the newspaper flat on her dining table – and immediately felt sick.

Banker stung in honeytrap vice ring, screamed the headline. *US political hopeful and German minister also ensnared by escort girl conspiracy.*

She skim-read the text, hoping against hope that it was not her story, but it was. The story she had given David about the three escort girls who had brought down powerful men. He'd stolen it, taken it on and, from her quick scan of the feature, managed to find the link between the girls and a 'Mr Big' who was taking money from the men's rivals to set up the stings. Ruth's palms were damp as she grasped the newspaper, smearing the ink.

'If only you were bringing in things like this,' said Isaac, 'I could definitely justify keeping the London bureau.'

She dug her fingernails into her palm and tried to control her temper. There was no point explaining to Isaac what had happened, how the story had been her idea. How she had seen the link and come up with the theory that it turned out had been true. There was no point because it wasn't her story any more. It was David's.

'I agree,' she said, struggling to stay composed. 'It's exactly the sort of story we need to be generating. In fact, I've got something even better brewing for you, Isaac. It's a good one, a big one. It's going to make David's honeytrap story look like a local rag story about a park bench.'

'Now you're talking, kiddo,' said Isaac, a little of the warmth and humour returning to his voice. 'So when can I expect you to file it?'

'I'm still working on it,' she said. 'But soon, very soon.'

She hung up her phone, double-checked it wasn't still connected, then took a deep breath and screamed, crumpling up the paper and throwing it across the room.

'Bastard!' she yelled. 'I'll cut his balls off!'

In her fury, she swept the rest of the papers off the table, sending a coffee mug smashing to the ground. She couldn't remember when she had felt more angry. She was furious with David, furious with Isaac for being taken in by him, furious with that slut Susie for giving David the excuse to back-stab her. But most of all, she was furious with herself. It was her idea, *hers* – no one else had seen the link between those escort girls, no one else *could* have seen it – but instead of pursuing it and taking the glory for herself, she had got bogged down with this stupid Riverton murder story. And right now, that was looking like a bad decision. A very, *very* bad decision.

She stalked into the bathroom and turned the cold water tap on full, splashing it over her face.

'Think,' she said to herself. What was her next move? She couldn't let David win, not now, not when he'd already humiliated her with another woman – *a younger, prettier woman*, her mind mocked.

Consumed by rage, she went back into the living room and snatched up the phone, determined to ring David, confront him. She forced herself to calm down. What would it achieve? She'd been right first time: it was David's scoop now. No amount of yelling about feeding him his entrails would change that fact. In fact, Ruth was pretty sure hearing his voice would only make her feel lousier than she did already. And what if Susie answered? That would really cap her week. She was just about to chuck the phone down when she noticed there was a text message from Chuck. She clicked it open. 'Urgent,' it read. 'Call me.'

She dialled Chuck's home number.

'What's up?' she asked.

'I got hold of the CCTV footage.'

'Fantastic!' she said, her mood lifting, marginally.

'Not exactly high-definition, is it?'

'It's security film, Chuck, not a Spielberg movie.'

'Look, I know it's Sunday and everything, but do you want to come round? I've got something I think you should see . . .'

Ruth was dressed and out of the door in five minutes, munching a piece of toast as she ran to the tube station. Chuck lived in a shared house a few minutes' walk from Clapham Common. It should have been a short hop down the Northern Line, but engineering works and cancelled tubes meant a twenty-minute journey took over an hour. By the time she reached Chuck's place, Ruth's patience levels had sunk to zero.

'I'll get the coffee then,' said Chuck as he opened the door, catching Ruth's mood. 'I saw the paper. I'm sorry, must be galling.'

Ruth gave a wry smile.

'Just a little bit. All water under the bridge, hey?'

'Yeah, right,' laughed Chuck, leading her up the stairs. 'After you've slashed his tyres and sent his suits to Oxfam. Anyway, I've got something that might just cheer you up.'

He showed her into his room, a large sunny space, immaculately tidy – just like Chuck himself, in fact. A Yale pendant was tacked up on one wall, and photographs of Chuck's family were dotted around the room. There was a desk in one corner, set up with a computer. Chuck pulled up another chair for her and they both sat down.

'So what is it? What did you find?' asked Ruth.

'I've been through seventy-two hours of footage since eight o'clock this morning.'

He was angling for a pat on the back, but Ruth was going to save it until she'd seen what he'd found.

He clicked on a file and a window opened on the screen.

Ruth leant forward, fascinated: it was grainy and washed-out, but it was film of the hotel's lobby, shot from above the main door. And according to the time code in one corner, it was from the morning of the murder.

'How the hell did you get this?'

'Money,' said Chuck matter-of-factly.

'But isn't this in police evidence?'

Chuck shook his head.

'No, that's the beauty of modern technology – no tapes. The hotel just made a copy for the police.'

'This is brilliant,' said Ruth, feeling a rush of excitement as she watched the scene.

'Here,' said Chuck finally, touching the screen. 'This is Sophie Ellis leaving the hotel.'

They watched as the girl, evidently flustered, rushed through the lobby and out of sight. Chuck pointed to the time counter: 7:19. He let the film run on; there were a few people in hotel uniforms crossing back and forth and around a dozen people getting into and out of the elevators.

'So do we see anyone going up to Nick's room?'

Chuck pulled a face.

'Nope, only people getting into the lift, and there's no way to prove which floor they go to after that, let alone which room. Which is presumably why the police weren't that interested in this.' He froze the film at 7:32 and tapped the screen.

Ruth leant forward: it was too grainy to make much out, but it was a tall woman with long hair.

'That isn't . . . ?'

'Lana Goddard-Price?' said Chuck. 'It did cross my mind.'

He handed Ruth a folder. Inside were pictures cut from the party pages of glossy magazines: Lana Goddard-Price and her husband Simon at the David Cornish fund-raiser, Lana Goddard-Price attending the Cartier polo, Lana Goddard-Price laughs with designer Roman LeFey. It was impressive work considering she'd only given Chuck the brief twenty-four hours ago.

She held one of the pictures up to compare it with the image on the screen. It *could* be her. They both had dark wavy hair and a slim build, but she was facing the lift, away from the camera.

'Dammit,' said Ruth. 'I wish we had a better view of her.'

'Wait,' said Chuck, fast-forwarding the footage until the time code read 7:59. 'Watch the lifts.'

And there was the woman again, exiting the lift and hurrying through the lobby. She was wearing dark glasses and carrying a bag, but just as she was about to pass directly in front of the camera, a man in hotel uniform entered the building, blocking the shot. Ruth swore.

'There's no way Fox is going to arrest her on that evidence,' she sighed. 'We just can't see her face well enough.'

'Well don't look at her face then,' said Chuck.

'What do you mean?'

He pulled out another file and spread some printouts on the desk.

'These are stills from the footage you've just seen,' he said. 'I used some software to enlarge the images.'

Ruth looked: they were a little clearer, but they still had the same problem – the woman was facing away from the camera.

'All right, forget her face and look at her handbag.'

In the enlarged version, Ruth could see the bag was dark, textured, possibly woven.

'Sorry, I can't really enhance the image,' said Chuck. 'But it's obvious enough that it's a Nicholas Diaz bag, right?'

'How do you know that?' frowned Ruth, secretly impressed. Ruth knew nothing about designer labels and carried all her stuff around in a large Muji tote bag.

'My mum and my sister have them,' shrugged Chuck. 'They are colourful woven things, based on Peruvian peasant coats, I think – look, you can see it here.'

'Very interesting, but how does that help us?' asked Ruth.

'Well, I got in touch with a society photographer. We occasionally bump into each other when I have to cover gallery openings and things.' Chuck pulled a face. 'Anyway, he had loads more photographs of Lana. Look at this one,' he said, holding up a glossy print. 'It's Lana at some shop launch earlier this year. See her bag? It's definitely a Diaz, and it looks like the same colour and design as the one this woman's carrying at the hotel.'

'Trouble is, there's got to be thousands of women with the same bag.'

Chuck shook his head. 'Uh-uh. Not this one. Nicholas Diaz is a pretty big name now from dressing women on the red carpet, but his studio is still very small and exclusive. I'd bet there're only fifty of these bags in London right now.'

Ruth must have shown her scepticism, because Chuck turned back to the hotel lobby footage.

'Okay, now look at the woman's blouse. It's Gucci, last season. See the gold pattern around the neck?'

Ruth looked at him incredulously.

'Are you sure you haven't got anything to tell me, Chuck?' she laughed.

He held up his hands. 'My sister's an intern at *Vogue*. I emailed it over to her and she identified it immediately. And look . . .' He held up another society photograph. 'See? This is Lana at some charity garden party. The same pattern, the same Gucci blouse.'

Ruth looked from one picture to the other, narrowing her eyes.

'It is her,' she whispered. 'It bloody *is*!' She threw her arms around Chuck and kissed him on the cheek.

'Hey!' he laughed. 'I thought we weren't doing that any more?'

'Chuck, you're a genius,' she said, stuffing the pictures into her bag.

'Yeah, well just remember that when you're writing my references,' he smiled.

He turned his chair as Ruth grabbed her things and headed for the door.

'Hey, where are you rushing off to?'

'To see Inspector Fox,' she said, then pointed at him. 'Oh, and cancel all your plans for tonight – and tomorrow, too. We've got a story to write.'

43

It didn't look like home. Sophie peered out of the window as Lana's jet banked, dipping its wings towards the dark North Sea. There were droplets of rain on the glass and the clouds they had just descended through were grey-black. Beneath her the lights of Inverness airport glittered in the dusk, like stars reflected from the sky. To her right was the vast rippling plain of the sea, cut off by the lights of Inverness, and beyond, the brooding sketched outline of the Highlands.

She tensed as there was a thump underneath her feet and Josh squeezed her hand.

'Just the undercarriage going down,' said Lana in the seat opposite. 'Don't be so jumpy.'

That's the pot calling the kettle black, thought Sophie. Lana had been edgy and tense ever since they had met her at Miami airport, snapping at the slightest thing and chewing on her once immaculate nails. They had considered going to Scotland without her, but they had a deal with her to find the money together, and besides, she had the private jet to get them there.

Sophie had expected Lana to be excited and grateful when they had met at the Gulfstream and Josh had told her he had cracked the code, but she had been quite the opposite, making sniping remarks about 'Daddy's lucky girl' and her 'childish treasure map'. Sophie would have confronted her about it, but she was terrified that Lana might simply leave her and Josh on the tarmac. After all, she knew the map co-ordinates, all she had to do was go and pick up the loot, but Josh pre-empted any plan to maroon them by pointing out that as the clue had been given to Sophie, there was always a chance that the money – or whatever was waiting in Scotland – would have to be collected by her too.

So they had made the eight-hour journey from Miami to Inverness in near silence, each of them brooding on what they might find at the end of their long quest. Sophie guessed that Lana had probably been unsettled by the idea that the Russians were also on the trail: if Josh could work out that Ben Grear was a mountain, so potentially could Sergei. Perhaps she was picturing Asner's millions slipping from her grasp; that could make anyone snappy.

Sophie sat back in her seat as the jet bumped on to the runway, turning to watch the grey rain-lashed airport buildings as they taxied towards them.

'Not quite Florida, eh?' said Josh, looking past her out of the window. 'This is what we call summer in Scotland, I'm afraid.'

'Let's just find this damn mountain and get this over with,' said Lana, picking up her overnight bag. One of the many things they had neglected to discuss on the flight over was what happened if they did find the money at the foot of Ben Grear. Was Lana planning on just taking her investment and disappearing back to her house in London? Sophie doubted that very much; in fact she was sure that Josh's assessment of the situation was correct: Lana intended to take the lot. How she would do that, Sophie hadn't the foggiest, but as Josh had pointed out, they would have to deal with that when it happened. Right now, Sophie was only concerned with getting through customs.

Numbly, she followed Lana and Josh as they walked across the wet tarmac into the terminal building. Aside from being allowed to go down the mostly empty 'fast track' lane, this time they had to follow the same security procedures as everyone else. Sophie glanced at a clock on the wall as she handed her passport to the border guard: almost eight o'clock in the evening UK time. Would she be in a jail cell talking to Inspector Ian Fox by nine? she wondered, then realised she actually wouldn't mind. She was tired: tired of running, tired of lying, tired of trying to work out what everyone was thinking. All she wanted to do was curl up and sleep for a month, and at this moment, a hard bench and a thin blanket would be just fine.

'Miss?' said the guard. Sophie looked up, fully expecting someone to put their hand on her shoulder and lead her away. 'Your passport?' he said, holding it out for her.

'Sorry,' she stuttered. 'I was miles away.'

'Long journey, huh?'

Sophie gave a thin smile. 'You could say that.'

And then she was gliding through customs and out into the rain. She was back, she was home. It just didn't seem real, like she had been plucked from one place and dropped into another. The difference in temperature from Cap Ferrat, Miami – even the balmy London night – was shocking. Her thin T-shirt and jacket were no protection from the night breeze whipping down from the mountains.

'Josh, what happened?' she said, shivering. 'How come we got through?'

'Feels weird, doesn't it?' said Josh, taking off his jacket and draping it around her shoulders. 'I guess Hal Stanton thought our theory about finding the missing Asner millions via a name scrawled in a file was somewhat ridiculous.'

Sophie gave a grim smile.

'When you put it like that,' she nodded, 'I suppose it does sound like a wild goose chase.'

'Exactly. So why would he waste time trying to trace your mobile or talking to foreign policemen? He probably forgot all about us the moment they pulled out of the diner car park.'

Sophie shook her head and turned her face up to the now dark sky, feeling the misty rain on her face. It felt good, actually. It felt familiar – even the taxis queuing up outside the arrivals hall smelled different from the ones in France or America; they smelled *right*.

'Are you two going to stand out there in the rain all night?' They both looked up; Lana was climbing into the passenger seat of a black Range Rover. As Josh and Sophie ran over, the driver got out and handed Josh the keys.

'You'll be driving, sir?'

'I suppose so,' said Josh, looking at Lana.

'I have a migraine coming,' she huffed. 'And I can't be expected to drive in these conditions.'

'I wouldn't want to be out in this either,' said the driver, as he helped them load their bags into the back. 'You folks going far?'

'About forty miles north,' said Josh, his accent noticeably stronger, 'up towards Lairg.'

'Over the Bonar Bridge?' said the man. 'You'll be lucky if it's open in this weather.'

As he waved them off, Lana turned to Josh, her eyes flashing.

'Don't listen to him,' she ordered. 'We're going straight to the mountain.'

'Look, Lana, I grew up around here,' said Josh. 'When the storms come, it's like God has had a really rough night and is taking it out on us. We don't want to be on the roads in this if we can help it.'

'Do as I say,' she snapped.

'Okay,' sighed Josh. 'You're the boss.'

It was slow going. Even with the windscreen wipers on full, the rain reduced visibility to about twenty yards, and more than once Josh had to swerve to avoid some debris blown into the road. By the time they had left the coast and limped inland towards the bleak and scattered stone outbuildings of Lairg, the roads were awash and they could all feel the gusting wind from the north broadsiding the car when they topped a rise.

'Look, Lana,' said Josh, 'there's a sign for Ben Grear just up ahead. But even if we make it, we're not going to be able to see a bloody thing. I know you're worried about the Russians getting there first, but if they're here – and that's a big if – they're in the same boat.'

'Very well,' said Lana. 'There is somewhere we can stay just past Lairg. We'll start for the mountain at sunrise.'

They turned off the main road and on to a low single-track road, skirting the dark waters of Loch Shin, so wide it looked like an inland sea. Finally they pulled up at a grey stone building; from what Sophie could see, it looked like an old hunting lodge.

'This belongs to Edward, one of Simon's friends,' said Lana as they got out. 'I told him I might be stopping by. I think you'll find it comfortable enough.'

Sophie stepped out of the car. The rain had eased at least. Circling her shoulders to relieve knots of tension, she breathed in the cold Highland air. It was gone nine, although her body clock was telling her it was mid-afternoon. Still, she felt dog tired. Lana went round the side of the building and returned brandishing a large brass key. As she pushed it into the lock of the heavy oak door, they were met by a gush of warm air.

'Wow,' said Sophie. She had been expecting some spartan shack with musty carpets and no electricity. Instead it was like a ski chalet imagined by Ralph Lauren. There was a moose head over a huge fireplace, dark wooden floorboards and sumptuous leather furniture. It even smelt good – of heather and hollyhocks and cinnamon, like drawing up close to a rich man wearing really expensive cologne.

Lana went over to the wall, where there was a framed map of the area.

'We're here,' she said, pointing to the southern tip of the loch. 'Ben Grear is here, beyond the north-west side, but there's a direct road around the loch.'

'Yeah, it's maybe forty minutes away, weather permitting,' said Josh, looking over her shoulder.

'We leave as soon as it's light,' said Lana briskly. 'I'll take the master suite in the attic; you can have the double at the top of the stairs.'

Shrugging, Josh took their bags and went upstairs.

'Drink?' said Lana to Sophie, crossing to a well-stocked bar next to the fireplace. 'I'm sure Edward has some rather fine whiskies.'

'No thank you,' said Sophie, tight-lipped.

Lana shrugged, pouring herself a tumbler of the amber spirit.

'You hate me, don't you?' she said over the rim of the glass.

'Not really,' replied Sophie wearily. 'I blame you for turning my life upside down, for putting me through so much. But hate? No.'

She wanted to tell Lana the truth, of course: that she loathed her for everything she had done, for playing with her life in such a cavalier fashion, for making her fall in love with a man who wasn't even real, for putting her life in danger again and again. But what would that achieve? What was it Josh always said? Give them the story they want to hear. Until she could see how the game was going to play out, she needed to keep Lana on side.

'But then if it wasn't for you,' she added, 'maybe I'd be dead already. Sergei's men would have found me first and I might have ended up like Nick. And for that I'm grateful.'

Lana nodded. 'Nick did care for you, you know.'

Sophie flinched at that. Days earlier, they were words that she would have given anything to hear. She had felt so used and betrayed that even the glimmer of hope that Nick had really felt anything for her would have been a lifeline, something to grasp with both hands. But now she didn't want to hear it, because it made her feel cheap and guilty. Yes, her affair with Nick Beddingfield had been a fabrication, a lie he had created, just another job, but Sophie had really liked him – or so she had thought. And yet now, only days later, she had slipped into a relationship with someone else. Josh. *A relationship with Josh?* She almost laughed out loud. Tomorrow this would all be finished. Tomorrow they would find the money and this crazy roller-coaster ride would be over. Could she really expect Josh to be there for her? In that dark motel room in Miami as he had held her, their skin still slick from lovemaking, he had talked about them going to some exotic island together, of running away and leaving the world behind, just the two of them. But had that been the post-coital endorphins in his bloodstream, or maybe even just the romance of the situation? Had it just been the words of two people bound together in an extraordinary situation by excitement, danger and adrenalin? She just didn't know and it made her heart ache to think of it.

She looked at Lana for a long moment.

'What are you going to do with the money, Lana?'

She surprised herself by asking the question. The old Sophie Ellis of a month ago, maybe even a week ago, would never have dared be so direct. Nice girls didn't – it wasn't polite. But the past few days had hardened her. You couldn't do what she had done, see what she had seen, without coming out the other side a different person.

'That's for me to negotiate with the authorities,' said Lana briskly.

'For *us* to negotiate,' said Sophie firmly, meeting Lana's gaze. 'I have a stake in this too.'

'Oh yes?' said Lana. 'And what exactly will you be asking for?'

'I want all lines of investigation against me dropped and I

want my mother to receive a lump sum that will make sure she doesn't have to sell her house, plus a decent income for whatever time she has left.'

'My, my,' smiled Lana thinly. 'Aren't we the little Donald Trump?'

'I'm getting there.'

Lana folded her arms and stepped towards Sophie.

'So seeing as we're playing twenty questions: did you kill him?'

'Kill who? Nick?' said Sophie incredulously. 'No!'

'So what was it?' said Lana. 'An accident whilst you were making whoopee in the bathtub?'

Sophie shook her head. 'It was Sergei's men.'

Lana raised her eyebrows. 'Really? Did you ask him?'

Sophie frowned; she realised that they hadn't.

'No, but it's the only thing that makes sense,' she said. 'The Russians came looking for me and found Nick instead.'

Lana gave a cruel laugh. 'Do you really think Nick Beddingfield protected you? He would have told them everything he knew to save his skin.'

'And maybe he told them about you. Maybe they knew about you all along.'

She was pleased to see a momentary look of concern pass over the other woman's face.

'Why the surprise?' said Sophie. 'Nick would do anything for money, you knew that. Why wouldn't he have sold you out to another interested party if they paid slightly better?'

'So why kill him?' said Lana, recovering her composure.

'I don't know,' said Sophie, suddenly feeling very tired. 'Maybe he asked for too much money, maybe he screwed Sergei's wife, who knows? There're a lot of things I don't know, and I'll be honest with you, Lana, I'm sick of asking questions.'

She gave a weary shrug.

'I'm going to bed. I'll see you at sunrise.'

Stupid, thought Sophie as she climbed the stairs. So much for keeping Lana on side. But she'd been so smug, so condescending, Sophie hadn't been able to stop herself. *Standing up for yourself now? Another new side to mousy little Sophie Ellis*, she thought with a smile. She wanted to talk to Josh about it, but as soon as she entered their room, she could tell he was already asleep, his back turned towards her.

Suddenly Sophie was filled with sadness. Were the barriers already up? Would she ever share a room with him after tonight? They had barely known each other more than a handful of days, and yet already she felt this man was a part of her. She stood there for a minute watching his chest rise and fall, then slowly pulled off her jeans and slid in next to him. She leant forward to kiss the back of his neck. He twitched but he did not waken, and Sophie lay there listening to the rain on the glass.

44

'You're pretty determined not to let me have a day off, aren't you?' Fox stood at the door of his Albert Embankment flat wearing a navy polo shirt, jeans and a mischievous smile.

'Well, are you going to let me in or aren't you?' said Ruth, wedging her shoe in the door.

'Are you always this forward?' he said, standing back to let her pass.

'Only when I want something,' she replied. She was about to say something more, but her mouth fell open. 'I don't believe this place, you lucky sonofabitch.'

She walked through the flat's spotless open-plan living room, her eyes wide. Ahead of her were floor-to-ceiling windows giving an uninterrupted view of the Houses of Parliament silhouetted against the sunset.

'Fox! Why didn't you tell me you were loaded?' she said, looking back at him with amazement.

Fox smiled.

'Not loaded,' he said. 'No kids, no wife, not many vices and an interest-only mortgage. Plus I don't have any free time to spend my vast income.'

Ruth was too busy looking at the view to listen properly. She walked right up to the window, where dusk was falling over the city. It was magnificent.

'Do you need a lodger?' she asked, peeking into the other rooms, each equally neat.

'We'll work up to it,' said Fox. 'Could we start with a drink?'

'I think I need a big one after this shock,' she laughed.

'How about a glass of wine?'

Fox went over to his chrome fridge – of *course* he had a chrome fridge – and got out a bottle of white wine, quickly opening it and pouring Ruth a glass.

She leant against the breakfast bar and giggled.

'You are a dark horse, Fox.'

She couldn't help smiling. She was a journalist, so she was genetically predisposed to being nosy about the way people lived, but this had blown all her preconceptions about Fox out of the water. If she was honest, she had expected him to live in some scruffy apartment in Stockwell with a full sink and a clothes horse in the bath. But this, this had turned her image of the inspector completely on its head.

She walked over to examine a group of photographs tastefully framed on a nearby wall. Family photos, a couple of Fox in various energetic poses: skiing, sailing with a group of friends. In one he was running with a rugby ball, surrounded by the distinctive dark and light blue shirts of an Oxford–Cambridge Varsity match.

'Oxford?' she said, surprised.

'I was sporty,' he replied. 'Of course, I've let all that slide now.'

'But you were a rugby blue.'

'Very observant for a journalist.'

Ruth slapped her forehead.

'Fox – you're a trust-fund babe! Oxford, this apartment? How did I miss it?'

'My family aren't filthy rich, if that's what you mean,' he said, embarrassed now. 'The deposit for this place came from an inheritance, and yes, I went to Oxford. You think because I've got a northern accent I should be living in a bedsit? Looks can be deceiving.'

'So you're rich. You're clever. In fact I bet you're one of those fast-tracked inspectors. You know, I might have to start calling you Sherlock Holmes.' She smiled, giving him a long, lingering look.

Ruth had never been materialistic. She preferred the company of the newsagent to most newspaper editors. But Fox had more layers than she had at first thought and she wouldn't mind getting to unpeel them.

She lifted an apple from the fruit bowl and bit into it. Fox observed her and laughed.

'Well, I suppose I should be flattered that you feel so at home already.'

'Oh, sorry,' said Ruth. She realised she hadn't eaten anything all day.

He went back to the fridge and pulled out a bag of fresh pasta.

'Now this takes five minutes,' he said, reading the label. 'Do you think you can wait that long?'

'Yes, please,' she said, suddenly ravenous. She watched closely as Fox set to work, pulling out shiny pans and expensive-looking knives. He was ordered and meticulous, even when he was making pasta sauce: the onions were diced like a pro.

'So what's so urgent, Ruth?' he asked as he added them to the pan. 'You sounded pretty excited when you rang.'

Ruth hesitated, not sure how to play it. She didn't want to come on too strong, yelling about how she had cracked the case, but then she desperately needed his help and he wasn't going to do what she asked without proof.

She pushed her glass to one side and picked up her bag, pulling out a file.

'Look at this,' she said, taking out a print and putting it on the counter. 'This is a still from CCTV footage of the Riverton lobby,' she said, stabbing her finger against the photo. 'This woman with the bag is getting into the elevator at 7.32.

'Now look at these pictures of Lana Goddard-Price. Same bag, same blouse, same build, right?'

She slapped down another sheet.

'This is the same woman leaving the hotel twenty-five minutes later. And look at the shape of her bag. It's fatter. What's the betting it's got the other half of a smashed champagne bottle in it? Maybe even Nick Beddingfield's laptop.'

Fox was about to respond, but Ruth held up a hand.

'There's more,' she said, putting down another photograph. 'Here – a picture of Sophie's dad. Lana Goddard-Price's housekeeper identified Peter Ellis as Lana's lover.'

'What?' said Fox. 'How did you . . . ?'

But Ruth ploughed on, holding up a picture printed from the Red Heart gym website.

'This is Mike, he worked with Sophie. He told me he felt Lana was targeting Sophie, lavishing her with attention, asking her to house-sit; he thought she had deliberately sought Sophie out. Now doesn't that sound suspicious when you know her connection to Sophie's father?'

Fox was looking at the pictures, deep in thought. *At least he's considering it*, thought Ruth.

'But Lana was married to a hugely wealthy man,' he said. 'What did she need Peter for?'

Ruth shrugged. 'Maybe he was just a really good screw. Or maybe she wanted something from him. Apparently Lana and Simon's marriage is on the rocks; maybe it was her escape plan.'

'But then Peter had no money, remember?' said Fox. 'He lost it all in that American investment thingy.'

Ruth pulled a face, frustrated. She knew that, taken on their own, none of these points held much weight, but she was hoping that putting them all together would sway Fox enough to at least question Lana.

He picked up the still pictures of the CCTV footage.

'Have you got any more of these?' he asked.

'Loads,' said Ruth, opening the file and handing him the pile of printouts she'd picked up at Chuck's. He stood there examining them carefully, comparing them with the photographs of Lana.

'I don't know, Ruth. It could be her, but what do you expect me to do with this – get Interpol to put out a red notice and haul her in from her St Tropez sunlounger?'

She threw the file down in frustration.

'What do you mean, *I don't know, Ruth*? What sort of evidence are you after?'

'Something more tangible than a few fuzzy photos looking a bit like a few fizzy party pictures.'

'You mean like fingerprints?' she said slowly, a light bulb coming on in her head. 'Do you have a sandwich bag around the kitchen?'

'What?' asked Fox, looking utterly perplexed.

'A sandwich bag.'

Shaking his head, he retrieved a small plastic freezer bag from the cupboard.

'You found fingerprints on the fragments of champagne bottle in Nick Beddingfield's bathroom, didn't you?'

Fox nodded. 'They've already been sent to New Scotland Yard's Scenes of Crime branch. There was no match on the system.'

'But you search against your database, don't you? Fingerprints that are already in the system.'

Ruth already knew the answer; she'd spoken to enough SOC officers to know how it worked. Once prints had been retrieved, they were searched against the police national computer, which collated possible matches with the prints of known offenders.

'Yes,' said Fox. 'And against any local suspects. As we'd guessed, we found Sophie Ellis's fingerprints on the glass fragments, but then she told us she'd been drinking the champagne with Beddingfield the previous evening. It doesn't point to much.'

'But what if I asked you to run a match between the champagne bottle fingerprints and another sample?'

Ruth delved into her handbag and pulled out the biro she had taken from Lana's bedside cabinet. She'd only used it to write down her phone details for Cherry, but somehow she'd absently put it in her handbag with her notebook.

'Exhibit A. One biro belonging to Lana Goddard-Price,' she said, putting it in the freezer bag.

'What on earth are you doing?'

'There'll be prints on the pen's outer casing. Can you check them against the fingerprints you found at the crime scene?'

Fox looked at her aghast.

'You're unbelievable, you know that?'

'Look,' said Ruth defensively, 'I know you won't be able to use them in court, but just trust me. Lana Goddard-Price is the doer, Ian. I can feel it.'

'Where – in your waters?' he said sarcastically. 'I'm not sure that will stand up as evidence in front of the CPS.'

'So lift the prints off the biro and do a quick match, then you can go get official evidence.'

He barked out a laugh.

'Quick match? Ruth, these things can take weeks.'

Ruth felt her patience snap.

'For God's sake, Fox, pull your damn finger out. Get someone to run it against computer software to get a *probable* match – something! We haven't *got* weeks. Sophie Ellis's life could be in danger here; I'm not asking for fun, you know.'

Fox looked at her, startled.

'Bloody hell, Ruth. You can be fierce, you know that?'

He reluctantly picked up the biro with the plastic bag.

'Not exactly a professional evidence collection, was it?' he said doubtfully, then caught Ruth's frown. 'I have a friend at one of the borough fingerprint labs; I'll get her to take a look off the books, okay? But it's not going to be high priority.'

She wasn't sure which bit she felt more piqued about. Her low-priority evidence or the mention of a female friend in the lab. She could picture the scene now. Fox and his pretty forensics officer, sexy in her glasses and white lab coat, flirting over an exhibit. He'd invite her for a drink and they'd end up back at her cosy cottage for a glass of Chablis in front of a roaring fire.

Stop it, she told herself. *You're a journalist, not a Mills & Boon author*. But she could feel herself getting upset and she didn't know why.

'Look, Fox. I know you don't take me seriously,' she said. 'I know you think I'm one of Dan Davis's silly female hacks he keeps on a lead so he never has to buy a round. But I want this story. I need it. They're closing down the bureau and this is all I have. My boyfriend has left me – shafted me actually, stolen one of my stories and used it to get his own promotion whilst I'll probably be out of a job by Friday. So you might question my methods, but never question my commitment.'

Fox handed her a bowl of steaming pasta.

'Nice speech,' he smiled. 'Now eat up before it gets cold.'

It smelt delicious, but suddenly she wasn't hungry.

'You know, we've got dark hair samples taken from the hotel suite,' he said, as if he was thinking aloud. 'And we could do a cell-site analysis too . . .'

'What's a cell site?' said Ruth.

'The geographical area of a phone when calls or texts are made or received. In cities, you can pinpoint it to within a few hundred feet.'

'Can you do that retrospectively?'

He nodded. 'Or we could just get her mobile phone records.'

Ruth felt a sliver of hope.

'So you're going to question her?'

Fox turned to look out at the river, glinting like black ice from the lights on the bank.

'We've got to tread carefully,' he said. 'If she thinks she's under suspicion, she might never come back from the South of France.'

'And what if the prints match?' she pressed. 'Can't you get Interpol to bring her in?'

'Ruth, it's illegally obtained evidence. I couldn't think of getting an arrest warrant using it. You might have your standards, but I've got mine.'

Ruth jerked back as if she'd been slapped.

'What's that supposed to mean? That the police are all suddenly whiter than white? Bullshit!'

'It means I've got to toe the line,' said Fox, glaring at her. 'You know the Met are under the microscope for corruption and collusion with the press.'

'Well maybe if you paid a little more attention to—'

Brrring-riiing.

Fox's mobile was vibrating angrily on the breakfast bar.

'Are you going to answer that?' said Ruth. 'Or do you need me to show you how to do that too?'

'Ruth, I—'

'Oh, answer the damn phone!'

He snatched it up and walked away from her, over to the window.

'Fox,' he said, putting the phone to his ear. He listened for a long moment, then glanced back at Ruth. His whole demeanour had changed; Ruth was instantly on alert. *Who was he talking to*?

'Where are you?' said Fox, striding back over to the breakfast bar, urgently mouthing the word 'pen' to her. She pulled one out of her handbag and Fox began scribbling on the back of one of her printouts. 'What time?' he said; he paused, then, 'We'll be there.' Ruth could see him thinking, his face serious, as he put his phone down.

'Who was that?'

Fox looked at her.

'I'll tell you on the way,' he said, grabbing his jacket from the back of a chair. 'The pasta will have to wait.'

'On the way to where?' she said, quickly stuffing her papers into her bag.

'Scotland. We've got until sunrise to get there, and if you want your story, I suggest you come with me.'

45

Sophie woke with a start, her hands clutching at the covers. She looked around the room, disorientated and lost. *The hunting lodge, of course*, she thought, focusing in the grey light. *I'm in Scotland. I'm safe.*

She had been dreaming, a vivid, disturbing dream where she'd been back in Miami, at Sergei's house. But instead of watching Josh plunge into the pool, in her dream they had switched places and Sophie herself had been the victim, feeling the terror and impotence as her head was pushed into the frothing water again and again.

'Only a dream, Sophie,' she whispered to herself. 'Only a dream.'

It was then that she noticed she was alone. When she had slipped in beside him, Josh had been sleeping against the wall, but now he was gone. She looked at the armchair in the corner of the room; his clothes were gone too. Panicking, Sophie grabbed her watch: 4.55 a.m.

She got out of bed and, pulling on a towelling robe she found hanging behind the door, tiptoed to the landing. The house was in silence and the purple light of the fading night seeped in through the windows.

Where the hell was he? As quietly as she could, she padded up the stairs to Lana's room and peeped inside, where she could just make out the shape of Lana's slumbering body in the bed. That was something at least.

Sophie crept back down to the ground floor – as empty and still as the rest of the house – her mind searching for explanations of where Josh could be.

He had given a copy of *I Capture the Castle*, complete with its front-page annotations, to the Russians. She had no idea if Sergei would ever work out that the scribbled numbers were map coordinates, but perhaps Josh had been worried they might get there first. Sophie pushed a curtain back and peered outside. The rain had stopped and there was a vague glow around the surrounding mountains: dawn was almost upon them. Perhaps Josh had decided to get a head start; *or* – and she could barely bring herself to admit this notion to herself – or he had decided to get the money for himself. She shook her head, ashamed to even entertain the idea. *No*, she thought fiercely, *no, he wouldn't do that*. Not Josh.

Well, there was one way to find out. She moved towards the front door, her bare feet chilly against the stone floor. If he'd gone to find the loot, he'd have taken the car. The key was in the door and she turned it, stepping out into the cold.

And then she saw him. Sitting on the top of the porch steps, oblivious to the bitter wind blowing in from the mountains. Her shoulders sagged with relief.

'Here you are,' she hissed. 'You scared the hell out of me.'

'Did you think I'd gone to get the money?' he asked without bothering to turn round.

'No, of course not,' she said, sitting down next to him, wrapping the robe around her knees.

'You don't trust me, do you?' he said, glancing across at her. 'Not really.' He looked tired and disappointed.

'I was just panicking,' she said truthfully. 'I thought maybe you'd decided Sergei could have worked out the co-ordinates and wanted to get ahead of him.'

Josh didn't reply, just carried on staring out at the dark shapes of the mountains and the deep curve of the loch.

'I'm cold,' said Sophie, beginning to get up, but he put his hand on her knee.

'Stay with me and watch the gloaming.'

'What's the gloaming?' she said. It seemed like a suitable word for how she was feeling: uncertain and restless.

'It's an old Scottish word,' said Josh. 'It's that little window of time before sunrise or after dusk when everything's still. There's no place more beautiful than the Highlands in the gloaming.'

She shuffled closer, pressed up against him, and watched as ribbons of silver light twisted up from the horizon. It was eerie and yet quite magical, like viewing the landscape through a dark blue filter, when everything felt suspended and full of possibility. And then the sky lightened just a touch and the moment was gone.

Sophie squeezed Josh's hand, about to speak, when she heard a creak behind them.

'Go and get ready,' said Lana, standing in the doorway, fully dressed. 'I want to leave in ten minutes.'

By the time Josh and Sophie came back downstairs, Lana was standing on the driveway, the Range Rover's engine idling, the heaters on full blast.

'You drive,' she said to Josh, and handed the map to Sophie. 'You can navigate.'

'Yes, ma'am,' said Josh, tugging at an imaginary cap and rolling his eyes at Sophie. They may have been hundreds of miles north of Knightsbridge, but Lana still clearly believed she was entitled to the luxury of staff.

They drove towards Ben Grear in silence. Perhaps the others were thinking of what they might expect at the other end of the single-track tarmac road, but Sophie was entranced by the landscape around them. She had never been to the Highlands before, and the storm had obscured everything the previous night, save for what was in their headlight beams. But the clouds had lifted this morning and the colours cast by the rising sun were quite astonishing: the mauve, deep orange and emerald of the heathered moorlands swept up to the distant crags, which seemed to tower over them, their naked rock slopes a hundred shades of purple.

'Are you following the map, or are you looking at the flowers?' said Lana irritably from the back seat.

'It's all under control,' said Sophie, praying she was reading it correctly. 'Around this next bend, then two or three miles and we should see Ben Grear.'

'We don't want to see the mountain,' said Lana. 'We want the building. We don't even know what it is.'

'It's a castle,' said Sophie.

'How can you possibly say that?' scoffed Lana. 'I've studied the map, it isn't even marked.'

'No, it's a castle,' said Sophie, pointing straight ahead. Even from this distance, she could see it: a tiny castle built on an outcrop of land that jutted into a small loch, the glassy surface of the water reflecting it back like a mirror, the dawn sky casting a pink glow over it.

Josh tapped the GPS on the dashboard. 'Yep, that's it,' he said. 'Matches the co-ordinates exactly.'

He glanced over at Sophie, then pressed down on the accelerator.

'It's beautiful,' said Sophie as they wound up the little access road cut into the side of the mountain. It wasn't a *castle*, the kind you would visit on a school trip, with a moat and arrow slits and a drawbridge; it was more like someone's idea of what a fairy-tale castle should look like. It was made out of pale weathered stone, with a darker slate roof, tiny windows and two Rapunzel turrets bookending the building. A folly, perhaps, or some long-dead landowner's Highland fantasy; it didn't matter: to Sophie it had all the romance and magic she had dared to hope for. She had known instantly that this was her castle, the 'X' on the pirate map, the place her father had so carefully led her to, because it was exactly as they had talked about. Even now, she could hear her father's voice, day-dreaming with his daughter about where they would one day live.

Our own little magical castle, he had promised. And he had kept his word. But at what cost? She closed her eyes and thought of her father: the kind, generous man who had been her hero and protector, the clever, smiling youth so full of promise that she had seen on Miriam Asner's Super 8 footage. How could such a decent man, with so many wonderful qualities, have got mixed up in Asner's plan? How could he have been involved in a theft of that magnitude? A theft that had stripped so many innocent people of their money. Was money such a destructive, corrupting force? Of course, she knew that it was. What she would never know were her father's reasons, his justifications for getting involved.

'Look for a key,' said Lana, getting out and slamming the Range Rover's door. 'Whatever's here, it's going to be inside.'

Sophie tried the obvious first: she looked under the mat in front of the wide oak door, then along the top of the door frame and under flowerpots. Nothing.

Lana emerged from the back of the property, her hands empty.

'Do *you* have the key?' she said.

'Of course I don't have the bloody key,' snapped Sophie. 'Do you think I'd come all this way, then somehow forget—'

She stopped as they heard a grunt, then a crash. Running to the side of the house, they saw Josh's legs disappearing through a window. Sophie swore under her breath. What if he was about to wake up a couple of honeymooners, or worse – an angry Scottish laird with a shotgun? It would be just typical to chase thousands of miles only to be arrested at the last moment for breaking a window.

'No one's home,' said Josh two minutes later as he opened the creaky door from inside.

Sophie pursed her lips, but thought better of telling him off; things were tense enough without adding petty squabbles to their problems. She followed Lana inside. It was basic, almost spartan, with a thin layer of dust on most surfaces and a cold, damp smell coming from the bones of the house. There were a few personal effects – books, old maps and dark oil paintings on the walls – but it didn't look as if anyone had been there for a while.

'Now where?' said Lana. She looked wound up, on edge. Had her jibe about Nick betraying Lana to the Russians got to the woman? wondered Sophie.

'There's not much here, so check everything,' said Josh, coming back from a quick look around. 'Lana, you take the kitchen and living room. Sophie, you take the bedrooms upstairs. I'll do everywhere else.'

There were three bedrooms on the first floor. Sophie took the largest one first, which at least looked as if someone had been in it within the last thirty years. There was a fishing rod in one corner, some leather-bound Dickens novels on the shelves, but not much else. *So what exactly am I looking for?* she wondered. If there was money hidden here, it would take up a lot of room, and even if Asner's loot had been converted into diamonds or something else valuable, she was pretty certain it would be something of size. *A suitcase, perhaps?* she thought, looking under the bed. No. Not even a shoebox. In the corner of the room was a small built-in wardrobe, but there was nothing inside apart from a rather mildewed overcoat and a pile of equally mouldy linen. *In the movies, the safe is always hidden behind a painting*, she thought to herself, walking over to a picture above the washstand – and found herself looking at a photograph of a boat.

'*Iona*,' she gasped, recognising her father's beloved boat. 'So you *were* here.'

She stood there in shock for a moment. She had guessed that this had been her father's place, had *expected* to find something of his here, in fact. But even so, she found her heart beating hard in her chest, knowing he had stood where she was, that he had slept in this bed and, after all the running and dead ends, that this was exactly where he had wanted her to come.

'Where would you hide something, Daddy?' she asked.

And then it came to her. At Wade House, her father had installed a wall safe in the back of a wardrobe; she could remember him on his knees with the drill. She stepped back over to the wardrobe and pushed the overcoat and the mottled sheets out of the way. There it was, the same colour and shape as the safe they had at home, with a four-digit electronic PIN lock.

'Josh! Lana!' she shouted.

She heard Josh's heavy footsteps coming up the stairs two at a time.

'Good girl,' he said when he saw the safe. 'Have you tried to open it?'

'Not yet,' she said. She bent to tap in the combination of the safe they had at home. It beeped twice: wrong number.

Lana burst through the door.

'Have you found it?' she gasped.

Josh nodded to the safe. 'Yes and no. We don't have the code.'

'Try the number from the book,' said Lana.

Warily, Sophie pulled the paperback from the pocket of the waxed hunting jacket she had borrowed from the lodge that morning. She wanted to get inside, of course, but she didn't like the feeling of having Lana hovering behind her.

She tried various combinations of the map co-ordinates, but still the safe door refused to budge.

'This is ridiculous!' said Lana. 'Josh, do something.'

'What do you expect me to do?' he said. 'Blow a hole in

it? All I know about safe-cracking I got from *The Italian Job*.'

Tuning out their bickering, Sophie turned back to the first page of *I Capture the Castle*. Was there anything else on it except the name and coordinates?

Of *course* there was.

To my dearest S, read this and think of our castle. Happy birthday. All my love always, Daddy.

Her birthday. The fourth of September – it had to be. She bent over the panel and tapped in '0409'. There was a second's pause, then the safe whined open. She could hear Lana gasp behind her. Sophie looked inside: it was empty. No, not quite: there was a plain Manila envelope sitting on the bottom. She opened it and pulled out a sheet of paper.

'A certificate?' she said, looking up at Josh.

She had been expecting bricks of bank notes or gold bars; at the very least a black velvet bag full of diamonds. This looked like a fancy version of the guarantee which came with a washing machine.

'It's a bearer share certificate,' said Josh, taking it from her.

'What's that in English?' said Sophie, standing up to get a better look.

'Have you ever heard of bearer bonds?'

She nodded. 'They're what Hans Gruber was after in *Die Hard*, right?'

Josh didn't smile. 'Exactly, but you don't just get them in Hollywood. They used to be used by banks to transport large amounts of money, but they became popular with criminals as a way of concealing funds. If you have a bearer bond, it's like owning cash, except it's pretty much untraceable. Whoever physically holds the bond can redeem it for cash.'

'So what's this?' asked Sophie.

'This,' said Josh, waving the paper, 'means you own a whole company, rather than just cash. You turn up at the issuer's bank holding this, it means you – and you alone – have full access to the company's accounts. Your dad was clever, Soph. Putting Asner's money into this offshore company meant it was almost impossible to track down because it leaves so little paper trail.'

'So where is the bank account?'

Josh examined the certificate.

'Vanuatu, by the looks of it. It's an offshore banking centre in the South Pacific.'

Lana stepped forward.

'Very good, Josh,' she said coolly. 'You're smarter than I thought. Now how about you give it to me and then I suggest we hurry along.'

Josh handed Lana the certificate.

'I'm sorry, Sophie. I think it's better if you stay here,' said Lana slowly. 'And if you think of squealing to the SEC about where Mr Asner's hidden money has gone, you'll have more than some angry Russians on your tail.'

Sophie looked at Lana and then at Josh. She felt time slow down as she realised what was going on.

'Josh, what's happening?' she croaked, a sense of dread filling her chest.

Lana gave a gentle little snort.

'He's doing his job, aren't you, Josh? Now are you coming or do you want to stand around admiring the view?'

'W-where are you going?' said Sophie, still looking at Josh.

Lana shrugged, putting the certificate back into its envelope.

'Oh, I believe the first stop will be Vanuatu. It's an island in the South Pacific, one of the most privacy-conscious offshore banking centres in the world. That's where Peter told me he'd hidden the money. All I have been trying to do is work out where the bearer share certificate was. It's useless trying to claim the money without it.'

Sophie felt the floorboards beneath her feet shift. Her brain couldn't take it all in.

'You spoke to my father?'

'Frequently,' said Lana with a spiteful smile. 'Usually in bed, actually.'

'You liar!' screamed Sophie, lunging at her. Josh stepped forward and grabbed her, pinning her clawing arms to her sides. 'My father wouldn't go near someone like you!' she spat.

Lana pouted.

'I was your father's mistress for almost two years,' she said mildly. 'Before my husband, of course – well, mostly before.'

Sophie struggled against Josh again, but he held her tight. 'You bitch!'

'Funny, that's what your father said when I told him I was marrying Simon. He said it was only because Simon was richer than he was, which was probably true, actually.'

She gave a small laugh.

'But then poor Peter began to beg; he told me he was going to come into a lot of money too, but I didn't believe him. Why would I? He was just some accountant from nowhere.'

'Screw you, Lana,' said Sophie. 'You never knew him.'

'Actually, you do have a point,' said Lana. 'It turned out that Peter had hidden depths after all. When Simon found out I couldn't give him children, he told me he wanted a divorce. So I went back to Peter and asked him straight – "What money?"'

She laughed, shaking her head.

'He was only too happy to tell me about Asner's fraud. According to Peter, we just had to sit tight for a couple of years until the scandal blew over, and we could go to Vanuatu and retrieve the money.'

'So your family never lost money in the Ponzi scheme?'

'Don't be silly,' she laughed. Then her face clouded over. 'But then that idiot Asner got himself killed and Peter fell apart. He couldn't handle the stress. I visited him in hospital, gave him a little incentive to tell me how to get to the money, but the bloody-minded fool wouldn't tell me.'

'You killed him!' roared Sophie, jerking towards Lana, almost slipping from Josh's grasp. He pulled her back and pushed her on to the bed, standing between the two women.

'Don't, Sophie,' he said. 'You'll only make it worse.'

'Worse?' she spat, her voice cracking. 'How could it possibly be worse?'

Lana looked at her watch and put the envelope into her bag.

'Come on, Josh, we can't stand here all day.'

Together they turned towards the door, leaving Sophie crumpled on the bed in misery.

'And you're working for her, I suppose,' she hissed at Josh.

Lana spoke for him. 'Nick did such a shabby job of getting information from you; he always was too easily impressed by pretty things. But then I met Josh in Cap Ferrat and I knew that he could be more helpful than Nick had ever been. So I persuaded him to work for me.'

Hot tears were running down Sophie's cheeks.

'Sophie,' said Josh, his eyes pleading. 'If you'll just let me explain . . .'

'Get the hell out of here!' screamed Sophie. 'I don't want to even look at you, let alone listen to any more of your lies.'

'Sophie, I'm sorry.'

'Get out!' she sobbed. 'Get *out*!'

Josh bowed his head, then turned and walked out of her life.

46

Ruth felt like she was in the Cannonball Run. She'd been up all night, tearing along motorways, A roads and now narrow, winding country lanes, the endless white lines in the cone of the squad car headlights blurring into one. At first it had been exciting to put on the spinning blue lights and the 'nee-naw' siren and watch the traffic ahead part like the Red Sea, but they had now been on the road for five hours and the novelty of the high-speed pursuit had long since worn off. Ruth had always considered Great Britain to be a small country; after all, her home state of North Carolina was bigger than the whole of England alone. But as the past few hours had shown her, the road from London to the Scottish Highlands was a very long one indeed, even when you were exempt from the speed limit. It hadn't helped that by the time Josh McCormack had called Fox at his flat, it had already been too late to fly north, and trains from London to Scotland reverted to the slower overnight sleeper variety after ten o'clock. Short of requisitioning a police helicopter – 'You would not believe the paperwork involved,' said Fox – the only solution had been to get a fast train to Manchester, then continue the rest of the way in a squad car, speeding up the motorway as far as Glasgow, then picking their way cross-country.

Ruth popped another can of Coke and leant against the car, staring across at a distant farmhouse, the only feature in an endless expanse of gorse and heather. They'd taken a pit stop in a lay-by so Fox could make some calls. He was tense, jittery; she could tell he knew his career was on the line if he got this wrong. She turned as he tapped on the windscreen, and slid gratefully back inside the warmth of the car.

'Everyone's in position,' said Fox as he gunned the engine back to life. 'Let's hope it's all worth it. I'm going to look such a bloody banana if this was a crank call.'

'This Josh McCormack's got no reason to lie,' said Ruth, inspecting the road map one last time. She had been staring at it for so long, she felt she could ace a quiz on any of the towns and villages they had passed through that night.

'Okay, take the next right,' she instructed. 'We should be coming to the head of a loch. My guess is that we'll see it pretty soon.'

Fox slowed down as they reached a sharp turn at the bottom of the road and Ruth smiled to herself: he was still signalling, despite the fact that they hadn't seen another vehicle in about an hour. Almost immediately the steep pass opened out in front of them and they could see the small castle high on their right, hanging over the loch beneath the glowering crag of Ben Grear.

'Look, tyre tracks,' said Fox, nodding towards a muddy strip where the loch road and the drive up to the castle met. 'Looks like someone has been and gone.'

Ruth swore under her breath. 'Don't say we've come all this way and missed them.'

Fox gunned the engine all the way up the narrow roadway, skidding to a halt in front of the castle's wide porch and running for the door.

It creaked open and he immediately raised a hand to stop Ruth. He put a finger to his lips. 'Shh . . .' he whispered as they went inside. 'Did you hear that?'

Ruth shook her head, listening. It was quiet and still, except for the distant call of a bird, out through the open door.

'Is anyone here?' shouted Fox. 'The sound came from up

there,' he hissed, motioning towards the stairs. 'Maybe you'd better wait here.'

'Screw that,' whispered Ruth. 'I'm sticking with you.'

They walked up the stairs, wincing at each creaking step.

'Police!' called Fox. 'Inspector Ian Fox from the Met.'

Ruth followed him through a door and found herself in a bedroom. She stared in amazement as a door in the corner creaked open and Sophie Ellis stepped out of the closet.

'Sophie,' Ruth gasped. 'What the hell are you doing in there?'

'I thought you were the Russians,' she said, her voice shaking. Ruth immediately saw that the girl's eyes were red from crying, and she stepped over and pulled her into a hug.

'Everything's okay now,' she said, guiding her over to the bed to sit down.

'But it's not,' said Sophie, dissolving into tears. 'Josh was working with Lana.'

Ruth looked up at Fox.

'Sophie, we . . .' she began, but Sophie wasn't listening.

'They set the whole thing up to get Michael Asner's money. You've heard of Asner, right?'

Fox nodded.

'It was hidden here,' said Sophie.

'You found it?' asked Ruth, her pulse racing. 'You found the money here?'

'Not the actual money, something called a bearer share?' said Sophie shaking her head. 'Apparently it's like a passport to get the cash. The money is banked in some South Pacific island. Vanuatu? Something like that.'

'Vanuatu,' said Ruth excitedly. She'd read about the offshore tax haven in some *Vanity Fair* article.

'So where is it now, Sophie?' said Fox.

'Josh gave the certificate to Lana and they've gone.' Her shoulders slumped. 'It doesn't matter any more. Nothing matters.'

Fox knelt down in front of her.

'No, Sophie, this could be very important,' he said urgently. 'Where did Josh and Lana go? Back to the hunting lodge?'

'Yes. How do you know?' said Sophie, frowning at him. 'How did you know I was here?'

'Because of Josh,' said Fox gently. 'You think he double-crossed you, but actually he was setting up Lana. He called me last night and explained the whole thing. He was the one who gave us the map coordinates for this castle.'

Sophie stared at him, her mouth opening and closing. She turned to look at Ruth, her face a mixture of hope and disbelief.

'It's true, Sophie,' said Ruth. 'Josh is the one who sent us.'

'So you know what happened?' said Sophie, her eyes wide. 'You believe me?'

Fox nodded.

'Josh told me everything. About Sergei Kaskov and Lana's search for Michael Asner's money. He begged me to get an Armed Response Unit to the shooting lodge in case the Russians appeared.'

'An Armed Response Unit? You mean, like a SWAT team?'

'Exactly,' said Fox, straightening up and holding out his hand to Sophie. 'Which is why we need to get moving. If Josh went back there, then he's in danger.'

Ruth noticed the distraught look on the younger woman's face. Whoever this Josh was, Sophie was in love with him, she could tell that immediately. 'Come on,' she said. 'Let's go and get him.'

Fox drove as fast as the twisting road along the loch would allow; mercifully it was free of traffic, with only one heart-stopping moment when they topped a rise to find a stag blocking their way. Luckily for both parties, Fox went left and the stag went right, disappearing into the bracken.

As they drove, Sophie told them the whole story: her escape from the Russians by the Thames, their journey to Paris and Cannes to track down Nick's secret business colleague, and her shock when she discovered it was Lana Goddard-Price. And her discovery that her father had been involved in Asner's fraudulent scheme. Ruth cursed herself for not putting that final piece in the jigsaw. She thought of the whiteboard in her living room and the spidery web of connections. She knew Nick and Lana had both been after something from Sophie: money, most likely. She knew of Peter Ellis's connection to Lana and Lana's to Nick – she had even been able to prove that particular one with the CCTV footage. She had even known about Peter's connection to Michael Asner and their friendship at college. And yet who would make the leap between that seemingly casual association decades ago and being intimately involved in a huge financial fraud? Ruth supposed that was why Asner had asked Peter in the first place. Who would suspect someone as ordinary as Peter Ellis?

As they closed in on the hunting lodge, Fox's phone rang. Thinking it could be the Armed Response Unit, he switched it to loudspeaker.

'Ian, it's Gilly, how are you?' said a female voice. Flirty, smiling. Ruth was immediately on edge.

'Hi, Gill. Listen, I'm a bit busy at the mo, can I—'

'Won't be a tick,' said the woman. 'Just wanted to let you know we ran those prints from the biro.'

'Wow, Gilly, that was quick,' said Fox.

'I was on the night shift. Besides, anything for a friend,' said Gilly warmly.

Anything for a friend, thought Ruth, wanting to strangle the woman.

'Anyway, I ran it through the biometric software analysis. The sample was very poor, and completely inappropriate for court use, but from the shapes of the ridges and grooves of the print, I'd say it was a match with the print on the champagne bottle from the Riverton.'

Ruth felt triumphant. Lana Goddard-Price had killed Nick. It wasn't exactly a smoking gun, but it proved she had picked up the bottle – an empty bottle, Sophie had testified to that. Even a mediocre barrister could make a jury see that there really was no reason to pick up the bottle other than to use it as a weapon.

Fox cut the forensics woman off abruptly for another call coming through. It was the team leader from the Armed Response Unit saying that three men had arrived at the lodge.

'Is Lana Goddard-Price there?' asked Fox urgently.

'Affirmative. White male, thirties, with her.'

'Can you identify the three men?' said Fox.

'Sorry, sir,' said the voice. 'They're on the move. Spotter's seen a gun, we're going in.'

'They must be Sergei's men,' said Sophie.

'Shit,' cried Fox, banging his hand on the steering wheel. 'How far do you think we are, Sophie?'

'Not far,' she replied. 'I recognise the farm over there; we can only be a mile away at most.'

'Let's see how fast this thing can go,' he mumbled, adding a burst of speed that jerked them all back in their seats.

They reached the lodge within a minute. It was surrounded by Armed Response Unit vehicles, and at least ten officers in bulletproof jackets and helmets. As the car screeched to a halt, Ruth's eyes widened as she saw Lana Goddard-Price on the porch steps, being held in a stranglehold by a shaven-headed man.

Fox jumped out of the car and ran to an officer holding a walkie-talkie. Welded to their car seats, neither Ruth nor Sophie dared move. The air was so quiet, Ruth could hear the rustle of wind in the trees.

'Has he got a weapon?' hissed Sophie.

'They suspect so,' said Ruth, seeing the gentle arch of Lana's back, as if she had the barrel of a gun pushed into it.

A crackly voice through a loudspeaker pierced the silence.

'Drop your weapon,' it ordered through the static.

'He's going to kill her,' gasped Sophie, hearing the loud coordinated click of the armed officers cocking their weapons.

The facial expression of the shaven-headed man soured.

'No he's not,' said Ruth, watching him drop his gun on to the stone steps with a clatter.

Lana collapsed on to the ground as the police moved in. Two more of Sergei's men ran out of the house and put their hands behind their heads. Ruth and Sophie got out of the car and ran towards Fox as another officer and a WPC helped Lana off the floor. She had her hands cuffed behind her and she was weeping, her make-up smeared, any hint of the aloof socialite gone.

'Sophie!' she cried desperately when she saw the girl. 'Tell them this is all a misunderstanding; tell them I was only trying to recover my money.'

'We know everything, Mrs Goddard-Price,' said Fox bluntly. 'And I know you killed Nick Beddingfield.'

Ruth expected the woman to deny it, but her face seemed to crumple and her shoulders sagged.

'It was an accident,' she sobbed. 'You have to believe me. Nick was . . . well, we had a few difficult phone conversations, so I flew back from France and checked into the hotel next to the Riverton. When Sophie left him on Monday morning, he called me to arrange a meeting. I went round, we argued . . .' Her voice trailed off at the memory.

'You killed him?' screamed Sophie.

'He wanted to pull out of our arrangement. I lashed out, grabbed the bottle on the bath. I didn't mean to hurt him . . .' She looked over at her house-sitter. 'You believe that, don't you?'

Sophie didn't say anything; she just stepped forward and slapped Lana across the face.

'Put Mrs Goddard-Price in the squad car,' said Fox to the detective.

Ruth could still hear Lana shouting as she and Fox walked into the lodge, leaving Sophie with a WPC.

'Hey, nice place,' she said. 'Almost as nice as your flat.'

'Don't start,' smiled Fox.

'So who are the goons that had got Lana?'

'Mercenaries for hire, I suspect,' said Fox. 'Sergei Kaskov wouldn't have had time to dispatch his own men to somewhere so remote. And anyway, he's too clever, wouldn't want to take the risk when he will have been aware Lana and Sophie were being watched by the Met and the SEC at the very least.'

Ruth nodded; she had heard Fox talking to Hal Stanton on the way up to Manchester, getting briefed about the Russian crime lord and the US authorities' suspicions about his link to the Asner money.

Through in the kitchen, they could see Josh sitting talking to a detective, giving a statement.

'What are you going to do with him? He hasn't broken any laws, has he?'

'Leave the police work to me,' smiled Fox.

'Yeah, *right*, Sherlock,' she teased. 'We'd have wrapped this case up days ago if you'd just shared a bit more information, like I suggested.'

'At least you got your story,' he said.

'Actually, I didn't just get one story, I got two,' said Ruth, the truth of the statement only just sinking in. For what seemed like forever, she had been trying to find out who killed Nick Beddingfield. It had consumed her every waking hour, because the future of the bureau, and by extension her career, depended on it. And in pursuing it so doggedly, she had uncovered something else, something even more amazing: Michael Asner's missing millions. She had solved a high-profile murder and one of America's biggest financial riddles in one go. *Screw you, David*, she smiled. *See if you can beat that*, she thought, knowing, with satisfaction, that she had saved the London bureau.

'Listen,' she said, feeling bold. 'When I've filed the story and you've made your arrests, how about you take me for dinner to say thank you for all my help? And somewhere nice, seeing as you're loaded.'

'*I'm* the loaded one?' laughed Fox. 'You're going to be so hot after this story, CBS are going to be poaching you for some highly paid Diane Sawyer role.'

Ruth shook her head.

'Nah, I'm a newspaper girl, not a television journalist. Besides, I like London and I like the bureau too. I think I'm going to be sticking around.'

'I'm glad about that,' said Fox, his blue eyes meeting hers. Ruth felt her pulse quicken, surprised by how much she liked this man.

'Next Tuesday,' he said suddenly.

'Next Tuesday what?'

'That's when we're both going to take the day off. I reckon we deserve it after all this overtime.'

Ruth raised one eyebrow.

'We're going to take the day off?'

'Yes, us, together,' he said. 'Unless you don't want to, of course.'

His phone began to ring. Fox didn't move, his intense gaze focused on Ruth.

'Shouldn't you answer that?' she said, the ghost of a smile on her lips.

'It'll wait. So are we on for Tuesday?'

Ruth laughed.

'I'd like that,' she said, adding to herself, *I'd like that very much indeed.*

47

Sophie was standing on a slope to the side of the lodge, looking out towards the loch, when she saw Ruth Boden approach.

'How are you doing?' asked Ruth, putting an affectionate hand on her shoulder.

'I'm okay, thanks.' Sophie smiled. 'It feels weird seeing you again. All this time I thought I was out there on my own, and all the time you were thinking about me, trying to find me.'

'I always knew you were innocent,' said Ruth. 'Although I have to admit, I didn't guess that Lana killed Nick until right at the end.'

Sophie looked away. She didn't want to think about it, not right now, not yet. She had held Nick's body as the life ran out of him, and whatever he had done, no one deserved to die like that. And all for what? Money? Sophie felt sick to think that she had once seen money as the answer to all her problems too. Was that how her father had thought? Was it ultimately his undoing? Sophie supposed she would never know if Lana had been directly responsible for her father's death – and part of her didn't really want to know. Lana Goddard-Price had already caused so much destruction and pain, she wasn't sure if she wanted to unearth anything else.

'Listen, Sophie, I have a story to write,' said Ruth awkwardly. 'I don't suppose you'd grant me an interview . . . ?'

'I guess I owe you something.' Sophie smiled, then hesitated.

'I feel there's a "but"?' said Ruth.

Sophie nodded, meeting the journalist's gaze.

'Ruth, I know what my father did was wrong. Very, very wrong. But he's dead, he's had his punishment. Please, don't make this any worse for our family than it has to be.'

'I'll be sensitive,' said Ruth, holding up three fingers. 'Scout's honour.'

'Good,' said Sophie. 'Then you won't mind me saying this: no interview unless I have final copy approval.'

She saw Ruth's surprised reaction. Clearly she hadn't expected little Sophie Ellis, the flighty Chelsea girl, to drive such a hard bargain. But she wasn't mousy Sophie any more; she had changed. For better or worse, she was a different woman from the one who had run for the taxi outside the Riverton that morning. She knew Ruth would agree to her terms; what choice did she have? Sophie was in control now – that was the difference. She was in control.

'Let's talk later, okay?' she said. Across the field, she had spotted Josh sitting on a dry-stone wall. When Ruth had gone, he came over.

'Can we talk?' he asked.

'Let's walk down to the water,' said Sophie.

They took a path that ran down to the edge of the loch and walked out on to a small wooden jetty. Josh sat down next to her, their legs dangling over the water.

'Why didn't you tell me what was going on?' she said finally.

'I wanted to protect you, Sophie. From the minute you left my houseboat and saw those Russians, that's all I wanted to do. I figured the less you knew, the better, at least until I had worked out what to do.'

'Protect me?' she said bitterly. 'You agreed to work for Lana.'

'I only *told* her I was going to work for her. She asked me on the plane over to New York when you were asleep. I mean, there was the slight suspicion that she might kick me off the Gulfstream mid-air if I didn't agree, but mainly I figured I would find out more from the inside.'

'You could have been killed, Josh. *We* could have been killed. And I assume it was you who told the Russians to go to the shooting lodge? Why the hell did you do that?'

'The same reason I gave them a copy of *I Capture the Castle*,' he said. 'I had to. If they thought we'd stiffed them, they'd have come and killed us.'

'But you *did* stiff them.'

'Not really. I gave them everything we had: first the clues in the book, then when we got to the lodge, I called Sergei and told him that Lana had worked out where the money was, but that he needed to be careful as the SEC, the FBI and the Met were on her tail. His men would have to be clever if they were to get to Lana first.'

'And you think that's going to get us off the hook with Sergei Kaskov? You stitched him up.'

Josh shrugged. 'My guess is that he's going to stiff *me*. I asked him for a finder's fee for telling him all about Lana, because I knew that's the kind of back-stabbing double-dealing he'd respect. But now the money's gone up in smoke, I suspect he'll stop taking my calls.'

Deep down, Sophie knew she believed him. She had spent plenty of time questioning his motives and his morals, but all along, the truth was that Josh McCormack had been constant: he had defended her, supported her, even put his life on the line for her. Even so, she couldn't get that image out of her mind of him following Lana out of the bedroom in the castle. She had thought her heart had been torn in two, and if she was honest, it still hurt, however much he had meant to protect her.

They sat in silence for a while, watching flycatchers

swooping over the water for midges. It was so beautiful, so still there, Sophie couldn't stay angry.

'You know, I think there might be something going on between Fox and Ruth Boden,' she said.

Josh smiled.

'I spotted that too. Maybe they should check into the shooting lodge when they've packed the criminals off. It's pretty romantic.'

'Says he!' she replied. 'I left you for twenty minutes last night and when I came upstairs you were snoring your head off. Not even my most seductive neck kisses could wake you up.'

'You're going to have to show me that trick later.'

He took her hand, and suddenly Sophie felt that everything was going to be okay.

'Listen, Sophie, I'm sorry, so very sorry if I hurt you at the castle, sorry for keeping you in the dark, I'm even sorry for being distant last night. When I realised there was no way to get to the map coordinates that evening, I knew I had a few more hours to work out what to do. I had to cover all the bases, juggle Sergei and Fox . . .'

'Ssssh,' she said, putting a finger to his lips. 'None of that matters any more.'

'Honestly?' he said.

'Honestly.' She looked out over the loch and smiled. 'All that matters is that we made it through – together. And just look how beautiful it is out here. Even my dad's castle was just as I'd always imagined it to be.'

Josh gave her a sideways look.

'Well I'm glad you like it, because it's yours.'

'What?'

He nodded.

'Remember when we were searching the castle looking for the safe? I found a load of paperwork in the library. The title deeds to the castle were there – and they were in your name.'

Sophie wasn't sure she could breathe all of a sudden.

'You are making this up,' she said uncertainly.

'Really, Sophie, I swear it's true. And not just the castle but five thousand acres around it. Oak and pine forests, moorland, even part of the loch.'

'*I own a loch?*' she squeaked.

'It's owned through an offshore company which is held in trust for you.'

He shifted his hips and pulled something out of his back pocket. It was a pale blue envelope.

'And there was this,' he said, handing it to her.

She stared at it for a moment. Her name was written in small, neat handwriting. Her father's handwriting.

Josh stood up. 'I'll leave you to read it,' he said.

Sophie watched him go, feeling numb and sick at the same time. She turned the envelope over in her hands, not knowing what to do, excited that her dad had left something for her, yet terrified of what it might contain. Steeling herself, she tore it open and pulled out a letter.

My darling Sophie,

So you've found your castle. You were always such a clever girl, I knew you would. You have always been so much more resourceful, brilliant and beautiful than you ever knew. Now you've discovered it, never forget it. Never doubt yourself. Be the best person you can be, because Sophie, I know you are capable of anything. Maybe you realise that too now. I hope so.

If I haven't given this letter to you personally, then I fear it means that I'll be off sailing *Iona* in the sky. I knew there were risks, so I'm sorry if I disappointed you and your mother, but hopefully my business transaction with Michael might make up for it. Or perhaps it will disappoint you more. That's why I left the clues for you to follow, so that you could do with the certificate what you will. It represents a $100 million fund, the money we siphoned from Michael's main investment pot – what we called our 'rainy day fund'. If it's in your hands, I guess it means it's raining for Mike too. So it's up to you now. Keep it and be richer than you ever dreamt you could be, return it to Miriam Asner who knows nothing of this money, or hand it over to the government. Perhaps you will want to do a little of all three.

Don't judge me for what I have done with Michael. For many years I felt a failure. I was never good enough for your mother, she made that pretty clear. But there are no excuses. Michael gave me an opportunity to help him. I had the choice to turn it down, but as our money was in his investment fund, a Ponzi scheme as it turned out, I took it.

Either way, the castle is yours, just as I always promised you. Every penny it took to buy it was legitimately earned over forty years, saving and investing. I don't expect you to live in it. But keep it. Be inspired by it. Come and write the poems and the stories I know are inside of you. Find someone you want to share your life with and enjoy it together.

I love you always.

Dad x

Sophie gulped and folded the letter carefully back into the envelope. She closed her eyes and let a thousand emotions pinwheel around her.

She felt Josh come up behind her, threading his arms about her waist and kissing her neck.

'I love you, Sophie Ellis,' he whispered into her ear, and she leant back against him, feeling his strength, his warmth. Feeling at home. She opened her eyes and she could see more clearly now. There was no point looking towards the past.

There was no place for regrets. There was just the future. She turned round, grabbed his hands and kissed him back.

'I love you too,' she said. It was the only thing that mattered.

Acknowledgements

Continued thanks go to my agents and wise counsel Eugenie Furniss, Claudia Webb and Dorian Karchmar. To the terrific team at Headline, especially Sherise Hobbs (welcome back!), Imogen Taylor, Lucy Foley, Jane Morpeth, Vicky Cowell, Jo Liddiard, Emily Furniss, Laura Esslemont, Aslan Byrne and the lovely Sales team – you are all such a pleasure to work with. To the talented design team Patrick and Yeti, to Jane Selley, Penny Price and Rebecca Kerby, who copyedited and proofread the novel, and to Darragh Deering and all the Headline teams overseas – you might be a long way away but your efforts to get my books sold in far-flung corners of the globe are much appreciated!

A big thank you to everyone who helped me with the research for this book, especially corporate-wizard Andy who helped me sort out a crucial plot hole. Thanks also to my school-gate medical advisor Ranil, Ian 'Minty' Johnston, and to Kathryn Rowe for making sure Fin had fun when I was right up against my deadline. Thanks to Penny Vincenzi, Kay Burley, Alison Kervin and Polly Chase for lovely suppers and book chat. To Big Davey Jones for his digital design flourishes and to Claire Taor and Dina Belemlih who *parlez francais* much better than I do. To Mum, Dad, Far, Digs and Dan: thank you, thank you, thank you. To my son Fin for the smorgasbord of artistic delights that brighten up my writer's garret. And for your ideas! Six years old and already a master storyteller! Last, but not least, thank you to John. For everything. I never felt magic as crazy as this.

Read on for an exclusive extract from
Tasmina Perry's thrilling new novel,

Deep Blue Sea

Prologue

Twenty years ago

'*Who is she?*' screamed her mother from downstairs. For the past twenty minutes, from the moment Rachel Miller had come home from swimming practice and been ordered to her room, she had been unable to hear the precise contents of her parents argument. She had closed her bedroom door intentionally, not wanting to pick out the abuse and accusations, but there was no mistaking the fact that her father was now being confronted. '*And don't lie to me . . .*'

Rachel had known this argument was coming. It was almost as if she had been able to feel it in the air, like a brewing storm.

It hadn't always been like this. There was a family photo downstairs on the TV cabinet that said otherwise. Mum, Dad, Rachel and her big sister Diana, all crammed together on the sofa, big toothy smiles. You could almost hear the laughter and cries of 'cheese!', arms wrapped around each other as if they would never be apart.

Or had that been a lie too? Somehow, somewhere down the line, it had all gone sour. The bickering over little things, stupid things. Resentments growing into arguments, rows growing into all-out war. There had been a particularly bad confrontation before Christmas; her parents' voices so full of hate and fury that Rachel had gone to the bedroom and prayed for it to stop.

And in some ways her prayers had been answered. The rows had stopped, only to be replaced by a hostile silence, a constant tension in the house that was like the drip-drip of a tap, splashing one drop at a time until the bath finally overflowed.

Rachel reached over to her bedside table, scrambling round the drawer for her new compact disc player, her fingers stabbing at the buttons to switch the thing on and drown out the noise. She crept under her duvet, pulled her knees up to her chest and stuck her nose into her copy of *Just Seventeen*. It had been returned to her that day following a week of confiscation after she'd been caught reading it in Double Physics.

'Rach?' She jumped at the sensation of her headphone being pulled away from her ear. She looked up to see her sister standing by the bed. She hadn't seen her since school and it was a relief she was here. Diana had her own room next door. A bigger one than her own, with pink and white Laura Ashley wallpaper covered with pictures of Matt Dillon and Christian Slater, but they often bunked in each other's rooms when her parents rowed.

'I should have stayed out,' said Diana quietly, pulling back the duvet and creeping in next to her sister.

'Where have you been?' asked Rachel, happy to be talking about anything else.

'Paul's.'

Paul? Rachel's eyes widened – for the moment, everything happening downstairs was forgotten. Paul *Jones?* Diana had been at Paul's house? Paul Jones was the king of Ilfracombe comprehensive, the resident heart-throb: dark eyes peering out from under a floppy fringe, captain of the football team.

Paul Jones even had a motorbike. Every girl in the school was a little bit in love with him and Rachel – in secret, in her dreams – was a lot in love with him.

'Is he . . . is Paul your boyfriend now?'

Diana shrugged her slim shoulders. 'I'm just going with him.'

Rachel nodded, trying to appear casual, though her mouth was dry and her stomach felt hot. What did 'going with' someone mean, exactly? She was pretty sure it was kissing. Proper kissing on the mouth with tongues, the thought of which still freaked her out a little bit. But she was going to be thirteen next week and she was curious to know for sure.

'Is it easy?'

Diana smirked, one eyebrow raised.

'Is what easy?'

'Kissing.'

Diana laughed. She had a pretty laugh; everything about Diana was pretty – it was so annoying. But Rachel knew Di would never laugh at her, she was never unkind. 'I've never really thought of kissing as easy or hard,' she said. 'But it's fun.' She caught sight of Rachel's furrowed brow. 'Don't worry, you'll get the chance soon enough.'

Diana smiled at her, and Rachel felt a little of her jealousy ease. It wasn't Diana's fault that Paul Jones fancied her instead of her younger sister, was it? If she was Paul, she would probably have picked Di too.

There was a loud crash. It sounded like the whole dinner service hitting the floor.

'What are they rowing about anyway?' whispered Diana, moving closer to her sister. Rachel was always surprised at how small her sister's voice was. People expected Diana to have a big personality – perhaps because of her beauty and her popularity with the cool crowd – but she was quiet, sensitive, sitting for hours with those stupid romantic books she liked to read.

'I don't know. Dad was already here when I got home.'

Who is she? . . . Rachel was not a stupid girl. She had picked up on what her mother had suggested. Her father had found somebody else, somebody else to love. But she didn't want to tell Diana that. Not tonight.

'I hate it,' said Diana. 'I hate the shouting.'

'I know,' said Rachel quietly, putting her arm around her sister.

People often mistook Rachel for the older Miller sister. It wasn't just her height and her large feet, that had finally come in so useful for swimming. Diana looked like a doll compared to her.

They could hear the noise of a door slamming shut. The two girls glanced at each other: they both knew it had been the sound of the front door.

'He's gone,' said Rachel. It was out of her mouth before she had time to think about it.

'Gone?' said Diana, a note of panic creeping into her voice. 'How do you know? What do you mean, "gone"?'

Diana scrambled out of the bed and ran to the window. Rachel didn't need to hear the car engine gunning away to know he had left them. Sometimes Rachel just knew things, knew what people were thinking, what they were going to do. She didn't like it much, it made her feel like a storybook witch.

'Rach, *do* something!' screamed Diana, her eyes flooding with tears, her beautiful, solemn face as white as a ghost's.

Rachel puffed out a small breath, trying to convince herself that things would start getting better from now on – just the three of them. 'We should see if Mum's okay,' she said finally. She took her sister's hand, knowing she had to keep calm, keep strong, because she had a funny feeling that her mum and her sister weren't going to.

'Let's go and see if we can help sweep up the pieces.'

1

'So who's up for climbing Everest?'

Diana glanced around the table, not sure which of her guests had said it, which friend had thrown down the gauntlet. It could have been any of the men sitting at the neat round of twelve, even a couple of the women. Their friends were like that: accomplished, ambitious, competitive. It wasn't money, it was the alpha mind-set. Bigger, better, higher. Two weeks scaling the Himalayan giant was for her guests what rock climbing at Center Parcs was to most people.

'Well I'm in,' said Michael Reynolds, her husband Julian's close friend. Diana knew Mike was winding them up: he was three stone overweight, not to mention a world-class bull-shitter, but she was immediately concerned that it would only encourage Julian. Climbing a mountain was not what he – not what *they* – needed right now.

Michael leant forward in his chair. 'No, I mean it,' he said, his eyes sparkling. 'Everyone thinks it's so hard, but I've been reading up on it and it is actually quite do-able. Just takes a bit of determination.'

Julian sipped his Armagnac, letting the amber liquid roll around his tongue before he finally spoke. 'I'm not sure,' he said to Diana's great relief. Her husband was an adventurer at heart. He had trekked across deserts, motorbiked across continents, but it was all done – as everything in his life – with great consideration, planning and thought. 'I just think it's too busy these days.'

'Too busy?' laughed Michael knocking back his own brandy. 'It's not the ski lifts at Verbier we're talking about here, Jules.'

Michael's wife Patty swatted him on the arm. 'Well, I think Julian's right. So many people want to do it . . . they're even doing corporate trips up to Base Camp these days. It's like the adventure equivalent of a Birkin – you have to put your name down, wait for years and pay through the nose for the privilege.'

Everyone began to laugh as coffee cups were refilled by Diana's fleet of caterers. The glorious smell of arabica beans mingled with the scent of honeysuckle and roses. Diana had been unconvinced about moving the party into the garden but when numbers had necessitated five tables of twelve, outgrowing the available space in their dining room, there was nothing else for it.

'Jules doesn't need to go to the top of the world,' added Bob Wilson, a fund manager, distinguished by his unconvincing hair weave. 'You're already there, aren't you, Denver? Say, is it true the company's buying Jura Motors?'

Julian gave a long, slow smile. As CEO of the Denver Group, one of Europe's biggest and most highly valued conglomerates, he was used to fending off rumour, speculation and shameless mining for information from their investor friends. 'Don't believe everything you read, Bob. I think we've all learnt that the hard way.' He reached over and took Diana's hand, resting his fingers over hers on the table. She felt all eyes land on her, which made her feel a little uncomfortable. 'Speaking of the Himalayas, I think it's time we go and check out the vodka ice-luge my wife's had sculpted. I've been promised it's not in the shape of Michael's penis,' he added, with a wink.

'Shame!' shouted Patty as the guests stood up and dispersed around the gardens.

Diana stood up, smoothed down the white lightweight wool of her shift dress and sighed a small sigh of relief that the dinner had been a success. Her favourite caterers had come up trumps again. She had personally selected the menu herself with Liam Donnell, the company's head chef. There was king crab, liquorice panacotta in the palest of blue and she had been particularly proud of the canapés – white miso glazed prawns – soft, delicate little bites. Certainly, she hadn't seen anything left on anyone's plates; always a good sign among gourmands like these.

The garden also looked ravishing. Julian liked to refer to their detached, four-storey Notting Hill villa as their 'London crash-pad'. Their main home was now Winterfold, a grand three-hundred acre estate in Oxfordshire, but the garden here was still impressive for this part of town, where multi-million dollar homes usually had to make do with a communal garden square. Tall poplars framed either side, with a sloping lawn to the centre and a kidney-shaped pond full of Koi reflecting the fairy lights strung from every bough and bush. In the balmy early summer evening, it was like a Victorian schoolgirl's vision of a fairy grotto – which was exactly the effect Diana had been hoping for. She had been nervous about entertaining after all this time, but the night, so far, was going down a storm.

'Oh, darling,' said Patty, approaching her on the terrace. 'It's gorgeous out here. I don't know why you don't spend more time up in town.'

Diana looked down at her glass. 'Oh, I much prefer the country nowadays. I feel so hemmed-in in the city,' she said, not entirely honestly.

Patty gave a gentle smile and touched her arm. 'Of course,' she said. 'I do understand. But we miss you, you know.'

Patty was being kind – and of course, she *did* understand;

Patty and Michael knew all about Diana and Julian's 'problems', as they were ever-so-politely referred to. But the truth was, Diana had been relieved to move out to the country three years ago. She had never felt entirely at ease moving in the sort of circles Julian so loved: the bankers, the industrialists, the gilded elite – exactly the sort of people he had invited this evening. Which was why she had insisted that this, their first appearance on the social scene in nine months, stay small and intimate. If you could call sixty friends and colleagues and a five course dinner *small*.

Diana and Patty walked down to a raised seating area overlooking the pond and turned to watch Julian, Mike and a group of the men talking enthusiastically about 'chartering a chopper' and 'yomping across Nepal.'

'Don't they ever get bored of that macho grandstanding?' sighed Patty. 'Climbing Everest indeed. None of them can find a space in their diaries for a round of golf, let alone an expedition to Shangri-La.'

Diana giggled.

'More to the point, none of their wives would stand for it,' added Patty with a sigh. 'I want flip-flops on my feet on holiday, not crampons.' She gave Diana a reassuring tweak. 'Are you having a good time, darling? I'm so glad you're, well, out and about again since . . . all the trouble.'

How we love our euphemisms, thought Diana. In the long months since 'all the trouble', she had come to realise how hard people in her world found it to discuss real issues. Stillbirth, miscarriage; it was all too serious, all too real for these people. *My child died inside me*, she thought, *why can't you say it?* But Diana knew Patty was only trying to be kind. And besides, tonight wasn't the time to be dwelling on the past. Tonight was a time for laughter and happiness, looking to the future, not the past. She glanced over at Julian who looked to be having a good time with his friends, and so hoped so.

'I won't pretend the last year was one of my all-time favourites,' said Diana, 'but I promise I won't hide away in the country the whole time.'

'No one would blame you if you did,' said Patty kindly.

Diana was grateful for her words. Even though Patty was at least fifteen years older than she was, she was one of the few wives on the circuit she felt she could talk to. She was ferociously bright and successful – on the board of a Swiss bank – but she didn't wear it on her sleeve. Together with Michael, who headed up an influential hedge fund, she was part of a financial power couple. So much so that they had decamped to Geneva the previous summer, where they lived in elegant splendour in an eighteenth century villa by the lake. No-one mentioned that Patty was from an ordinary background in the North because it didn't matter: she was one of them now. Diana wished she could pull the same trick. Not a day had gone by since she married Julian when she hadn't feel judged for where she had come from.

'You should go back into this professionally,' said Patty.

'Back into what?' Diana had let her thoughts wander again. It was getting to be a bad habit recently.

'Event planning, darling,' said Patty. 'Isn't that where you started?'

'Hardly. I was temping at Julian's company and I got roped into organising the company's summer party.'

The temp that got lucky, she thought to herself. That was what the bitchy wives and girlfriends said about her with ill-disguised jealousy. *The temp that bagged the boss.*

'You should start your own company,' said Patty. 'Seriously. I'd hire you in a heartbeat. We don't entertain quite like we used to but we could certainly make use of the fairy dust you sprinkle on your parties.'

Diana shook her head ruefully. 'Did anyone ever tell you that you're very bossy?'

Patty's eyes sparkled. 'Yes, and I don't take no for an answer, either. Ask Mike.'

Diana had always envied the relationship Patty and Michael had. Uniquely in their circle, apparently, they seemed to actually like each other's company. They bickered endlessly, of course, always making jokes at each other's expense, but there was an unmistakable feeling of warmth and respect between them. They just seemed happy together.

'Patty, I can't think about starting a business right now,' said Diana. 'I have a child . . .'

'Charlie is a teenager,' interrupted Patty. 'A teenager who is at boarding school.'

'Okay, but I want to get pregnant again. You know how difficult it has been for us. I don't need any stress.'

Patty waved a dismissive hand. 'That's what everyone said to me when I was going through IVF. Give up work, relax, it's the only way to get pregnant. You know what I did? I gave up IVF, went back to work – hey presto! – had Jack at forty-two.'

'So you're saying I should get a life?' said Diana with a wry smile.

Patty inclined her head towards a group of three women, gossiping by the French windows. 'No I'm saying that you don't want to turn into one of *those* women.'

Diana had been thinking the same thing. Dressed in a uniform of high-end labels, their hair and nails primped and polished, their eyes constantly monitoring their husbands and each other, these women were trapped in an endless cycle of one-upmanship. Yes, they had shoes and bags and Italian marble work-surfaces in their architect-modelled Kensington homes, but they lived their lives on a privileged hamster wheel and in a state of constant anxiety. She looked at the hard-faced blonde standing next to Greg Willets. Greg was one of Justin's oldest friends, a hugely successful investor who treated girlfriends like fast food.

'I see Greg has a new lady-friend,' said Patty pursing her lips. 'Where do you think he met this one? A massage parlour?'

'Patty!' gasped Diana.

'Come on,' smiled her friend. 'Greg is an ordinary man with an extraordinary-sized bank balance. A woman that blonde and gym toned wouldn't be with him if he was a bin man. And do you really think Greg is looking for a career woman or an intellectual equal?'

'She could be a high flying lawyer for all we know.'

'If she is, I'll eat Greg's Bentley,' snorted Patty.

Diana held her tongue. For one thing, Patty was probably right. Julian's single friends tended to date former models and glamorous PRs, not brain surgeons. And for another, she was in no position to criticise those girls. Because the truth was, she was one of them.

She accepted a top up to her glass of champagne from the waiter. She had been sober all evening, but what the hell? Patty was right, it was time to start enjoying herself.

'I envy you and Michael,' she said, suddenly.

'You know what the secret is to making us tick?' Patty answered sagely. 'We're both busy. We have enough money to stop working tomorrow, but we choose not to because we want to keep interesting.'

She motioned over to Greg Willet's blonde. 'These girls get chosen because they seem to be good wife material: attractive, unchallenging, good enough in bed. They get married, they run the house, they go to the gym, shop. And you know what happens? They get boring. So their husbands, who aren't totally stupid – not even Greg – they get bored, especially when their wives start losing their looks and their perkiness. So they upgrade. I mean, is that all they have to look forward to?'

Diana frowned. 'I thought you were supposed to be cheering me up.'

'Oh, I don't mean *you*, darling. You and Julian, it's different.'

Diana looked over at her husband, who was laughing at something Michael Reynolds had just said. 'Is it?'

Patty turned to look at her meaningfully.

'Yes, it is. He *adores* you, Diana. Seriously. I know it hasn't all been plain sailing for you, but Julian loves you. And don't take this the wrong way, but you're most certainly not a trophy wife.'

Diana burst out laughing. 'That's supposed to be a compliment, is it?'

'Damn straight it is,' said Patty, holding her gaze. 'And that's what I've been saying all night; you're too bright to do nothing. Get out there, do something. Set up an events company, get a job. It's good for you. And it's good for your relationship too.'

She nodded, but Patty's words seemed alien to her. Diana had never been told she was bright. Beautiful, exquisite, yes. But brainy? It was her sister who was the brain-box. The smart, hard, ruthless one who would be good at business. *Too ruthless*, she thought, stamping out an unwelcome memory.

'Promise me you'll think about it,' said Patty.

'I'll think about it.'

'*Do*. Because Julian has his faults, but he's a good one. Speaking of which, I had better go and rescue my husband from that women's tits, because if he keeps staring at her cleavage I fear that he's going to fall in.'

It was gone midnight when the party finally broke up. Diana left Julian saying goodnight to the last stragglers at the front door, and walked back through the house into the dining room. The caterers had almost finished up, the tables dismantled, crockery, linens, glassware and food miraculously cleared away into the van parked on the street.

She stood at the French windows that overlooked the

gardens, and took a moment to admire the scene. The fairy-lights were still twinkling like a thousand shining Tinkerbells. In fact, Peter Pan had been the inspiration for tonight's theme. Diana had happened upon the book, left behind in her son Charlie's room. He was thirteen now, and in his first term as a border at Harrow. Children's stories, however classic, were not the sort of thing a self-conscious teenager would want in his dorm. It was an old copy – fifty or sixty years old, ragged and worn – but it had particular resonance for Diana. She had bought the book from a junk shop on her first year in London, when she had arrived with no money, a twelve-month-old child, and nothing more than her looks and a determination to better herself.

She turned. Julian was standing in the doorway, the first three buttons of his shirt undone, and it made her heart jump.

He was a handsome man. Not perfect, of course: his dark eyes were perhaps a little too narrow, his lips not quite full enough, his nose perhaps a little too strong, but beauty was more forgiving in men, wasn't it?

'Hey,' he said, stepping over to her and putting his arms around her. 'Why so sad? I thought it went really well tonight.'

She relaxed into his embrace, leaning her head against his shoulder. She loved his smell, his touch. When she was in his arms she felt she could do anything.

'Why did you marry me?' she said softly.

'What?' he replied, with evident surprise.

'Answer the question,' she said, turning to look into his eyes.

He took a moment to reply. 'I chose you because you are kind and beautiful. And I asked you to marry me because I fell head over heels in love with you.'

'Good answer.' She smiled playfully, feeling completely reassured by his answer. 'So no climbing up mountains, okay? Forget busy – it's *dangerous*.'

'But what about Base Camp?' asked Julian seriously. 'It would be amazing, and we could take Charlie with us.'

'He's almost 14,' scoffed Diana. 'Next summer, all he's going to want to do is go to Ayia Napa with his friends, not Nepal.'

'You underestimate our child, Di. I think it would do Charlie good to go on an adventure.'

Our child. It had taken her a long time to think of Charlie as theirs, but Julian had never treated him as anything but his from day one. She thought of Patty's words: 'Julian has his faults, but he's a good one.' He *was* a good one. Yes, there had certainly been dozens of reasons not to marry Justin Denver. Most of them were tall, leggy and blonde, like half the women she saw around Notting Hill. Diana knew there would always be women who would bat their eyelids and roll their hips and she knew it would always be tempting for a man like Julian who liked sex, liked women and had the looks and money to attract them. Diana had been brought up to believe that men were unfaithful, and she had gone into their marriage knowing that there was always a risk that someone might get their long claws into her husband – that he might even welcome it. On that score, of course, she had been proven right, but they had got through it, pulled their marriage back to stable ground, because she believed that they loved another.

'I love you,' she said quietly, voicing her thoughts out loud.

'What's brought all this on?' he said, lifting her chin. 'I've been watching you all night, I thought you were having a good time. You sure you're okay?'

'Yes, yes I'm fine. And you?'

She knew tonight was going to be hard. Julian had been quiet all week, and she wondered if he had been as anxious about the party as she was. But at least people had been discreet about their absence from the social circuit.

He nodded and pulled her closer. As she leant against his

warm body, Diana felt a flicker of lust, which was sudden and unexpected. The past eighteen months had almost extinguished their sex life, except for the solitary purpose of getting pregnant again. Two miscarriages and the horrible trauma of the stillbirth – the one she had been forced to carry to term – had not made her feel sexy. It had made her feel like a failure.

And yet tonight, she felt a lick of desire, a flicker of promise. Tonight she wanted to make love to him. Not just because she wanted his child, but because she wanted *him*. She tilted her head and kissed him softly on the lips.

'So are you coming to bed?' she murmured.

'You go up. I've got something to do first.'

She tried not to let her disappointment show. In her mind's eye, she had seen him unzipping her dress right here in the doorway, peeling off her lingerie as he backed her into the dining room, finally pushing her back on the table, sweeping aside the imported silver . . .

'Sure. But don't be long, okay?' she said.

As he walked into his study, he stopped, turned back. 'I love you too,' he said with feeling. 'No matter what.'

The bedroom was warm after the garden, the deep white carpet soft between her toes as she kicked off her shoes and unpinned her hair. Catching a glimpse of herself in the dressing table mirror, even she could admit how lovely she looked, petite and slim with long dark hair that fell between her shoulder blades. She unclipped her brand-new Sabbia Rosa half-cup bra, which, under any other circumstances would be just too lovely to take off.

For the first time in – well, a long time – Diana could feel the heat of desire spreading through her until even her fingertips were tingling. Peeling off her thong, she slipped into bed, turning off the bedside lamp, loving the feel of the crisp sheets on her skin, sliding her long legs back and forth. She felt so aroused that one hand slipped up to her breast, feeling the nipple rise to the touch.

Come on Jules, she thought, imagining his strong arms around her, his lips on her. *Put down that bloody phone*, she thought, *come upstairs*. She stretched her arms above her head, feeling warm and more relaxed than she had in ages. The last thing she thought was: *maybe I shouldn't have had that champagne*.

When she woke, the bed next to her was empty. *Julian?* she thought sleepily, reaching out to touch his side. She opened her eyes, and wondered where he was. Perhaps he had gone to the bathroom to get a glass of water – he often got dehydrated after he'd been drinking, but no: the sheets on his side felt cold and unslept in.

Diana closed her eyes, but she was unable to fall back to sleep. Inhaling sharply, she rolled onto her side and squinted at the small digital clock by the bed – part of some expensive but never-used Bose system Julian had installed last Christmas. 04.37, she read.

Lifting her head towards the en suite, she saw there was no crack of light in the doorway, no sign of anyone in the room. Nor were his clothes over the bedroom chair where he usually put them after undressing for bed. *Where is he?* She thought crossly. *Surely he isn't still working?*

Feeling groggy, she propped herself up on the pillow, her mind running through the possibilities. Julian could quite easily be on a call. But there were other possibilities, darker thoughts that were also easy to believe. Diana swung her legs out of the bed and reached for her robe. She had gone to sleep thinking how much she loved her husband, but she still had to be realistic. She was the wife of a billionaire, a man who had barely touched his wife sexually in the past six months. Julian was a catch to end all catches; why wouldn't she suspect he was up to his old tricks? She walked out onto the landing and cocked her head, listening. Nothing.

Stop it, Diana, she told herself. Where did she expect him to be? On a Skype call to a secret mistress? In the garden on a booty call with a hooker? They had put all that behind them; they had to. How was a marriage to survive if there was no trust? She almost laughed. Eighteen months of marriage-counselling after Julian's 'indiscretion' and where had it got her? Standing by her bedroom door, imagining Justin having some late night tryst under her nose. *Thank you Dr. Crabb, full marks*. She padded down the stairs, all her senses alert.

Compared to Winterfold, their West London home was almost small, but at night it seemed cavernous. She was too practical a woman to believe in ghosts but there was still something unsettling about walking through an empty house lit only by the dim light from the early grey dawn leaking through the windows. She stopped on the bottom step and held her breath, hoping that she would detect some sound or movement to indicate where her husband might be.

'Where the bloody hell are you?' she whispered, her disquiet turning to irritation. She turned on a downstairs light and walked through the dining room and across to Julian's study, half expecting to find him jabbering into his phone, scrolling through columns of financial hieroglyphics on his computer screen. It wouldn't be the first time: it was late morning in the Far East, early afternoon in Australia and Julian seemed to have business interests in every corner of the globe. But not tonight. The room was dark, with only a half-empty whiskey glass sitting on his desk to show he had been there.

Something about seeing that glass made prickles appear on Diana's arms.

'Julian?' she called out, louder, moving through the house, switching on lights, opening doors. She was actively worried now. Had he left the house? But why would he, at this time of night? And anyway, how? He had certainly drunk far too much at the party to drive.

The car, of course. She had to check on the car. Diana

went to the back door and slipped on the first footwear she came to – Julian's scuffed up old walking boots, which felt cold and over-large on her bare feet. She fumbled the keys into the lock and stepped out into the garden, the fairy wonderland of the party now cloaked in dark shadows and strange shapes. It was cold, and a light sprinkle of early dawn dew had settled on the lawn. *Keep going,* she told herself, clumping along the path that led towards the large brick garage at the back of the grounds. *If his car's gone, then you'll know.* But know what, exactly?

The door to the garage was closed but unlocked. 'Julian?' she called, as she peeped her head inside. She could make out the outline of the two cars that they stored here – her own silver Range Rover runabout and Justin's dark blue Mercedes, which at least meant he hadn't driven anywhere.

Now she was puzzled. Shaking her head, she resolved to call him on his mobile and go back to bed. Closing the garage door, she turned back to face the house and noticed a crack of light from one of the lower ground floor rooms.

It was a part of the house she rarely went to. There was a utility room down there, an overspill dressing room, and a small, sparse library – they had moved most of their book collection to Winterfold – where Justin kept his drum kit and collection of vinyl. She hurried inside and took the stairs to the basement. Like the rest of the house it was still and silent, but down here, it made her feel especially anxious. She pushed the library door open and stepped inside. The room was in semi-darkness, bathed in a low silvery dawn light from a gap in the curtains. She turned to look for the lamp switch, gasping in disbelief at the sight in front of her. Julian slumped and kneeling on the floor, a noose attached to a book shelf tied around his neck.

She didn't even hear herself scream.

COMING SOON

Passionate. Explosive. Impossible to put down.
Sunday Times **Top Ten Bestseller Tasmina Perry is back with her most spectacular novel yet.**

Deep Blue Sea

**Beneath the shimmering surface
lies a dark secret . . .**

Diana and Julian Denver have the world at their feet. With a blissful marriage, a darling son and beautiful homes in London and the country, Diana's life, to the outside world, is perfect. But nothing is at it seems . . .

When Julian dies suddenly and tragically, Diana is convinced there is more to it than meets the eye. She calls on the one person she had never wanted to see again – her sister, Rachel.

A former tabloid reporter, Rachel appears to be living the dream as a diving instructor on a Thai island. The truth is she's in exile, estranged from her family and driven from her career by Fleet Street's phone-hacking scandal.

For Rachel, Diana's request opens old wounds. But she is determined to make amends for the past, and embarks on a treacherous journey to uncover the truth – wherever it may lead . . .

headline
review

TASMINA PERRY

Private Lives

Rumours can be deadly . . .

A young associate with a glamorous media law firm, Anna Kennedy is the lawyer to the stars, hiding their sins from the hungry media. But when Anna fails to prevent a damaging story being printed about heart-throb movie actor Sam Charles she finds herself fighting to save not only his reputation, but also her own.

Soon Anna uncovers a scandal more explosive than even Sam's infidelities. A party girl is already dead and those responsible are prepared to silence *anyone* who stands in their way. Not least a pretty young lawyer who knows too much . . .

Step into a world where games are played to mask the truth. Where there is no one you can trust. And where being too good at your job could put your life in danger.

'A thrilling, sun-drenched beach blockbuster' *Glamour*

'You won't want it to end! *****' Closer

978 0 7553 5846 5

headline
review

TASMINA PERRY

Kiss Heaven Goodbye

IT WAS SUPPOSED TO BE
THE PERFECT SUMMER . . .

On the luxurious private island of Angel Cay, four
privileged students toast the end of their exams.
Miles, Grace, Alex and Sasha have the world at their
feet. But one dark night will change their perfect
lives for ever.

As the friends move into glamorous careers – fashion,
music, politics – each tries to put the past behind
them. But no matter how high their stars rise, they
cannot escape the dreadful truth. And, for one of the
four, there is a terrible price to be paid . . .

'Takes you to the most glamorous corners of the globe
while keeping you on the edge of your seat' *Glamour*

'Exotic, decadent, sexy and full of surprising twists . . .
Irresistible' *Closer*

978 0 7553 4842 7

headline
review